IN THE
SHADOW OF
THE BRONTËS

Books by the same author:

They Must Have Seen Me Coming

IN THE
SHADOW OF
THE BRONTËS

Louise Brindley

St. Martin's Press
New York

192 6096

Library of Congress Cataloging in Publication Data

Brindley, Louise.
   In the shadow of the Brontës.

   1. Brontë family—Fiction.   I. Title.
PR6052.R444715 1983   823'.914   83-2928 FIC
ISBN 0-312-41167-7

First published in Great Britain by Frederick Muller Limited.

First U.S. Edition

10 9 8 7 6 5 4 3 2 1

For Raymond Fieldhouse, with gratitude

My thanks are due to the following: the Yorkshire Arts Association for its generous help towards the cost of research; the Curator and staff of the Brontë Parsonage Museum for their hot coffee and sympathy, and to the ever helpful Bryan Berryman and his staff at Scarborough Library, for their unflappable calm and smiling good manners.

CHAPTER ONE

April 1820

It was a chilly spring day when the Reverend Patrick Brontë, his wife Maria, and their six children left Thornton in Bradford parish to travel to their new living at Haworth.

Throughout the tedious journey, Mrs. Brontë held her two youngest children, Emily and Anne, close to her heart, while the older ones, Maria, Elizabeth, Charlotte and Branwell – fruits of eight years of marriage to tall Irish Patrick – gazed from the wagon, their sharp young eyes following the curve of the road.

Marriage late on in years – Maria was thirty and had believed herself destined to be an old maid when she met her husband-to-be – had brought to her the blessings of a full and happy family life. Patrick had proved himself not only virile but possessed of a burning zeal to educate and reform, linked to a gift for writing poetry, and even more eloquent prose, which he had spilled on to paper in his ardent love letters to his wife.

As the wagon rumbled on, Maria patted the shabby velvet reticule containing the ribbon-bound bundle of Patrick's love letters and reflected how stimulating her husband's new living would be to a man of his intellect. Haworth, although isolated, honed by cutting winds and teetering upon wild chasms of granite, was nevertheless a stronghold of religious zeal, its inhabitants strong silent folk whose way of living and thinking was moulded by the bleakness of their surroundings. As for herself, she tried to put aside the increasing physical weakness

7

which bearing six children late in life had imposed upon her frail constitution.

The baby stirred in her arms. Emily's head drooped against her shoulder. It was a pale cold day with patches of snow in the hollows and edging, like delicate lace, the wild hills surrounding them.

Maria thought of her old home in Penzance, of rooms flooded with sunshine; windows opened to soft sea-breezes, roses clustering thickly near a sun-warmed garden wall, and the sweet scent of thyme from her herb-garden near the kitchen door. She remembered June mornings when the sun shimmered on the calm waters of Mount's Bay, and where St. Michael's Mount, joined by a rocky causeway to the coast of Penzance, basked like a benign sea-monster.

Half asleep, lulled by dreams of Cornwall, Maria suddenly opened her eyes to reality. The sky was saffron now, an ochreous yellow seamed with menacing cloud, and there, winding up from the deep cleft of the Aire Valley was a street of such preposterous ascent that she held her babies more firmly lest they should be forced from her arms. Anxiously she called to the older children entreating them gently to grasp hold of her cloak.

Startled, the little things obeyed, all except Branwell who crept to the dashboard and, with a boy-child's delight at the drama of horses' hooves seeking purchase on the cobblestones, seemed likely to fall in his excitement.

Patrick leapt down and went to the driver's aid as the other wagons – six of them containing their household goods and chattels – lumbered on up the hill, a snorting, panting cavalcade of steaming horseflesh and grating wheels.

Trembling, Maria saw a church tower set against a darkening sky, and a long low house upon rising ground against a backdrop of wild moorland, a house fronted by a walled plot of garden containing a few straggling, dun-coloured bushes, and a churchyard which harboured its dead beneath monstrous flat slabs of granite.

The house was heavily roofed with slate to resist the winds of heaven which tore at it as though anxious to uproot it from its lofty position on the hilltop. Flat windows stared down at her. A

8

thin plume of smoke ascended from one of the chimneys. The wagon ground to a halt.

Patrick helped Maria down, and then lifted the children down one by one, bestowing an affectionate pat on Branwell's red head as he did so.

A village woman who had come to light the kitchen fire and sweep the house in readiness for its new occupants, opened the front door and mumbled a welcome.

Maria stepped over the threshold of her new home and stared round at the bleak interior. The flagged passage struck a chill through the soles of her shoes, and the rooms leading from the passage seemed oddly cramped to Mrs. Brontë after the house at Thornton and her old home in Penzance.

'Well, my dear, we are home at last,' Patrick said. 'Praise be to God.'

'Praise be to God,' Maria echoed, and yet she could not help glancing over her shoulder at the grim graveyard beyond the boundaries of the garden. She shivered at its proximity to the parsonage and felt crushed and fearful in that instant. Even from her bedroom window she could see nothing but those flat-topped gravestones sloping down to the door of the church, with no trees or flowers to soften their severity.

Haworth, 1821

How brightly the fire crackles in the gate, Maria thought. Propped up with pillows, she remembered how much she had disliked her new home the first time she saw it, but it was scarcely more than winter then, and she was tired after the long journey from Thornton.

Time had passed quickly since the day she and Patrick had come to live at Haworth. She recalled their first spring there, when the last of the snow had melted and the lilacs had come into flower. What a silly goose she had been to think that spring could never come to so bleak a place, but her heart had been too closely linked with Cornwall at the time, and perhaps it was wrong of her to have longed to be back in her old home once more.

And yet pleasant memories died hard. Even now she loved to

see the servant cleaning the grate in her bedroom with an onslaught of black-lead and brushes, for Sarah Garrs buffed away at the fireplace as a Cornish-woman would have done. She laid the fire and set the flames dancing with a laughing word that delighted Maria's fun-loving instincts, despite the weakness of her hands on the counterpane and the fears that beset her during the long, restless watches of the night when Patrick prayed at her bedside, and nursed her devotedly and tenderly.

It was then that she remembered such silly, inconsequential things; the familiar scents and sounds of the house in Penzance where she had lived with her two sisters, Elizabeth and Charlotte Branwell, the soft scrape of her shoes on the sea-sanded floors, and Elizabeth pegging out her starched caps to dry on the washing-line in the rose-scented garden.

And often, when Patrick was praying aloud, Maria's mind was teased with the differences between her sister Elizabeth's fervent Methodism and the softer teaching of the Church of England. On the one hand was the precept of love and salvation through the Lord Jesus Christ, and on the other an Old Testament fear of God and eternal damnation for wrongdoers.

Maria's parents had died within a year of each other. They were gentle people, kind and well respected. How could she bear to think that their souls might not be at rest? Then she remembered the night she had heard the sound which had made her sit up in bed, shivering – the sound of her father's violin playing the melody he had especially composed for her.

At first Maria had believed the sound to be a trick of the wind sighing round the casements, but when she got up and ventured on to the landing, the music had seemed much stronger. Slowly she had descended the stairs, drawn by the soft playing of that violin, and stood trembling by the parlour door where her father, Thomas Branwell, used to entertain his guests with music after supper. But when she opened the door the room was empty and the music faded. There was nothing but a shaft of moonlight across the floor and a soft wind rattling the window-catches.

As Patrick's prayers droned on by candlelight in the dark watches of the night, Maria's mind grappled hazily with that memory. Perhaps she had dreamed the sound of her father's violin playing the tune, which was evocative of the sea, of waves whispering upon some far-distant shore, and of the soft singing of the sailors aboard some ocean-going ship sailing out to face unknown dangers.

'Oh Lord Jesus Christ, grant Thy servant peace, and alleviate her suffering upon earth,' Patrick prayed earnestly.

Maria stirred restlessly, her wasted fingers plucking the counterpane. Peace? How could she be at peace knowing that she was dying, and that her six little children would be left motherless? How would they fare when she was gone? Would Branwell be a good boy?

She knew that her daughters would be good because the poor little mites seemed old before their time on her account, sitting as quietly as mice when they ought to be playing out there in the garden, but Branwell possessed a wilful streak and an excitability that worried her. The pain of the cancer which was eating her life away seemed to be so little compared to the pain of leaving her loved ones.

Perhaps after all she was not fit to die as a Christian soul when she wanted so much to live. She reached out her hand to touch Patrick's hair, and noticed how loosely her gold wedding ring hung on her finger. She knew that Death would not come as a friend, and yet she had always believed that the merest hair's breadth divided this world and the world to come, something as delicate as a moth's wings amongst the harebells on the moor, or as gentle as a breeze dispelling the summer mist on the crags above Haworth.

What she dreaded was being swept away on a gloomy tide that would bear her away, not to a gentle heaven, but to some dark place where she would be shut away for ever from her home and children.

CHAPTER TWO

Scarborough, 1839

The rain had stopped an hour since. Cobbles glistened in the pale sunshine of an April afternoon, and a cool capricious wind sent white clouds scurrying across a water-colour sky.

Now that the time had come to leave the workhouse, Lizzie Godolphin wished that she might stay there for the rest of her days rather than face an unknown future. A slim, pretty girl of nineteen, with fair hair, blue eyes and an anxious expression, she stood inside the workhouse gates clutching a bundle containing all her worldly belongings, waiting for the hired cab which would take her to Grayston Lodge, the home of her new master.

The cab was late, and Josiah Grice, the workhouse master, was not in the best of tempers as he strode across the yard muttering imprecations against the gentry who possessed no idea of time, and who didn't give a tinker's cuss whom they kept hanging about.

The girl paid him little heed. Grice's rough tongue did not worry her half so much as the prospect of working among strangers who might be harsh, cruel or indifferent. She could not know, as she waited in a state of nervousness bordering on despair, that another girl – Anne Brontë – had left the security of her home at Haworth that morning to travel to Blake Hall, Mirfield, as governess to Mrs. Ingham, and that Anne too dreaded her meeting with strangers.

Destiny had begun to shape their lives, but neither Anne

Brontë, arriving at Blake Hall, nor Lizzie Godolphin standing near the entrance of the Scarborough workhouse in Waterhouse Lane, could guess what fate held in store for them.

The other workhouse girls would have given their right arms to have been hired as scullery-maid to Edward Grayston, and they had made it quite clear that they envied Lizzie her good fortune.

'I saw him ride into the yard and dismount the other day,' said one saucily. 'You could tell he was a gent by the way he handed the reins to one of the lads to hold, then chucked him a shilling to look after his horse. And his boots were so shiny you could fairly see your face in them! I'd be laughing if I was Lizzie Godolphin, not skulking about looking as if I'd lost a penny and found a farthing.'

'She'll get some good grub up at Grayston Lodge,' said another, 'summat different from the rubbish we get here, I shouldn't wonder.'

'Ay,' added the first maliciously, 'an' mebbe a good thrashing now and then to pay for it!'

As the minutes ticked by, Lizzie thought of the humiliation of lining up with the other girls for Edward Grayston's inspection. Of standing there in the long, cold workhouse room feeling herself to be as dumb and stupid as an ox, yet too proud to lower her gaze when he and the workhouse master had paced slowly down the line, and Grice had produced the grubby workhouse register and had started reading from it details of the inmates' poor, wretched lives.

Shame had eaten into Lizzie. Human beings should be treated with more dignity, she thought defiantly, but she had kept her eyes fixed unwaveringly on one of the uncurtained windows in the room she shared with thirty other women, refusing to give way to tears.

Why was it necessary for Mr. Grayston to be told that Hannah Mason was illegitimate, or that Jane Ogilvy had borne a child out of wedlock, and that the poor little mite had died before it could be baptised; that Sarah Skelton had once been convicted for assault on a man who had promised to marry her, who later turned out to be married after all?

But seemingly the workhouse master took a keen delight in

humiliating those less fortunate than himself. His eyes, as narrow as a pig's, darted down the pages of the register as he traced the entries with a grimy forefinger. And then came her own turn to be pilloried.

'Lizzie Godolphin,' Grice said thickly. 'This one's an orphan, admitted to the care of the Guardians when she was six years old. No known felonies . . .' He sounded almost sorry that she had no criminal record, Lizzie thought. ' . . . Let me see. Bound to one Captain Abraham Smith as a scullery-maid, then to a Mrs. Maidment of Merchant's Row . . .'

'Did you say Captain Smith?' Edward Grayston interrupted, 'Captain Smith of Princess Street?'

'Ay, that's right. Why, sir, is anything wrong?'

'No, not at all. Pray continue, Mr. Grice.'

'She left there when the Captain's house was closed for some reason. We kept her here for a few months, then she went to Mrs. Maidment, a very kind, Christian lady she was too by all accounts.'

'Then why did the girl leave such a kind, Christian lady?' Edward Grayston raised his eyebrows quizzically.

'Ah,' said Grice, 'that poor soul went to her Maker last December, so back she came to us again – the lass, I mean. Not that Mrs. Maidment was entirely satisfied with her. Oh no. There was a lot of trouble with her, I believe. But Mrs. Maidment, God rest her soul, was never one to forsake her Christian duty to one less fortunate than herself. Not that Lizzie Godolphin ever expressed any gratitude for kindnesses received. In short, sir, I believe her to be entirely lacking in any sort of gratitude towards the Guardians of this worthy institution, or anyone else come to that.'

'I see.' There was a moment's silence, then Mr. Grayston continued in a cool, decisive voice, 'Thank you, Mr. Grice, I'll take Lizzie Godolphin.'

It was then, and only then, that Lizzie dropped her eyes, met Mr. Grayston's level gaze and heard, as he walked away from her, the ribald comments of the toothless crones. Those too old to work any longer, who had watched the proceedings from the wooden benches near the black-leaded stove and who had cackled obscenely throughout.

'It's twenty past two!' Grice's voice brought the girl back to the present. 'Am I to be kept from my work all afternoon?'

Lizzie glanced at him scornfully, knowing full well that it was not his work Josiah Grice was concerned about, but a tankard of ale and a warm fire. The man was nothing but a hypocrite, as she knew from bitter experience. All that talk about the kind, 'Christian' Mrs. Maidment, when the pair of them had been as thick as thieves all the time, with Grice lying to his poor wisp of a wife to partake of Mrs. Maidment's hospitality whenever possible.

A cab drew up at the entrance. The cabman climbed down, grumbling, from his perch, to inquire tersely where the devil his fare might be, and stared in surprise as Lizzie stepped forward and mounted, without a word, into the creaking, damp-spotted interior.

When the driver had exchanged a few harsh words with the workhouse master, he hoisted himself back on his seat and cracked his whip. The cab jolted and began to sway. Lizzie heard the rubbing and jingling of the harness as the horse moved forward, clopped along North Street, manoeuvred, with difficulty, the narrow portal of Newborough Bar, and then swung left into Vernon Place.

Leaning forward in her seat, Lizzie's eyes were drawn up to the pale pinnacled tower of Christ Church. Just at that moment the carriage lurched as the wheels struck a pothole. For one agonising moment it seemed to the girl that the church had tilted and was about to topple. Then she had the curious feeling that, not only the church, but time itself had slipped out of focus.

As the cab passed by the heavy doors and the steps leading up to them, it seemed to her that shadowy figures moved there. Vague shapes dressed in black, holding handkerchiefs to tear-stained eyes. Then the moment passed, the church was behind her, the cab righted itself, and everything seemed normal again.

Giddy and frightened, Lizzie leaned back against the horse-hair seat as the horse moved on downhill, slipping and striking sparks from the rough limestone surface of the road, then it trod more easily across the base of the valley which cut Scarborough from east to west.

The sea, chequered with shine and shadow from the hurrying clouds, was now visible under the span of a bridge linking the shoulders of the valley. In a cluster of trees to her left was a little round museum with ribbon-like paths winding away from its base to the higher ground beyond it. Then the horse began to sweat and labour again as it attempted the steep incline of Ramshill. The driver cursed the animal soundly as a useless bag of wind and bones before leaping down to grasp its bridle and calling to his passenger to dismount.

Lizzie stepped down from the cab. The air was fresh and clean. Rain-starred hedgerows held a promise of spring. She smiled with pleasure and turned to look at the scene below her.

Caleb Smart, the driver, ashamed now of his taciturnity, reined in the horse and waited for the girl. She seemed a decent sort of lass, and she was very pretty.

'So,' he said heartily, 'you are going to work at Grayston Lodge, are you?'

'Yes, sir.'

'Are you an orphan?' he asked.

A hot tide of colour stained Lizzie's cheeks. The man averted his gaze and, to cover his embarrassment, he took out a handkerchief and blew his nose violently, wishing he had not asked the question. The horse, relieved of its burden, plodded on to the crest of the hill. When it arrived there, Caleb opened the door and bade Lizzie to get back in to the cab. Most workhouse girls, in his experience, were either too brazen for their own good or little short of idiotic, but this one was different.

He whipped up the horse with unnecessary vigour and turned its head into the Hull Road.

The wind was rising, rain threatened. Lizzie's apprehension was mounting. Suddenly, 'There it is!' the driver shouted, flourishing his whip. 'There's Grayston Lodge!'

Lizzie wished that the cab might drive on for ever, but it turned between high ornamental gateposts and stopped before a pillared portico.

'Well, here we are, miss.' Caleb jumped down from his seat.

'Should I knock, do you think?' Lizzie asked as she dismounted.

'Why, I hardly think so.' The man glanced doubtfully at the girl's clothes which bore the unmistakable stamp and smell of the workhouse, clothes cobbled together with no thought of style or comfort. Then, seeing that her fingers were trembling, he said, kindly, 'It might be best if you went round to the back door'.

There was no need of further consultation. A man dressed in black appeared round the corner and hurried forward, frowning. 'I had begun to think you were never coming,' he said. 'What the devil delayed you? I've been hanging round an hour or more to pay you the fare.'

'It's all very well for such as you with good horseflesh between the shafts,' Caleb grunted, 'but my old feller ain't as frisky as he used to be, more's the pity. I was obliged to walk him up Ramshill – and the lass as well. It's a fair pull up there.'

'Ay well,' said the man in black, his face clearing, 'here's your money, and if you take your animal through that arch in the lane yonder you'll see a trough. Best give the poor beast a drink before you set off back to Scarborough.'

'Thanks, I will.' Caleb pocketed his fare. 'But what about the girl?'

'What about her? She'll come with me, of course.' Tom Stonehouse, the man in black, turned to where the girl stood shivering in the cold wind.

'Why, bless my soul,' he murmured, visibly shaken, peering into Lizzie's face. 'Whatever are you doing here, Miss Brontë?'

Lizzie stared at the man uncomprehendingly, then shook her head. 'I'm sorry, sir,' she replied, 'I don't know a Miss Brontë. My name is Lizzie Godolphin.'

CHAPTER THREE

Tom's wife, Amelia, possessed a tongue sharp enough to bustle the domestic staff of Grayston Lodge about their business when necessary, and a heart as warm and ample as her bosom when they were in trouble. Today, however, she felt off-colour and strangely detached from her surroundings. Wearily she sat down in her rocking-chair to pull herself together.

Half-past three, and still no sign of the new scullery-maid. It would be lighting up time soon for the sky was overcast. I hope Tom hasn't caught his death of cold waiting for that carriage to arrive, she thought, and I wish the girl would hurry up and come. But what was wrong with her? It wasn't like Amelia Stonehouse to worry herself into a state of agitation over a workhouse girl, and yet the girl had been on her mind since she woke up that morning.

Amelia heard the back door slam and heaved herself from her chair. 'Oh, at last, and about time too,' she called out. 'Well, Tom, what's amiss? Why are you lurking there in the shadows? Bring the lass to the window where I can see her. Why, I'll be blessed!'

'You might well call down a blessing,' Tom chuckled. 'I've never seen such a likeness, have you? In fact, I called her Miss Brontë to her face, thinking the parson's daughter from Haworth had come to visit us.'

'It's uncanny,' Amelia faltered. 'Why, if I'd seen her walking down Church Lane at Haworth, I'd have said, "Good day, Miss Anne", never doubting it was the Reverend Mr. Brontë's youngest daughter I was addressing. But it's all very well you standing there laughing, Tom Stonehouse. Does the master know she's here?'

'I don't know,' Tom said, still chuckling. 'I suppose he must have noticed the carriage arrive, seeing the driver brought it to the front door.'

'Then go and find out,' Amelia said huffily. 'I've got work to do, and time's getting on. Well, child,' she turned to Lizzie, 'if your name isn't Anne Brontë, what is it?'

'Lizzie Godolphin,' the girl replied in a low voice.

'Godolphin?' Amelia puckered her forehead. 'That's a Cornish name, surely?'

'I – I don't know, ma'am.'

'Have you no relatives?'

'No, ma'am. None that I know of.'

'Eh dear, that's a sad state of affairs. Where did you come from, then?'

'I lived with Mrs. Menzies until she died,' Lizzie said, 'then I was taken to the workhouse.'

'But what about your parents? You must have had parents.'

'I never knew them, ma'am.'

'Oh dearie me!' Amelia tactfully changed the subject. 'Well, now that you're here, what do you think of my kitchen?'

The girl glanced round the room. 'It's beautiful,' she said simply, her eyes drawn to the fire blazing in the grate.

Amelia grunted, pleased and touched by the girl's answer. 'Well, go to the fire and warm your hands if you've a mind to,' she said gruffly. 'I've never been inside a workhouse myself, thank the Lord, but I hear tell they're dreary places. We had another girl here from the workhouse a while ago, Ginny Morrison. A right ne'er-do-well she was an' all, but I quite liked her for all that. I had all on to keep her from roasting her knees by the fire at times, but I couldn't blame the poor lass when she told me that there was now't but an old black stove to warm a room ten times the size of this one, and thirty or more women fighting to get near it in winter.'

Lizzie held her hands to the blaze, noticing how brightly the firelight winked on the polished copper skillets and reflected in the rows of shining dishes on the tall dresser.

'Ah, here's Tom,' Amelia said, 'and about time too. Well, what's to do?'

'The master's in the library. I'm to take the girl to see him at once.'

'Well, go on then,' Amelia said, catching Lizzie's appealing glance, 'he won't bite you.'

A more incongruous procession along the hall would be hard to imagine as Tom Stonehouse in his sober suit and white stock ushered Lizzie Godolphin in her plain grey dress, black cloak, unfashionable bonnet and clumsy boots, into the library for her interview with Edward Grayston.

Lizzie had not realised that there were so many books in the world. Her head swam as she looked up at the towering shelves crammed with leather-bound volumes. It was the most beautiful room she had ever seen in her life, with three long windows draped in soft blue brocade overlooking the driveway, and the floor strewn with thick Oriental carpets.

A coal fire burned brightly in an ornate fireplace beneath a gilt-framed hunting-scene. It was a man's room with models of ships in glass cases, fishing-rods propped up in an alcove, chairs strewn with copies of the London papers, and a burnished mahogany desk littered with books and documents. Behind the desk sat Edward Grayston.

'The new scullery-maid, sir,' Tom said impassively, and then withdrew.

'Ah yes.' Edward eyed Lizzie intently. 'I had begun to think, as the carriage was so late arriving, that you had either met with an accident or decided not to come after all.'

Lizzie flushed. 'I had no choice but to come, sir. I am bound to go where the Guardians choose to send me.'

'Whether it suits you or not?' Edward frowned.

'Yes, sir.'

'I see.' He got up and crossed over to the fireplace, stood in front of the fire with his back to her and stirred the coals with the toe of his boot. He was a tall, fresh-complexioned man in his thirties, with thick brown hair and the keen blue eyes of a sailor. His clothes were of the finest quality and fitted his lean, muscular frame to perfection, but there was nothing of the dandy about him, and his boots, which he was using alternatively as pokers, were polished to the sheen of horse-chestnuts.

'In view of your reply,' he said at last, turning away from the fire, 'it may be as well to remind you that, if you fail to give satisfaction here, your return to Waterhouse Lane could, and would be arranged without undue delay. Do I make myself clear?'

Lizzie bent her head. 'Yes, sir.'

'It seems to me that you possess an outspokenness which ill becomes your station in life. Perhaps I made the wrong choice after all, but your name was familiar to me. I remembered that your former employer, Captain Abraham Smith, spoke well of you. That is of no consequence, however, if you are unable to accept my authority. Well, have you anything to say?'

'No sir, except I am glad that Captain Smith spoke well of me.'

'Is that all?' The girl's unexpected replies irritated yet intrigued Edward Grayston. He walked back slowly to his desk, a man bedevilled by his own troubles, with no desire to add to them by attempting to understand the feelings of a workhouse girl.

'Yes, sir.'

'Well then, as you are here, willingly or no, I had better explain the running of the household. Mrs. Stonehouse is my cook-housekeeper, and her husband my personal servant and coachman. I also employ a groom, a governess, and two housemaids who live in. The other servants come in daily from the farms opposite. My wife is – ill – at the moment, therefore we live modestly and seldom entertain.'

He glanced at Lizzie, 'I shall expect you to be obedient to your mistress and to Mrs. Stonehouse in all things. Shirk your duties and you know what to expect. Now you had better come with me to meet your mistress.'

He strode from the room and led the way up a broad panelled staircase to the landing above. 'Wait there,' he said shortly, 'until I call you.'

From the window above the portico, Lizzie saw that the house faced a broad vista of fields and farm buildings. Loneliness engulfed her as dark clouds billowed across the sky chased by the rising wind. From the room on her left, Lizzie heard the sound of voices rising and falling, the petulant tones of a woman interspersed by the deeper tones of a man – presumably Mr. Grayston. They appeared to be arguing, but Lizzie was too unhappy to pay them much heed.

Presently the door opened. 'You may come in now,' Edward Grayston said.

Lizzie moved forward nervously, thinking that the room downstairs was nothing compared to this one with its red damask curtains and opulent furniture, white-canopied bed, mahogany dressing-table, long mirrors, delicate gilt-framed etchings, and a crimson velvet sofa pulled up to the fire, on which lay a dark-haired woman, wearing a loosely-fitting robe edged with swansdown.

'Arabella, my dear,' said Edward in a low voice, 'this is the new scullery-maid I told you about. But there is no need to tire yourself by explaining the running of the household. I have already done so.'

'Then perhaps you should also explain that I do not possess eyes in the back of my head,' the woman said irritably. 'How can I possibly see her if she will insist on standing behind me?'

Edward motioned Lizzie to step forward. In doing so, she caught the toe of her boot against a footstool, and stumbled. When she had recovered her balance, Mrs. Grayston wrinkled her nose in disgust at her appearance.

'Really, Edward, you should not have brought her to my room wearing those filthy garments,' she protested. 'They must be burnt at once! The smell of her sickens me! Take her away at once! She must be crawling with lice from head to foot!'

Edward caught the bleak expression in Lizzie's eyes, and felt a tug of pity for the girl. What if she were Cathy standing there, he thought, helpless to express her true feelings without inviting punishment, obliged to accept intolerance as her due, how would she react?

The question was hypothetical since his daughter, Catherine, was but six-years-old. Then he remembered that, when this girl was his daughter's age, she had been put into a workhouse.

'Well, Edward, didn't you hear what I said?' Arabella Grayston's fingers drummed nervously on the puffy silk eiderdown covering her legs; her diamond rings sparkled in the firelight.

'Yes of course, my dear. I'm sure Mrs. Stonehouse will find her something more suitable to wear.'

'I don't doubt it,' Arabella snapped. 'There must be plenty of old clothes in the attics left over from that wretched Ginny Morrison you chose to bring here. Really, Edward, I do feel that your sense of charity is grossly misplaced at times.'

Edward lightly kissed his wife's hand, and led the way to the landing. Lizzie followed him, close to tears.

'Come now,' he said briskly, 'there is no need to look so downcast. The next time your mistress sees you she will not know you, and when you have some neater shoes, you will not trip over every footstool that is foolish enough to stand in your way.'

Edward Grayston crossed the hall to the library and rang the bell for Tom Stonehouse. 'Now try to put your old life behind you,' he advised, 'and make a fresh start.'

'Thank you, sir,' Lizzie said.

Edward gave Tom instructions. Lizzie bobbed an awkward curtsey and followed Tom to the kitchen

'So you're to be bathed and given fresh clothes to wear, are you?' Amelia stood with arms akimbo. 'Right! Tom, stoke up the fire under the copper and drag that bath to the wash-house!'

As he hurried to do her bidding, she called after him, 'And tell Peggy Robson to find those old clothes belonging to Ginny Morrison. What's that you say? Where is Peggy? How should I know? Out in the yard, I expect, teasing the life out of Joseph Franklin!'

She bustled to the oven. 'Eh, what a to-do,' she said, 'and me with the dinner to see to, and my tea-cakes just on ready! What do they expect of one body, that's what I should like to know! Tom, when you've filled that bath, just warn young Joseph to keep his nose out of the wash-house, or he'll be sorry. Now, Lizzie, get those clothes off and wrap yourself in this blanket.'

When the bath was ready, Amelia laid beside it a cake of carbolic soap in an earthenware dish. The new clothes, which a dark-haired girl brought along with the towels, were put in front of the fire to air, and the old ones were gingerly thrown into the stable yard with a pair of firetongs.

'Mind you wash your hair as well,' Mrs. Stonehouse called out when Lizzie was in the bath. 'But come to think of it, I'd better do it myself. You'll leave the soap in, likely as not. Why, what's the matter, child? Why are you covering yourself like that? We're all made the same, aren't we? My God! Those marks on your back! No, don't struggle, Lizzie. Let me look!'

There was no mistaking the red weals that marked the girl's tender flesh. She had been severely beaten.

'Who did that to you?' Amelia demanded. 'Was it that brute of a workhouse master?'

Lizzie shook her head.

'Who, then?'

'It was Mrs. Maidment, my last employer.'

'Why? What had you done, Lizzie?'

'I-I brought a dog into the house. The poor creature was starving. It was so weak it could scarcely stand. I – I give it a few scraps of meat left over from dinner, not knowing that Mrs. Maidment wanted them for a pie.'

Flushed with anger, Amelia gave vent to her feelings by pouring a can of hot water over Lizzie's head and digging her fingers into the girl's scalp.

'The very idea,' she muttered, 'the very idea!' Then, when she had calmed down a little, she demanded to know what Mrs. Grayston had had to say to her.

'She said I smelt,' Lizzie admitted.

'Ah well, she was right about that. Terrible, it was. A queer sickly smell. Boiled mutton, grease and greens, I shouldn't wonder. Ginny Morrison smelt just the same when she came here. Pooh!' Amelia's stout bosom heaved as she rubbed and rinsed Lizzie's hair.

'The mistress seemed very short tempered,' Lizzie ventured when the tubbing was over. 'Is she always so angry?'

'Short tempered! Angry! She enjoys it if you ask me,' Amelia retorted. 'But no, I shouldn't have said that. The poor soul has been very poorly for a twelvemonth or more.'

'Who looks after her?'

24

'Who indeed! We do more's the pity! She had a nurse at one time, but she soon packed her things and left. Now Peggy and I do most of the fetching and carrying, but the brunt of madam's ill-humour usually falls on the master, who has the patience of Job to put up with it in my opinion. There now, stop asking questions and put those clean clothes on.'

When she was dressed, Mrs. Stonehouse looked at Lizzie with a sigh. 'Eh dear. Blessed if you don't look more than ever like Anne Brontë now you are clean and decent. You have the same colour hair and eyes, and her way of walking too. It is the strangest thing, but you are so much like Miss Brontë in every way that I have the feeling I'm seeing double. Why, whatever's the matter, child? You look quite faint.'

'I – I don't know.' Lizzie pressed the back of her hand to her forehead experiencing, once more, the sensation of having stepped momentarily into another dimension as she had done when the carriage jolted near Christ Church. Then the feeling passed off and she was looking into the housekeeper's anxious face.

'Tired, that's your trouble,' Amelia said gruffly. 'As soon as your hair is dry and you've had a bite of supper, off to bed with you. Oh, gracious me, I forgot all about that bundle of yours. I'd better give it to Tom to put on the bonfire.'

'No! Please don't do that!'

The housekeeper held the bundle at arm's length. 'Why, whatever's in it to cause such a to-do? If it's clothing, it's to go on that bonfire, or the mistress will work herself up into a frenzy.

'There are some clothes,' Lizzie admitted, close to tears, 'but please don't burn my book and my doll.'

'A doll?' Amelia dropped the bundle on a chair. 'Why Lizzie, I'm surprised at you. What does a big lass like you want with a doll?'

'Just to keep it with me to look at now and then. I've never been parted from it before.'

'Well, I never! Show me!'

The girl opened the bundle and took out a cloth doll with a crudely painted face and yellow woollen hair. The wretched thing, Amelia saw, was nothing more than a bundle of rags with a clothes peg for a backbone, but the girl held it as tenderly as if it were a living creature.

'Now let me see the book.'

Lizzie complied.

'But this is a Bible. Where did you get it?'

'The lady I lived with gave it to me before she died, and she made the doll for my fifth birthday.'

Amelia sighed. 'Well, the mistress said now't about burning books and dolls, but the clothes will have to go. Now I must look sharp with the dinner or that will be a fault. Here,' she thrust the objects into Lizzie's hands, 'but mind what I'm saying. Don't let on to anyone that I let you keep that doll. Take it upstairs with you and hide it.'

'Thank you, ma'am. Oh, thank you.'

When the dinner had been served, Lizzie's eyes grew heavy. The housekeeper bustled her off to bed with a buttered tea-cake and a mug of milk. An hour later she went up to the attic room where the girl lay.

'Not asleep yet, child?' Amelia sat down and felt the girl's hair to see if it was dry. Lizzie smiled drowsily, thinking that no one had done that since she was a little girl.

'Well, do you like your room?'

'Yes, ma'am. It is beautiful.'

Beautiful, the housekeeper thought, glancing round the narrow apartment with its uncurtained windows, empty fireplace, varnished wash-hand stand and cracked basin. What must the poor little soul have been used to if she thinks this is beautiful?

'I'll find some curtains tomorrow,' she said. 'It'll look better then.'

'Oh no, ma'am,' Lizzie's eyes were fixed on the window. 'I like to see the moon shining in.'

'Never mind the moon,' the housekeeper said gruffly, 'what about the wind? There's a terrible draught.'

'I don't mind that. I'm used to it.'

'Eh dear. Well it wouldn't do for me, but then I'm getting old and set in my ways.' Amelia got to her feet. 'Have you said your prayers?'

'No, ma'am.'

'Do you know what to say?'

'Oh yes, Mrs. Menzies taught me. Will you pray with me?'

'That I will, child.' On an impulse, Amelia bent down and kissed Lizzie's cheek. 'Now then, "Our Father, who art in Heaven . . ."'

CHAPTER FOUR

Anne Brontë alighted from Mr. Smith's gig, her skirts spattered with mud from the wheels, her face pinched with the cold, her hair and bonnet awry, praying that her nervousness would not bring on a bout of asthma or a fit of stammering. Not that she entertained many sanguine hopes of remaining calm in the face of meeting her employer, Mrs. Ingham of Blake Hall, for her breathing was already laboured and her mouth felt as dry as stale breadcrumbs.

'Well, Miss Brontë, here you are.' Mr. Smith, the driver, felt sorry for the girl, but wished to start on his seventeen-mile jaunt back to Haworth without undue delay, 'I wish you well, miss, and I'll tell the parson you arrived safely.'

'Thank you, Mr. Smith.' Anne watched the gig set off down the drive, feeling that she wanted to run after it. It took every ounce of courage she possessed to turn her back on it and walk up to the door of Blake Hall.

As she rang the bell, Anne clung on to her reasons for wanting to make her own way in the world; not only to earn money – although £25 per annum was not to be sniffed at – but to prove to her family that, although she had always been considered delicate, she was fit enough to pull her own weight and make good use of the education she had received at Miss Wooler's school at Roe Head.

It had not been easy to convince her father and Aunt Branwell that it was time she earned her own living but, having done so, she must not be found wanting. If only she might be allowed to tidy herself before meeting Mrs. Ingham, but the door was opening and she felt compelled to put on a brave face and march in as confidently as she could.

'I – I am expected,' she told the servant. 'My name is Anne Brontë. I am the new governess.'

The woman glanced at her coolly. 'Follow me,' she said.

The hall is very fine, Anne thought as she glanced around. It reminds me of Keighley Town Hall, full of marble busts and oil-paintings. Oh, what a sight I must look! I never thought the wheels of Mr. Smith's gig would throw up so much mud. I wonder what Mrs. Ingham will think of me? I did so wish to make a good impression, especially as my recommendation came from Miss Wooler's brother-in-law.

'Miss Brontë has arrived, madam.'

'Ah yes, Brown. Show her in.'

'How different Mrs. Ingham looks without her bonnet, Anne thought, advancing into the room. I did not realise that her hair was so dark or her complexion so sallow. She is taller, too, than she appeared in Roe Head Church, but then she was usually kneeling down when I dared glance in her direction. Oh dear, I must not let my mind wander.

' . . . and the older children join us at dessert every evening. You will see that they are properly dressed for the occasion. Miss Mary goes to bed at seven, but our son is allowed to remain until eight o'clock. When he returns to the nursery, however, you will find some little game or other to amuse him before settling him down for the night. Is all that quite clear?'

'Y-yes, ma'am.'

'After that, your own supper will be sent up to you. We usually provide cold meat and bread at that hour.'

'Yes, I see.' Anne wondered if Mrs. Ingham meant her to commence her duties at once. Evidently she did, for she concluded with the words, 'The schoolroom is on the second floor, Miss Brontë. The servant will show you the way. I trust that you will settle in quickly. We realise, of course, that you lack experience as a governess, but the Reverend Mr. Blake spoke highly of you, and we greatly admire Miss Wooler's educational system.'

'Th-thank you, ma'am. I w-will d-do my b-best to p-prove myself worthy of your c-c-confidence in me.'

Laying her heavily ringed hand on the bell-pull, Mrs. Ingham glanced curiously at her new governess. I had no idea, she thought, that Miss Brontë possessed a speech impediment. How unfortunate.

'God bless dear papa ánd Aunt Branwell. God be merciful to my dear departed mother and sisters, Maria and Elizabeth. Watch over my sister Charlotte, and please let Branwell succeed as a portrait-painter, for he has great talent, I know. And please, Lord, bless my beloved sister Emily, and our faithful servant Tabby Aykroyd. Amen.'

Her prayers said, Anne Brontë gave herself up to thoughts of home. Papa will have gone to bed now, she thought, and so will Aunt Branwell. Charlotte and Emily will most likely be in the dining-room, sitting close to the fire, and Emily will be playing with the kitten. Poor Tabby, she was aghast when I kissed that kitten goodbye.

Anne remembered Tabby's words, 'Eh, tha mun be daft, kissing a cat!' It was the old servant's way to scold her 'childer', not harshly, as Miss Branwell sometimes scolded them, but in her own inimitable Yorkshire fashion which had forged a loving bond between them. The young Brontës were in awe of Aunt Branwell, but they adored Tabby, and the old woman's remonstration about the cat, Anne knew, had simply been her way of softening the moment of leave-taking.

On that April night, with the wind sighing among the trees and a fitful moon shining through the branches, two destinies drew even closer as Anne Brontë at Mirfield, and Lizzie Godolphin at Grayston Lodge, Scarborough, blew out their candles.

The next morning, Lizzie flushed crimson as a handsome young fellow, wearing leggings and with a red handkerchief knotted about his neck, came into the kitchen carrying two heavy scuttles full of coal.

'Good morning, miss,' he said, giving her a saucy wink.

'This is Lizzie Godolphin, the new scullery-maid,' Amelia

told him, 'and I'll thank you to keep your winks to yourself, Joseph Franklin, and get on with your work.'

Joseph chuckled, 'Ah, you're only jealous because I wasn't winking at you, Mrs. Stonehouse, but I might give you a kiss if you let me have a slice or two of hot bread to put me on till breakfast.'

'You'll not get round me,' Amelia cried. 'Be off with you, and save your kisses for those daft enough to want them.'

Joseph went off, laughing, just as the two maids, Peggy Robson and Beatrice Godwin, appeared with their boxes of cleaning materials.

'Is breakfast nearly ready?' Beatrice demanded. 'I'm starving.'

'Starve on then,' Amelia said without rancour, 'the table's not laid yet.'

It was a bright, windy morning. The scent of freshly-baked bread blended sweetly with the freshness of springtime meadows and the tang of the sea. Lizzie heard the jingling of the harness in the stable-yard, the clatter of hooves on the cobbles, the crackling of the kitchen fire, the clatter of pans and skillets, the chattering of the two girls who had started setting the table, and the creak of Amelia's rocking-chair as the housekeeper sat down for a minute to pour herself a cup of tea from the brown pot on the hearth.

The baize door to the passage opened suddenly and a thin woman entered the room, an expression of haughty disdain on her pinched features.

'Now, Miss Blackledge,' Amelia said, looking up, 'what brings you to my kitchen so early?'

'I am not bound to give an account of myself to you,' said the woman sharply.

'Well, you haven't come here for the pleasure of my company, I'll be bound,' Amelia retorted. 'You must want something.'

'Very well then. You will oblige me by sending up one portion of breakfast only this morning. Miss Catherine is not to have any.'

'Why not? Is the child ill?'

Miss Blackledge tossed her narrow head with its coils of dark oily hair. 'More ill-tempered than ill. Going without breakfast is to be her punishment for being so naughty.'

'Is it indeed?' Amelia rose from her chair indignantly, 'Well you're a wicked woman, in my opinion, to deprive a six-year-old child of her breakfast for some childish prank or other.'

'You can keep your opinion to yourself, Mrs. Stonehouse,' the governess flared. 'The child is in my charge, not yours, and I have the mistress's permission to punish her as I see fit.'

'Oh, have you? We'll see about that! If you deprive that child of food I'll go straight to the master.'

Jessica Blackledge's face flushed to the colour of beetroot. 'I am here to teach the girl and teach her I will! She must learn discipline. Madam knows that she has picked up rough ways from romping with the fishermen's brats – and the master's to blame for taking her down to that shipyard of his . . .'

'You dare stand there and criticise the master to me?' Amelia trembled with rage. 'Why you're not fit to black his boots! As for Miss Cathy, a sweeter child never lived. No, don't interrupt me, miss! I'll stick to my guns. Starve that child and not one more bite will *you* ever get from this kitchen. You can try starving and see how you like it!'

'Oh!' The governess turned on her heel and stormed out of the room.

'I don't know what this house is coming to,' Amelia cried, stirring the porridge as if she intended to knock the bottom clean out of the pan. 'Whatever is the mistress thinking about to set a harridan like that in charge of a six-year-old mite? Well, what are you gawping at?' Her glance fell on the two maids who had hidden in the pantry while the row was going on. 'You look like dying ducks in a thunderstorm! Sit yourselves down, the breakfast's just on ready!'

Tom and Joseph came in from the stables as hungry as hunters, discussing how much feed the master would need to order for the horses. Lizzie, who had just finished scouring the scullery floor, noticed that Joseph's eyes kept straying to the dark-haired Peggy with her heart-shaped face and tip-tilted nose, and that she feigned indifference to his glances, as she chatted to Beatrice.

'Stop clacking, you two! Tom, say Grace and then we'll begin!'

'For what we are about to receive, may the Lord make us truly thankful,' Tom intoned.

'Now pass the porridge.' Toying with her food, for the harsh exchange with Miss Blackledge had taken away her appetite, Amelia fell into a reverie about her old home at Haworth, thinking that her life there had been peaceful compared to this.

'You haven't eaten much, Mrs. Stonehouse,' Peggy observed when the meal was over. 'Are you feeling poorly?'

'No I am not!' Amelia spoke sharply to hide her feelings. 'Well, are you going to sit there all morning? The master will be down directly and he won't thank you for flapping about with your dusters when he's having breakfast. And you, Beatrice, can stop staring at me and see to the library fire.'

'Yes, Mrs. Stonehouse.'

'As for you, Lizzie, clear the table and start the washing up. The soda's under the sink. Only be careful and don't cut your fingers on the knives.'

Lizzie smiled. If the housekeeper had ordered her to cut off her right hand she would have done so willingly.

Joseph, grooming the master's carriage horse, was singing a popular song of the day.

'Humph,' Amelia muttered, '"My Dwelling is no Lordly Hall" indeed! That lad doesn't know when he's well off, and that's a fact!'

Ladling hot water from the copper to the sink, Lizzie thought about the housekeeper's spirited defence of little Cathy Grayston. How brave she was to have spoken up in that fashion. Mrs. Stonehouse reminded her of Agnes Menzies, her foster-mother, who had given her the doll and the Bible. Not that she could read the book. There had been no opportunities to learn how to do anything save scrub floors and scour pots and pans during her short lifetime.

The sink faced a window that looked out on the stable-yard and framed what Lizzie thought of as a small world in itself; a cheerful world with polished tack glinting in the sunshine, and the stalwart figure of Joseph Franklin striding over the cobbles carrying water for the horses.

Two labradors lay sunning themselves near an arch leading to a lane, glossy creatures with liquid eyes and lolling tongues. Suddenly a smaller dog – a spaniel – raced into the yard followed by a pretty, dark-haired child holding the lead from which the animal had escaped. Lizzie noticed that the girl's hair streamed in thick, unruly curls as she ran.

'Dido!' she called breathlessly. 'Come back, you naughty dog!' But the spaniel refused to be caught and bounded into the lane followed by the two labradors.

The child spun round, caught her foot against a stone and fell full-length in a pool of water, soaking her dress. Wide-eyed, she sat up and tried to scramble to her feet as she heard her governess calling, 'Catherine! Where are you? Answer me directly or I shall go straight to your mother!'

Lizzie supposed that the woman was in the passage behind the hall, and guessed that in another minute she would flounce through the kitchen to the stable-yard. There was no sign of Joseph who must have gone upstairs to his apartment over the stable. Whatever happened, the governess must not see Catherine with the front of her dress soaking wet.

Impulsively, Lizzie picked up her skirts and ran outdoors. Miss Blackledge had not yet appeared, but there wasn't a moment to lose. Helping the little girl up, she whisked her quickly into the scullery. 'Hush,' she whispered, pressing her fingers to her lips as the back door slammed, the governess stalked out into the stable-yard, and stood staring around her with pursed lips and an angry expression on her thin face.

'Ah, the coast is clear for the minute,' Lizzie said. 'Now slip through to the kitchen and ask Mrs. Stonehouse to take you up to the nursery. Will you do that, Miss Cathy?'

The child nodded. 'Yes, but what about Dido? She has run away.'

'I daresay Joseph will find her, but you'd better hurry before your governess returns.'

Cathy ran to the scullery door, then, on an impulse, she turned back, threw her arms round Lizzie's waist and hugged her. 'What's your name?' she asked.

'Lizzie. Lizzie Godolphin.'

When Cathy had gone, Lizzie stood with her back pressed

against the door. I could be sent away for this, she thought. If the mistress finds out what I have done she will send me back to the workhouse. Then, lifting her chin, she knew that she didn't care.

No matter if she was sent away, nothing would ever take from her the spontaneity of Cathy's embrace, or the knowledge that, for once in her life, she had acted not as a servant but as a free human being.

CHAPTER FIVE

The schoolroom clock chimed midnight. Anne Brontë passed a weary hand across her brow, and attempted to rekindle the fire from one remaining ember.

It had taken her but a few short days to discover that Joshua and Mary Ingham were desperate little dunces whose sole pleasure in life was tormenting their governess.

Anne's life had resolved itself into one long tussle. She had expected to instil into her charges a sense of goodness and fair play, believing that all children possess a natural core of affection. It was now evident that the young Inghams did not. And yet, if it was possible to rekindle a fire from one coal, surely it was possible to kindle an ember in a child's heart? If only she might win an affectionate kiss from Mary, and contrition for a naughty act from her brother. Anne was young and eager enough to hope that she might yet curb their wild intractability; their careless disregard of her lessons.

Gazing at the flames licking the tiny pyramid of sticks, Anne wished that she might have some respite from her charges during daylight hours to renew her energy, but there was no hope of that. At mealtimes she had to restrain their noisy quarrelling over food, and in the evenings force their wriggling limbs into their best clothes; attempt to brush their hair and tie bows which they undid as fast as she tied them. Then, exhausted by her efforts, she felt obliged to present a calm, smiling image of an efficient governess to their parents who made not the slightest effort to back her authority.

With a clatter of sticks and cinders, Anne's brave little fire collapsed; the last spark was extinguished. With a desperate sigh, she got up slowly, went to bed and tossed restlessly on her pillow.

Were the confused images of Haworth dreams or reality? Was it April or November? Was the fog which hung like an impenetrable curtain over the moors near her home a dream or something acutely real?

Suddenly it seemed to her that she was kneeling at the kitchen sink in the parsonage, peeling apples, when Aunt Branwell opened the door and accused her of not tidying her bed.

'Pray, Anne, why not?' Her Aunt's face was long and pinched, framed by the frills of her white cap.

'I'm s-sorry, aunt. I f-forgot.'

'Forgot? Really Anne, I fail to see how you could forget such an important matter. Where is Emily?'

'I don't know, aunt.'

'Well, I must say! This household is completely disorganised. Anne! Are you *kneeling* on that stool?'

'Y-yes, Aunt Branwell.'

'Young ladies do not kneel on stools, Anne. I've told you so often enough before.'

'Yes, aunt.'

'Neither do lessons learn themselves nor beds tidy themselves. You and Emily spend far too much time making up silly fairy stories and laughing together. What your poor mamma would say if she were alive to see you I cannot imagine. Goodness knows, child, I have done my best to guide you in her stead. Is this how you repay my sacrifice in coming here to look after you?'

'I am s-sorry, aunt.'

'Never forget, Anne, that God sees all and He will punish the wrongdoer. Chasten yourself before Him lest it be too late. Be ever watchful and on your guard not to fall into irreparable sin which cannot be forgiven you.'

'Help me, Emily! Help me! Tell me that God is a God of love, not vengeance!'

Anne opened her eyes and stared wildly into the darkness.

37

She had been dreaming after all, but the choking sensation was not a dream. She sat up, fighting for breath.

Daylight, which heralded for Anne Brontë a renewed battle with Joshua and Mary Ingham, ended the despotic rule of Jessica Blackledge over little Cathy Grayston. The woman's boxes stood strapped and ready in the hall of Grayston Lodge, waiting for the ten o'clock coach to Hull, and if Amelia Stonehouse felt some degree of satisfaction at Miss Blackledge's departure, she kept a still tongue in her head.

It was the red-haired Beatrice who had the most to say on the subject. 'Well there was bound to be a bust-up sooner or later,' she declared, 'and I'm glad that governess is leaving. I'll never forget the master's face yesterday when he came downstairs after all the rumpus. But if you ask me, Miss Blackledge cooked her own goose, when she locked Miss Cathy in that cupboard.'

'Nobody *is* asking you,' Amelia replied sharply, 'so get on with your breakfast.' But Beatrice was too wound up to take heed. 'Eee, there was a first-class row between the master and the missis,' she continued, 'You heard it, didn't you Peggy?'

'Beatrice!'

'Yes, Mrs. Stonehouse.' Beatrice dropped her glance.

'Have you finished your porridge, Lizzie?'

'Yes, ma'am.'

'Pass your dish, then.'

Lizzie complied, but refused the plate of bacon and dip the housekeeper handed her.

'What's the matter with you?' Amelia asked. 'Are you sickening for something?'

'I don't think so.' How could she explain that her stomach was so churned up with worry that she could not face food? Her own part in aiding and abetting Cathy was certain to be discovered before long, and she had already made a bad start with her new employers.

Edward Grayston pushed aside a ledger and glanced with distaste at the deeds, documents and accounts which littered his desk. He crossed to the window and stared out at the Hull road which shone as bright as a silver ribbon in the clear morning air.

The Four Inside Magna Chărta, bound for Hull, bowled briskly along the highway, its wheels catching the sun, and drew up outside the gate. A thin figure in black stepped jerkily into the roadway and mounted the coach. Edward watched Miss Blackledge climb into the vehicle with a sensation of loathing, then the driver cracked his whip and the coach continued on its journey.

When it was out of sight, Edward returned to his desk and stood looking at the deeds to his shipyard and Grayston Lodge – the legal paraphernalia he had been about to sign to placate his wife.

With an impatient gesture he swept the papers into a drawer and turned the key on them. What madness was he contemplating? And it would be madness to sell the home and the business he loved. He knew that now.

Presently he rang the bell for Mrs. Stonehouse. 'I know you are busy,' he said with a faint smile, 'but you and I are old friends, Amelia, and I owe you a debt of gratitude.'

'I'm glad you think so, sir,' the housekeeper replied. 'To tell you the truth, I was afraid I had overstepped my position in warning you of the governess's treatment of Miss Cathy.'

'You may forget that notion,' Edward said grimly. 'I am indebted to you.'

'But what about the mistress? I never thought she'd take on so about the woman leaving, and that's a fact.'

'The mistress is not herself at the moment, Amelia. But that is my problem, not yours.'

'Yes, I suppose so. But I am worried, Mr. Grayston, and so, I believe, is poor Lizzie.'

'Oh. What part did she play in all this?'

'Perhaps I shouldn't have mentioned it,' Amelia said unhappily.

'Well now that you have, you had better continue.'

'I don't wish to get the girl into trouble. The poor little soul has had enough trouble already, but she was the one who brought Miss Cathy indoors when Miss Blackledge was seeking her, and smuggled her through to the kitchen.'

'I see,' Edward said slowly. 'But what do you mean by "trouble enough already"? I found the girl somewhat proud and ungrateful.' He glanced at Amelia shrewdly. 'I take it that you have seen something in the girl which I have failed to.'

'I have seen the welts on her back,' the housekeeper said indignantly, 'put there by her last employer.'

'You seem to have taken to her, Amelia.'

'Well yes, I can't deny it. There's something about her I can't put my finger on, but she's a cut above any servant I've ever known before.'

'Oh come now, Amelia, you are exaggerating.'

'Perhaps I am, but I couldn't bear it if the girl was sent back to the workhouse for a kindly action.'

'You know me, Amelia. Do you believe me capable of unjust punishment?'

'Of course not, sir.'

'Very well. But I have kept you from your work long enough.'

As she was about to leave, Edward said, 'I believe that all the girl's clothes were burnt?'

'Yes they were. She's wearing Ginny Morrison's old things for the time being.'

'In that case, why not take her into Scarborough on Monday and buy her some prints for the warmer weather? And while you're about it, you may as well buy her a decent cloak and bonnet, and some new shoes.'

Lizzie turned her face to the sun, glad of the scent of fields and hedgerows. The wind that sent white clouds scudding across the sky made her borrowed cloak billow about her like the sails of a ship. She asked Mrs. Stonehouse if she had lived in Scarborough all her life.

'Bless you, no. I'm a country woman born and bred at Haworth, and the landscape there is as different from this as chalk from cheese. Tom and I came to Scarborough when the mistress married Mr. Grayston.'

Lizzie listened entranced as the housekeeper talked about Haworth, that village set high among the wild Pennines, and laughed as the woman gathered up her skirts flattened by the wind against her legs.

'This is what I am used to,' Amelia cried joyfully, 'the wind cutting like a knife, and the clouds flying as they used to on Haworth Moor! I often wandered there all day and never met a living soul except the Brontë children and old Tabby Aykroyd. Those poor little mites went out on the moor every afternoon unless the weather was unfit. Tabby was like a mother to them. "My childer" she called them – for all they teased the life out of her at times.'

She paused a minute to draw her breath, then went on, 'Those bairns would have had a thin time of it if it hadn't been for Tabby, for their aunt was always preaching hell-fire and damnation, and their father became something of a recluse after his wife died, taking all his meals alone in his room. Poor Mrs. Brontë, it was a tragedy when she died, for she was a bright, bonny little thing.'

A nameless melody whistled suddenly on the wind. Lizzie shivered. Brontë, she thought, I know that name, and then she remembered the day of her arrival at Grayston Lodge when Tom had mistaken her for a Miss Brontë. But there was something beyond that – a half-familiar tune played on a violin; a sudden feeling of kinship with the bright and bonny Mrs. Brontë.

She shivered again, as if a goose had walked over her grave, and remembered when Mrs. Stonehouse told her she looked so much like Anne Brontë that she might be seeing double. That was when she had the strange feeling of confusion, of having swung momentarily into another dimension. But as she and Amelia walked on down the sloping road to the valley, Lizzie forgot her disquieting thoughts in her contemplation of the view spread before her.

The sea, whipped to countless white-capped wavelets by the wind, ruffled like blue lace to a clear horizon. Mrs. Stonehouse pointed out the master's shipyard near the harbour, but all that Lizzie could make out was a blur of masts no thicker than pencils at that distance. She had often walked along that way when she was in service to Captain Smith of Princess Street; she had seen the hulls of ships on their wooden cradles, and the long lines of sail-lofts behind timbered fences; she had watched, in fascination, brawny men swinging their hammers as they drove home the iron bolts, and had sniffed the scent of hot tar from cauldrons suspended over glowing braziers.

'No wonder the master's rich if he owns a shipyard,' she remarked. 'But being rich hasn't made him happy.'

'You're right,' Amelia admitted. 'But when it comes to money, the mistress is even richer than the master. Her father owned a fine textile mill at Keighley, and he left everything to her when he died, including their old home, Crossways Grange. Mrs. Grayston's aunt, Miss Blakeney, still lives there.'

'Look!' Lizzie cried. 'There is the little round museum! I don't know why it fascinates me so, but it does. One day, perhaps, I shall pluck up enough courage to look round it!'

The housekeeper had no breath to reply as she toiled up the steep path to St. Nicholas Cliff. Matching her pace to her companion's, Lizzie looked with interest at the bridge spanning the valley, and the toll-house where rich people paid their sixpences to cross it.

This was the place she liked best of all. The houses were so fine, especially the building opposite; Wood's Lodgings, although the row of cottages adjoining it were small by comparison.

The Cliff was deserted. There were no carriages in the roadway and no pedestrians other than herself and Amelia, and yet as they crossed the road Lizzie heard the clop of horses' hooves and saw a carriage drive up to one of those cottages.

Two women stepped down from the carriage, and then a third whose movements were so slow, so weak, that she required all the support the others could give her.

Standing stock still, Lizzie gazed with rapt attention at the group of figures as they moved towards No. 2, The Cliff – a neat little house with sandstoned steps and crisply-starched curtains and then disappeared from view.

'Lizzie! Whatever's the matter? Are you ill?'

Turning her head, the girl realised, with a shock of disbelief, that the road was empty of carriage or driver, and came to herself to see her companion's eyes wide with fright.

'For pity's sake, child, what were you looking at?' Amelia cried. 'I called you three times, but you might have been deaf for all the notice you took of me!'

Lizzie swayed and would have fallen had it not been for Mrs. Stonehouse.

'Come, love.' The housekeeper helped the girl to a bench, and searched in her reticule for sal-volatile. 'Now tell me what you were looking at.'

'At a carriage drawn up in the road over yonder.'

'Go on.'

'I saw three women alighting from the carriage.'

'What else?'

'That is all, except that two of the women were supporting the steps of the third. But that third one! Oh, Mrs. Stonehouse, it was pitiful to see a frame so wasted. She seemed to be dying on her feet!'

'Could you see her face?'

Lizzie shook her head. 'No, and yet – I *knew* her! I'm sure I knew her.'

'Have you ever seen anything like this before?'

'Twice,' the girl said. 'Once on the way to Grayston Lodge, the second time in the kitchen there.'

'Try to explain, child. You can trust me.'

'The first time was when the carriage passed Christ Church,' said Lizzie in a low voice, 'I saw people on the steps; people dressed in black, but they did not seem to me to be real people, just – shadows. Then, at Grayston Lodge, when you said I looked so much like Miss Brontë that you might be seeing double, I seemed to be in another room – a much smaller apartment; a kitchen with a bright fire. A young woman was kneeling up on a stool, then a thin woman wearing a white cap with frills came into the room, a rather cross lady whose shoes made a strange clicking sound . . .'

'Mercy on us,' Amelia cried.

'I'm frightened, Mrs. Stonehouse. What does it mean?'

'I'm not sure, child. Perhaps it has to do with you being Cornish. At least I suppose that your forebears must have been Cornish or how would you have come by a name like Godolphin? And folk from that part of the country are very often fey.'

'But I never saw anything of the kind until I went to Grayston Lodge,' Lizzie murmured, 'although I have felt, at times, that there exists a person close to me, someone I have

43

sought all my life and never found – and sometimes I hear a tune in my head which tantalises me, a sweet tune played on a violin.'

'Bless my soul,' Amelia said faintly. 'But we have sat here long enough. The wind is blowing up a gale, and we'd best be moving. You must come to my parlour one evening when Tom goes out. We shall be able to talk better there.'

Suddenly the sky darkened and the first spots of rain began to fall.

CHAPTER SIX

That same afternoon, Edward visited his old friend Captain Abraham Smith.

'Edward! My dear boy! Come in, come in!' The old man rose to meet him, hands extended. 'Draw up a chair to the fire! I'll ring for Maggie to light the lamp. What time is it? I must have dozed off. That is one of the penalties of old age, Edward, dreaming of the past when there is no foreseeable future.'

'Don't bother with the lamp unless you've a mind to,' Edward clasped Abraham's veined hands warmly in his. 'I can't stay long, and I like the firelight.'

The captain chuckled. 'I know you do. I remember you as a lad, lying there on that very rug, staring into the coals. I often wondered what you were thinking about, but I never liked to ask. Confidences cannot be forced, I know that. But I am your friend, Edward, and I have worried a great deal about you, lately.'

Rain pattered on the windows, and streamed like tears down the panes.

'Is anything wrong at the shipyard?' Abraham sounded anxious.

Edward smiled. 'No. I have work enough and to spare, thank God, and as fine a workforce as any man could wish for.'

'But you are worried for all that? I can tell.'

Edward stared into the fire. 'Yes, you are right, Abraham. I can't deny it. Arabella is not well. Oh, the doctor assures me that there is nothing physically wrong with her, but the fact is

45

that she dislikes Scarborough and thinks that we should move to London where our child would benefit from what she chooses to call a more "civilised" environment.'

'London? But what of you, Eddie? Could you be happy there?'

'No, I think not. Shipbuilding's my life, but Bella cannot understand that. She is a wealthy woman in her own right and hankers after a gay social life with plenty of excitement . . .'

'All the things that you in fact, detest.'

'Yes.' Edward bowed his head.

'But what of your child? Would she benefit from your wife's notion of a civilised environment?' The old man leaned forward in his chair.

'I doubt it, Abraham. Cathy loves the sea as much as I do. The trouble is, she is fast becoming, not an object of affection, but a bone of contention between Bella and me, and that is bad for the child. But I must not burden you with my problems!' Edward smiled at the old man. 'Come, let us talk of other things! Do you remember a girl called Lizzie Godolphin?'

'Lizzie Godolphin?' The captain's forehead creased with the effort of recollection.

'I believe that she once worked here as a scullery-maid.'

The captain chuckled. 'Ah yes, now I remember! The little girl who wanted to learn to read! Oh what an upset that caused! I will never forget my housekeeper's indignation when she found the child attempting to read one of the books in that case yonder. The trouble was, the poor little thing was holding the book upside down! Maggie called me in to read the Riot Act to the girl, to make her see the error of her ways, but she was such a pretty little thing, with so much spirit and determination, that I found myself promising to give her reading lessons instead.'

Edward laughed. 'And did you?'

'Unfortunately no. I received my sailing orders shortly afterwards, and dismissed all the servants except Maggie. When I returned two years later, I made enquiries at the workhouse, but the girl had been sent elsewhere by that time. Why do you ask?'

'Because Lizzie is now at Grayston Lodge, and has already

46

become embroiled, to some extent, in a domestic argument between Bella and me.'

'That sounds like Lizzie,' the captain said, leaning back against his cushions, 'but there is no harm in the girl. Indeed, there was something about her which puzzled me . . .'

'In what way?'

The old man frowned. 'It is difficult to say. I simply felt that she was no ordinary servant; that she had sprung from good stock.'

How strange, Edward thought, that is just what Amelia said. Then, noticing that his friend seemed tired, he got up to leave.

The old man's eyes flickered open. 'No, Eddie, don't go. Stay just a little while longer. You have been as dear to me as my own son. Your presence comforts me.'

Raindrops scurried against the windowpanes; the fire sank lower. Edward smiled to himself, thinking that the captain had gone to sleep there in the firelight.

The rain turned later to a sullen persistent downpour. Arabella drew her shawl more closely about her shoulders and listened to the whine of the wind in the chimneys. Where was Edward? Why was he so late? She pushed aside her supper tray and tugged savagely at the bell-rope.

'Why ma'am,' Peggy said when she answered the summons, 'you haven't touched a bite.'

'I'm not hungry.'

'Have you any other preference? I'm sure Mrs. Stonehouse has some cold chicken in the larder.'

'If I had wanted cold chicken I would have asked for it! Take the tray from my sight. Tell me, is my husband in the dining-room?'

'Yes, ma'am. He's just finishing his dessert.'

'Then ask him to take coffee here with me.'

'Yes, I will that.' Peggy hurried from the room, pitying the poor master.

Arabella stared into the dressing-table mirror. Oh God, she thought, what would my darling parents think if they could see me so pale and haggard? Why did I throw myself away on the first man to ask me to marry him?

47

'There's something wrong with the master,' Peggy confided to Mrs. Stonehouse. 'He's done now't but pick at his food, and when I gave him the mistress's message he shoved his plate aside and ran his fingers through his hair as if he was right-down weary. Then he bade me bring the coffee and said he would take it up to her himself. I never saw a man look so downcast – as if he'd just lost his best friend.'

'Never mind that,' Amelia said tartly. 'Just put the coffee on a tray, and make haste about it.'

Peggy had no way of knowing that she had hit on the truth. Captain Smith, Edward's oldest friend, was dead. As he walked upstairs with the coffee, the only crumb of comfort seemed to him to be that the captain had not died alone, and that his passing had been as peaceful as sailing out at twilight on a calm sea.

'What, Edward? Have we no servants to wait upon us?' Bella turned from the dressing-table when her husband entered the room.

'I brought the coffee myself to save Peggy the trouble of coming upstairs again,' he said patiently.

'Indeed? Well, as you are playing the part of a servant, you might as well draw the curtains closer together. The draught is unbearable.'

As the rings grated on the brass rods, Bella continued, 'I had nearly given you up! But I suppose the time will come when you'll spend not only your days but all night at that precious shipyard of yours.'

'I wasn't at the yard, Bella. I went to see Captain Smith . . .'

'I might have guessed. Well, it is all too evident that you preferred his company to mine!'

'You don't understand. The captain is . . .'

'Oh, for heaven's sake, Edward, pour the coffee. I'm tired of your excuses.'

'As you wish.' He smiled grimly as he poured his wife a cup of coffee, and a glass of Madeira for himself.

'You are smiling,' Bella said sharply. 'Do you think a smile will placate your idiot of a wife who is no longer mistress in her own home?'

'If you are referring to the fact that I dismissed the governess

48

without your leave,' Edward said, 'I cannot believe that you would have wished me to do otherwise.'

'Miss Blackledge came well recommended,' Bella sipped her coffee. 'You were with me at the interview and agreed that her qualifications were excellent – French, history, needlework . . .'

'Not to mention incarceration and starvation,' Edward interrupted savagely. 'Dammit, Bella, what use is education allied to brutality? Thank God I found out that Miss Blackledge's notion of educating a helpless child included locking her up and starving her.'

'That does not alter the fact that you dismissed the woman without first consulting me!' Bella's dark eyes flashed.

'I was angry. That is why I sent Miss Blackledge packing, not as you suppose to undermine your authority. Oh my dear, I cannot believe that you misunderstood my motives.' He took his wife's hand into his where it lay as dry and cold as a winter leaf. 'There was a time when all you desired was my love and protection. Have you forgotten?'

'Oh that's right,' she cried petulantly, 'throw that up at me.'

'I had no intention of so doing.' He kissed her inert fingers. 'I hoped to remind you how much we once meant to each other.'

'As if I needed reminding of that painful episode! I was young, and beside myself with grief at losing my parents.'

'I know that, my dear, but you seemed to need me, and you were so very lovely.'

'I was *blind*! Lettie told me so at the time. "What do you know of Edward Grayston?" she asked. "A man who owns a shipyard in some Godforsaken town in the North of England. Don't you think it a little odd that a man whose business in London has to do with borrowing money should sweep an heiress off her feet and propose marriage within a week?"'

'Lettie was blind if she thought that.' Edward set down his wine glass. 'The money I borrowed was to increase the output of my shipyard, and it was paid back within six months of our marriage, as you very well know.'

'Perhaps. But I never thought the day would dawn when you would care more for this place than you care for me, or that life would become so dreary and commonplace.'

'I was born in Scarborough. Is it so unusual to feel strongly about one's birthplace? Don't you remember your home with as much affection?'

Bella sank down on the sofa in front of the fire. 'Certainly, but life was different then. Dear papa always insisted that mamma and I wintered in Italy, believing, quite rightly, that the fogs and chill winds of Haworth would be ruinous to our health, and it aggravates me past bearing to think that, save for your blind adherence to that wretched shipyard of yours, we might winter at Lake Garda.'

'Take care, Bella!' Edward's patience was wearing thin. 'You seem to forget that my shipyard turns out some of the finest craft in England; that it built Grayston Lodge, and the income from it provides a great deal of comfort for us, and a secure future for our daughter.'

'And you seem to forget that what your shipyard provides is a drop in the ocean compared to what my money could provide if you were not so stubborn and unreasonable.'

'What? Live on your money and prove Lettie Railton right in her opinion of me as a fortune-hunter? No, Bella. As long as I live I will provide for my wife and family in my own way. Anything else is unthinkable.'

'Where are you going?'

'To say good night to Cathy. Won't you come too, Arabella?'

'No, I am far too upset. Tell Catherine that mamma is not well enough to see her tonight.' Her face puckered self-pityingly.

'So be it. Good night Bella.' With a heavy heart, Edward walked upstairs to the nursery.

'Papa?' Cathy knew his step at once.

'Not asleep yet, darling?'

'I couldn't go to sleep without saying good night to you, papa.' The child turned up her face to be kissed.

'Have you said your prayers, my Cathy?'

'Yes, papa, Lizzie heard me.'

'Lizzie?' Edward frowned. 'But I thought Mrs. Stonehouse was going to sit with you.'

'She did for a long time, then she went down to see to Uncle Tom's supper, so Lizzie came instead.'

'I see, darling. And where is Lizzie now?'

'In the schoolroom. You are not cross, papa, are you?'

'No, love, only it is time you went to sleep.'

'Where's mama? Isn't she coming to say good night to me?'

'No, angel. She isn't very well tonight, I'm afraid, but she sent her love to you.'

The little girl's face saddened. 'Poor mamma. I wish she could get well again soon.'

'Good night then, Cathy.'

Stepping quietly from the room, Edward saw, through the half-open door of the schoolroom, a shadowy figure in grey beside the dying embers of the fire. 'Lizzie,' he said softly.

'Sir?' The girl rose and came towards him.

'I understand that you are relieving Mrs. Stonehouse?'

'Yes, sir.'

'In other words, you were bound to go where you were sent?'

'No. I asked permission to come. I wanted to come. I am sorry if you think otherwise and believe me ungrateful.'

'I could scarcely think that,' Edward observed drily, 'since you befriended my daughter when she needed help.'

'Oh that, sir!' Lizzie blushed. 'I did not stop to think.'

'Not stopping to think appears a failing of yours.' Edward walked to the fireplace and rested his arm on the mantelpiece. 'Apparently you did not stop to think the day you invaded Captain Smith's bookcase and attempted to read one of his volumes upside down.'

'H-how do you know that, sir?'

'Because the captain told me.' Edward paused. 'Lizzie.'

'Sir?'

'Were you fond of the captain?'

A smile played round Lizzie's lips. 'Indeed I was. He was always kind to me. You know, sir, he used to talk to me of so many things. The sea and ships. I was so unhappy when he went away.'

'Will you pray, then, for the repose of his soul?'

Edward saw, by the dim light of the fire, the sudden anguish in Lizzie's eyes. 'Oh, he's not dead, is he?'

'I am afraid so.' Edward bowed his head wearily. 'He died late this afternoon. I was with him at the last.'

Lizzie's eyes filled with tears. 'Poor Captain Smith. I hope he did not suffer.'

Edward looked up with a faint smile. 'No, thankfully he did not. His end was a sailing forth to calmer waters, and so peaceful that even I did not realise he had gone. He simply fell asleep in his chair by the fire.'

'God grant him a safe passage, then.'

'What?' Puzzled by her words, Edward looked down at the girl's face, and saw the tears on her cheeks.

'I only meant, sir, that I hope the captain will come to a safe harbour, and find all his old comrades waiting there to greet him.'

'I'm sure he will. Good night, Lizzie.' Edward walked slowly from the room, scarcely able to control his emotion, yet strangely comforted by his servant's tears.

CHAPTER SEVEN

Two evenings later, Mrs. Stonehouse invited Lizzie to her private parlour. Tom had gone out to 'wet his whistle', and Peggy was looking after Cathy.

'Eh dear,' Amelia plumped down in a chair, 'I scarcely know if I'm on my head or my heels at present. I'm worried to death about the mistress, and I only hope the new governess she has engaged will suit. She's never forgiven the master for sacking Miss Blackledge, but he did quite right, in my opinion, to send that besom about her business. But what's the matter, child? You look down in the dumps tonight.'

Lizzie sighed. 'It is just that I thought rich people had everything to make them happy. Now I think that money brings nothing but misery.'

'You puzzle me at times, child,' Amelia said. 'You speak like an educated person, and yet you can't even read or write. Have you ever wished you could?'

'Oh you don't know how much, for I seem to be locked up inside myself with ignorance.' Lizzie clasped her hands round her knees. 'The day I came to Grayston Lodge and saw all those books in the library, my head started to spin, and I wished with all my heart that I could read even the titles.'

Amelia laughed. 'Well, I'm not what you could call an educated person, far from it, but I know the alphabet. What would you say if I taught you the letters?'

The look of pure joy on the girl's face touched the house-keeper. 'Nay, don't thank me, lass,' she said in some confusion.

'I'll be glad to do it, and you'll learn quickly I'm sure of that.' She glanced sharply at Lizzie. 'I know I keep harping on about it, but have you no idea at all who your parents were?'

Lizzie shook her head. 'The only person I remember is Mrs. Menzies. I called her "Aunt" but she was not related to me. I think she knew who my parents were, and that she would have told me when I was old enough, but she died before I was capable of understanding anything except the little games she invented for me.'

The housekeeper leaned forward to stir the fire. 'There are times,' she said, 'when life makes no sense at all. Take the mistress, for example. She has everything in the world to make her happy – a good husband, a lovely daughter, and plenty of money, and yet she isn't content. It's a pity, for she was a pretty, lively young girl when I first knew her. Perhaps her parents were too soft with her.'

Mrs. Stonehouse put down the poker and opened the sideboard cupboard. 'I take a drop of stout at night,' she explained, 'to buck me up. Now, where was I?'

'You were telling me about Mrs. Grayston as a girl.'

'Ah yes. Well, she was the apple of her parents' eye, and money was no object since her father, Mr. Blakeney, owned the biggest textile mill in Keighley. Life was one long round of pleasure for Miss Arabella and that fancy cousin of hers, Miss Lettie. Then Miss Lettie married a London banker, Mr. Percy Railton, and went off to live in a place called Well Walk, Hampstead. The name always sticks in my mind.'

Amelia paused to swallow a mouthful of stout. 'When Miss Lettie had gone, there was no consoling Miss Arabella. But that was just the start of her troubles, poor lass. Later that year, her mother took the fever and died.'

'The mistress must have been very upset,' Lizzie said.

'Upset? I thought she'd go off her head with grief. But that wasn't the end of her misfortune. Six months later, Mr. Blakeney took the typhoid. That was the summer of the bad epidemic when people were dying like flies. I'll never forget it as long as I live, the procession of carts and coffins up to the churchyard, and everyone living in fear of catching the disease. There weren't no proper drains, you see, and some of the

54

villagers weren't all that particular about their middens.'

'It must have been terrible.'

'It was.' Amelia finished her stout with a sigh. 'No wonder Miss Branwell – the Brontë children's aunt – wore pattens to keep her feet from the filth of the main street. Of course lots of other particular people wore them too, but Miss Branwell even wore them indoors, so Tabby Aykroyd told me, to stop the cold striking up through the soles of her shoes. Poor Tabby always knew when Miss Branwell was coming, for she clickety-clacked wherever she went.'

A clicking sound, Lizzie thought. One of them wore shoes that made a strange clicking sound!

'After Mr. Blakeney's funeral,' Amelia continued, 'Miss Arabella went off to London to stay with her cousin, Mrs. Railton, leaving her aunt, Miss Blakeney, at Crossways Grange with Tom and me and two other servants to look after her.

'Those were unhappy, anxious days for us, Lizzie, in that old house, with the blight of two deaths hanging over us; solicitors coming and going, taking stock of everything, and Miss Arabella far away in London. Then one day Miss Blakeney told me that her niece had inherited everything – the mill and the house, but that Mr. Blakeney had stipulated in his will that his sister should stay on at Crossways Grange for as long as she lived. Not that Miss Blakeney herself was a pauper, far from it. She had plenty of money of her own, but the old master didn't want her uprooted from her home at her time of life.

'Two months later, out of the blue, come a letter from Miss Arabella, saying that she was to be married to a Scarborough shipyard owner. You can imagine the shock we had, Lizzie. We feared that she had fallen prey to some fortune-hunter who had taken advantage of her highly-strung state. Poor Miss Blakeney wept in my arms the day that letter arrived. But when Miss Arabella – Mrs. Grayston, that is – brought her husband to Crossways Grange to meet us, we were greatly relieved to find him a man of character who would make her happy. And the mistress *was* happy then. I never saw anyone so radiant, with those dark eyes of hers sparkling, and her cheeks like roses.'

The housekeeper sighed. 'That is why it is so hard to understand what has gone wrong between them. But it is my opinion that the mistress has begun to hanker after the old days when she was the belle of every ball she went to.

'She's still a child in many ways. I think everything happened too suddenly for her – bereavement, marriage and motherhood – then finding herself shut off from all the old pleasure and excitement; the parties and dances, picnics and wintering abroad. Now she hates Grayston Lodge, for she has told me so. But the master hasn't changed. He's as steady as ever he was. The fact is, he never knew the real Arabella. That's the tragedy, and where it will all end the good Lord only knows.'

Mirfield, June 1839

Anne Brontë paused to take in the beauty of her surroundings. Blake Hall, in its setting of lush parkland, was so lovely that she forgot her charges momentarily. But her sweet moments of forgetfulness were soon interrupted by their insistent voices.

Oh no, she thought, they cannot mean to dabble in that old well. Why will they persist in playing there when there are other, more attractive places to explore?

'Mary! Joshua!' she called desperately. 'Do come away from there!' and glanced back fearfully over her shoulder lest Mrs. Ingham, sitting in a chair by the open drawing-room window, should venture out to discover the cause of the commotion as the children, yelling and hallooing, broke off branches from nearby bushes to stir up the murky water.

'How can you bear to tear off such a pretty branch of lilac, Miss Mary? And you, Joshua, are you not ashamed to disturb nesting birds in that cruel fashion? Look what you have done! That little nest you have so wantonly brought down is a miracle of Creation . . .'

With a heartbroken cry, Anne ran forward to see Joshua Ingham, not attempting to restore the nest to another branch, but stoning the tiny occupants to death.

She knelt beside the broken nest, her heart so full of misery that she felt she would choke. In that instant of shock and horror she perceived, not just a broken nest and three dead birds, but a Universe where the innocent were condemned to

56

suffer and perish as Aunt Branwell had predicted.

Emily, she cried inwardly, Oh Emily, where are you? I need you so! But there was no Emily on hand to comfort her. She was alone, and was forced to draw upon her own reserves of strength and courage.

The children, far from being aware of her agony, were churning up the water of the well with the broken branches of lilac; paddling their feet in the muddy water that slopped over the edge, and laughing at her.

One day, Anne resolved, I will write a book about my experiences as a governess. I will cease to write what Aunt Branwell called 'fairy stories' and write about reality. This knowledge brought a strange feeling of comfort in the midst of her present suffering.

Having satisfied himself that all was well for the launching of the barque, *Titan*, bound for Newcastle to carry coal, Edward walked up Paradise to St. Mary's churchyard.

The name of the street intrigued him. Assailed by a sense of timelessness, he stood gazing out to sea thinking of the days when rich merchants and beggars alike had trooped into Scarborough to set up their stalls and awnings in the fetid, straw-strewn streets near the harbour, bringing with them pack-horses strapped with pedlars' merchandise, rich silks, cloth and leather. He could imagine them even now, those shoemakers, tailors and wood-turners, clowns and tumblers, bound for Scarborough Fair. But that was hundreds of years ago, when hooded Franciscan friars paced the twisting alleyways in their leather-thonged sandals.

Now the town was spreading its boundaries further afield. Since the building of the Cliff Bridge, Scarborough was waking to its full potential as a bustling holiday resort and soon, by all accounts, coach and horses would be replaced by George Stephenson's railway. When that happened, Grayston Lodge might be swallowed up in a rash of new houses, for the green fields of Ramshill would not remain sacrosanct when the developers moved in.

He walked on slowly. At least today there were no fashionably dressed visitors about, no carriages bringing be-ruffled ladies and top-hatted men to Sunday service, only the quiet grey church of St. Mary's dreaming in the warmth of an early summer afternoon, and two small boys playing 'tig' among the gravestones, who scampered away at his approach.

Pushing open the churchyard gate, Edward trod the springy turf to Abraham Smith's grave near the south wall.

Staring down at the mound of earth, he remembered that it was not his wife who had provided comfort in his hour of need, but a servant girl. The thought troubled and perplexed him.

A letter addressed to Mrs. Grayston, bearing a London postmark, effected her sudden, almost miraculous cure.

Beside herself with excitement, the invalid became at once animated and impossibly demanding in her requirements, for her cousins, Lettie and Percy Railton, were travelling to Yorkshire to attend a wedding at Malton, and they had declared their intention of spending a night, en-route at Grayston Lodge.

Sending for Amelia, she gave orders for the entire house to be turned upside-down, every nook and cranny gone into with brushes, mops and dusters, curtains taken down, washed and re-hung within the compass of a few days, and the kitchen taken apart and put together again.

'Eh dear me,' Amelia panted, 'it's a good job the weather's fine. How we'd have got those curtains dry otherwise I just don't know.'

But the housekeeper had more to worry about than curtains. The mistress made out and tore up so many menus that Amelia's head was in a spin, and on the very day of the Railton's arrival, when she thought the matter of food was settled, Mrs. Grayston sent word that she had changed her mind about dinner yet again.

'Lord love us,' Amelia groaned, sitting down at the kitchen table with her head in her hands. 'Whatever shall I do now? Apart from the soup and the vegetables, I've none of these new items she's ordered.'

Tom drew his watch from his waistcoat pocket, glanced at it, and finished his mug of tea without more ado.

'Where are you off to?' his wife asked.

'To the smithy at Seamer,' he buttoned his coat, 'and I'm late as it is.'

'But can't you go into town for me?'

'I'm sorry, love, I can't. I shan't be going back to Scarborough till four o'clock this afternoon, to pick up the master.'

'That will be too late!'

'I know, but I'm obliged to go to Seamer. What a pity the mistress didn't make her mind up sooner, then I could have brought the groceries back with me this morning.'

'Make up her mind!' Peggy butted in. 'What a hope! She's like a flay-crow! Doesn't know her own mind from one minute to the next! I wish those fancy cousins of hers had been going to a wedding in Timbuctoo, for I'm sick and tired of all this rushing about.'

Beatrice giggled. Tom strode to the door. Amelia stared in perplexity at the paper in her hand.

'What has she ordered this time?' Peggy asked, picking up her box of cleaning materials.'

'Turbot, which she wants cooked in a wine sauce, a saddle of moor lamb rubbed well with salt and fat before it goes into the oven to make the skin bubble, a selection of cheeses, and some of that special coffee from Lawson's in St. Helen's Square,' Amelia said, 'but she might have to make do with the goose she ordered yesterday as things stand, and devilled kidneys instead of the turbot.'

'Didn't you tell the mistress that you couldn't change the menu at such short notice?' Beatrice said in that vacuous way of hers. Amelia treated her to a withering glance.

'*Tell* the mistress? That I did not! It isn't up to me to *tell* Mrs. Grayston what's to be done in her own house. Why, she'd go up in the air and never come down again. I never saw a woman in such a flummox.'

'I don't see as how you've much choice in the matter,' said Beatrice, 'seeing that a saddle of moor lamb is scarcely likely to gallop up to the front door on its own.' She giggled. 'I'm glad I'm not in your shoes, Mrs. Stonehouse, and that's a fact.'

Lizzie wondered if she dare suggest walking to Scarborough to do the shopping, but held back because she did not understand the value of money. Standing beside the sink, she did not hear Joseph come into the scullery, and cried out when she felt a pair of strong arms around her waist.

'Oh,' she cried frantically, turning round and pushing him away with her clenched fists. 'Go away! Let me be!'

'Come on, Lizzie, give me a kiss.' The lad laughed, not one whit put off by her struggles. 'There's no harm in it, is there?' he said, bending forward and brushing her cheek with his lips. But he got more than he bargained for when Lizzie stamped on his foot and, taking advantage of his surprise, twisted away from him and fled to the kitchen.

'Why, whatever's come over you, child?' Amelia looked up in astonishment as the girl suddenly appeared and blurted. 'I'll go to Scarborough for you if you like.'

'Well, that would solve the problem to be sure. But why are you so hot and bothered all of a sudden?'

'I'm not! It's just that . . .'

'Oh, I see!' Amelia got up and rushed through to the scullery. 'It's that young devil Joseph up to his tricks again!' But the scullery was empty for Joseph had beaten a hasty retreat to the safety of his room above the stables. 'I'll settle his hash for him one of these days!'

'No! Please don't say anything to him! Only let me go to Scarborough for fear he comes back. And don't, I beg you, say anything to Peggy.'

'It would serve him right if I did,' Amelia grumbled. 'Eh, I don't know, if it's not one thing it's another. But I would be pleased if you would get me that fish and the lamb – if you are sure you can manage on your own. As for the coffee and cheese, well you must just do your best and trust to luck.'

Lizzie set off to walk to town clutching a leather purse so tightly that the hasp dug into her palm. She thought of Joseph, and turned to look over her shoulder to make sure he was not following, but the road was empty and she slowed her pace. There was no badness in Joseph, she knew that, but it was the first time a man had attempted to kiss her, and besides, he belonged to Peggy Robson.

On that bright June morning, when hedgerows burgeoned with white hawthorn and the ditches with straggling campion and cow-parsley, a lark climbed, singing, to the blue sky, then dropped suddenly to the green meadow below.

The glad clear song of the bird reminded Lizzie of Mrs. Stonehouse's description of Haworth Moor; the larks that sang there, and the wild waste of heath which sprang miraculously to life in the springtime, with fresh green bracken lightening the dun colours of winter, and blue harebells fluttering near the rough outcrops of granite.

As these thoughts crossed her mind, she felt herself drawn to another being whose spirit reached out to hers, but Lizzie was not afraid. This was no vision but a warm feeling of companionship as if some richer mind was linked to hers – a mind which knew and understood her love of home. A soft warm wind blew suddenly against her cheek, bringing with it an inexpressible sense of gladness.

'Emily,' she murmured softly.

But who was Emily?

The seashore was like a painted canvas, bold in design, rich in colour. Donkey-carriages with ragged urchins in attendance wove intricate patterns on the crowded beach, but some of the boys were far too harsh with their patient beasts, and she could scarcely bear to see the way they whacked the animals' rumps with short bamboo canes.

Someone else seemed to share her opinion, for in one of the carriages a young woman leant forward to admonish the boy in charge – a small ruffian who had flourished his cane too carelessly for her liking.

The woman's back was turned towards Lizzie, but there was something familiar about her. It crossed Lizzie's mind that the woman must have expressed a wish to drive the donkey herself, for her hands were holding the reins. But those hands! How thin and weak they looked, and yet there was a firmness about her shoulders, a fragile resoluteness which touched Lizzie, and the boy was looking up at her as if he not only heeded but respected her words. She was so prettily dressed, too, in a pale lavender gown, a dove-grey bonnet and a grey silk shawl.

Seized by a strange desire to see the woman's face, Lizzie looked back over her shoulder, but the donkey-carriage, the urchin with the cane and the frail woman in the lavender dress had disappeared.

Lizzie's heart began to race. Had she imagined the scene? But no, that was impossible. The woman in lavender had been quite real and must have driven away to another part of the sands. This was no phantom. She had seen the design on the woman's shawl, the sheen of her curls and texture of her dress.

I am being foolish and too imaginative, Lizzie thought as she walked on towards the fish market near the harbour where the stalls were set out with fresh catches of herring and haddock, and where the fishermen's wives made a brilliant splash of colour in their bright aprons and kerchiefs. Then, with faltering footsteps and a feeling of dismay, she wondered how she would fare when it came to choosing and paying for the fish.

Bedevilled by her own ignorance, she loitered near the stalls, dreading the moment when she would have to throw herself on the mercy of one of the fishermen's wives and confess that she did not know one fish from another, or a shilling from a sixpence.

'Well, Lizzie,' said a familiar voice at her elbow, 'are you spoilt for choice?' She turned to find Mr. Grayston standing beside her.

The girl blushed. 'No, sir. The truth is, I am here to buy turbot for your dinner, but I can't tell which is turbot, and I don't understand the value of money.'

The master laughed. 'Well at least you are honest,' he said. Then, turning, he called one of the fishermen over to him.

'Now then, Mr. Grayston,' the man said with a slow smile of recognition. 'what can I do for you? I've got some nice fresh lobsters in my creel.'

'Not today thanks, Seth. What I want is some nice fresh turbot.'

'You're in luck, then, sir. There's some over yonder, brought ashore this very morning.'

Lizzie got out her purse, opened it, and spread the coins it contained on her outspread hand.

'You may put that away,' said Mr. Grayston, 'I'll pay for the fish.'

When the parcel was safely in her basket, the girl turned to hurry away.

'Now where are you going?' Mr. Grayston called after her.

'To the Shambles to buy some lamb. A saddle of moor lamb, not a leg or a shoulder, Mrs. Stonehouse said. Then I have to go to St. Helens' Square for some special coffee and cheese.'

Edward frowned. 'And why has the purchase of these comestibles fallen on you? Why didn't Tom Stonehouse take them home with him this morning?'

'I suppose he would have done,' said the girl uncomfortably, 'except that the mistress changed her mind about the menu at the last minute.'

Edward's face darkened. 'Indeed, well, the Shambles is no place for you to go by yourself,' he said shortly. 'I'd better come with you.'

It was a stiff walk up Bland's Cliff into town, and a relief to stop halfway to allow the Malton coach, pulling into the yard of the Bell Inn, to pass by. Lizzie pressed back her skirts as an avalanche of yapping dogs descended after the vehicle, and she glanced up to see the master looking down at her with a strangely puzzled expression on his face. Perhaps her bonnet was awry or the strings had come undone, she thought, putting a hand up to feel.

The coach drew up, the dogs wandered off to find some other moving object to chase, and Lizzie walked on silently beside the master, still worried about the state of her bonnet, yet thankful, when she saw the crowds milling about the stalls, that he was with her, knowing that she would not have felt at all confident in that busy thoroughfare with the stallholders intent on inching every penny from reluctant purses. But how their attitude changed when confronted by a gentleman; how civil and attentive they became as they brought out their best meat for his approval, and he proffered a crown in payment.

When the lamb was nestling beside the fish in her basket, Edward said that he would bring the coffee and the cheese home with him that evening. Then he remarked that it was about time the Shambles was done away with, for the stench of offal was a disgrace to the town.

'One day,' he said, dusting his hands with his handkerchief, 'a decent market-hall may be built here, but I doubt if it will be in my time.'

'Oh yes, sir, it will,' Lizzie said confidently as they pushed their way through the crowd. 'And a very fine building it will be, with steps leading up to it, and columns – pillars – I don't know the proper name, and a sort of pointed roof like a pyramid – an apex – and all the stalls will be under one roof.'

'And how the devil do you know that, Lizzie Godolphin?'

Colour drained from the girl's face when she realised that she had described a building she had seen in her mind's eye, and had used unfamiliar words to press home the description.

'Come with me,' Edward said sharply, and the girl followed him down Bland's Cliff to the seashore.

'Now then,' he said when they were alone, 'what do you know of architecture?'

'Nothing, sir,' she said in a low voice. 'Nothing at all.'

'But you spoke of columns, pillars, and an apex. Do you take me for a fool?'

'N-no. I swear that I do not! Oh sir, you are not angry with me, are you?'

'Angry? No, but I *am* puzzled. Just who are you? Where did you come from?' Amelia, he remembered, had said that this girl was a cut above any servant she had ever known, and so had Captain Smith. He had been disinclined to believe them. Now he was not so sure.

'I – I don't know what you mean! Oh please, sir, don't be angry!' She was close to tears, a scrap of a girl in a print dress and a dowdy bonnet.

Waves ran in and broke up on the sand. Striding along by the water's edge, Edward felt baffled, powerless to understand his feelings. He recalled the first moment he had set eyes on Lizzie in that long ugly room in Waterhouse Lane. Had he really chosen her because of Captain Smith, or was there some other reason? He could have chosen one of a dozen girls to be his scullery-maid. One of the poor creatures had even gone so far as to loosen the strings of her blouse to gain his attention, but it was Lizzie, the small fair-haired girl whose eyes had remained riveted on the high blank window, whose chin was lifted with so much spirit and determination who had caught and held his

64

attention, and he had known, even before the workhouse master started reading from that damnable register of his, that Lizzie Godolphin was the one he would take, and it would not have mattered one iota if her record had been as black as sin.

'I have something to tell you, Lizzie,' he said at last. 'I intend to replace you as my scullery-maid.'

So the master was angry with her, she thought. She had displeased him and that meant she must go back to the workhouse. Scarcely knowing how to bear the blow which had befallen her, she took refuge in that instinctive gesture of defiance which had so moved him. Raising her chin, blinking back her tears, she said, 'I am sorry, sir, that I have disappointed you.'

'Disappointed me? But you haven't, Lizzie.'

'I – I don't understand.'

Their footprints, he noticed, had begun to fill with water at every step. 'It is simply that Mrs. Stonehouse and I feel that you have earned something better.'

'Sir?'

He smiled. 'You know that my wife's cousins are coming to spend a night at Grayston Lodge? Well, it is evident that they intend to come again, later on in the season, on a more extended visit. When that happens, Mrs. Stonehouse will need someone to help her with the cooking . . .'

'You mean – you are not going to send me back to the workhouse?'

'No, Lizzie. You are going to learn how to make tea-cakes. Do you like the idea?'

'*Like* it! Oh, sir, I cannot thank you enough!'

Her footsteps in the sand, Edward noticed, wavered from side to side as carelessly as those of a happy child.

'I must leave you,' he said. 'But your basket is heavy. Can you manage it all the way back to Grayston Lodge?'

'Heavy?' she replied, laughing, 'But it isn't in the least heavy. It seems as light as a feather to me now. Look!' She swung the basket high in the air. 'I feel I could carry it to Kingdom Come and back for the sheer pleasure of it!'

'Your arms would drop off long before you arrived there,' Edward said drily, as he left her. But when he had walked back a little way along the seashore, he could not forbear to glance over his shoulder, or to smile as he saw her snatch off her bonnet and swing it, by its strings, against the summer sky.

CHAPTER EIGHT

Lettie Railton clung to Arabella's arm and expressed her delight in everything she saw. 'How thoughtful of you to have lit a fire,' she prattled, 'for the evenings always come in chilly. You have no idea, Bella, how much I am looking forward to coming back here later on in the season.'

'No more than I am,' Bella said in a low voice, 'I only wish you had been able to stay longer this time.'

'Why Bella, is anything wrong? I know that you haven't been well lately but I never thought to find you so depressed.'

'I need a change of scenery,' Bella said irritably. 'I wished to go abroad last winter, but Edward refused to accompany me. The truth is I am bored to distraction with this place, this house . . .'

'But it's a beautiful house, darling! Close to town, but just far enough removed from it to provide a restful country atmosphere. It will do my little Julia so much good to come here for a visit, for the poor little girl has been quite peaky all winter.' She flitted round the room like a pink satin butterfly, admiring the furniture. 'Oh what a charming cabinet! I had no idea Edward collected snuff-boxes. And isn't that rosewood table from the Grange? It's such a *warm* room. Those globes are really delightful. I must try to find some just like them when I return to London.'

With a whirl of her pink skirts she tripped over to where her husband stood talking to Edward. 'Come now,' she insisted, 'we must have your full attention. You must not talk business tonight. Bella and I wish to be diverted.'

Linking her arm in her husband's, she drew him to the fire knowing that firelight flattered her creamy skin to perfection. Surely Edward would notice how beautiful she was in contrast to Bella who looked quite haggard these days.

'Sorry, m'dear.' Percy Garforth Railton, exuding amiability, allowed himself to be led. 'What do you want to talk about?'

'The theatre for one thing,' Lettie fluttered her lashes. 'You know of course that our dear Queen Victoria has set the vogue for theatregoing in London? And I understand that your Theatre Royal, Edward, is extremely enterprising. Is it true that there is to be a promenade concert there in August? They are all the rage at Drury Lane. Oh what fun! I shall look forward to that and to the races on the sands. Tell me, Edward, shall you enter a horse for the sweepstake?'

'Edward does not care for such frivolous pastimes.' There was an edge of bitterness to Arabella's voice. 'All he cares about is building ships.'

Lettie laughed, refusing to take her cousin seriously. 'We'll see about that. I shall insist on Eddie taking a holiday in August. He must be persuaded to take us to the opening of the Spa Saloon. You will won't you, Edward?'

Lettie looked up at her host, who smiled but would not commit himself to any future plans. What an attractive man he was, Mrs. Railton thought, with that courteous but remote air of his which so excited her. Something had obviously gone wrong between him and Bella as she had always hoped it might, but if Edward belonged to her she would twist him round her little finger.

Amelia rocked gently by the fire. The Railtons' driver had gone with Tom to see to the horses, Peggy had disappeared with Joseph who had been hanging about the yard an hour or more trying to get a word with her, while Beatrice was minding Cathy. Lizzie finished putting away the pots and pans and then she went through to the kitchen to sit with Mrs. Stonehouse.

It had been the happiest day of Lizzie's life. She would never forget walking into town to do the shopping, or that warm feeling of kinship with – Emily.

68

'Why are you smiling?' Amelia eased her shoes from her swollen feet.

'Because it has been such a beautiful day.' Lizzie's eyes shone in the fireglow.

'I thought you were put out because of Joseph.'

'I was at first, but he was just being foolish because Peggy leads him such a dance.'

'You're right there. Joseph's a good lad for all his cheek, and he'd be a sight more settled if Peggy would agree to marry him. He has asked her, but she will not say yes, the stubborn thing.'

'Perhaps she will tonight.' Lizzie gazed dreamily at the patch of fading light beyond the window, thinking that there was magic abroad in the June twilight.

Amelia stirred comfortably, enjoying the moment of peace with Lizzie beside her. The girl was so pretty and gentle, just like Anne Brontë. No sooner had the thought come into her mind than Lizzie looked up and said, 'Mrs. Stonehouse, who is Emily?'

'What was that? What do you know of Emily?' the housekeeper's eyes darkened with alarm, for who could Emily be but the Reverend Brontë's second daughter? That proud creature whose eyes looked beyond this world to some private realm of her own conjuration.

'I know nothing. But you know her, don't you? Won't you tell me about her, for I felt some warmth flowing between her spirit and mine – or that is how it seemed to me.'

In that instant Amelia knew that she was the catalyst, that Lizzie's clairvoyance had to do with herself. 'There is only one person I know called Emily,' she said, 'and she is Anne Brontë's sister, a tall, dark, proud person who keeps herself to herself, though Tabby Aykroyd has always been very fond of her.'

'Tabby Aykroyd? You mean the lady who used to walk on the moors with the Brontë children? The one who is friendly with your sister at Haworth?'

'Yes. Tabby has always said there are two sides to Emily Brontë, and I suppose anyone who thinks as much of birds and animals as Emily does must have a softer side to her nature.'

'Her nature is warm and compassionate,' Lizzie said simply.

69

Lord have mercy on us, Amelia thought, what does it all mean? And where did she come into it, an ordinary woman like herself?

'I'm tired, Mrs. Stonehouse,' Lizzie sighed. 'I'll go to bed now, if you don't mind.'

'Good night then, child.'

Lizzie undressed slowly and put on a thin cotton nightdress, then she unbraided her hair and brushed it until it stood out like a golden nimbus. Her heart sang like a lark in her slender body. Opening the drawer of her dressing-table, she spread the few items it contained on the counterpane – her doll and Bible, a pencil and a few scraps of paper, and began to copy the letters of the alphabet the housekeeper had taught her.

'Lizzie, will you come at once?' There was a sharp knocking at Lizzie's door, and Beatrice's moon face appeared round the edge of it.

'Why, whatever's the matter?'

'It's Miss Cathy. She's crying as if her heart will break. I tried my best to comfort her but it weren't no use. It's you she wants.'

'I'll be there in a minute!'

Not stopping to rebraid her hair, Lizzie slipped from the room to the nursery and found Beatrice hovering helplessly near the sobbing child. Cathy's hair was wet with tears.

'What is it, love?' Lizzie gathered the little girl tenderly in her arms.

'I dreamed I was l-locked in a cupboard, and it was all dark.' The child's arms tightened round Lizzie's neck. 'Then mamma came to let me out, but when she unlocked the d-door, she was angry with me and said she did not love me.'

'Hush, pet, it was nothing but a horrid nightmare. You are quite safe now.' She felt the trembling of the poor little mite's body, and the salty taste of Cathy's tears on her own lips.

'Where is papa?' Cathy whispered.

'Why I believe he is downstairs,' Lizzie said. 'Don't you remember, your aunt and uncle from London are here, and you were allowed to have dinner with them? Your mamma was very proud of you, darling. Peggy told me how nicely you behaved at table. You weren't unhappy then, were you?'

'N-no,' Cathy faltered.

'Perhaps you got over-excited,' Lizzie said, 'and that is why you had a bad dream. Won't you go back to sleep now, thinking happy thoughts?' She wiped the little girl's face with her handkerchief and smoothed the damp hair from her forehead.

'C-could I have Dido in bed with me?' Cathy asked anxiously. 'I'd feel safe if she were with me.'

'No, angel,' Lizzie imagined what the mistress would say if she found the dog in bed, 'but you could have my doll if you like.'

'Your doll?'

'Yes, my magic doll.'

'Magic? How magic? What does she do?' Cathy's tears were forgotten as Lizzie explained that she brought sweet dreams to good little girls and kept them safe from harm.

'Oh, I should like your doll to cuddle!' Cathy snuggled down in the bed-clothes. 'What is her name?'

'Cathy, the same as yours.'

'Will you bring her now?'

'Yes, darling, I'll be back directly.'

Placing the doll in the child's outstretched arms was the sweetest thing Lizzie had ever done; her first present to another human being. Bending down, she kissed the little girl, and knew that she loved Cathy with all her heart.

Mirfield, December 1839

'Come in, Miss Brontë, and close the door behind you.' Mrs. Ingham's voice lacked its usual patronising cordiality. 'Sit down if you please.'

She glanced coldly at the governess, and continued, 'What I have to say may not come as a total surprise to you. It concerns my children's education.'

'Ma'am?' Anne's eyes clouded.

'My husband and I have come to the painful conclusion that you have failed to grasp what we required of you. No, just a moment, do not interrupt me. You have displayed a remarkable lack of firmness and perseverance on our children's behalf which leads us to the only possible conclusion. We intend to find another instructor as soon as you have packed your things.'

'But ma'am, I h-have d-done my best . . .'

'I don't doubt it, but your best has not proved good enough. My children have scarcely benefited at all from your teaching. We are naturally disappointed, especially as you came to us so well recommended, but their manners remain uncultivated and their tempers unruly.'

Tears sprang to Anne's eyes. How could the woman speak so when she had worked so hard and been so sorely tried?

'Well, Miss Brontë, have you anything to say before we part company?'

What is the use of saying anything, Anne thought, twisting her fingers in her lap. Better to lift my head and say nothing at all than to plead and grovel. But oh, dear God, to have failed so abysmally when I tried so hard to succeed. What will my family think, especially as my own failure has followed hard on the heels of poor Branwell's failure as a portrait-painter?

'No, I have nothing to say – except that I am sorry.'

'I am sorry too. But no matter. It is almost Christmas. You will go home, of course.'

'Yes, Mrs. Ingham.' In spite of her failure, a sudden warmth invaded Anne's heart as she thought of going home to her family; of the firelit parsonage, the scent of baking from the kitchen, the sound of the piano in papa's study, and the red-haired Branwell striding down the lane to play the organ in church on Christmas Eve.

Mrs. Ingham would never know with what relief she would turn her back on Blake Hall; with what loathing she would remember her cruel, insensitive monsters of children.

'Very well, Miss Brontë, that is all.'

Anne rose to her feet with a smile. When she had gone, Mrs. Ingham felt nettled by the governess's reaction to her dismissal. One would have thought the wretched girl to be almost happy to return to that dreary parsonage at Haworth instead of spending her days in the luxurious surroundings of Blake Hall. But most governesses, she pondered, were half-witted creatures at best. Even so, one expected more humility from a paid servant.

CHAPTER NINE

Scarborough, 1844

The young red-haired man had no interest in the museum. He had been there many times before and knew all the finer points connected with its history and style of architecture. It seemed ridiculous to Branwell Brontë that he should spend his time wandering round the exhibits when Lydia was promenading the Spa pleasure gardens with her husband and children.

His mind was in a turmoil, his every thought centred on Lydia Robinson, the wife of his employer, with the sick introspection of a lover whose eyes could scarcely bear to contemplate anything except the face of his beloved.

He wished for a nip of gin to give him courage, for he felt himself sinking deeply into one of his bouts of depression. If only Lydia had included him in the Spa outing, at least he would have had the pleasure of looking at her; imagining her warm lips on his.

How heartily he wished himself back at Thorp Green Hall, the Robinsons' home near York, where opportunities for his being alone with Lydia occurred more frequently when they discussed young Edmund's lessons and when, on some pretext or other, he was bidden to Mrs. Robinson's private apartment for a blissful interview with his mistress.

His mistress! Suddenly Branwell's spirits lightened; his mood swung from despair to elation as he remembered what had already taken place between himself and the glorious

Lydia. Why, her deliberate refusal to let him accompany the family on their afternoon outing was nothing but a ruse to divert suspicion! How clever she was, how wise to have dismissed him so coolly in front of her husband.

In his newly acquired mood of mental intoxication, Branwell was prepared to devote his attention to the relics on display, thinking that his life had been as dry and desolate as those fossils until Lydia had come into it. Yet his life might have been very different, he considered, if his father had not insisted on teaching him at home, and leaving him for hours on end with only his books for company, or if the 'Old Man' as he secretly called his father, had understood that his son possessed no particular aptitude for study. Little wonder, in those circumstances, that he had broken away as often as possible to keep company with the lads of the village, who teased the life out of him for being tied to the apron strings of so many women.

Leaning upon his cane, Branwell pushed aside his feelings of guilt connected with his family. They had no right to treat him as a child, particularly Charlotte with whom he had once spent many absorbing hours plotting affairs of state in their make-believe kingdom of Angria. Now he felt himself to be both misunderstood and under-rated, forever surrounded by reproachful eyes both at Thorp Green and here in Scarborough, for in both places his sister, Anne, in her role as governess to the young female Robinsons, was always present, regarding him with those gentle blue eyes of hers, filling him with a sense of his own failure to live up to the standards expected of a parson's son. But then, he thought, at least he had Anne to thank for her recommendation which had taken him to Thorp Green as Edmund Robinson's tutor which, in turn, had brought about his meeting with his lovely Lydia.

Glancing up, he saw to his surprise that Anne was standing but a few feet away from him, closely studying a shelf full of fossils. How odd that she had not spoken, but perhaps she had not noticed him. Assailed by a sense of guilt, his thoughts coloured by the debt of gratitude he owed her for bringing him into Lydia's orbit, he regarded her fondly, forgetting the times he had raved inwardly at her constant vigilance which so irritated him. Poor Anne, perhaps he had been too harsh with her at times. Smiling, he tiptoed to her side and kissed her lightly on the cheek.

'Sir!' The startled blue eyes were so like Anne's that he could scarcely credit his mistake. But the girl confronting him, whose cheeks were crimson with confusion, was not Anne after all.

'I – I beg your pardon,' he said, feeling more than a little confused himself, 'but you must believe me when I tell you that I mistook you for my sister.' He stared disbelievingly at the girl he had kissed. 'I swear I have never seen such a likeness between two people before.'

Lizzie smiled. 'You, I take it, are Mr. Brontë?'

'Why yes,' Branwell raised his eyebrows in surprise. 'But how did you know that?'

'I have been mistaken for your sister before today.'

'Well, I'm dashed! But we cannot possibly talk here – all the old fossils are staring at us! Shall we find a seat in the fresh air?'

He was not a handsome man in the accepted sense, but so vital, so golden with youth and high spirits, so confident, that it mattered little that his chin was weak and his nose rather too large. His hair shone like newly-minted copper and sprang wirily from his high forehead, making him seem taller than he was, but his charm lay in his manners and easy flow of conversation. As Lizzie sat beside him on a bench, she was entranced by his soft, cultured voice, and flattered by the attention he was paying her.

In a matter of minutes he had found out her name and where she worked. 'So you know Mrs. Stonehouse of Haworth, do you?' he said. 'What a coincidence! I shall write a story about this intriguing encounter, Miss Godolphin, for I am a writer among other things.'

Branwell expanded in the girl's admiring look. 'A writer? You mean that you have had your work published?'

'Why yes, some of it,' he bragged easily, 'mainly poetry, although I have in mind a full-length novel which I believe will bring my name into public prominence when it is completed.'

'What a talented person you must be,' Lizzie sighed. 'I wish that I could write poetry.'

'It is a gift with some people, I suppose. My father too has known some success as a poet, but I have enjoyed my chief success as a portrait-painter. I left Haworth at one time, you know, to study at the Royal Academy in London.'

He neglected to add that he had never gone near the Royal Academy; he squandered the money entrusted to him for his education there, and returned home penniless. Then, feeling that he should change the subject, he slapped his hand on his knee. 'But it has just occurred to me that I must introduce you to my sister! I cannot wait to see her look of bewilderment when the pair of you come face to face.'

Lizzie's heart hammered against her ribs. 'You mean that she is here in Scarborough?'

'Naturally, seeing that we are tutor and governess to the same set of brats.' Branwell pushed the thought of the 'brats'' mother to the back of his mind as he spoke. 'Anne was sitting on a seat near Wood's Lodgings when I left her an hour ago, writing a letter to Emily.'

'Emily?'

'Why yes,' Branwell's tone betrayed a slight impatience. 'She is another sister of mine.' He rose from the bench. 'Will you wait here, Miss Lizzie? I will find Anne and bring her to you, but I shall not tell her why for that would spoil the fun.'

As she watched his slight, animated figure hurry away up the path towards St. Nicholas Cliff, Lizzie's apprehension mounted, and the implications of the meeting began to dawn on her. I cannot stay, she thought, I cannot, but she seemed rooted to the spot. Then it was too late. She saw Branwell coming back down the path towards her, walking a little way ahead of his sister, and guessed that he intended to wait until they were almost face to face before he stood back with a flourish.

It happened as Lizzie supposed. When Branwell had come as close to her as he could without actually knocking her down, he stepped aside with a dramatic gesture. 'Miss Godolphin,' he said in a voice high-pitched with excitement, 'may I introduce my sister, Anne Brontë?' and he began to babble how he had met Lizzie in the museum, and kissed her before realising his mistake, but Anne was not listening. Her eyes widened momentarily as she looked at Lizzie, then she held out her hand simply and trustingly.

It was if a mirror swung between the two women, a mirror

which reflected the same image. Eyes, nose, mouth, complexion were startlingly alike, but Anne's face was thinner; her eyes sadder, as if she had undergone some recent sorrow. She did not speak at once, but her beautiful eyes spoke for her in that moment of meeting. It was as if she looked into the face, not of a stranger, but that of an old, well-loved friend.

Branwell's disappointment would have been evident if they had noticed it. He had expected exclamations of surprise: some embarrassment even, and was totally unprepared for Lizzie's reaction; her words, 'Miss Brontë, what a long time it has been.'

Anne put her head slightly on one side inquiringly. 'Why, Miss Godolphin, have we met before? I am sure I should remember if we had.'

'No, we have never actually met . . .' As she gazed into Anne's eyes, Lizzie recalled a bright June morning five years ago when she had walked to Scarborough to buy fish from the market on the sands. The memory of a young woman in the donkey-carriage was still clear in her mind, and even though the woman's face had been turned away, there was no mistaking the set of the slim shoulders, the movement of her head, the dove-grey bonnet and lavender dress.

'I saw you in the summer of 1839,' Lizzie explained. 'You were driving on the sands in a donkey-carriage, saying something to the boy in attendance. You wore a lavender gown very like the one you are wearing now, a similar bonnet, and a grey silk shawl.'

A puzzled frown appeared between Anne's eyebrows. 'You are mistaken,' she said softly. 'I was at Mirfield in the summer of 1839. My first visit to Scarborough did not occur until 1841 and,' she added with a smile, 'I have never owned a grey silk shawl in my life.'

'I – I beg your pardon, Miss Brontë,' Lizzie said slowly, 'it must have been someone else.'

Branwell could not forbear to butt in. 'Well, Anne, how does it feel to possess a doppel-gänger?' he said with a laugh, to mask his disappointment.

Anne shivered. 'Please, Branwell, do not use that expression. I am sure that what Miss Godolphin saw was not a phantom or wraith of a living person, or an apparition of herself, but a visitor to the town whom she mistook for me.'

Branwell shrugged, piqued because his prank had not provoked the response he had hoped for. 'Why must there always be a simple explanation for everything when the not-so-simple explanations are much more interesting?' His spirits flagged; his thoughts returned to Lydia Robinson who might have returned, by now, from her Spa promenade. His demeanour changed from moroseness to excitability as he reminded his sister that it was time they were getting back to Wood's Lodgings.

'I suppose you are right, Branwell.' Anne sighed, her own spirits sinking at the prospect of the noise the young Robinsons would make when they bounced back into the lodgings full of sea air and devilment. 'It is time we were going.'

'I hope we will meet again,' Lizzie said, reluctant to part from either of them.

'I hope so too. If you are passing this way next Thursday afternoon, I will look out for you,' Anne said. 'Goodbye for the present, Miss Godolphin.'

Lizzie watched Anne and Branwell out of sight, certain that she had seen Anne before. But if not on the sands in the summer of 1839, where?

CHAPTER TEN

The past five years had brought about unwelcome changes in Edward's life. Driving home from his shipyard, he recalled his fears that Grayston Lodge might eventually be swallowed up by those anxious to develop Scarborough as a fashionable watering place, and the encroachment had already begun since a consortium of businessmen eager to attract wealthy visitors to the town had built the Crown Hotel and, through shrewd advertisements in the London papers, had succeeded in weaning some fashion-conscious people from the German, French and Italian 'Spaws', Lettie Railton, Bella's shrewd and fashionable cousin amongst them.

Lettie, with a pretty, marriageable daughter on her hands, had not been slow to take advantage of Bella's invitation to the Railton family to spend their summers at Grayston Lodge, and every season during the past five years, Edward had been obliged to endure their invasion of his home and privacy. Not that he disliked Railton, or his pretty little niece, Julia. It was the idea of the entire entourage, and Lettie in particular, that he found disquieting; the fact that his house was taken over when they were in residence, and no corner of it was solely his any longer.

The only advantage, so far as he was concerned, was the marked improvement in Bella's health. That and the fact that she no longer wished him to part with their home which she now saw as a decided asset. And yet the shipyard remained a bone of contention between them, and Arabella still could not understand Edward's steadfast refusal to give up his means of livelihood – especially since shipbuilding in Scarborough was on the decline.

Only yesterday she had returned to the attack and demanded to know why, when he could play the country squire, he would insist on building ships.

In equally attacking mood, Edward had retorted, 'I don't wish to "play" at living, Bella! I've told you a hundred times that nothing on earth would persuade me to live on your money!'

'But most of the smaller yards have already been closed, and your own workforce has been reduced by half!'

'I am well aware of that fact, Bella, but the men left to me rely on the yard for their living!'

His wife had rounded on him savagely. 'I have never been able to understand the philanthropic streak in you, Edward, or your strange penchant for championing the underdog! I simply do not understand you at all! Most people advertise for servants, but not you! Oh no, every time we need a scullery-maid, off you go to the workhouse, when we could just as easily get a reasonably tidy and educated person from the Amicable School!'

She turned away to pat a stray hair into position in front of her dressing-table mirror as she spoke. 'There was that wretched girl Ginny Morrison, for example. You brought her here from the workhouse, and I haven't forgotten the bother she caused us in getting herself into trouble under this very roof!'

'For heaven's sake, Bella! You are harking back seven years or more!'

'What of it? The girl was nothing but a common little slut!'

'Why delve into past history? The girl got herself into trouble, but the lad responsible married her . . .'

'I should think so too! Now there's Lizzie Godolphin!'

'What about Lizzie?' Edward felt his hackles rise. 'You can't find fault with her surely?'

'Oh, I suppose she works well enough,' Bella said grudgingly, 'but she has high-faluting ideas above her station, if you ask me, and she is far too thick with Catherine. Have you forgotten that wretched doll she gave her?'

'From the kindest possible motives, Bella. After all, the child had suffered a nightmare!'

'Kindest possible motives indeed! The child might have been contaminated! And what a fuss Catherine created when I made her get rid of the nasty thing!'

'You are being totally unreasonable,' Edward flared. 'All that is water under the bridge!'

Now, leaning back in his carriage, Edward reflected deeply on his life and circumstances. Nothing, he knew, would ever reconcile Bella to his means of earning a living, but, as hard as it was for him to hold out against her constant badgering, thank God it had lain within his power to help those worth helping.

Lizzie Godolphin had grown, under Amelia Stonehouse's guidance, into a fine cook. Moreover, the girl had struggled hard to educate herself. Smiling, he remembered that day five years ago when Amelia confessed to him that she had taught Lizzie the alphabet but was puzzled to know where to turn next.

'Would it help if I passed on some of Cathy's primers?' he asked.

'Oh lor, sir, that it would! Lizzie would be over the moon!'

'Very well, Amelia. But it is to remain our secret.'

When Lizzie had mastered the primers, he suggested to Amelia that the girl might be allowed to borrow books from his library. That arrangement had also been kept a secret.

In sight of Grayston Lodge, Edward saw what appeared to be a blue muslin and satin waterfall cascading down the front steps. Lettie, Julia, Arabella and Cathy were going for a drive.

'Oh wait!' Cathy begged the Railtons' coachman. 'Here is papa! We are off to Oliver's Mount. Won't you come with us?'

'I have too much sympathy for the horses,' Edward laughed. 'Besides, I should crush those pretty dresses.' He doffed his hat and walked towards the carriage.

'Won't you change your mind?' Lettie glanced up provocatively under the brim of her blue bonnet.

'I'm afraid I can't. I have some work to attend to.'

Arabella regarded him coolly. 'Don't forget that we are going to a concert at the Town Hall after dinner,' she said, 'and that dinner will be an hour earlier than usual.'

'Indeed,' Edward replied, 'it's the first I've heard of it!'

'I have just given Mrs. Stonehouse instructions, otherwise we should never get to the concert on time.'

'But it is late already!' Edward consulted his watch. 'How long do you intend driving?'

'As long as it takes to get there and back, I imagine!' Bella put up her parasol to indicate the end of the conversation.

'Very well, but as we have put Mrs. Stonehouse to the trouble of hurrying on our account, we must see that she is not kept waiting at the last minute.'

Damnation, he thought, as the carriage drove off, it is simply not good enough. Bella must know that it is Lizzie's afternoon off and that Amelia will be hard pressed to bring the meal forward.

He went to the library and poured himself a glass of Madeira. What an intolerable situation it was to be sure – the house overrun with the Railtons and their servants, and his own servants scarcely knowing where they were half the time. Had Bella stopped to consider the extra work that fell on Amelia's shoulders when she issued such ridiculous orders, and the fact that the housekeeper was not as young and sprightly as she used to be.

Depression hung over Edward like a cloud. He had tried to rekindle Bella's affection, but it was useless. His suggestion that they might one day have another child, had met with a blank refusal.

'What? Go through all the pain and nastiness of giving birth again?' she cried. 'Why, it would kill me! No, Edward, I have done my duty as a wife. I have given you one child who, God knows, seems more yours than mine, but I will never have another! It is quite impossible!'

'But Bella, this house was meant for children. Don't you recall how happy you were when you knew Cathy was on the way?'

'Oh yes!' she had turned on him bitterly. 'But I had no idea then how wretched I would feel later on. I thought I would die when Catherine was born! So did Dr. Binns, and so did *you*! But you've forgotten that now, haven't you? The answer is no, Edward. Never!'

Lizzie found Amelia basting capons, and sensed that the housekeeper was angry, and resentful.

'What's the matter, Amelia?'

'You might well ask,' the housekeeper snapped. 'The mistress has just sent word that dinner's to be put forward an hour, and I haven't even started the fruit pies. I'll never get done in time!'

Throwing aside her outdoor clothes, Lizzie harnessed herself with a white pinafore, and hurried off to fetch the baking things.

'And what do you think you are doing?' Amelia wiped the perspiration from her forehead and glared at Lizzie. 'It's your afternoon off, isn't it?'

'And do you really suppose that I could go upstairs to my room and sit there with my feet up leaving you to struggle on alone?' Lizzie said lightly.

The housekeeper dabbed her eyes with her apron. 'The fact is, I'm fair worn out with all this extra work and having the Railtons' servants under my feet all the time. If that Hannah Skinner has been through this kitchen once today, she's been through it twenty times! And a right bit of an uppity chit she is too!'

She had scarcely finished speaking when the woman in question stalked in from the yard carrying a pile of newly-dried linen. 'There,' said Amelia, 'what did I tell you? I suppose she heard every word I said, and will report me to Mrs. Railton. Not that I care! Why, for two pins I'd hand in my notice and go back to Miss Blakeney at Crossways Grange. At least I'd be appreciated at Haworth!'

Haworth, Lizzie thought. How odd that Mrs. Stonehouse should mention Haworth when she had just met Mr. Brontë and his sister. Working swiftly and silently, she recalled every moment of that meeting; her first horrified reaction to Branwell's kiss, then the feeling that she was drowning in the warmth of his personality. Why had he searched her face so intently, she wondered. Was it merely to trace her likeness to his sister, or could it have been more than that? Was she a fool to hope that it might have been more?'

'You're very quiet, Lizzie.' Amelia's voice broke in upon her reverie. 'You are not upset, are you? I'm sorry I spoke so sharply when you came in.'

'Oh no, Amelia. It is just that I have some news for you.'

'News? Not bad news, I hope,' Amelia said anxiously, feeling that her world was bounded by bad news.

'No,' Lizzie laughed. 'Interesting news! Something to cheer you up!'

The housekeeper attended to the capons once more. 'I could do with something to cheer me up and that's a fact. Will you come to my parlour when Tom drives the master and mistress to the Town Hall? We shan't be disturbed then.'

When dinner was over and the carriage had driven off, Lizzie followed Amelia to the cosy parlour which contained all her favourite bits and pieces of furniture and ornaments.

'Now then,' the housekeeper said, slipping off her shoes. 'I'm all agog. Tell me your news!'

'I met Mr. Brontë in the museum this afternoon,' Lizzie began, and recounted the rest of the tale.

'Lord love us,' Amelia beamed, 'the novelty of that situation would suit Master Branwell down to the ground. But what's the matter, child? You are blushing.'

'It's the fire,' Lizzie said awkwardly. She had thought it best not to mention the kiss.

'My dear,' Amelia admonished, 'do you think, in all the years I have known you, that I have not understood your every mood and expression? Something has disturbed you. What is it?'

'Oh, Amelia,' Lizzie said, 'I have never met anyone like him before. I cannot forget his voice or the way he looked at me . . .'

'Branwell? You are talking of Branwell Brontë?' Amelia interrupted.

'Yes. Why, what is wrong?'

'Nothing – except . . .'

'What?' Lizzie slipped from her chair and knelt at her friend's feet.

Amelia shrugged helplessly. 'Why, I scarcely know how to put it.'

'If there is something wrong, you must tell me.'

The housekeeper shook her head. 'If there is one thing in this world I could not bear, it would be to lose your confidence. But

84

I must warn you, child. Branwell Brontë is not for you. It would be foolish of you to read any hidden meaning into the way he looked at you.'

'Why?'

'I'll try to explain in my own way, but I beg of you to remember that I am your friend. Nay, more than that, I could not love you more if you were my own flesh and blood, and I would never do anything to hurt you. But Branwell Brontë is a strange person. Oh, I'll not deny that he is as full of charm as an egg is full of yolk, but that charm is like the streams that bubble on Haworth Moor – pretty when the sun is shining, but dark and sinister on a winter afternoon.'

'Branwell, *sinister*?' Lizzie laughed. 'Oh no! You must be mistaken. There could not be anything sinister in that frank, open countenance. Why he exudes nothing but goodness, boyishness, high spirits. Apart from that he is a poet, an artist! He told me that he once left Haworth to study at the Royal Academy. He was not lying, was he? And his poetry has been published?'

'Ay, two sonnets in the *Halifax Guardian*,' Amelia admitted. 'But the art venture came to nothing. He was back at Haworth within a week, and rumour has it that he never went near the Academy . . .'

'Rumour! Do you think I care for rumour? He is brilliant, I tell you!'

'Oh yes, I'll grant you that, and if he persisted in what he undertook to do he might become famous one day, but persistence is not one of his virtues. Poor Branwell.'

'You must be mistaken! If you had seen his face. . .'

'I have seen Master Branwell's face a good deal oftener than you have,' Amelia reminded her tartly. 'I have known that lad since he was three-years-old, and I like him – but liking isn't loving, and I would do anything to spare you the agony of falling in love with Branwell Brontë.'

Lizzie blushed crimson. 'Falling in love? That is – ridiculous.'

'I think not, child. I have been in love myself and I know all the signs. Oh I daresay it will seem daft to you, but when I fell in love for the first time – not with Tom, but a young ne'er-do-well from Oakworth, what a to-do there was. Nobody could talk sense to me. There I was, blushing and weeping, with my head stuffed full of romantic nonsense, and all because of a pair of bonny eyes and a head of dark curly hair.' Amelia sighed.

'I might have done as he wanted and run off with him. Then someone told me that he had got some girl into trouble and had promised to marry her. Did I believe it? Not I! Not until the poor little lass came to me and begged me not to come between them; that the banns had already been called. That cured me, I can tell you. But the day he married that girl I thought I would die with the pain of it. So you see, I *do* know.'

'I know you mean well,' Lizzie rested her cheek against Amelia's skirts, 'but the truth is I have never met anyone like him before, and I never will again.'

'You are right there. Young Branwell has a way with him that could charm a duck off a wall, and I know that there are times when he seems to be nothing more than a cheerful, high-spirited young fellow. But there is more to Branwell than that. He is *too* high-spirited. He . . .' She stopped fearfully.

'Please go on,' Lizzie said. 'I have no wish to hear anything against Mr. Brontë, only to speak in his defence. I cannot believe that there is anything so dreadful in his character that I must be warned against him.'

'Nay, I'll not tell you. I have said all I'm going to say. You have known Mr. Brontë for a few hours, you have known me for five years. You must draw your own conclusions.'

Tom returned at that moment. 'Don't run away because I've come,' he said, but the girl pleaded tiredness and went upstairs to her room, her brain in a turmoil.

Her encounter with Branwell had kindled feelings of such intensity that her mind seemed like a wild bird caught and caged. She remembered that bright, animated face which had laughed into hers; his dry, light kiss on her cheek. All those things, linked to the magnitude of his intellect and that warm, cultured persuasive voice of his, filled her with a singing happiness and despair which she could scarcely contain.

The sky was radiant with moonlight. She rested her head on the windowsill, her eyes bright with tears, her heart and mind straining towards some intangible truth which eluded her.

The faint warm sigh might have been the summer breeze murmuring among the trees. Lizzie lifted her head and listened. There it was again. The very air around her seemed charged with a strange intensity and power.

'Emily,' she breathed softly. 'Emily.'

Emily Brontë looked out with dark brooding eyes to the gravestones crowded thickly in the moon-washed landscape. She was thinking of Anne at Scarborough, willing her spirit across the miles that separated them to carry a message of hope and comfort to her beloved sister.

The house was quiet. Her father had gone to bed early as usual, pausing to wind the clock on the landing before retiring for the night. Emily wondered if Charlotte was asleep. Probably she was not. Their conversation before they came to bed was not conducive to slumber. Branwell's dismissal of his post as clerk on the railway was a subject which never failed to disturb them.

Emily did not believe for one moment that Branwell had stolen the money missing from the railway funds, but nothing could alter the fact that the books showed a deficiency of £11.1.7., and that her brother had been sacked for carelessness. They all knew why. Branwell had been drinking when he should have been on duty. It was unforgivable.

Emily stared out of the window, weighing her judgement. Unforgivable? No. Nothing in the entire Universe was unforgivable. If God's compassion encompassed all his creatures, who was she to withhold forgiveness from her own brother?

But while she could not condemn him, Emily wished with all her heart that her father and Aunt Branwell had been spared the agony of Branwell's disgrace when he came home from Luddenden Foot a ruined man, weak and shaken at having dishonoured the name of Brontë.

She imagined that homecoming. With herself and Charlotte in Brussels, and Anne away at Thorp Green, how lonely Branwell must have felt. Little wonder he had collapsed under his burden of guilt, left alone to face the reproachful eyes of his father and Aunt Branwell.

Branni wasn't like her, Emily knew that. He hated the

solitude essential to her own well-being. His mind was not strong enough to withstand solitude, while she craved it; pined without it. Nor could Branwell enjoy what gave her pleasure – her passionate love of home; the humble daily tasks which enriched her very existence.

The dog lying near her bed got to its feet. Bending down, Emily cradled his brindled head. 'Down, Keeper,' she said softly, and the dog sank to its haunches, ears pricked to obey her slightest command.

Emily looked out at the vast dark line of hills adumbrated against the bleached summer night. With daylight gone, what remained seemed a distillation of colour, pure and holy. Her spirit seemed drawn towards the cold moon. A strange ecstasy invaded her. Stars burned their elemental fire into the recesses of her mind. Her being seemed contained within that fire.

The dog whined uneasily. Emily turned away from the window; a traveller returning home from a long journey beyond the stars. As she made ready for sleep, her tiny room seemed peopled with those beings who would one day spring to life through the power of her pen and her fertile imagination.

She wondered if Anne was sleeping, and fell asleep thinking of her.

'Emily?' Lizzie whispered. But the dark, brooding presence was gone, and yet she felt an inexpressible sense of comfort in the moments when their minds met.

CHAPTER ELEVEN

Anne had had a difficult morning. Her pupils were more than usually fractious, complaining at being shut up indoors when they might have been on the beach poking into rock-pools in search of crabs and starfish. She had found herself as frustrated as the girls by their lack of attention and babyish behaviour, their quarrels over a shared book which Bessie declared she could not see properly because Mary kept pulling it away from her deliberately. Even Leila, the oldest girl, had created silly games from the least diversion.

Anne wondered if Branwell was having such a tussle with young Edmund in the room across the landing, and dreaded any thought that she might be required to accompany the Robinsons to the Spa that afternoon to keep an eye on the children. But Anne had been dismissed when lessons were over, and had brought her writing-case to the seat overlooking the beach where she had promised to keep a look out for Lizzie Godolphin.

Branwell, who had seemed charmed by the girl at their first meeting, when reminded that it was Thursday – Lizzie's afternoon off – had lost all interest in her. 'Oh, the doppel-gänger,' he said airily. 'No, you must make my apologies. It would be too deucedly embarrassing sitting between the pair of you. I should feel like a pet dog between two fairings. Besides, I'm off to the Spa this afternoon to see that young Edmund behaves himself.'

'It is harsh of you to refer to Miss Godolphin as "the

doppel-gänger",' Anne said, sensing in her brother's careless reply his impatience to follow Mrs. Robinson. Branwell merely laughed, then dashed upstairs to collect his hat and cane.

Anne had meant to start a letter to Charlotte and Emily, but could not concentrate on her task. Her mind felt stultified with worry over Branwell. Although he seemed much valued in his situation as Edmund's tutor, that was not enough for Branni. After a quiet enough start in the Robinsons' household, it was not long before he began to expand in the atmosphere of warm affluence.

At first, Anne had failed to perceive the effect he had on Mrs. Robinson. Now that lady's flirtatious attitude towards Branwell filled her with shame and foreboding. Branni, always attractive to women, now basked in Lydia Robinson's favour, and it grieved Anne to witness her brother's infatuation for a married woman seventeen years his senior. The situation was dangerous. She could not help observing Mr. Robinson's growing dislike of Branwell, or the way the servants had begun to snigger behind his back. Now she blamed herself for having recommended her brother as tutor to young Edmund Robinson, and wished Branni had never gone to Thorp Green at her instigation.

As she hurried towards the trysting place, Lizzie felt a growing excitement. Passing the Rotunda Museum where she had met Branwell, she glanced towards it hoping that he might have taken it into his head to wait there for her, but he was nowhere to be seen.

Putting aside her disappointment, the girl mounted the steps of Museum Terrace and saw Anne on the seat near Wood's Lodgings.

'Miss Godolphin!' Anne smiled up at her, 'I am so glad to see you again.'

'Please, my name is Lizzie. I'm not used to being called "Miss Godolphin".'

'And I am Anne. But you must be t-tired after your long walk.'

'I am used to the distance. It does not trouble me, and I enjoy walking.'

'Would you like to sit here and rest for a while? It is such a glorious view,' Anne smiled. 'The sea reminds me of the moors at Haworth. Both are equally vast and unfettered. Have you ever seen the moors, Lizzie?'

'No, but Mrs. Stonehouse, the housekeeper at Grayston Lodge, has described them to me. She used to live at Haworth.'

'Mrs. Stonehouse? Why, I remember her. We met her occasionally during our walks, and Tabby Aykroyd has often spoken of her. Did she not work, at one time, for Miss Blakeney of Crossways Grange, and doesn't her sister Abigail still live at Haworth?'

Lizzie beamed. 'Yes, that's right. She'll be pleased when I tell her you remember her.'

'You seem very fond of Mrs. Stonehouse,' Anne observed.

'I am. Indeed, she has been like a mother to me.' Lizzie paused, knowing that she could confide in her new friend. 'You see, I have no recollection of my own mother. I don't even know who my parents were.'

'I am sorry,' Anne said, 'and I understand your feelings. My own mother died when I was a baby.'

Lizzie closed her eyes momentarily, hearing the distant music of a violin; a sound as soft and insistent as summer rain, buried deep within herself.

'Tabby Aykroyd has been to me what, I imagine, Mrs. Stonehouse has been to you,' Anne continued. 'When my mother died, my aunt came from Cornwall to take her place, but Aunt Branwell died two years ago.'

Her head drooped forward like a flower on a slender stalk as she recalled the anguish of being called home to Haworth too late to say goodbye to her aunt, and how that second blow had fallen one short month after the death of her father's happy-go-lucky young curate, William Weightman, the man she had loved with all her heart. 'What my sisters and I, and Branwell, would have done without Tabby I cannot bear to think.'

At the mention of Branwell, Lizzie turned her head away, hoping against hope that Anne would not notice the flush which mantled her cheeks, but Anne was quietly observant of the tell-tale colour and guessed, with a sinking heart, the reason for it.

'Branwell asked me to proffer his apologies for not coming this afternoon,' she said. 'He has gone to the Spa with our employers.'

What more could she say? And yet she felt she ought to say more, remembering Branwell's casual dismissal of Lizzie as the 'doppel-gänger'.

Love is the cruellest of emotions, Anne thought, especially when there is no hope of reciprocation, and fingered her writing-case where William Weightman's Valentine card lay among her most treasured possessions. If only Willie had meant all those pretty speeches he had made to her. She remembered the way he had looked at her in church, and how she had scarcely dared lift her head for fear of meeting his eyes. But Willie had made pretty speeches to Charlotte and Emily too, and to Charlotte's friend, Ellen Nussey, when she visited the parsonage. It would be cruel not to warn Lizzie that Branwell often made pretty speeches without meaning them.

'My b-brother is not entirely well at the moment,' Anne said slowly. 'Aunt Branwell's death had a profoundly disturbing effect on him, and he lost, almost at the same time, a very dear friend of his, my father's curate, who was a g-great f-favourite with all of us.'

'I am sorry to hear it.' Lizzie remembered Amelia's strange warning concerning Branwell. Now, it seemed, Anne was adding a subtle warning of her own. 'Perhaps I am being foolish, but your brother made a great impression on me.'

'Branwell seldom fails to make an impression,' Anne observed.

'I should like to explain my feelings if it lies within my power to do so,' Lizzie said. 'When I went to Grayston Lodge, I could neither read nor write, and I cannot tell you how deeply I suffered on that account. I felt like a prisoner in a dungeon. My ignorance seemed like chains to me. Then Mrs. Stonehouse taught me the alphabet, scrawling the letters on the hearth with a piece of sandstone.

'When I had mastered them, Mr. Grayston lent me books from his library; essays and poems – I particularly loved the poems of Mr. William Wordsworth. Then I began to read the newspapers that were put out to be burned, and they seemed like gold to me. It was then I began to glimpse a world I never knew existed; of other towns and countries, great cities, and people I had never heard of before. Clever people, writers, painters and politicians . . .'

Lizzie's eyes shone at the memory. 'Then I met Branwell, and when he spoke to me of his own painting and writing, I felt that I wanted to write too if only I knew where to begin.'

'I understand,' Anne said. 'That creative urge is strong in myself also. Without the mental absorption of putting one word after another, I might have gone mad long since with grief and frustration.'

'Then – you are a writer?'

Anne flushed. 'Yes, but not a successful one – and I doubt if I ever will be.'

'You are wrong there,' Lizzie said simply, 'you will be successful one day.'

Anne glanced up, puzzled. 'You speak as if you knew.'

'But I *do* know.'

Anne shivered suddenly despite the warmth of the day, and her hands began to tremble.

'You are cold,' Lizzie said. 'I am sorry if I have said anything to upset you. Perhaps I should not have spoken about Branwell as I did, and yet . . .' She got up slowly from the seat and, clasping her friend's hand in hers, realised that this was the person she had waited for all her life long. Gentle Anne Brontë, who seemed a part of her own being. 'I must go now,' she said in a low voice.

'But you will come again, won't you, Lizzie?'

'Oh yes, I will come again!'

I will never leave you again in this life, she thought as she turned away. Wherever you are, whatever you do, I will be with you in spirit.

Lizzie walked unsteadily towards Museum Terrace. Approaching the Cliff Bridge, she saw Branwell walking across it, but he did not notice her. His eyes were fixed on a buxom woman handsomely dressed in a gown of violet silk with cherry-coloured ribbons, holding a black lace parasol.

A dour-looking man in sober dress walked beside her, and

behind them trooped three girls in muslin and a thick-set boy, wearing a tasselled cap.

Branwell sauntered behind the group, but his eyes never deviated from their contemplation of the beautiful woman in the violet dress.

Lizzie understood that look so well. It was the same look Joseph Franklin had once directed across the breakfast table at Grayston Lodge towards Peggy Robson, now his wife. A silent but unmistakable declaration of love.

CHAPTER TWELVE

Amelia knew that she must talk to Lizzie. The girl was fretting about Branwell Brontë, and the housekeeper believed that it was all her fault for warning Lizzie without giving her reasons why.

'Come to my parlour, child,' the housekeeper said that evening. 'I have something to say to you.'

'Why, is anything the matter?' Lizzie asked, her eyes heavy from lack of sleep.

'You're the best one to answer that, my dear. I know something is wrong between us, and I want to get to the bottom of it.'

'Nothing is wrong. Nothing ever could be wrong between us, Mrs. Stonehouse.'

'I'm relieved to hear it,' Amelia felt in her pocket for a handkerchief, 'but I was foolish to warn you against Branwell and then leave you in mid-air. The truth is, he's addicted to drink and to opium. Oh, the drug's harmless enough taken in moderation, but Branwell takes nothing in moderation. There now, I've told you!'

'Poor Branwell,' Lizzie said bleakly. 'Oh, God help him! But are you sure? There was nothing about him to suggest addiction to anything save a love of life.'

'I am sure. I've heard it from Tabby Aykroyd herself. The poor soul's beside herself with grief over it. Branwell is as dear as a son to her, and she cannot bear to see him wasting his life.'

Lizzie brushed her hand across her eyes, remembering

95

Anne's veiled warning concerning Branwell; her words, 'My brother is not entirely well at the moment'.

'It's the poor rector I feel sorriest for,' Amelia said heavily. 'He sets such store by his only son. Eh, Lizzie, it's a tragedy. Now do you understand why I warned you about the lad? I couldn't bear to think of you giving your heart to someone who isn't worthy of it.'

Branwell doesn't want my heart, Lizzie thought, but if he did I would not withhold it, nor my help if ever he needed it. But she kept the thought to herself.

Lydia Robinson swept into Todd's music shop in St. Nicholas Street to order a pianoforte.

'I wish to rent one for the season,' she informed the manager in an off-hand manner. 'Have you anything suitable in stock?'

'Certainly, madam. This is a very fine instrument – solid mahogany, splendid tone, overstrung, with pure silk ruching and solid brass candle-holders.'

Madam did not make up her mind immediately. Ladies of quality, the manager knew from bitter experience, seldom did, and this one seemed more pernickety than most. He followed her obsequiously as she rustled around the shop, remarking a scratch here, a flatness of tone there, and finally deciding upon the first instrument he had pointed out to her, although she expressed some dissatisfaction with the colour of the ruching.

When all was settled, she said that the pianoforte must be delivered to Wood's Lodgings before three o'clock that same afternoon.

It is always the same with the confounded gentry, the man thought angrily as she swept out of the shop to her carriage, wanting everything done in five minutes.

Even so, the piano was installed in Mrs. Robinsons' suite by half-past two. The furniture removers, who had lumped it up two flights of stairs, wiped the sweat from their brows and stared round the sumptuous apartment as they caught their breath, taking in the soft carpets, rugs and sofas, sideboards and mirrors, and the tall windows overlooking the sea leading on to a handsome wrought-iron balcony. Then, doffing their caps as Mrs. Robinson swept into the room, they stared in open admiration at her generously swelling bosom beneath the folds of an apricot silk bodice, and thanked her profusely as she handed them a shilling for their trouble.

When they had gone, Lydia ran her fingers across the keys, and did not hear the door open. A pair of hands covered her eyes. She stopped playing and said impatiently, 'You idiot! Have you gone completely mad?'

'I knew you were alone,' Branwell whispered. 'I saw you enter the room, and waited until the removers went downstairs. Oh, my darling, I have been on fire for this moment. Kiss me!'

'Branwell,' she remonstrated sharply, 'what if you had been observed? You must *not* put me in jeopardy! I have told you before that it is not safe here. Why can't you learn to be patient?'

Rising from the piano-stool, Lydia touched the tutor's cheek lightly with her fingertips, a careless gesture which inflamed his desire to fever pitch. Attempting to catch hold of her, he received a smart tap for his pains. 'Don't presume too far,' she said tartly, and then, relenting, she continued in a sweeter tone, 'You do not comprehend the danger. Why, at any moment the children might burst into the room, then our lives would be made intolerable. You do realise that?'

'It depends how you look at it,' Branwell cried excitedly. 'Would it be so intolerable to free ourselves of this subterfuge? I don't think so. Why, for two pins I'd proclaim our love from the roof of Wood's Lodgings. I would shout it aloud to the sea and sky and be rid of these stupid fetters.'

'Please, Branwell! You must be more circumspect – for the time being at least.'

'Not until you kiss me.' The expression in Branwell's eyes frightened Lydia. Unless she pandered to him, he might well do what he had threatened.

'Very well,' she acceded, 'but I beg you to hurry. One kiss, and then you must go. Promise?'

'I promise.' Branwell would have promised the world, the sun, moon and stars, for the delight of holding Lydia in his arms. He took the kiss lingeringly, passionately, while she glanced over his shoulder, ready to break away in an instant. But, ah God, his lips were sweet. She ran her fingers through his hair and gave herself, for one ecstatic moment, to his embrace, then pushed him away, shaken by the depth of feeling he aroused in her. What had begun as a pleasantly mild flirtation with Edmund's tutor threatened now to engulf her. But it must not. It must *not*!

Torn between her desire to throw caution to the wind and take the strangely exciting young man to her heart, Lydia felt herself drawn ever deeper into a whirlpool of indecision, and resorted to her old trick of placating Branwell with promises of delight to come – when the time was ripe – and spurning him because the time was not ripe. After all, she had her position to think of, her security, her good name.

'Go now, my darling boy,' she whispered, pulling away from him, 'and please, *please* be patient for my sake.'

Her bewitching smile and her plea for understanding and forbearance worked now as it always had. Branwell, ready to fall down at her feet and worship, withdrew his arms, kissed her hand, and went out of the room dizzy with delight, believing that the time would surely come when his patience would be rewarded.

Later, Lydia sped from room to room overseeing the arrangements for the evening's entertainment. When all the details had been settled to her satisfaction, she sat down in front of her dressing-table mirror and gazed at her own reflection. Her new dress, from London, was superb – midnight blue velvet trimmed with the palest pink aigrettes.

Calling to her maid to dress her hair, Lydia reflected that it was going to be a delightful party. The sea beyond the open windows shimmered under a full moon. She could not help thinking of Branwell. How ardent he was, how tender, gay and original in comparing her eyes to the stars, her beauty to that of dusk, dawn and sunset, her voice to the sighing of the night wind. She adored his flattery but refused to have her head turned by it, knowing full well that Branwell had come into her life at a time when she needed stimulation. Her family was complete, and her days seemed, at times, becalmed in waters too unruffled for her liking. Good works were all very well – and she counted herself a philanthropist – but they did not compensate for the conquests of youth.

98

Therein lay Branwell's charm. He had awakened in her memories of what it was like to be young and carefree; had brought to her a fresh feeling of youth which sat oddly with her status as mater-familias to a fast-growing brood of children and the wife of a sour, often difficult husband, but that did not mean that she envisaged a permanent relationship with the fiery-haired tutor. Indeed, she would be foolish to do so if that meant giving up her comfortable life as mistress of Thorp Green Hall and her place in society.

At Grayston Lodge, Arabella, Edward and the Railtons were dressing for the Robinsons' soirée. Percy Railton sang as he buttoned his shirt, and the sound irritated his wife. She could not help comparing her own husband to Edward Grayston, and sank down on her stool remembering the first time she had seen Edward, twelve years ago, a cloaked stranger standing in the hall of her London house, a tall man, lean, handsome – and remote.

Percy had warned her that he was bringing a guest to dinner – a shipbuilder from Yorkshire – and she had yawned, bored to distraction at the thought of entertaining some rough-tongued John Blunt from the North of England, for all Yorkshiremen, she believed, possessed a strange predilection for 'calling a spade a spade', and must surely be wanting in charm and culture.

She had walked downstairs expecting to meet a gnarled yokel who would guzzle his soup and drop his bread into it. Instead she had found a tall, bronzed man who seemed as much at home in her London drawing-room as he would have been on the deck of a ship.

I remember so well, Lettie thought how he bent to kiss my hand, not fawning over it as most men would, and how, as he looked up from it, Arabella came downstairs, holding up her black dress in one hand, the other resting lightly on the banister. 'This is my cousin, Miss Arabella Blakeney,' I said, and at that moment I wished her back at Crossways Grange.

Then, as we went in to dine, I heard Percy explaining that Arabella had suffered, not one but two bereavements, and noticed, during dinner, that Edward's eyes scarcely left Bella's face. Oh it was so damnably unfair. She scarcely uttered a word, just sat there toying with her food, looking fragile and helpless, while I did my best to be amusing.

Then, the next day, his flowers arrived – not for me, but for Bella. All I received was a 'thank you' note. And while Bella pretended not to be excited by the flowers, I knew that she was, for she pinned a rose to her bodice – one splash of crimson against that black dress of hers, and she was for ever sidling over to the window, expecting his carriage to draw up outside the house, and of course it did.

I knew then what the outcome would be – that they would marry, despite my warning to Bella that she knew nothing about him, that he was probably a fortune-hunter. I raised every objection under the sun because I wanted him for myself, and if I had not been married to Percy I would have found some way to win him. If Edward had paid court to me, I would have gone to the ends of the earth with him.

The atmosphere of Wood's Lodgings was oppressive despite the open windows. Edward wished that he had possessed the moral fibre to excuse himself from attending the party, but Bella would never have forgiven him had he done so.

Railton, he noticed, was deep in conversation with a group of men at the far side of the room, and he could guess what their talk was about – stocks and shares; bonds, making money.

Arabella was ensconced on a sofa with a dowager whose name he had forgotten. Edging his way through the crowd, Edward stepped on to the balcony, heard the faint wash of the tide on the beach below, and saw the moon riding high above the water. Resting his hands on the cold iron, he felt a sudden longing to be out at sea, one of the ship's company, hearing the faint music of an accordion played below decks.

'Edward?' The voice at his elbow brought him back to reality. A woman's white dress shimmered vaguely in the moonlight.

'Why, Lettie,' he said, 'so you also felt in need of fresh air?'

'You could put it like that, I suppose.'

Edward frowned lightly. 'Oh? I'm not sure that I understand.'

'No, Edward, I don't suppose you do. But then, you have never really taken the trouble to understand me, have you?'

Edward knew in that instant that Lettie had drunk too much wine. Her eyes were too bright, her hand trembled as it touched his sleeve.

'Darling Edward,' she murmured, 'if you only knew how much I have longed to be alone with you.'

'I think we had better go inside,' he said urgently, realising the danger of the situation.

'Oh yes, that's right,' she flared. 'It would never do, would it, to be seen alone together? Someone might jump to the conclusion that you care for me. But you don't, do you?'

'Of course I care for you, Lettie. You are Bella's cousin – and mine also.'

'Cousin!' she said bitterly. 'Don't you understand what I am saying? I don't care for you as a cousin! I care for you as a woman – a woman who could give you everything! No, Eddie, don't turn away from me! I know that you and Bella are not happy together, that you no longer sleep together. But I could make you happy, my darling, if only you would let me.'

Edward said coldly, 'So you've started listening to backstair gossip, have you?'

'No! I swear that I have not! Bella herself told me!'

Sick with disgust, Edward turned to go indoors, but Lettie clawed at his sleeve, imploring him to stay, to listen, to talk to her.

'We cannot talk here. In any case, there is nothing more to be said.'

Lettie's eyes flashed, 'Ah, at least I've made you angry!'

'Please let go of my sleeve, Lettie,' he said, patiently, making allowance for her intoxication. 'Let us go back to the party and forget this ever happened.'

'I can't forget it, and neither can you now. Oh, Eddie, we *must* talk!'

'Very well, but not here. Not now.'

'You promise?'

'You leave me little choice.'

'When?'

'I don't know. When I have had time to think.' Someone else

was coming out on the balcony. 'For God's sake, Lettie, go back indoors! Think of your reputation!'

The urgency of his tone penetrated her muddled brain. She relinquished her hold on his sleeve and slipped back through the french windows.

Edward gripped the railing. He must get out of that place; must be alone to think. He entered the drawing-room and pushed his way to the door. Someone was about to sing. Guests were drawing up chairs for the recital. He found his way to the landing; heard the pulsating murmur of voices through the closed doors, and then a light ripple of applause.

The landing was dim. All the noise and artificiality was contained in the overcrowded room he had just left. His one thought was escape. Suddenly a pale shadow stepped from the deeper shadows near the stairs, that of a young woman with serious blue eyes and a certain neatness of step which he recognised at once.

'Lizzie,' he muttered hoarsely, 'what are you doing here?'

'You are mistaken, sir,' the girl said, 'I am not Lizzie Godolphin, my name is Anne Brontë. I am governess to the Robinson children.'

'But that is incredible! I have never seen two people more alike!'

Anne smiled. 'I know. Even my own brother failed to tell us apart.'

'You know Lizzie, then?'

'Yes, sir, we are friends.'

'Pray forgive me, Miss Brontë,' Edward said quietly. 'You must think me boorish. My name is Edward Grayston.'

'Ah yes. Lizzie has spoken of you.'

Edward's heart lifted suddenly.

'But I must bid you good night, sir,' Anne said. 'The younger children are restless tonight on account of the party, and I believe I heard Miss Mary calling to me.'

'Good night, then, Miss Brontë, and – thank you.'

Anne glanced up in surprise. 'But sir, I have done nothing to merit your thanks.'

'I think that you have.'

'Oh? Then I am glad.'

'If you had not appeared when you did,' Edward said, 'I would have left this house, walked home alone, and caused a domestic crisis in so doing.'

'I see.' Anne's serious blue eyes met his. 'But do you not think, sir, that the good Lord, in His wisdom, often puts the right person in the right place at the right moment?'

'I have never considered that possibility before. But yes, Miss Brontë, I think that you are probably right.'

The girl turned away and moved, with a whisper of grey skirts, towards a room at the end of the corridor.

CHAPTER THIRTEEN

Mrs. Robinson handed the shopping-list to Anne Brontë, not quite meeting her eyes.

'Miss Mary needs two yards of narrow lace to re-trim her petticoat,' she said carelessly, 'and there are a few other trifles besides, as you will see.' Lydia was never entirely at ease with Branwell's sister.

'Yes, ma'am.' Anything, Anne thought, would be better than going to the Spa and pushing her way through the crowds of fashionably-dressed promenaders, even standing dumbly at the counter of one of the shops in St. Nicholas Street, waiting to be served by an assistant who, realising her humble station in life, ignored her for as long as possible, preferring to show off the braids and ribbons to more elegantly-dressed women.

It was a hot, airless afternoon. Approaching St. Nicholas Street – the busiest and most fashionable street in Scarborough – Anne's footsteps wavered and she walked instead towards Vernon Place, drawn by the peace and solitude of Christ Church.

A cart containing barrels of sea-water lumbered past her into the courtyard of Harland's Baths, polished phaetons rolled by, the sun glinting on their wheel-spokes. Sick at heart, weary of noise and confusion, Anne made her way to the church where she often worshipped, and entered by a side door.

The noise of traffic, the rolling of carriages and landaus, the lumbering hooves of cart-horses pulling heavy drays from the brewery in St. Thomas Street, and the voices of passers-by faded as she stood inside the church. Brilliant shafts of colour streamed down from the stained-glass windows upon the high pulpit and empty galleries; dappled the altar cloth, stained the lilies, and touched with fire the outspread wings of the lectern-eagle.

She slipped into a pew and knelt there, remembering Willie Weightman. If only her father's curate had lived, he might have restored Branwell's faith in himself and led her brother to better things. Willie was such a good person, full of compassion for the failings of others, never preaching on the follies of sin and wickedness, but lifting the fallen to a sense of their own worth in the eyes of God.

Is it wrong to think of Willie? Anne wondered. To remember, in this house of the Lord, how much I loved him? To recall the first time I saw him?

It was a December afternoon, just after she had been dismissed from Blake Hall. The parsonage was decorated with holly for Christmas, there was the scent of hot mince pies from the kitchen, and the sound of laughter issuing forth behind the closed door of the dining-room, but she had hung back in the flagged passage, scarcely able to bring herself to join the rest of the family. Then, when she had plucked up enough courage, she opened the door to see Willie Weightman smiling down at her.

How easy it was to read into that smile of his more than he ever intended to convey. How foolish she was to believe that he thought more of her than her sisters, yet how happy she was in her state of euphoria. What silly dreams she had conjured, for his very presence had lightened her sad heart.

Was it wrong to grieve so because he was dead, because she would never, in this life, see his handsome smiling face again? Was it wrong to wish him still alive?

Clasping her hands together, Anne knew that her own life had seemed to end when Willie died; that she would carry to her grave a burden of loneliness and regret.

'Oh God,' she prayed, 'forgive me. I know that I am wrong to feel so. Forgive my puny anger. There is nowhere to turn except to Thee. Teach me humility to accept Thy will. Grant me courage to face whatever the future may bring.'

'Papa.'

'Yes, darling?'

'I wish I had been born a boy!'

Edward glanced at his daughter. 'Now what is going on inside that little head of yours?' he asked. 'Why did you say that?'

Cathy sighed. 'Because, if I had been born a boy I should not have been obliged to wear skirts and have my hair curled. I would have worn breeches and come to the shipyard every day.'

Edward laughed as the girl placed her arms akimbo and swaggered a few paces, emulating the rolling gait of a sailor. 'And you would have sent me to sea to learn all about ships, as Grandpa Grayston sent you, papa, and I should have come home knowing all about masts, spars and rigging, fore-topgallants and mizzens, and how to read a compass.'

'I don't doubt that for a minute,' Edward said, amused by his daughter's antics, 'but you might have wished yourself safely ashore when the decks began to slip and slide under you. I know I did.'

'Oh, I should not care about that,' said Cathy. 'Why cannot a girl go to sea and learn how to build ships?' She turned her head to stare at the hull of a new vessel on the stocks, and the workmen who were busy putting the finishing touches to it. 'You know, papa, I think that building ships is the most exciting thing in the whole world! How wonderful it must be to know that every bolt, every drop of tar, and every square inch of canvas, when they are all put together in exactly the right way, will make a ship fit to sail to the far corners of the world and back.'

How tall she is growing, Edward thought, and how beautiful. Her skin is like porcelain. But she possesses something more valuable than mere beauty. My girl has character.

'Now then, Miss Cathy.' The voice belonged to Zach Mainfaring, Edward's overseer. 'What are you doing here?'

'I've come to look at the new ship, Uncle Zach. She's lovely, isn't she?'

'Ay lass, that she is!' Zach grinned. 'She'll mek a right splash when she hits the tide tomorrow.'

'I wish I could be here to see her,' Cathy pulled a long face, 'but I have to go to a picnic to Rain Cliff Woods, and I shall hate it because mamma will expect me to sit just so, with my feet tucked up under me, or play at battledore and shuttlecock with those silly Robinson children who will make no end of a fuss if I beat them. Oh, papa, couldn't I come here tomorrow to see the ship launched?'

'You know you couldn't,' Edward replied sympathetically as Zach went about his business. 'You've just said so yourself. You must go on the picnic.'

'But *why*?' Cathy looked at her father appealingly. 'Oh, I know what you are going to say. Because mamma would be upset if I didn't!'

'Yes, darling, I rather think that she would.'

Cathy turned away to hide her disappointment. 'I don't understand grown-ups at all,' she murmured, meaning that she did not understand Arabella. 'Why is it that I must refer to Uncle Zach as "Mr Mainfaring" at home, and never mention my dearest friend of all, Lizzie? Is it because mamma thinks they are not worth mentioning? Oh, I cannot fathom it. Why cannot mamma be more like you, papa? Why can't she see that people are *people*? I know that some have to serve, and the rest to give orders, but it doesn't seem right to me that . . .'

'Hush, Cathy. That's quite enough.'

'I'm sorry, papa, but it's true, isn't it?'

'You are very young, my darling,' Edward drew the child into his arms, 'and you will learn, as you grow older, that nothing in life is as simple as all that; that no two people are entirely alike in what they think and believe.' He hesitated. 'Life itself has a way of changing people.' He thought briefly of the Arabella he used to know. 'Unhappiness has never touched your existence, my Cathy, nor tragedy. Don't try to grow up too soon, my love. Enjoy what life has to offer in the springtime of your days. Try not to apportion blame without just cause.'

The girl stared up at him, not fully understanding what he was saying to her. 'Have I made you angry, papa?' she asked.

'No, Cathy. You could never make me angry.'

'I didn't mean to spoil our afternoon together,' she said. 'I'll go on the picnic tomorrow and keep my feet tucked out of sight if that will please mamma. I'll be a credit to you, I promise. But that does not mean that we cannot enjoy today, does it?' Her eyes sparkled with fun as she stepped away from him. 'Oh, papa! Let us stand on the deck of the ship together and pretend that the tide is coming in! Then, if we close our eyes and pretend hard enough, we'll feel her running down the slipway, and the spray on our faces when she hits the water, and that moment will be ours for as long as we live!'

Branwell Brontë pondered bitterly his servile status.

An hour since, he had watched Lydia drive away with her family to a picnic in Rain Cliff Woods. Sunlight dazzled on the carriage-harness; the horses champed impatiently at their bits as Lydia – a picture of loveliness in a white gown and broad-brimmed hat tied with scarlet ribbons – took her place beside her husband.

There had been some slight delay. Mary, the youngest child, had developed a sore throat and could not go on the outing. Branwell had heard the commotion from the landing, the little girl's tears, and Lydia's voice telling her that she would have a special treat later on to make up for her disappointment, then he had watched, from a landing window, the scene in the street below; the flurry of skirts as Leila and Bessie got into the carriage; the stocky figure of young Edmund, and then Lydia's husband – the skeleton at the feast.

Branwell flung himself on his bed. How could his beautiful Lydia endure the proximity of such a Philistine? That boorish pedant who possessed no sensitivity, no regard for talent, no ear for poetry, cadences or lyricism, who was jealous of his own scholastic prowess and his friendship with Hartley Coleridge, the poet, who had commented in glowing terms on the manu-scripts he, Branwell, had sent for his consideration. But whenever he mentioned his friendship with Coleridge, Bran-well perceived no flicker of admiration in Robinson's eyes. Quite the opposite – a cold hostility, even disbelief.

Now, as a servant, he was disbarred from the kind of jaunt which would have given him so much pleasure. If only he might have ridden in the carriage in Robinson's place.

A low sob escaped Branwell. Thoughts of lying in Rain Cliff Woods with Lydia beside him drove him mad with desire. He could almost smell the scent of wild garlic, young bracken, sap and earth; all the scents of a hot summer day trapped in deep cool woods, with the trilling of birds and the hum of bees.

There, with Lydia's fingers teasing his hair, he would have known a drug more potent than opium, headier far than wine, and she, amid all that dappled, dim enchantment, might have forgotten once and for all that she was the wife of a choleric country squire, and that he was nothing more than their son's tutor.

Turning his face from the light, he hid his face in the pillow. His spare frame trembled with passion, his copper hair burnt like a flame against the white slip. He was the son of a Cambridge scholar, a poet, an artist! Didn't Robinson realise that his name was destined to go down in the annals of English literature; that he would be remembered long after Robinson had been forgotten?

When a light knock came to the door he feigned sleep, so deeply sunk in his own wretchedness that he could not bear to face a living soul. Whoever had knocked went away, and he lay shuddering and sighing, sunk in his delusions of grandeur.

Covering his face with his hands, Branwell wished himself back at Haworth, at the Bull Tavern, where his fame as a raconteur stood supreme, where his brilliance increased as the evening wore on, and where he was listened to with respect, not dismissed as a servant. Oh God, to be there now, straddling the hearth, a measure of gin in his hand, the flickering firelight and smoky oil-lamps shutting out the darkness beyond the tavern door.

Anne slipped out of Wood's Lodgings in the hope of seeing Lizzie, but there was no sign of her, nor was there any sign of Branwell at whose door she had knocked to ask if he would keep an eye on Mary.

With a sigh of frustration she went back indoors. The child was asleep now, but she herself was weary with her afternoon-long vigil, and the room, with its drawn blinds, swam with a strange green light.

Sitting by Mary's bed, Anne realised that serving the Robinson family was slowly but surely undermining her health, and yet she had taken up the post with so much hope and enthusiasm, for Willie was alive then, and it had seemed a sensible plan to earn her keep and put aside a little money for their future together.

The Robinsons, she had believed at the time, were thoroughgoing gentry, but Mr. Robinson, although ordained as a minister, had never taken up a living, swore like a trooper, and preferred hunting to any other activity, while his wife, accustomed to flattery and social success, had given her children no moral training whatever, and they were, in consequence, just as indolent, vain and selfish as their mother.

Governesses, Anne knew only too well, were not highly thought of. The other servants treated her with scant respect, and during those first difficult months at Thorp Green two things alone had sustained her – her dreams of one day being married to William Weightman, and the possibility of starting a school at Haworth. But the school project had come to nothing – and Willie had died.

For three long years now she had tried to shut her eyes to the unpleasant glimpses of human nature she had experienced at Thorp Green, and had clung to the Robinsons' annual visits to Scarborough as the one bright oasis in an arid desert, for Scarborough seemed a haven to her, and she felt drawn to it, not only because of its beauty, but by the strange feeling of destiny which she sensed there. Even so, she could not go on much longer.

Four o'clock, and still no sign of the Robinsons' return. Branwell stirred. His room felt like an oven; his mood of self-pity clung to him like a shroud; it was the mood of a child who, denied a treat, has sulked itself into a torpor. Then, unable to bear the heat any longer, he rinsed his hands and face and went down to await Lydia's return.

'Oh, there you are, Branwell. I thought you had gone out.' Anne slipped out of Mary's room, closing the door behind her.

'I fell asleep. I was exhausted,' he said sullenly.

'You are not the only one,' Anne chided. 'I have been tied to Mary's room all day! Branwell, would you do something for me?'

'That depends,' he said non-commitally.

'Would you walk as far as the museum and wait there a while? I promised to meet Lizzie this afternoon. I know she walks home that way, and if you do see her, would you explain what has happened?'

'Very well,' Branwell said dully, 'but I can't promise to hang about there for long. I have Edmund's lessons to prepare.'

Lizzie had walked into town to do some shopping for Amelia. Now, tired and thirsty, she dreaded her long trudge back to Grayston Lodge. Her clothes clung to her, and she could feel the blistering heat of the pavements striking up through the soles of her shoes.

Something must have prevented Anne coming out today, she thought as she passed Wood's Lodgings and glanced up at the windows, scarcely noticing the man coming up Museum Terrace towards her.

'Mr. Brontë!' The girl was shocked by his appearance. This was not the ebullient Mr. Brontë of their first meeting. His face was haggard, his shoulders stooped.

'Anne asked me to come,' he explained. 'She has been kept indoors all day. One of her charges is ill, and her parents have gone off to a picnic in Rain Cliff Woods.'

'Oh yes, the picnic. I know all about that,' Lizzie said. 'My mistress and her guests have gone to it also.'

'Really? The woods will be somewhat crowded, then!' Branwell's tone was bitter. 'What a pity that you and I were not invited to swell the numbers. Don't you agree?'

'No, Mr. Brontë,' Lizzied said decisively. 'Oh, I'm not denying that I should like to visit Rain Cliff Woods, or any woods come to that, on such a hot day, but I could not bear to go there with so many other people. I should prefer to be alone, wouldn't you?'

'Not at all,' Branwell snapped. 'If I went there, I should like to go with one other person. Someone who would understand my every thought and mood. What pleasure would there be in wandering alone in such idyllic surroundings? To whom could one express an appreciation of beauty? Do you not think that beauty shared is beauty enhanced?'

'Not necessarily, but it would depend entirely on one's companion.'

'That is what I meant,' Branwell said feverishly. 'One person entirely in tune with one's self! One's alter ego if you like!'

'I understand what you mean, but how often does one come across such a person?'

'Not often,' Branwell admitted. 'In my own lifetime I have known but two. One a man who played David to my Jonathan, a wonderful person who died some time ago. The other a woman, a beautiful woman, not in the least understood and appreciated by those closest to her, in whom I have found an awareness, an intellect equal to my own. And yet, Lizzie, if I were to tell you what barriers exist between that person and myself, you would not believe me. How could those people who should best love and understand her, mistreat her so? It is incredible, I swear, how blind and self-righteous they are.'

Poor Branwell, Lizzie thought, why didn't I see, at first, how excitable he is, how moody and irritable? If only I could do something to help him.

'You know, Lizzie,' he said despondently, 'apart from the person I have just mentioned, who loves me, I swear, to distraction, I doubt if there is another person in the world who would care a jot if I died tomorrow.'

'You are wrong there, Mr. Brontë.' Lizzie could not help betraying some sign of emotion as she spoke. 'Have you forgotten Anne? She loves you a great deal, I know. And you have other sisters, have you not?'

'To be sure,' he said with a sigh, 'but Charlotte, the sister I was once closest to, thinks little of me now, while Emily, I believe, often regards me as a hopeless being.'

'And what of your father?'

'The Old Man?' Branwell gave a mirthless laugh. 'Well, I doubt if he entertains many sanguine hopes on my account. I gave him a bad shock, you see, two years ago, when I was dismissed – without just cause, I assure you – from a piffling post as clerk to the railway at a place whose name I cannot even recall. And so, you see, there is no one, except the person I mentioned, who would give a damn if I were at death's door, or who would come to me in my hour of direst need to give me succour and support.'

'I would come,' Lizzie said quietly.

'*You*?' Branwell stared at her in disbelief. 'But why the devil should you?'

'Because . . .' Lizzie began, then changed her mind. 'Why, to dispel, for one thing, your absurd notion that no one else cares for you, which I do not believe for one moment.'

'You look and sound so much like Anne,' Branwell said, 'that I feel damnably uneasy. But I must be getting back now.' His expression became more animated when he remembered that Lydia might have returned to Wood's Lodgings. He would know at once if she had, for rooms which had seemed empty all day would be full of noise and movement; the sweet sound of Lydia's voice calling to her children, the bustling of servants, the clutter of picnic hampers on the landing, and Lydia's broad-brimmed hat with the scarlet ribbons flung carelessly on a chair.

'I shall see you again, I suppose?' he said off-handedly, anxious to be gone.

'One day, perhaps, who can tell?' She watched him walk away from her, and when he was out of sight she stumbled blindly down the slope to the valley, knowing that Branwell Brontë would never care twopence for her, but that she would always care, more than a little, for him.

CHAPTER FOURTEEN

Leila, the Robinsons' eldest daughter, fairly danced into the schoolroom. 'I'm going to the theatre on Tuesday,' she cried, 'with mamma's friends at Grayston Lodge, and I'm to have a new dress!'

Bessie immediately set up a wail because she could not go. 'Don't be silly,' Leila said patronisingly, 'you are not old enough!'

'I am, I am!' Bessie sobbed. 'It's not fair!'

With a sinking heart, Anne realised that the morning's lessons would prove a fiasco, and she was right. There was something in Leila's demeanour she could not understand. The child was all a-tremble – as if she were in love, blushing and starting by turns, gazing out of the window with stars in her eyes.

Later, in her room, the longing to be back at home struck Anne forcibly. She thought wistfully of the grey parsonage set among hills with the moors behind it; the solitary paths, glowing colours of bracken and bilberry, the contours of earth and rock, and the place where a waterfall tumbled over mossy ledges to a deep pool which Emily had christened 'The Meeting of the Waters'.

It was there, in that tiny oasis amid trackless miles of purple heather, that one heard the smallest sounds in the stillness; the chirping of birds which fluttered down to take the crumbs Emily scattered for them, the soft insistent splash of water into the pool.

Anne loved Scarborough. The sea, even in its angriest moods, calmed and soothed her, but she missed Emily whose presence gave her strength, whose mind was a fertile treasure-house, whose awareness of Nature matched its austere simplicity. Neither she nor Charlotte possessed one iota of Emily's inner calm, she knew that. Charlotte was often prey to nervous headaches and depression, while she herself waged a continuous war with her conscience.

Only Emily had succeeded in remaining calm and resolute in face of all the hidden rocks of life.

She *must* go home soon!

Edward dressed slowly. The thought of spending a hot summer night at the theatre depressed him unutterably, and since the night at Wood's Lodgings there had been an increasing sense of strain between himself and Lettie Railton.

What am I doing, he thought, dressing for a performance I have no wish to attend? Where is this so-called round of pleasure leading? He remembered the scene on the balcony with a sense of unease, Lettie's tipsiness, the bright, false atmosphere of the Robinsons' soirée, the inane chatter and laughter of the guests gathered in that overheated drawing-room.

In those few minutes on the balcony, Lettie had destroyed something that Edward had taken for granted – his wife's loyalty. He could scarcely believe that Bella had discussed their relationship with her cousin but she had done so, and the knowledge sickened him. Moreover, Lettie had extracted under duress his promise to talk to her at some later date, but what could he possibly say to her?

There was a tap at the door. 'Come in,' he called, thinking it would be Tom Stonehouse. But it was not Tom. Lettie Railton slipped into the room, her eyes shining, one hand clutched to her breast in her excitement.

'I had to come, Eddie,' she said breathlessly, 'we cannot put off talking a minute longer!'

'Are you out of your mind, Lettie? Don't you realise the risk you have taken in coming here to my room?'

'Risk?' she asked innocently. 'What risk? Percy is dressing. I simply told him that I wished to consult Arabella on the choice of a necklace. He suspected nothing, why should he? And I *have* consulted Bella. No one saw me slip along the landing from her room, and if someone comes to the door, don't answer. They will think you have finished dressing and gone downstairs. You see, darling, how easily these matters are arranged?'

'Oh yes, I see that,' he said scornfully, 'but where does honour come into it?'

Lettie frowned. 'What have I done that is so dishonourable? I cannot help my feelings. It would seem more dishonourable to me to deny them or attempt to hide them.'

'And yet you lied to Percy to come here.' Then, seeing the dull flush which mounted her cheeks, he checked his anger. 'I'm sorry, Lettie,' he said quietly. 'I have no wish to offend you, it is simply that I am at a loss to understand your motives.'

Stung by his reply, Lettie retorted, 'My motives, as you choose to call them, are based on a desire to find happiness in each other's company. Is that so wicked? I have always been attracted to you. It was when I knew that you and Bella had become estranged that I felt it time to confess that attraction.'

'And what of Percy and Julia?' he demanded. 'What of Arabella and Cathy?'

'Oh come now, Edward.' Lettie swirled forward confidently in her forget-me-not blue gown and laid a slender, be-ringed hand on his arm. 'It is not unknown for two people to form an alliance – discreetly of course. Would it surprise you to know that even that pillar of Yorkshire society, Lydia Robinson, is having an affair with her son's tutor? Not that I blame her for that. She is just as tired of her husband as I am of mine, and Branwell Brontë is a very attractive young man.'

Edward's temper rose. 'I have heard enough! So marital infidelity is a kind of game is it? I would have given a great deal to have spared you the humiliation of asking you to leave this room, but I have nothing more to say to you.'

Lettie's eyes blazed. 'By God, Edward,' she cried, 'now I know why your marriage has failed. You are incapable of loving! I should have listened to Bella. She told me how hidebound, stern and intractable you were! I feel sick with shame that I squandered my emotion on you!'

She swung round, her pendant earrings catching the light of the dying rays of the sun through the window. 'Men of distinction have sought my favour but I cared nothing for them. It was you I wanted. God knows why, for you are nothing but a Yorkshire peasant!'

He felt almost sorry for her at that moment, understanding what it must mean to a beautiful woman to be spurned, and Lettie was very beautiful.

Turning at the door, she made her parting shot. 'I shall never forget how you have mistreated me! But remember, Edward, that loathing is just as powerful an emotion as love! The day will come when you will remember that!'

The Theatre Royal was stifling. The red plush box, as the Robinsons' party entered it, was the cynosure of all eyes, yet how little the nudging folk in the gallery knew of the flesh and blood people beneath their finery, Edward thought.

It is we who should be down there on stage, he told himself, and the actors up here applauding our brave attempts to conceal what we really are.

He glanced at Lettie Railton, clinging to Arabella's arm and laughing as if she hadn't a care in the world. What a consummate actress the woman was. And what of Arabella? No one looking at her could guess the discontent which ate into her like a maggot into an apple, spoiling the clean white flesh. Only he knew her secret fears and regrets, the way she had of rejecting happiness.

Then his gaze fell on Lydia Robinson, possibly the most striking figure present, who possessed the outward perfection of a portrait by Reynolds but who, if what Lettie said was true, concealed a treacherous heart beneath her charming, flawless façade.

Edward's face softened as he looked at the two girls, Leila Robinson and Julia Railton. Life had not yet had time to mar their happiness, or to etch anything save laughter on their lips. He was fond of Julia who, despite her mother's attempts to push her into a suitable marriage, remained impervious to the charms of the various 'suitable' young men with whom Lettie had brought her into contact. She will marry, when the time comes, Edward thought, for love, not for wealth or convenience. He had no way of knowing that Leila Robinson was already enamoured of young Harry Roxby whose father owned the theatre, and that she would one day elope with him.

And what of himself? Edward smiled grimly, a man approaching his fortieth birthday. He too was acting a part – the role of a happy husband.

He glanced at the programme. The first item would be a farce entitled, 'Is he Jealous?' to be followed by the 'Virginian Mammy' and 'Jump Jim Crow', none of which interested him. Then his eye was caught by the name Henry Godolphin, the celebrated Shakespearean actor, who would present 'Gems from the pen of Mr. William Shakespeare,' excerpts from his most famous roles as Henry V, Hamlet and Othello, with Miss Henrietta Jacobs as Portia, Ophelia and Desdemona.

As the lights dimmed, Lettie dropped her fan at his feet. Edward bent down to retrieve it, knowing that it had not been dropped accidentally. For all her rage, Lettie's glance held a dumb appeal as he handed her the object. Then, reading pity, not love in his eyes, she snatched the fan, with a toss of her head.

Edward leaned back in his chair, letting the farces wash over him, his mind busy with the name Godolphin. Lizzie's name. Could this man, this distinguished Shakespearean actor, possibly be connected with her?

Images flitted swiftly through Edward's brain. Lizzie Godolphin, the enigmatic personality who so baffled him; the courageous workhouse waif who had battled her way from illiteracy to learning; the girl who betrayed, despite her unknown parentage, undeniable traits of good breeding and intelligence. Cathy's beloved Lizzie.

The footlights shone on the figure of a man in doublet and hose. A man whose silver-blonde hair crowned a magnificent leonine head. When Henry Godolphin raised his head and began to speak, the audience was held in thrall. His features, Edward saw, were finely chiselled. It was an aesthetic face with a compassionate mouth and strangely compelling eyes, and his voice was an instrument from which he drew, not words but music.

'To be or not to be – that is the question;'

When the soliloquy ended, the audience reacted with thunderous applause. Then the curtain dropped and a woman, dressed in the neat apparel of an advocate, stepped from the wings. She was dark, of Jewish descent, and declaimed Portia's speech from the *Merchant of Venice* with a well-rehearsed intensity which pleased the audience.

When she had taken her bows, the curtain rose again, and Godolphin, arrayed in a jerkin of chain mail, sword held aloft, now radiated all the vitality of young King Hal before Harfleur, urging his troops on to victory. His voice rang out, vibrant, clear and confident. The audience could scarcely forbear to shout and clap its approval even before the magnificent battle-cry rent the stifling air:

'The game's afoot;
Follow your spirit; and upon this charge
Cry "God for Harry, England and Saint George!"'

Godolphin turned to the audience unsmiling, his sword held aloft in salute, and then – with an instinctive gesture that Edward knew so well – he lifted his chin, just as Lizzie Godolphin had lifted hers that April day when he had chosen her to be his scullery-maid.

Lizzie ironed the crumpled paper firmly with the palm of her hand, and when it was as smooth as she could make it, she picked up the scissors and cut it carefully, but the scissors went blunt and made a jagged edge. Frowning with concentration, she continued to cut the blue paper – an empty sugar-bag which Amelia had thrown away as rubbish – fashioning from it a cover for the scraps of paper on which she had carefully copied some of her favourite poems by William Wordsworth, and the entries in her diary of events at Grayston Lodge.

The fire in the schoolroom was nearly out by the time she had finished her task, but Lizzie smiled, for there, in her hands, lay her first, her very own book.

Suddenly Dido, in her basket near the fire, lifted her head

and began to wag her tail. She then leapt from the cushions and flung herself ecstatically into Cathy's arms.

Lizzie turned her head as the girl crept into the room. 'What are you doing here?' she asked, 'I thought you were fast asleep.'

'I was, but I'm awake now!'

'So I see!'

'But what are you doing, Lizzie? What's that you are holding?'

'It's a book. Not a proper book of course, but a kind of book.'

'May I look?'

'I'm not sure, Cathy.'

'Why not? Oh, I know! Because you are grown up and I'm just a little girl.' The child pulled a face. 'And you don't love me at all as you pretend to do!'

'Don't say that even in jest, Cathy.'

'I won't then, Lizzie, for I do love you! Next to papa, I love you better than anyone else in the whole world!'

'You musn't say that either.'

'Why not? It's true. I do love you Lizzie. I love you better than mamma! Better than Dido even, and that's saying a good deal.'

'You are talking nonsense and you know it,' Lizzie said. 'You are half asleep and your brain is muddled.'

'You haven't shown me the book,' Cathy replied. 'Why can't I see it? Is it a secret?'

'No, only rather – silly.'

'Let me look, then.'

'Very well. Take it. Read it, if you must.'

'Oh Lizzie! I did not know that you liked poetry! What kind of a book is it meant to be?'

'It's a – diary.'

'What is a diary?'

'A daily account of one's life, allied to one's private thoughts and feelings.'

'Which is why you did not want me to look at it?'

'Perhaps.'

'I'm sorry, then. I should not have pressed you to show it to me, but I thought I knew you so well. Have you many thoughts and feelings that you have kept hidden from me?'

'As many, I imagine, as you have kept hidden from me.'

Cathy sighed. 'Isn't it strange that there are so many secrets in the world? That even the people one loves best are not always what they seem to be? Take papa, for instance. I love him, and he loves me. He pretends so hard to be happy, but I know that he is not.'

'Hush, Cathy,' Lizzie said softly. 'It is well past your bedtime. You must not trouble your head about such things.'

'But I *must*! Oh, I know that I seem a child in years, but I think a great deal, which is why I cannot take much pleasure in the society of children of my own age who care for nothing but dressing up and going to parties. I vex mamma, I know, and that makes me unhappy because I cannot please her no matter how hard I try.'

'Cathy!'

'It's true! She would love me much more if I would sit as mum as a wax doll and she could show me off to her friends, but I hate sitting mum, so I am always disappointing her. Poor mamma!'

The girl put the dog back in its basket and siezed Lizzie's hands. 'If I show you something,' she whispered, 'will you promise never, never to tell anyone, or to write about it in that secret book of yours?'

'How can I answer that until I have seen what it is?'

'Very well, you may write about it when you are an old lady if you wish. Come with me, Lizzie.'

'Don't make a noise, then,' Lizzie countered, moving towards the door. 'You know your governess is poorly, and will be cross if we disturb her.'

She wouldn't mind that,' Cathy said airily. 'Miss Broderick is as different from Miss Blackledge as chalk is from cheese.'

The nursery wing was dim and quiet as the two girls tiptoed along the passage to Cathy's bedroom. It must be ten o'clock or a little after, Lizzie supposed, but the Graystons would not be home until midnight for they would return to Wood's Lodgings with the Robinsons for supper after the theatre.

Cathy crept forward to her cupboard. 'Will you lift me up, Lizzie? What I have to show you is on the top shelf right at the back.'

'Can't it wait until another time?' Lizzie felt worried about the governess asleep in the adjoining room.

'No. This is the moment! There will never be another moment as right as this one!'

'Very well, only don't start laughing or we'll both end up in trouble.'

'Wait until you see what it is! Now grasp my legs firmly and hoist me up – and don't you start laughing or I shall fall on top of you. There, I've got it!'

'What is it?' Lizzie frowned. 'A bundle of old newspapers?'

'Yes. Let us go back to the schoolroom and spread them out on the table.'

Lizzie laughed at the girl's excitement. 'And why,' she demanded, 'have you taken to saving old newspapers? This one is dated 1839. That's five years ago!'

'You'll see! Now close your eyes and see what God has sent you!'

'Very well, but if it's a trick – a frog or a dead mouse – I shall scream.'

'It isn't a trick, Lizzie. Now you can open your eyes.'

'Oh Cathy! It – it's my doll!'

'Yes, Lizzie. Your magic doll. The one you gave me that night you came to comfort me when I cried so.'

'But I thought – I thought . . .'

'I know what you thought, dearest Lizzie. You thought the doll had been burnt. Well it would have been if I hadn't poked it from the fireback with a pair of tongs. Why Lizzie, you're crying. I thought you would be pleased. But you *are* pleased, aren't you?'

'Oh Cathy, my love, my little love!'

The child was in Lizzie's arms, trembling and laughing.

'And you did that for me?' Lizzie fingered the girl's hair. 'Oh my darling, my darling!'

'Mamma was so angry when she found it in bed with me the next morning. I tried to explain that it was a magic doll but she would not listen, and threw it on the schoolroom fire. I knew it was naughty of me to disobey mamma, but when she had gone downstairs I rushed into the schoolroom. The poor little thing was lying on the ledge at the back of the fire, and when I had rescued it, I hid it. Later on I heard Aunt Amelia say that it was a crying shame to throw it away when it meant so much to you, but I didn't say a word to anyone. Why does it mean so much to you, Lizzie?'

'Because it was given to me by someone I loved very much.'

'And yet you gave it to me? Why did you?'

Lizzie touched the doll tenderly. 'Because you needed it more than I did, I suppose.'

Cathy sighed dreamily and slipped her arm round Lizzie's waist. 'You won't ever leave me, will you? I want you to stay here for ever and ever.'

'That is not up to me, pet,' Lizzie replied softly. 'Servants cannot always choose for themselves.'

'But you are not a servant! You are my friend! I would never let you go away from here, and neither would papa!'

'Hush, darling. We have talked long enough. Your eyes are heavy, and even Dido is fast asleep.'

'Very well. Only tuck me in, Lizzie, and kiss me good night. I do love you so.'

'And I love you, Cathy.'

CHAPTER FIFTEEN

The alleyway was dark and cool, shaded from brilliant sunshine by a high brick wall on one side, and the Theatre Royal on the other. Edward slowly walked towards the open stage door, pondering the wisdom of seeking out Henry Godolphin, yet strangely convinced that the man was in some way connected with Lizzie.

Inside the building all was dim and quiet, and as he crossed the threshold, the smell of the theatre met him – greasepaint, cheap powder, dusty scenery and extinguished oil-lamps. He stood in the wings and, looking out at the well of the auditorium, saw in vague outline, the plush-edged box where he had sat the night before.

'Who's there?' cried a hoarse voice. 'What do you want?'

Edward turned to see the figure of an old man in the shadows. 'Oh beg pardon, sir. I couldn't make out whether or not you was real.' The man chuckled. 'This place is haunted, you see.'

'I'm sorry to disappoint you,' Edward said drily. 'I am no phantom I assure you – just someone looking for Mr. Henry Godolphin. Have you any idea where I might find him?'

'Godolphin, eh? Why, is he a friend of yours?'

'No. I wish to speak to him that's all. Is he in the theatre?'

The old man rubbed his unshaven chin. 'Nay, he's not. There's none of 'em here at present, not at this time o' day. You'll likely find him at his lodgings in Queen Street. I forget the number but it's a door or two from the Talbot Inn. Most of 'em stops there with a Mrs. Maddern. Nice and handy for the theatre. It's a big house with steps to the front door, just to the left of the Talbot. You can't miss it.'

'Thank you.' Turning, Edward slipped him a shilling.

'Oh, thank *you* sir!' The old man touched the peak of the greasy cap pushed to the back of his head. 'Don't forget the name, Mrs. Maddern.'

So far so good, Edward thought, walking down the alleyway to where Tom Stonehouse waited, like Patience on a Monument – the perfect servant, discreet, loyal and trustworthy. He smiled inwardly at Tom's expression, knowing that he was bursting with curiosity.

'Now drive me round to Queen Street,' Edward said, 'to a house two doors or so removed from the Talbot Inn. A theatrical boarding house.'

'Yes, sir. Giddup, Bess!' A theatrical boarding house, Tom thought. What's the master up to? He's never taken a fancy to one of those actress women has he? Nay, I don't believe it. The master's not the type to play fast and loose.

'Stop here, Tom, I think this must be the house. If not, I'll walk along until I find it.' Edward dismounted and stared up at Number Seven, a brick house with stucco quoins and tall windows. Laughing, he turned to Tom. 'Don't look so shocked, man, I'm not going courting.'

'I never supposed that you were,' Tom called back to him.

'The truth is, I may be on a wild goose chase, and I have an uncomfortable feeling that I am interfering in something that is not strictly my business.'

Tom watched his master stride up the steps of Number Seven, saw the door open, and Mr. Grayston doff his hat as he stepped inside.

'There's a gentleman to see you, Mr. Godolphin.' The servant handed Henry a visiting card.

'Oh Lord. Does the room look very untidy?'

The girl giggled. 'No more than usual, sir. Shall I clear a space on the sofa?'

'Thank you, m'dear.' Henry watched as the girl whisked away an untidy pile of garments and thrust them into a cupboard. 'Now you can show him in.' Godolphin smoothed his hair with his hands. 'My dear sir,' he said cordially when the visitor entered, 'won't you be seated? Pray forgive the room's disorder. I am not, by nature, a tidy person. No matter, at least I can offer you a tolerable Madeira.'

The man seemed to fill the room, not only in stature but with the warmth of his personality, so that his surroundings were scarcely noticeable. The larger-than-life aura of the great actor was etched in every line of Godolphin's face; his every gesture, movement and utterance. Indeed the disorder of the room complimented rather than detracted from that aura, and the man appeared to overflow not only the furniture but his own massive frame.

'And now, Mr. Grayston, your very good health. I see by your card that you are a resident of this town, and an uncommonly fine town it is. Are you a theatregoer, sir?'

'I was at the theatre last night,' Edward acknowledged 'which brings me to the purpose of my visit.'

'You intrigue me, sir. Pray continue.'

'I scarcely know how,' Edward said. 'It will strike you as odd, I'm sure, that a stranger should turn up on your doorstep to inquire into your family background, but that is precisely why I am here.'

'Now I am more than ever intrigued.' Godolphin gave him a quizzical look. 'Are you perchance a detective?'

'On this occasion I suppose that I am. The mystery concerns a young lady – a member of my household – someone who bears your surname, whose parentage has never been discovered.'

'I see. Do you mind if I draw the blinds a little? It's infernally hot in here. More wine, Mr. Grayston? Let me refill your glass. Wine has the advantage of loosening tongues has it not? Speak freely, sir. Tell me more about the lady.'

'Thank you for putting me at my ease,' Edward smiled, 'for to tell the truth I felt damnably uneasy when I entered this room.'

'That much was apparent to me.' Godolphin considered his guest shrewdly. 'It is a part of my profession to interpret human expression. You struck me at once as a gentleman of a serious disposition bent upon a delicate mission, and I was right. I will do all in my power to help you solve your mystery.'

'Five years ago,' Edward told him, 'I engaged, as a scullery-maid, a nineteen-year-old girl called Lizzie Godolphin. The girl's history is a sad one. She was taken, on the death of her foster-mother, to the Scarborough workhouse. I shall not dwell on the agonies the child must have endured – she was but six years old at the time. Suffice to say that, when she came to Grayston Lodge to work, I was struck by her air of breeding – something intangible – I cannot quite put my finger on it, allied to a quick intelligence, and something beyond that – a baffling ability to look into the future. Why, what is it?' for Godolphin had risen from his chair, spilt his wine, and not even realised that he had done so.

'My God! It cannot be! David's child! She must be my cousin David's child!' Godolphin's eyes burned with excitement.

'You do know her, then?'

'It is incredible! I only wish my unfortunate cousin was alive to hear of this, and my dear Aunt Rachel Godolphin. But what of Hepzibah? What became of her?'

'Hepzibah?'

'The girl's mother! David's wife!'

'Lizzie's mother is dead, I'm afraid. That much is certain, I am sorry to say.'

Godolphin strode to the window. There was the sound of traffic in the street below; the crunch of wheels and the clatter of hooves as the Malton coach swept into the inn yard. Raising the blind which he had just lowered, Godolphin stared down at the pavement. His every movement was filled with a restless energy. 'What a tragedy,' he muttered. 'Poor little Hepzibah! My aunt begged her not to journey alone from Cornwall in her condition, fearing that the rough jolting of the coach would precipitate the birth of the child she was carrying, fearing some dreadful occurrence, but the poor creature, beside herself with grief at the death of her husband, pleaded to go home.'

Turning away from the window, Godolphin paced the room, holding his forehead as he did so. 'Oh it was natural enough,' he continued, 'for the dear girl to want to be among her own kith and kin when her child was born, but Hepzibah never reached her home. She simply disappeared from the face of the earth. No one ever found out what became of her although inquiries were made at York and Leeds where the coach stopped. But Aunt Rachel foresaw the tragedy of that I'm certain. Rachel Godolphin, Lizzie's grandmother, possessed the gift of sight to an unusual degree, but it killed her in the end. The poor soul could not live with that accursed "gift" of hers.'

Godolphin stopped pacing and rested his hands on the mantelpiece. 'Now I can hazard a guess that Hepzibah's child was born prematurely, and that somebody befriended her. Someone who cared for the babe after the mother was dead.'

'That seems more than likely,' Edward replied. 'I know that Lizzie was inordinately fond of her foster-mother, and that no one could have been kinder to the child, if that is any comfort to you.'

'It is, sir, it is! Perhaps you would care to hear the whole story?'

'Indeed I would.'

'You are probably aware,' Godolphin continued, 'that Methodism had its earliest roots in my native Cornwall. John Wesley himself instituted the ordination of ministers for work in America; and my cousin David studied hard for the ministry, became ordained, and went out to America to preach the Gospel there. Unfortunately his wife, because of her condition, was unable to accompany him at that time. David would not allow it, and because there was no telling what rough conditions she would be called on to face, plans were made for the birth of their child at my aunt's house in Polperro.

'In the seventh month of Hepzibah's pregnancy,' he went on, 'word came that David had died of septicaemia following the amputation of a limb. Can you imagine, my friend, the effect of that news upon a pregnant woman? The poor creature seemed almost demented. Aunt Rachel, despite her advanced age, stood ready to accompany Hepzibah to her own home in the North of England, but the dear child cared deeply for Rachel and would not hear of her risking such a long, tedious journey.

'Hepzibah was a delightful girl, a brave little thing with serious eyes of the deepest blue, fair hair, and a lovely complexion. Her father and his father before him were silversmiths. Tell me, Mr. Grayston, is the child, Lizzie, much like her mother?'

'Yes,' Edward said slowly, 'she is. Her eyes are almost violet in colour, her hair shines like gold with the sun on it, and she possesses an abundance of courage and common sense.'

'Indeed?' Godolphin glanced sideways at his companion, thinking that the man must be in love with her, whether or not he was aware of the fact.

Edward continued, 'But I must warn you, Mr. Godolphin, that Lizzie knows nothing of this visit, and I want nothing done in haste. Your niece has no knowledge of her past history, and news of it must be broken to her gently.'

'Of course.' Godolphin pondered the situation. 'But I should like to meet her, for I am convinced that she is David's child. A certain remark of yours struck home at once. You spoke of the girl's ability to see into the future. That is a family trait. Aunt Rachel possessed the gift of sight to an unusual degree – but I repeat myself. I have already told you that that gift of hers destroyed her in the end, for it broke her heart. She never forgave herself for allowing Hepzibah to travel alone.'

'I am very sorry.'

'Thank you, Mr. Grayston. But there is some urgency in this matter. I am leaving for Richmond on the Sunday morning stage. Today is Wednesday. It is my intention to take Lizzie under my wing, but all depends on you to arrange a meeting between us. Will you persuade her to visit me here tomorrow afternoon?'

'I will do my best.' Edward rose to his feet.

'Good. That's settled, then. God bless you for coming, my dear sir. You have put fresh heart into me.'

On his way downstairs, Edward wished that his own heart felt as light as Godolphin's.

CHAPTER SIXTEEN

Lizzie trudged home to Grayston Lodge, aware as never before of the patterns of the town she loved; the shapes of the buildings, the way shadows slanted obliquely from the shop blinds; aware too of sounds and movements, the swish of skirts brushing the pavements, the tap-tapping of heels, the clip-clop of horses' hooves, the jingling of harness; the shrill cries of children trundling hoops, vendors crying their wares at the marketstalls in Newborough Street. She thought that she would never again see Scarborough as she saw it now, or love it so much.

The sun beat down as she began the long ascent of Ramshill, and she remembered the day she had come from the workhouse to Grayston Lodge. The hedges were not fresh and springlike as they had been then, there were no billowing clouds overhead now, only the aching blue arch of the sky and the fierce sun turning the ground to dust beneath her feet.

Shy violets and primroses had peeped from the hedgerows that day. Now overgrown weeds choked the ditches, and there was spindly purple campion and foaming masses of white lady's lace where she had once glimpsed the dancing green tails of catkins, and spied soft grey velvet sprays of palm. Yet all seemed precious to Lizzie, a part of the pattern of life which was hers, and when the rain came all would bloom afresh. Then the perfume of the summer hedgerows would blend entrancingly with the tang of the salt air, and the lady's lace and campion would stand tall again, and beautiful, rain-washed against the straggling dog-roses and convolvulus.

Soon there would be other hills to climb, other patterns to adjust to. But now that the time had come to spread her wings and fly away, she wondered if she would be entirely happy away from her beloved Scarborough.

Dust spurted up under her shoes as she walked on. The hill had never seemed so steep before; her eyes ached in the shimmering glare, her head throbbed from the bewildering meeting with her uncle who had towered over her like a monolith, and yet wept like a child when he spoke of her parents.

For nigh on two hours he had talked of his old home in Cornwall, and of his aunt – Lizzie's grandmother, Rachel Godolphin. Lizzie herself had wept when she heard how her father, David Godolphin, had died far away in a strange land, and how her mother, Hepzibah, had undertaken that long, difficult coach journey alone.

After a while, Godolphin's mood had changed. He became more jovial and thrust a volume of Shakespeare into her hands. 'Have you ever acted, Lizzie?' he cried. 'No, I don't suppose you have. Forgive me, child! I was forgetting how different your life has been to mine. I imagine that you cannot even read or write.'

Lizzie could not forbear to laugh at his woebegone expression. 'I cannot act, uncle,' she said, 'but I am able to read.'

'Are you indeed?' His face lightened. 'Then you are Cleopatra, Queen of Egypt, and I am Mark Antony! Read your part, Lizzie! Don the mantle of Queenly dignity. Let the words roll from your lips:

> 'Ah dear, if I be so, from my cold heart let heaven
> engender hail.'

She had read the passage self-consciously.

'No, child, that is not the way,' Godolphin groaned. 'But no matter. I shall make an actress of you yet.'

He begun to pace up and down, making plans. 'My last performance here is on Saturday,' he said. 'On Sunday the company moves on to Richmond. The stage leaves the Talbot at ten o'clock. You shall join me there. Just think, my dearest child, a new life awaits you in Richmond. An end to the miserable servitude you have been obliged to endure in the past.'

She had left the house in a dream, almost hypnotised by her uncle's words and overwhelming personality. It was when she began to walk through the streets of Scarborough for the last time that she realised that servitude had become a way of life to her, that she neither resented nor regretted the years she had spent at Grayston Lodge.

She heard the slow clip-clop of horses' hooves. A carriage drew level and stopped. Edward Grayston leapt down. 'Get in, Lizzie,' he said brusquely. 'You look exhausted.'

'But sir, I . . .' How could she explain that she would feel out of place riding in her master's carriage.

'Do as I say.' Edward helped her into the carriage. 'Right, Tom,' he called, 'you can drive on now.'

'Poor Bess.' Lizzie smiled wanly, referring to the horse.

'Never mind Bess, she'll manage. She had a good feed and a drink before she left the yard.'

Leaning back against the blue leather seat, Edward wondered what was going on in Lizzie's mind. Had she seen Henry Godolphin? He forbore to ask, knowing that she would tell him in her own good time, but he noticed that her fingers were trembling in her lap.

The carriage swayed on, a small intimate world on wheels to the accompaniment of jingling harness. He had never been physically closer to Lizzie before, and there would be the devil to pay if Bella saw a servant riding in her place, but he knew that he would not give a damn for his wife's disapproval.

Bess reached the top of the hill where Tom rested her a while before turning into the Hull road. Upon the rise, Lizzie looked out at the green fields, spreading to left and right, and shimmering in the hot bright sunshine. A dusty cart was driving into the yard of Newton's Mill; men were sitting on sacks of grain, wiping their brows with spotted 'kerchiefs, horses nosed in a water-trough, a woman in a green print dress shaded her eyes from the glare, and waved as the carriage passed by.

The mill made another pattern, a high conical pattern with a hard-blocked shadow falling away from it. An old man dozed on a bale of hay.

Lizzie's eyes stung with tears. As Tom clicked to the horse, she said in a low voice, 'Sir I think this is the last time I shall ever come this way. I have promised to go to Richmond with my uncle.'

The storm broke at midnight. Lightning slit the dark canvas of the sky. Rain began to patter on the dry earth.

Edward heard the commotion in the stables as the horses reared up and crashed their hooves against the sides of their stalls, and saw the flicker of a lantern as Joseph clattered down from the loft to attend to them. Flinging wide his bedroom window, he peered out, glad of the tumult which echoed his own inner turmoil, the drumming of his heart, the complexity of his emotions.

Roses swayed and bent beneath the deluge. He heard the bellow of a cow in some distant outhouse, the shrill bark of a dog, and whinnying of the frightened horses. Rain dripped on to the carpet as the storm rose to a crescendo above the chimneys of Grayston Lodge. Then hailstones thumped down like bullets, cutting runnels in the dykes, washing away the soil, carrying with them in a quick scurrying flood, branches, twigs and tiny nocturnal creatures.

Edward had excused himself after dinner and had retired to his room to wrestle with his own dark thoughts, wondering how he had endured through five courses of Percy's long-winded account of a business transaction to do with the purchase of a stallion from Sir George Egmonton of York, and Sir George's invitation to spend the weekend at Egmonton Hall to clinch the deal.

'What, Edward,' Bella said coldly when he refused coffee, 'are you tired of our company already?'

Now, as he stared at the bobbing lanterns in the stable-yard, he heard a sudden urgent knock at his door, and Bella's voice calling him to let her in. He strode across and turned the key. His wife pushed past him, her eyes dark with terror.

'I cannot bear it,' she cried hysterically. 'I think the roof is coming in!' Then, seeing the open window, she uttered a startled cry. 'For God's sake, Edward, are you mad? Close the window at once and draw the curtains. We shall be struck on the spot!' She stared at her husband. 'I thought to find you abed,' she said sharply. 'You were so intent upon having an early night, yet here it is well past midnight and you have made no move towards undressing.'

'I had problems on my mind to do with the shipyard,' he replied grimly. It was the truth. Tomorrow he would be obliged to lay off more men. The thought was not a pleasant one, nor was the realisation that the day was fast approaching when sand and mud would silt up the slipways, when the stanchions would rot, the padlocks rust in the salt air, and all that had been built up with so much pride over the years by his father and his grandfather before him, would cease to exist.

'Problems! It is always problems with you!' Bella sank down in a chair. 'Why can't you forget your problems for once?' She flinched as another flash of lightning cut through the summer night. 'But you will come to the Egmonton's house party, won't you? We are all invited, and Lettie is over the moon because the Honourable James Hennessy, the Egmonton's nephew, wants to meet Julia.'

'Not now, please, Bella. I thought I heard Joseph calling. I had better go down and see if he needs help with the horses.'

'Damn the horses! What about me? I want an answer!'

'I haven't time to discuss it now,' he said urgently. 'Something is wrong down there. Bella, I must go. Seek out Percy. Tell him to come down and lend a hand. I believe one of the horses has broken loose.' Edward threw on a coat and hurried downstairs.

When dawn came, Edward surveyed the night's havoc with a heavy heart, knowing that worse havoc awaited him at the shipyard. Even so, he could not help feeling sorry for Percy whose favourite carriage-horse had broken a leg in its frenzied efforts to quit its stall, and had been put out of its misery by a quick and merciful bullet through the brain.

At five o'clock, he bade Joseph saddle one of his older hacks and, without stopping to eat or drink, he mounted and rode to Scarborough, dreading what he would find at his journey's end.

It was far worse than he had anticipated. Mud and sand

silted up from the harbour bottom lay as thick as treacle over the entire area of Sandside. Tethering his horse in Merchant's Row, Edward picked his way down to the yard, mud oozing over his insteps and almost sucking the boots from his feet.

Zach Mainfaring was there before him, gazing grimly at the wreckage of the launching cradle.

'Well, Zach, we'll have our work cut out to clear this lot,' he said.

'Ay, master,' Zach's tone was lugubrious. 'But Tindall's Yard is worse hit! He's lost two ships, and there's now't left of his sail-loft.'

'The poor devil,' Edward said bitterly. Tindall's Yard was the biggest of the lot, and old Mr. Tindall had been his father's friend.

'Well, sir,' Zach said gruffly, 'this ain't the first mess we've cleaned up together, and I doubt if it'll be the last.'

'Let's hope you are right, Zach. Is Mr. Tindall at his yard?'

'Ay, sir. He come just afore you did.'

'I'd better get along, then, and have a word with him.' As Edward turned, he saw that his workmen were beginning to filter into the yard. Not one of them was due for another two hours, but there they were, picking their way through the mud to begin the work of clearing up.

It was just after eight when Edward returned to Grayston Lodge and gave the horse to Joseph to unsaddle and rub down.

'Is it bad down yonder, sir?' Joseph asked, taking the reins.

'About as bad as it could be,' Edward replied, going indoors through the kitchen entrance. 'I'll have a bite to eat first, then I must get back as quickly as possible.'

Lizzie was in the kitchen. 'You must be famished, sir,' she said.

'Famished? I'm starving, Lizzie.' He threw his coat on to a chair and spread his hands to the fire.

'Could you eat some ham and eggs?'

He laughed. 'I fancy I could eat at least six eggs and a side of bacon, but I'll settle for two eggs, a couple of rashers, and one of those oven-bottom cakes spread thick with butter.'

Sitting down in Amelia's rocking-chair, Edward watched the

girl as she moved quickly about the kitchen. What have I done, he thought. Why the hell did I interfere? I'm a fool, a blundering fool. What right had I to approach Godolphin? What made me think that I was acting in her best interests? Now it is too late, she is going to leave me.

'Will you eat in the dining-room, sir?' Lizzie set the skillet on the fire as she spoke.

'Not in these boots, and I'm far too tired to change them.'

'No sir,' Lizzie smiled, 'they are not your boots, are they? I remember thinking – that day in the workhouse – that I had never seen such shiny boots as yours in all my life. They reminded me of autumn leaves, or glossy chestnuts when they have just changed colour.'

The bacon curled in the skillet. Edward watched Lizzie closely, noticing the neat way she worked, setting his knife and fork, cup and saucer, the way she cut the bread, stirred the porridge, and cracked the eggs with the skillet held a little to one side so that they did not lose their shape or run together in the breaking.

'Shall you be happy in Richmond?' he asked. 'And where will you go after that?'

'I don't know, sir. To other towns, I suppose – wherever my uncle is booked to appear – then to London.'

'And have you any idea what you will be doing from place to place?'

'I'm not sure. My uncle spoke of making an actress of me. He made me read a passage from *Antony and Cleopatra*.'

Oh God, Edward thought, Lizzie an actress. That tender child standing on some stage or other with waxen flowers in her hair and make-up on her face. It is unthinkable, and I'm to blame. I wish I had never set foot inside that theatre, but it is too late for regrets. Today is Friday. One more day and she will be gone . . .

'All is ready. Will you eat now?'

He took his place at table. Thank God, he thought, that Bella and the Railtons are going to York this weekend, and thank God that I have reason enough not to accompany them. Bella need not know that Lizzie is leaving, but she will not care. One servant is like another to her. But what of Cathy?

Lizzie appeared to have read his thoughts. 'I haven't told Cathy I'm leaving,' she said quietly.

'Why not? Why haven't you done so?'

'Because . . .'

Edward rose to his feet impatiently, pushing aside his plate. 'Forget that I am your employer,' he said. 'Tell me the truth! You are not a slave, you know, and the day after tomorrow you will no longer be called upon to serve me or any member of my household.'

'I know.' The girl stifled a sob. 'But it is not easy to change in a matter of hours. I cannot forget my upbringing so easily. Now I know who my parents were, and I am glad, but that knowledge has not changed *me*! It has not changed the happiness I have known here at Grayston Lodge, or the way I feel about Amelia and Peggy and Tom and Joseph. The truth is, they seem dearer to me than my own kin. How could it be otherwise? They are the people I have learned to love. As for Cathy – I do not know how I can bear to leave *her*. I love her so . . .'

'Lizzie!'

'Oh, I realise that I must tell Cathy that I am leaving, and I shall. But I would rather face all over again the deprivations of my own early life than cause her a moment's pain. Oh sir, what shall I do?'

'I cannot decide that for you, Lizzie,' Edward shook his head. 'The decision rests entirely with you. That is the price one has to pay for freedom – or what one chooses to call freedom. As for myself, I believe that I acted wrongly in visiting your uncle without first consulting you, but I did not know if there was any connection at the time, and it would have been cruel to build up your hopes to no purpose.'

'But you cannot think that I blame you for this dilemma? I know you acted for my good, and I am grateful to you.'

'Thank you, Lizzie. But I do not wish to add to your distress. Would it be easier for you if I told Cathy that you are leaving?'

The girl smiled faintly. 'Why yes, it would. It would indeed. And that would absolve me most honourably, would it not?'

'You mean . . . ?'

'I mean that I should never sleep soundly in my bed again if I took the coward's way out. I must tell Cathy myself.'

Edward sighed, strangely satisfied. 'That is what I thought you meant.'

Lizzie walked slowly downstairs, caressing the banister as if she would never again touch anything so dear to her, and stood for a moment drawing to herself for all time the smell of beeswax polish and lavender, and the scent of pot-pourri in a bowl on a sun-drenched windowsill.

Time was pressing, but she lingered a while in the kitchen; looking at the coal-skips, the shining dishes on the high dresser, the polished copper pans and skillets, and the black-leaded range with Amelia's rocking-chair beside it.

The house seemed strangely quiet and empty, with a Sunday morning sense of peace lying over all. She remembered, with pain, her leave-taking of Amelia and Cathy. Peggy and Joseph and their two children were, she knew, waiting in the drive to say goodbye to her.

Pushing open the hall door, she saw slanting rays of sunshine dappling the carpet with red and blue prisms from the stained-glass window on the landing, and she trod carefully, trying absurdly not to shatter the brittle colours at her feet.

Raising her hand, she knocked on the library door, heard Mr. Grayston bid her enter, and stood just inside the room, seeing her master through a veil of tears.

He was standing near the fireplace, his arms resting on the mantelpiece, and turned as she entered.

'Well, Lizzie, it's goodbye, then?'

'Yes, sir, it would seem so.'

'I cannot begin to express my thanks for all that you have done – for all that you have meant to – to everyone at Grayston Lodge.'

'It is I who should thank you, sir,' Lizzie faltered, 'for all that they have meant to me.'

'And Cathy? What of Cathy?'

'I think that she is very upset, sir,' Lizzie said slowly. 'I knocked at her door ten minutes since to bid her a last goodbye, but there was no answer.'

'Don't worry. I will go up to her directly.'

'Thank you, sir.'

'Well, goodbye Lizzie – and may God go with you.'

She turned as silently as a ghost, and was gone. When the door closed behind her, Edward rested his head on the mantelpiece.

I love her, he thought. My God, I love her. I suppose that I have loved her from the first minute I saw her, and never realised it until now.

As the carriage moved away down the drive, Lizzie sat stiffly, choking back her tears, holding a child's wilting posy of buttercups and daisies gathered by little Emma Franklin, and thrust into her hands as a parting gift.

Every bend of the road, every field, farmhouse, tree and dewpond, was dear and familiar to Lizzie as the carriage bowled along towards the turning into Ramshill.

Then suddenly it seemed not to be a summer Sunday morning any longer, but a bright, windy spring Monday morning five years ago, with white clouds scudding overhead, and Amelia crying, 'This is what I am used to! The wind cutting like a knife, and the clouds flying as they used to up on Haworth Moor.'

As that memory faded, it was a warm day in June, and she was striding along the road towards the market on the sands, glancing back over her shoulder to make sure that Joseph was not following her, and with the hasp of a purse digging into her palm. A lark was flinging its heart to heaven, and the air was filled with the name Emily . . . Emily . . . Emily!

Lizzie glanced up at Tom's ramrod back, then at the bundle on the seat beside her containing her doll and Bible, and her diaries.

Patterns, she thought bleakly, life is woven into patterns, and one break destroys the whole fabric. What am I doing sitting in this carriage, breaking the threads of my happiest days to face an unknown future?

My uncle is my own flesh and blood, and yet Cathy is much more to me than that. She is a part of my own fibre and being, as Anne Brontë, and Emily and Branwell are, although I cannot understand why, and my love for them has nothing to do with security. All I understand is what I *feel*. Security lies with my uncle, I know that, but my heart lies with those I have known and loved, and what I feel now is not happiness but anguish. Oh dear God, help me. Help me!

'Whoa, there! Whoa, Bess! Easy, old girl!'

The carriage ground to a halt.

'What is it, Tom?' Lizzie cried, lowering the window.

'It's young Miss Cathy!' Tom shouted. 'Gave me a fair turn, she did, springing up from the ditch like that. Whoa, Bess. Whoa!'

Staring from the carriage window, Lizzie saw the dishevelled figure of a young girl running across the road, her dark hair streaming in disorder beneath the brim of her straw hat.

'Cathy,' she cried, flinging open the carriage door.

'Lizzie!' The child hurled herself into the carriage, sobbing as if her heart would break. 'Don't leave me, Lizzie. Come back home! Oh do come back home!'

The seat and floor were scattered with wilting buttercups and daisies as Lizzie held the weeping girl tenderly in her arms.

Lizzie knocked on the library door.

'Come in.'

She scarcely recognised the voice of her master. He was still standing near the fireplace, his face turned away from her.

'Well, Tom,' he said despondently, 'has she gone?'

'If you mean me, sir,' Lizzie replied hesitantly, 'why no, I have come back.'

'Lizzie?'

As he turned to face her, an insistent chord, like far-off violin music, ran through her mind.

'Lizzie!'

'Yes, sir?' The melody increased in strength and power as Edward stepped forward, his face aglow with love, and took her hands in his.

'Lizzie! You have come back to me?'

'I could not for the life of me go away when the time came,' she said softly.

'Then you knew where you were most needed?'

'Why, I believe so, sir.'

'But – why?'

'Because, when Bess reached the turning into Ramshill, Cathy was there. She had waited an hour in the lea of a hedge, not to wave to me as the carriage passed by, but to beg me not to leave her. How could I refuse that appeal?'

'Oh, Lizzie.'

'I knew that I could no more leave Cathy than I could fly in the air, and so I asked Tom to continue to Scarborough to see my uncle; to explain to him why I could not be on that stage to Richmond. Then Cathy and I walked back along the road together, her hand in mine, the pair of us laughing and crying by turns.'

'Then it was for Cathy's sake only that you returned?'

'Well, no. There were other considerations.'

'Such as?'

'Why, Tom and Amelia, Peggy and Joseph, and . . .'

'Yes, Lizzie?' Edward said intently.

'I'm sorry, sir, I can't think of any other reasons. Well . . . none that I can explain.' The girl flushed and lowered her eyes.

'You just wanted to come back – home?' Edward said gently, releasing her hands.

'Yes.'

'Then all I can say is, thank God for bringing you back to Grayston Lodge. To Cathy, and to all those who – love you.'

'Thank you, sir.' Lizzie closed the door behind her, then leaned against it trembling, remembering that insistent chord of music she had heard when the master held her hands in his, and the undeniable current which had flowed between them.

I love him, she thought, staggered by the revelation. I love him! I believe that I have loved him from the first moment I saw him. Then she knew something more – that Edward Grayston loved her.

CHAPTER SEVENTEEN

The Robinsons' apartments at Wood's Lodgings were already shorn of the personal belongings which had marked them as their own during the long, hot weeks of summer.

Lydia's silver-backed hairbrushes and tortoiseshell trinket-set had gone from the mahogany dressing-table in her room, the inlaid wardrobe was empty of gowns, trunks and valises stood packed and ready to be loaded aboard the carter's wagon. The piano with the brass candleholders had been returned to Todd's music shop in St. Nicholas Street.

Sitting beside Lizzie on her favourite seat overlooking the South Bay, Anne Brontë admitted that she found something infinitely sad about the end of summer; the decline of golden days to the dreariness of winter. 'I hate the thought of leaving Scarborough,' she said, 'and I dread leaving you, Lizzie.'

'But we will meet again, Anne,' Lizzie said, taking her hand. 'There can be no end to our friendship. All is crystal clear between us, and even if we never set eyes on each other again during our lifetime, the flame that burns between us could never alter, never diminish.'

'You seem so sure of the future,' Anne said despondently, 'as if you could see it quite clearly. I wished that I possessed the smallest part of your confidence, but my spirits are at a low ebb, and I have long harboured a notion that my twenty-fifth year will bring about a crisis in my existence. I may prove a true presentiment or a superstitious fancy – and I shall be twenty-five on the seventeeth of January.'

'You seem far from well, Anne. What is troubling you?'

Anne sighed. 'My sisters and I had planned to open our own school at Haworth, and I had set my heart on going back there to teach, but the project has failed dismally. Not one pupil has applied. Now my life seems overshadowed by disappointment. I can see nothing in the future except failure. But how dreary you must think me. How lacking in courage.'

'No, Anne. If you can only believe it, the school project you had set your heart on would have proved disastrous in one sense, and you would have missed your true vocation.'

'My true vocation? I don't understand. What *is* my true vocation?'

'As a writer, of course.'

'A – writer?' Anne faltered.

'And you may forget any fears you entertain concerning the year ahead.' Lizzie said quietly, 'nothing untoward will happen to you. Indeed, you will find release from a troublesome situation. You will return to Haworth, not as a governess but as a free soul. You will teach, but not in the way you anticipated, and your lessons will be handed down to coming generations to learn from.'

'How can you be so sure, Lizzie? Are you clairvoyant?'

'Oh, Anne. That word frightens me. But I do, at times, seem to possess some inner knowledge. Now I think I understand why, for my uncle told me that my grandmother, Rachel Godolphin, possessed the gift of sight to an unusual degree. Such gifts, he said, are passed on, sometimes missing a generation, then recurring. And so it seems that I have inherited a legacy I had rather done without, but it is mine and I cannot deny it.'

Thank God, Edward thought, that the summer season is nearly over, that the Railtons will soon be leaving. As his carriage bowled briskly towards his shipyard, he contemplated the wide shining beach, and drew comfort from the knowledge that autumn would bring an uncluttered peace to the streets of Scarborough.

Life was difficult, he pondered, but would seem infinitely less so when Lettie had departed. Then he noticed a familiar figure in grey walking along the sands, and frowned. What was Lizzie doing so far away from Grayston Lodge at this hour of the morning?

'Stop, Tom,' he called. 'Set me down here, I'll walk the rest of the way.'

He hurried along the beach calling, 'Lizzie! Wait, Lizzie!' But when the figure in grey turned, he realised that she was Anne Brontë. He laughed and doffed his hat. 'So I have mistaken you yet again?' he said.

'I'm afraid you have, Mr. Grayston.'

The girl, he noticed, looked pale and drawn. He fell into step beside her.

'I am saying goodbye to the sea,' she said wistfully. 'I am going back to Thorp Green this afternoon.'

'You like the sea, then?'

'Indeed I do. I think that if it lay within my power to do so, I would sail out to that far horizon yonder, and leave the world behind me.'

'That is no uncommon wish, Miss Brontë. I have often thought of so doing myself, when life throws up problems which seem insoluble. Forgive my asking, but is anything wrong?'

'My dear father is not well,' she said. 'His eyesight is failing rapidly.'

'I am sorry to hear it,' Edward said, thinking how like Lizzie she was, with the same air of fragility laced with an underlying strength of character.

'But I must turn back now,' Anne said when they had walked almost to the fish-pier. 'There is some last-minute packing to do, and I dare not risk staying out too long.'

As they took their leave of each other, a barouche with one occupant, a woman in a blue dress, holding a parasol to shield her complexion from the sun and salt air, bowled along the sands. That woman was Lettie Railton, seriously out of temper after an altercation with her dressmaker. She recognised Edward at once, then saw that he was not alone but deep in conversation with a girl who seemed vaguely familiar to her.

Lowering her parasol, wishing to observe, not to be observed, she stared with narrowed eyes at the girl to whom Edward was talking so earnestly. My God, she thought, so that's it! Edward and that kitchen slut! That second cook, Lizzie Godolphin. Does Bella suspect what is going on under her nose? But no, she would have told me. I wonder what she would do if I told her?

On reflection, Lettie decided that it might give herself greater satisfaction to keep her discovery secret for the time being; to play the waiting game. One thing was certain, that wretched girl Lizzie Godolphin would live to regret her affair with Edward Grayston.

Arabella, lost and lonely after her cousin's departure for London, seemed likely to sulk herself into another decline until the arrival of a letter from Lady Ruth Bravington, a newcomer to Scarborough, who wished to make her acquaintance.

'Please do come to tea one day,' her ladyship wrote, 'and bring your little girl with you. I have two children of my own, Francis and Susannah, who are much the same age, and they will make ideal companions. My friend, Lady Margaret Egmonton, suggested that I should write to you. She and her husband, Sir George, are, I believe, acquainted with your cousins Mr. and Mrs. Percy Garforth Railton.'

Arabella replied at once, a date was decided upon, and she set off in high spirits with a less enthusiastic girl occupying the seat opposite.

'I do wish you would look more animated, Catherine,' Bella admonished. 'Why, when I was your age I had many delightful friends. You must learn the social graces, child. After all, you are nearly twelve-years-old now.' She paused, thinking what a fine match the Honourable Francis Bravington might make for her daughter in the fullness of time. 'Indeed Catherine, I wish you to make a very good impression today. Francis Bravington is a charming boy, I'm told. You will remember what I say?'

'Yes, mamma,' Cathy sighed, and absentmindedly pulled off her hat.

'Catherine! I despair of you! Now look at your hair! Are you deliberately trying my patience?'

'No, mamma. I'm very sorry. I'll try to be good.'

The carriage bowled up the driveway of Holl Beck Hall and clattered to a halt in front of an imposing terrace with steps to an arched doorway. Arabella dismissed Joseph, who was driving, with a gesture of her gloved hand, and told him to return at four-thirty.

'It was so thoughtful of Lady Egmonton to introduce us,' Arabella remarked over teacups.

Her hostess, a tall thin woman with a pinched bridge to her aquiline nose which imparted a somewhat haughty appearance to her face, smiled and nodded her head. 'Yes, she spoke warmly of you and your cousin, Mrs. Railton, and I believe that her nephew is quite besotted with your niece, Julia.'

Arabella's charm rose like bubbles on a glass of champagne as they chatted of this and that. Catherine, she noticed, was behaving beautifully, speaking when spoken to and keeping her feet tucked well out of sight. The Honourable Francis Bravington, she also noticed, could scarcely keep his eyes off her.

After tea, Lady Bravington suggested that the children went out of doors to play for a while. 'The fresh air will do them good,' she said, ringing for the servant to clear the tea things, 'and I should like to show you over the house, Mrs. Grayston, for it has many unusual features, including a rather charming minstrels' gallery which we shall use to full advantage at Christmas.'

'Now, Miss Catherine,' Francis said teasingly when they were alone, 'I'll wager you can't climb trees.'

'I can,' Cathy replied with dignity, 'only I musn't. I gave mamma my word that I would behave properly.'

'Parents are an infernal bore at times,' he said, aping the speech of a grown up. 'They spoil all the fun, don't you think so?'

'You shouldn't say "infernal",' his sister reminded him, 'that's a naughty word.'

'No, it isn't, Miss Prim and Proper,' Francis replied sharply, giving her a push. 'Papa often uses it, and you wouldn't dare tell *him* off, would you?'

'I dare climb trees, at any rate,' Susannah bawled, and shinned up one to prove her words.

'Miss Catherine is not interested in your monkey tricks,' Francis said loftily, 'but what are we to do to pass the time? I know! Let's go down to the pond.'

'I don't want to go there,' Susannah declared, her temper piqued because her brother had made her look foolish. 'I'm cold, and I am going back indoors to mamma.'

'Well go on, baby dear.' Francis, a tall boy with sandy eyebrows and fair eyelashes, pinched her arm. 'You are not cold, are you Miss Catherine?'

'A little bit,' Cathy confessed, beginning to dislike Master Bravington for his treatment of little Susannah, and wondering what her mamma would think of the 'charming' youth if she witnessed the push he had given his sister and the way he had pinched her arm.

'In that case, I know a game that will warm you in a trice,' the boy said gleefully, 'jumping over the pond! It's great sport, and requires a great deal of nerve. But I'll wager you haven't the nerve. Girls are as spineless as jelly fish when it comes to that kind of thing.'

'Where is the pond?' Cathy said.

'Take my hand. Let's run!' Francis pulled her along beside him. 'There's the pond. All you have to do is take a good run at it, then jump, but if you get your feet wet that counts as a penalty, and you must pay a forfeit.'

'What is the forfeit?' Cathy glanced doubtfully at the turbid stretch of water confronting her.

'Well, seeing that Susannah has gone back to the house,' Francis said boldly, 'what about a kiss?'

'A kiss?' Cathy stared at him in shocked disbelief.

'Why yes,' Francis threw back his head and laughed. 'You know what a kiss is, don't you?'

'Certainly. But I have no intention of kissing you.'

'Then all you have to do is jump over the pond without getting your feet wet.'

'But it's very wide, and I am wearing skirts.'

'That makes it all the more interesting.'

'Very well then.' Cathy pulled off her hat.

'You'd better stand well back and tuck up your skirts,' Francis teased her.

'No, I don't want to do it.' Cathy drew back, remembering Arabella's warning to behave herself. 'There must be other ways of keeping warm.'

147

'Ah, so you are a coward after all, most girls are.' Francis leaned against a tree and laughed at her.

'I'm not a coward!' Cathy flushed scarlet at his words.

'Very well. Prove it!'

I will prove it, Cathy thought determinedly, he shall not get the better of me. Tucking up her skirts, she marched back a few paces, drew a deep breath, and ran. The grass was coarse and uneven. As she approached the pond she knew that she would not clear it. Her foot caught in a tussock and down she came, slap into the muddy water.

'Catherine! Are you all right?' Francis was pulling at her hands, his laughter forgotten as she emerged, a sorry spectacle, drenched to the skin, her teeth chattering.

'I am not drowned if that's what you mean, but look at me!'

'I'm sorry,' Francis said. 'I never meant this to happen. You had better come back to the house directly. Mamma will see that you have a hot bath and a change of clothing. You are bigger than Sue, but her things will suffice until you get back home.'

'But you don't understand,' the girl cried. 'I promised my mother that I would behave myself. I cannot let her see me like this! She would never forgive me. Oh Francis, I must get home as quickly as I can. It isn't far, two miles at the most, and I know a short cut across the fields.'

'You can't go like that,' he wailed. 'You'll catch your death of cold.'

'I have no choice but to go.'

'But what shall I say? How shall I explain your absence?'

'Tell them the truth! No, don't. Say that I got my feet wet and went home to change my shoes. I don't care what you say, but I am not going indoors to disgrace my mother. I'll slip through the hedge, get home, and face the music there.'

'I take back what I said about you being a coward,' Francis murmured contritely. 'You are without doubt the bravest girl I have ever known.'

On an impulse, Cathy kissed Francis on the cheek, then she pushed her way through the hedge and started to walk back to Grayston Lodge.

'I have never been so humiliated in all my life,' Bella cried. 'What Lady Bravington thought I cannot bring myself to contemplate. The disgrace of it!'

'Never mind about Lady Bravington,' Edward said angrily, 'what of Cathy? Hasn't it occurred to you that our child is desperately ill?'

'It's her own fault! I *told* her to behave properly. But you have always taken her part against me!'

'It is not a question of taking "part", Arabella. The child is delirious! For God's sake, see reason!'

'Reason! Was it reasonable of a soaking wet child to attempt to walk home in the chill September air? Was it reasonable of her to get soaking wet in the first place? Oh, I swear I shall go off my head before long.'

'Bella, please go upstairs and try to make Cathy understand that you forgive her. Sit by her bed and, if she should open her eyes, she will see you there and feel comforted.'

'Lady Bravington, of all people,' Arabella whimpered, ignoring his plea. 'I did so want Catherine to make a good impression.'

'Damn Lady Bravington!'

'Edward, how could you speak so?' Bella burst into tears.

'I'm sorry, that was boorish of me. But the accident wasn't entirely Cathy's fault. If that wretched Francis hadn't teased her so, it would never have happened.'

'At least he admitted his fault,' Bella sobbed. 'In any case it was nothing but a little game he devised to entertain Catherine. It was scarcely his doing that she persisted in showing off . . .'

Edward quit the room, too sick at heart to continue the argument, realising for the first time that Bella possessed no real affection for their daughter. Or perhaps, he thought, as he went upstairs to Cathy's room, he had always suspected as much, but he would have given the world not to have had to admit it even to himself.

'I feel as if the house is frozen,' Peggy wept. 'As if we had all been turned into statues. It's like a bad dream. Oh, Mrs. Stonehouse, I'd give anything to see that door open and Miss Cathy come running through it.'

'Wouldn't we all?' Amelia rocked herself in her chair by the fire.

'I can't bear to go into the mistress's room.' Peggy wiped her eyes, 'It's unnerving to see her sitting there as if she was carved out of wood, but I suppose that's better than hysterics. I'll never forget how she carried on to the poor little soul when she came back from Holl Beck Hall that day. I thought she was going to strike Miss Cathy, she was so angry with her, instead of noticing how ill the child was.'

'The poor master must be fair worn out with all the worry,' Beatrice butted in, her eyes goggling. 'He hasn't left Miss Cathy's room since she was taken poorly. You'd think the mistress would take a turn, wouldn't you, instead of just sitting there in her room all the time?'

'I wish you'd keep a still tongue in your head!' Amelia rounded on her fiercely. 'The mistress would go to pieces in a sick room. She knows it, and so does the master. It's not her fault, she wasn't brought up to face illness. It frightens her after the death of her parents.'

'I meant no harm, I'm sure,' Beatrice sniffed. 'I'm sorry for the missis. She's as hard as nails, but I think she would go clean off her head if anything happened to Miss Cathy.'

'You must be tired too, Mrs. Stonehouse,' Peggy broke in. 'You've done your fair share of running up and down stairs these past two days.'

'I am tired,' Amelia admitted, 'but it's not myself I'm worried about, it's the master. If only he'd take some food and rest, but he won't hear of it. Now get about your business, you two. It's not up to us to sit shirking our duties. Rooms must be cleaned and food cooked whether anyone cares or not.'

As Peggy and Beatrice scurried away, Lizzie came into the kitchen.

'Is there any news?'

'Nay, love, none.'

'If only I could do something. I feel so helpless.'

'Perhaps you could.'

'Please tell me. I would do anything in my power.'

'Make the master take both food and rest,' the housekeeper advised.

'But how could I? I doubt if he would listen to me.'

'How do you know unless you try?'

'Very well, Amelia, I'll do my best.'

Lizzie hesitated outside Cathy's room. Behind that door, she thought, are two of the people I love best in the world, but what right have I to intrude?

A small forlorn dog trotted from the schoolroom, whining softly, wagging its tail. Lizzie caressed the dog's muzzle. 'Poor Dido,' she whispered, 'no one has given you a thought, but you love Cathy too.' She was fondling Cathy's dog when the door opened.

'Lizzie!'

'Sir? The girl stared in alarm at her master's haggard face.

'How the devil did you know that you were the one person I wished to see? Cathy is calling for you. Will you go to her?'

Gladly, if you will do something to please me.'

'What is it?'

'Take some food and rest, sir. Without them you might fail for want of strength.'

'I suppose you are right,' Edward said heavily. 'Very well, I'll do what you ask if you will sit with my child. She is in fever. Will you see that her brow is kept cool, and promise to rouse me at once if she regains consciousness?'

'With all my heart, sir.'

'There is no one on this earth I would trust with Cathy,' he said, 'except yourself and Amelia. I could not bear a stranger in the room.' He picked up Dido in his arms, and walked unsteadily along the corridor.

Arabella fluttered like a ghost on the periphery of the drama, staring with dark, tragic eyes at her only child whenever she could be persuaded to enter the sick room, and breaking into uncontrollable sobs as she was led away.

There was no fighting spirit in Arabella. It was Lizzie who fought, by Edward's side, for Cathy's life, constantly changing the cold compresses on the child's brow, sponging her body with warm water, attempting to administer the lung syrup Dr. Binns had recommended, rubbing her back and chest with a compound of eucalyptus and olive oil, dissolving Borax in water as a disinfectant, burning resin on a stove when Cathy's cough was most troublesome.

When the shadows began to fall, Amelia would come up from the kitchen to sit with the child by the flickering light of a candle while Lizzie rested for a while. At midnight, Lizzie would return to her vigil.

On the fourth day, Arabella announced that she had decided to send for Lettie Railton to give her sympathy and support.

'No, Bella!' Edward was adamant. 'Not Lettie! I absolutely forbid it! If you need support, and I am unable to provide it, I will send Tom to Crossways Grange to fetch Aunt Dora.'

'You are being unreasonable, Edward,' Arabella wept. 'I want Lettie! Aunt Dora is old and . . .'

'And very wise,' Edward reminded his wife. 'If she is able to come, I for one would be glad of her presence.'

Theodora Blakeney, a small dignified figure in black, arrived at Grayston Lodge on the seventh day of Cathy's illness. Having gone into mourning on the death of her brother and his wife, Theodora saw no reason to discard it or the jet necklace, brooch and mourning rings she wore containing locks of their hair. There was nothing, however, mournful about Miss Blakeney's outlook on life. She was a sensible, down-to-earth Yorkshire-woman.

Arabella met her at the front door and promptly burst into tears.

'There, there,' Theodora put her arms about her niece, 'You must try to be brave, my dear. Edward has need of your strength and courage in this crisis. It is up to you to set an example.'

Oh God, Arabella thought, leading Aunt Dora into the drawing-room, it is comfort I need, not a lecture on strong-mindedness.

'How is dear little Cathy?' Aunt Dora drew off her gloves.

'No better, aunt.'

'What does the doctor say?'

'That her lungs are affected.' Bella broke down completely. 'But Edward will not have a nurse. I have pleaded with him over and over again, but he will not listen to me.'

'No nurse?' Miss Blakeney lifted her eyebrows. 'Who, then, is looking after the child?'

'Servants! Amelia Stonehouse, the second cook, and – Edward.'

'I'm relieved to hear it,' Theodora said briskly. 'Amelia Stonehouse is worth a dozen nurses in my opinion. Nurses are all very well, Bella, but they usually require more looking after than the patient.'

'I'll ring for tea, aunt,' Bella said coldly, drying her eyes, offended because Theodora had not been more sympathetic towards her.

'Not until I have seen Cathy,' Miss Blakeney said firmly. 'My own needs must wait for the time being.'

'As you wish,' Bella said dully. 'I'll give Tom instructions to take your luggage to your room.'

'I have missed Tom and Amelia,' Miss Blakeney said. 'I often think that I was far too unselfish in parting with them.'

Arabella led the way to Cathy's room. Lizzie looked up from sponging the child's forehead, and curtseyed.

'Where is my husband?' Mrs. Grayston demanded.

'In his room, ma'am. He has gone to rest for an hour or two.'

'In that case I'll wake him and tell him you are here, Aunt Theodora,' Bella said, anxious to quit the sick room which so depressed her.

'Indeed you will not! Let the poor boy rest,' the old woman leaned over the unconscious child, 'but you may order tea, now, if you like. I will come down in a few minutes.'

The curtains were drawn to keep out the light. Miss Blakeney could not discern Lizzie's features, only the deftness of her hands. 'You must be the second cook my niece spoke of,' she said quietly. 'What is your name?'

'Lizzie Godolphin, ma'am.'

'I see. And can you tell me, Lizzie, why my nephew would not engage a professional nurse?'

'I think, ma'am, because the master preferred those who love Miss Cathy, not strangers, in her sick room.'

'Indeed? Well, Lizzie, you appear to possess a gentle touch. Do you love my great-niece?'

'I do, ma'am, very much.'

'I thought so,' Miss Blakeney said softly. 'Gentle hands, in my experience, betoken a gentle heart.'

Dr. Binns prepared the family for the worst. 'There is nothing more to be done for the child,' he said gruffly. 'I would have given ten years of my own life to save her, and to spare you this moment, but she is sinking fast. You should all stay by her bedside from now on, for the end will come in an hour or two.'

'I don't believe it! It isn't true!' Arabella cried hysterically, wringing her hands.

'Hush, my dear.' Edward attempted to hold her, but she pushed him away.

'You dare to tell me to hush when my child is dying? How could you be so calm, so unfeeling? You should have brought in a nurse! This would never have happened if you had listened to me!'

'Go up to Cathy,' Theodora said quietly. 'I will bring Bella along presently.'

Lizzie was sitting beside the bed. It was two o'clock on a bright early October afternoon. The girl glanced up as he entered, seeing him as a dim shape in the darkened room.

'Open the curtains, Lizzie,' he said. 'The light will not disturb Cathy now.'

'What are you trying to tell me, sir?'

'It is strange, is it not?' Edward fondled his child's dark curls spread out on the pillow. 'I cannot rid myself of the idea that she will get up soon and run out into the sunshine to play. Open the curtains, Lizzie. I don't want my Cathy to die in a darkened room, shut off from God's sunshine and fresh air. You see, there is no hope, Lizzie. Dr. Binns has just told us so.'

Blindly, the girl stumbled to her feet and drew back the curtains. A bright ray of sunshine fell across Cathy's face. All the fever had left her. She appeared to be sleeping peacefully.

'Oh God, Lizzie! How can I bear it? Help me!'

'I am here, sir. Always! I will never leave you!'

Edward groped blindly for her outstretched hand. 'If love had been enough, we would have saved her, would we not?'

'Yes. Oh yes.'

'You have been my right hand, Lizzie. My sword, my shield,

my armour. I can never repay you for what you have done.'
Edward longed, in that instant, to hold his child and Lizzie
together in his arms, to keep them with him for ever.

Knowing what was in his heart, understanding his distress,
Lizzie laid a finger to his lips. 'Hush, sir. You must not falter
now.'

'You are right, Lizzie,' he said, bowing his head, 'but I
cannot think of this world without her. I cannot, I cannot. And
do you know what troubles me most? That I would not let her
see the launching of a ship.'

On the advice of Dr. Binns, Arabella went directly to London
after the funeral, travelling there with the Railtons.

'Your wife has suffered a severe shock,' he told Edward
gravely, 'and it is my belief that you should consider taking her
abroad this winter to recover her health. She is highly-strung
and needs a change of scenery. It would be folly, in my opinion,
for her to spend the winter here. Would an extended tour be
possible?'

'Anything is possible in these circumstances,' Edward replied. 'I will make the arrangements at once.'

Sitting up late in his library, Edward made his plans. John
Howard, his designer, and Zach Mainfaring would look to the
shipyard in his absence, while Tom, Amelia, and the Franklins
would stay on, with Lizzie, at Grayston Lodge.

But a letter from Theodora Blakeney altered those plans.
The old lady begged that the Stonehouses and Lizzie Godolphin might be sent to her for the winter months.

> Their presence would be such a comfort to me, [she
> wrote]. My present housekeeper is anxious to retire, and
> nothing would please me more than to have Amelia here in
> her place – and Lizzie as my companion.
>
> My spirits are at a low ebb, and I long for company. Please
> lend them to me, my dear Edward, and I promise to give
> them back to you on your return from Italy. Knowing
> Arabella, she will insist upon going there.
>
> Your affectionate aunt, Theodora.

Lizzie wrote in her diary:

October 25th, 1844

Last night, on the eve of my master's departure for London, I stole down to the garden. There in the moonlight, at some unearthly hour, he came to me.

The air was thin, cold and heavy with the scent of bitter earth and dying roses. He did not see me at first – indeed he did not even suspect my presence there, but I had not been able to sleep for thinking of Cathy, and neither, I imagine had he.

He was hatless and trod softly. Merely the cracking of a twig beneath his boots warned me of his approach. I held myself against the trunk of a lilac, feeling its rough bark beneath my hands, fearing an intruder, then I saw my master coming towards me. His features were perfectly plain in the moonlight.

When he was almost near enough to touch me, he looked up, sensing my presence. Then he spoke my name over and over again, and kissed my cheeks, my hair, and my trembling lips.

To die then would have been to live for ever, with no more uncertainties, misgivings or pangs of conscious. I returned his kisses, not knowing how to deny myself the happiness of touching his face with my fingertips.

Then I turned away from him, aware that the spell of the moonlight and the soft sighing night wind had weaved so much enchantment that my senses were spinning away from me, and that if I stayed in the garden much longer I should never be strong enough to deny the passion I felt for him.

He stood close beside me and laid a hand lightly on my shoulder. 'You are trembling,' he said softly. 'You are cold, and the dew has soaked your slippers.'

'I must go, sir,' I replied. 'It is very late, and you have a long journey ahead of you.'

'Before you leave me,' he said, clasping me in his arms, 'I must tell you. I love you, Lizzie, I love you.'

'And I – I love you.'

At last, when the mist of early morning spread like a beggar's cloak between us, it was time to take our leave of one another. Before we parted, he kissed my trembling lips once more.

'Goodbye, Lizzie,' he murmured, as if the words were torn from his inmost being and self. 'Goodbye, my love, my heart's darling.'

'Goodbye.' I could say no more. I turned, sobbing, and hurried back to the house, my footsteps whispering in the dew-wet grass of that grey October dawn.

CHAPTER EIGHTEEN

Charlotte Brontë stared at herself in a mirror. Almost thirty years of age, she appeared to herself dwarfish and plain to the point of ugliness. The misery of unrequited love welled up inside her. How could any woman who had given her heart and been so cruelly rejected, who had begged for crumbs and received none, believe herself to possess the slightest physical attraction?

Since her return from the Rue d'Isabelle in Brussels fourteen months ago, Charlotte's thoughts had centred on Monsieur Heger – the director of the Pensionnat Heger where she and Emily had gone, in the spring of 1842, to further their education – her tutor and mentor, with whom she had fallen desperately in love.

Now it was all too apparent that Monsieur Heger did not love her, and as the months of their separation dragged by, Charlotte's thoughts, once bright and hopeful, had become tinged with melancholy.

Even Haworth failed to console her. The school project she had planned with her sisters had failed abysmally, and it would have been impossible to put the plan of opening a school at the parsonage into operation in any case, in view of Branwell's behaviour. His return from Thorp Green for the Christmas holidays had been little short of disastrous. Branwell's restless irritability when he was sober, and his unnatural levity when he was not, shocked Charlotte. Moreover, the reason for Branwell's conduct seemed shameful to his sister. How could he allow his infatuation for a married woman to poison his life?

Charlotte pushed aside the thought that her infatuation for a married man was equally poisoning her own life. At least she had not taken to gin and opium as a palliative. But there was a deeper, underlying grief. She could not bear to see Branwell so altered. Branwell, the pride of the Brontës, in whose talent she had pinned so much faith; her beloved 'little' brother; her dear childhood companion and fellow conspirator in their secret, make-believe kingdom of Angria, as close to her, once as Emily was to Anne. How could Branwell have forsaken her?

Lizzie turned her back on Grayston Lodge with a feeling of thankfulness, but the West Riding of Yorkshire with its towering granite outcrops, squat textile mills, lofty chimneys, smoke-blackened stones and sparse grass, was alien to her, and Keighley, a bustling town abounding in grey stone houses, seemed like a desert.

Crossways Grange, a sprawling stone mansion with latticed windows, beamed ceilings, and a garden full of monkey-puzzle trees, standing halfway between Keighley and Haworth, seemed ever hazed by smoke from the distant factory chimneys.

As the days shortened and the countryside was held in the grip of a savage winter, Lizzie longed for the softer fields of home, and the return of her master from Italy – the sight of his face and the warmth of his smile. And yet, she wondered, how could it be possible to return to Grayston Lodge when he did come home? How could she hide her feelings; how live with her conscience? One look, one loving look between them and all would be cheapened and spoilt if that look was observed. This she knew, she could not bear.

Perhaps I shall go to my uncle after all, she thought, or perhaps Miss Blakeney will keep me here as her companion.

'My dear Lizzie,' Miss Theodora said, 'I have a favour to ask of you.'

The girl looked up with a smile from the handkerchief she was hemming. 'Why, of course, I will do anything you ask of me. What is it, ma'am?'

'It is a matter of some delicacy, and I do not know quite how to put it, but I am expecting a visitor this afternoon, a quiet,

retiring gentleman of a serious disposition, a reverend gentleman from Haworth, and his eldest daughter . . .'

'You mean the Reverend Mr. Patrick Brontë and his
daughter Charlotte?' Lizzie asked.

'Quite so.' Theodora smiled.

'And you would wish me not to put in an appearance? Is that
it?'

'That is it precisely, my dear. You see I should not care to
embarrass the poor man by confronting him with an exact
replica of his youngest daughter, Anne. He is very old and
feeble nowadays, and keeps himself very much to himself, and
while I do not attend divine worship at Haworth – Crossways
Grange is nearer to Keighley – I do occasionally entertain the
Reverend Mr. Brontë and Charlotte to tea as a matter of
courtesy.'

'I quite understand, ma'am.'

'I thought you would, Lizzie, for I have not forgotten my own
reaction to seeing your face for the first time that terrible day of
Cathy's funeral. What is Miss Brontë doing here? I asked
Arabella, and she looked at me as if I had taken leave of my
senses. I did not pursue the subject of course, for it was obvious
that my niece had never seen Anne Brontë face-to-face.'

'I do understand, ma'am, and would never wish to embarrass either you or Mr. Brontë,' Lizzie said.

'Thank you, my dear.'

But Lizzie doubted if Mr. Brontë, when he arrived at Crossways Grange that afternoon – a tall, distinguished-looking man
with snow-white hair, wearing a high white stock about his
throat – would have remarked her resemblance to his youngest
daughter in any case, for he was obviously half blind, and
totally dependent on the lady in attendance, for Charlotte, his
eldest daughter, seemed half blind too, judging by the way she
ducked her head and peered short-sightedly into the dim recesses
of the hall, as if she was looking for something she could not find.

Edward walked slowly along the terrace fronting the villa Bella
Vista on the shore of Lake Garda, thinking of Cathy, and of
Lizzie. Since his arrival in Italy with Arabella, he had thought
of little else.

Lake Garda was beautiful, but the villa with its echoing salon and gilded furniture was not to his taste, and in the other villas along the shore, occupied by wealthy Italians, Swiss and Germans, and a scattering of English, he was aware of a decadance which distressed him. Surely there was more to life than this vain seeking after pleasure? What he needed most was to return to his shipyard and immerse hismelf in his work once more.

But this was a moment in the day that he could enjoy, when dawn broke over the lake, when wood-smoke began to curl from the chimneys, and the scent of burning olive boughs drifted like incense in the quiet air. From the terrace he could see the pink pantiled roofs of a village, and a slipway where rowing boats were moored. It was to that slipway, to Bella's disgust, that he turned most often during the long lonely days of his banishment from England, to talk to the peasants there; honest folk whose rough tongues and simple humour warmed his heart.

Edward's penchant for talking to the fisherfolk, and setting off on long lonely walks into the hills had caused more than one flare-up between himself and Arabella. He tried always to be fair to her, to remember that it was for Bella's sake that he had come to Italy, but he could not always comply with her plans to drive into Malcesine, the nearest town, to shop. He needed hard physical exercise in the fresh air to take his mind off his troubles; to shore himself up mentally for the endless soirées to which he escorted his wife.

Resting his hands on the iron railings, he gazed across the lake to what Bella referred to as 'the island' – a rocky tree-crowned protuberance with a gazebo – where they picnicked occasionally. Then his attention was caught by a rowing boat nosing its way from the nearby slipway, its bow biting into the tranquil water. The fisherman hailed him in a soft local patois. Edward smiled and raised him hand in greeting. 'Good morning,' he said in fluent Italian. 'I hope the fish will rise to your bait.'

'Thank God for a calm day,' the man called out to him, 'for then my life is made bearable. My wife does not grumble at me for bringing nothing to the table. But on a wild day,' he turned his eyes heaven-ward, 'oh, my friend, what a turbulence also in the kitchen!'

Edward smiled in sympathy as the man rowed away. He

knew all about 'turbulence'. Two cooks had given notice since Bella's arrival at the villa, and he had seen the lake when the wind whipped across its vast length and breadth, churning up the water and pitching the boats moored by the landing-stage at the end of the garden.

The boat was almost out of sight now, and only the ripples created by the oars ruffled the stillness of the lake. Suddenly the scent of coffee wafted up from the kitchen where an old, sharp-eyed servant prepared breakfast. Soon Bella would come down to the table in the belvedere, chattering incessantly of this and that, eating next to nothing, her dark eyes bright with a feverish excitement which Edward could not fathom.

Arabella seemed to him as volatile as a firework about to explode, and destined, when the last spark was extinguished, to sink to smouldering ash. This recent febrile excitement, Edward pondered, as he paced the terrace, had something to do with Stephen Florisent, a poet and artist of sorts whom Bella had taken under her wing, a pale, intense young fellow, almost girlish in appearance, whose garments – tight black breeches, long black velvet jacket and broad-brimmed hat – were meant to convey at a glance his artistic tendencies. But who the devil was Stephen Florisent, he thought, where had he sprung from, and what made his company so compelling to Arabella?

Later, at breakfast, Bella announced her intention of going to Malcesine to do some shopping. Wanting to please her, Edward offered to accompany her. To his surprise, she turned him down.

'No,' she said quickly, 'I have a deal of shopping to do for the party tonight, and you would soon be bored.'

'Oh, the party. I had forgotten about that.'

'No matter, but I have all the arrangements to see to and you would hinder me.' She hesitated, 'I thought you might prefer to go for a walk.'

'How thoughtful of you, my dear.' He smiled across the table at her, genuinely pleased then, wishing to reciprocate her generosity, he added, 'And if you like, we could row across to the island this afternoon to have tea there.'

A shadow flitted across her face as she replied, 'No, Edward, I shall be far too busy for that.'

As she rose, leaving her breakfast unfinished, Edward asked casually, 'Who is coming tonight?'

'Oh, the usual people,' she said, 'the Atkinsons, the Dominics, Sir Harold and Lady Shaw, the Count and Countess Ivichy . . .'

'And Mr. Florisent, is he coming?'

'Naturally, since he is going to recite to us after dinner. Why will you persist in questioning me? I find it extremely irritating.'

He watched her go, making no attempt to accompany her. Patronage of the arts, he knew, was fashionable among wealthy Italians, if somewhat unusual for a visiting Englishwoman. But why his persistent feeling that there was more to Bella's relationship with Stephen Florisent than met the eye?

The gilded salon, its windows open to the terrace, was lit by a myriad of shining candles and a glowing fire of fragrant olive branches. The great marble urns were filled with flowers, and in the long dining-room through an archway, the table was laid with the Derby dinner service, napery and silver-ware that Arabella had brought from England with them.

It reminded Edward of a scene in a play, wholly artificial and strangely unreal, and his wife seemed to him like an actress about to step on to the stage. He noticed how her eyes shone as she gazed at her reflection in one of the long ornate mirrors, twitched a wayward curl into place, and then revolved slowly to admire her shimmering purple dress, the cobwebby lace shawl about her shoulders, and her sparkling hair ornaments.

He thought of Cathy as he watched her, wondering how she could find pleasure in dressing up and entertaining so lavishly when their child was dead, and all he longed to do was excuse himself and go to his room. But Arabella would never forgive him if he did not play his part in the coming charade; he knew and accepted that fact.

'I think I hear the carriages arriving,' she cried excitedly, turning her head for a final glimpse of herself in the mirror. 'Well, don't stand there as if you had been turned to stone, Edward.'

He followed her reluctantly to the hall to welcome their

guests. The women resembled a bouquet of overblown roses in their colourful dresses. The Countess Ivichy, a tall woman in red, her throat encircled with a tight pearl choker, was both vivacious and flirtatious, and murmured to Edward behind her black lace fan that they really must sit together at dinner. She spoke shrilly in broken English, and rapped the Count's hands smartly with her fan when he protested that he was a jealous man by nature, and must challenge his rival to a duel if his darling preferred another man to him. Then the pair of them shrieked with laughter, while Lady Shaw, a faded English beauty wearing an unbecoming pink satin gown and too much rouge, turned pale under the pink daubs on her cheeks thinking, until her husband explained matters to her, that the Count Ivichy had really meant what he had said about duelling.

'I make the joke, that is all my dear madam,' the Count made his own explanation to the bewildered lady. 'You English have your sense of humour, we Italians have ours.'

Edward observed them quietly. The English contingent, he thought, seemed as out of place among the Italians as jet-jewellery would have been at a debutante's coming out ball. Then he caught sight of Stephen Florisent, a graceful, almost girlish figure in his tight black breeches, greyish shirt, and with a bow of some lightweight material knotted carelessly at his throat.

During dinner, young Florisent, seated next to Arabella, lost no opportunity of turning his calf-eyes in her direction. Glancing round the table, Edward wondered if the other guests were as embarrassed as he was by the poet's blatant flattery of their hostess.

The Italians appeared not to be. They were a careless lot intent on the food and wine, the spiced meats, the pastas in too-rich sauces, the fish and fowl imprisoned in quivering aspic, the sugar and cream-laced desserts sprinkled with almonds and brandy. They guzzled the food and wine with gusto.

But the English were a different breed altogether. Edward saw and understood their watchful expressions, their inbred dislike of upstarts and foreigners, and no matter how carefully they tried to conceal it, their innate disapproval of Bella and her poet.

They have come to winter in Italy, he thought, but they have brought with them, from England, all their inbuilt snobbery and shibboleths.

After dinner, when the women spread their skirts upon the gilded sofas, Stephen Florisent was exhorted by Bella to read his latest poem – a dissertation of great length – comparing the beauty of women to that of the lily. Nothing could have been more apt, or more boring.

> One noble, gracious lily, growing sweet
> Within a bosky dell, where slumbrous bees
> Inhale its fragrance, thus assumes a form
> Symmetrical as Dido's. Oh complete
> And beauteous flower, might I but take my ease
> Within thy stamened bosom, where the warm
> Sweet honey lies as yet unsipped . . .

The poet stood, completely at ease, declaiming his twaddle as confidently as Henry Godolphin had proclaimed Henry's speech before Harfleur.

The men, Edward noticed, fidgeted with their pocket watches, fingered their moustaches, and scratched their necks and noses, while the women, and Arabella in particular, gazed with rapt attention at the young man who stood before them – the son of a Leed's joiner, had they but realised it – an indolent young fellow who had broken his parents' heart in refusing to earn his bread by sawing up wood, who had stolen his fare to the Continent, and had sold himself time and time again for the price of a bottle of wine and a good meal; intent upon one day finding a wealthy benefactress who would recognise his own worth and talent.

Now he had found such a woman, and his spirits lifted as he recited his poetry.

When the guests had departed with kisses, handshakes, and what Edward felt to be exaggerated praise of the evening's entertainment, Bella moved quickly to the fireplace and held out her hands to the smouldering branches, keeping her face carefully turned away from him, but he could tell by the nervous movement of her shoulders and the flush on her cheeks that she was more than usually excited.

'What is it, Bella? Is anything the matter?'

'That depends on how you look at it,' she said, still not meeting his eyes. 'Oh, I know that you will not approve of the plan, but I have decided to offer Mr. Florisent the belvedere as a permanent home. It is quite detached from the house, and there is plenty of room in the upper storeys. It is quite clear to me that he must be given every facility to develop his talent, and I intend to see that he does.'

Edward felt inclined to laugh. 'You cannot be serious?' She had babbled the rigamarole as if she had been rehearsing it, rather like a child repeating a lesson.

'I knew that would be your reaction.' Her voice was high pitched, almost hysterical, 'But I don't care what you say. I intend to have my own way in this. Stephen cannot possibly continue to live and work in that revolting garret he occupies. Why, it is not fit for human habitation. The walls and ceiling are running with damp, and there are cockroaches everywhere.'

'You appear to be well acquainted with Mr. Florisent's accommodation.' Edward felt less inclined to laugh now. He moved slowly towards her, wanting to look at her face which she had kept half turned away from him.

Bella tossed her head, 'I went there to take him a hamper and a bottle of wine when he was ill, that's all. There was no harm in it. Carlo drove me there and carried the hamper upstairs.'

'Look at me, Bella.' Edward laid his hand on his wife's arm. 'I believe you owe me an explanation. Your attachment to young Florisent has puzzled me of late. I don't understand how it happened or why . . .'

'I told you at the time,' she retorted. 'I met Stephen in the market place at Malcesine soon after our arrival in Italy. I was stepping down from the carriage when I stumbled and dropped my reticule. He was charming, helpful . . .'

'And realised that you were rich, and might prove equally helpful to him.' Edward's tone was bitter. 'I can just imagine his reaction to having a wealthy woman falling quite literally into his waiting arms.'

She pulled her arm away from him. 'Faugh, you sicken me with your cheap jibes, Edward. You count yourself a philanthropist; spend hours consorting with peasants, but your philanthropy never extends to my friends. Stephen possesses gifts which you could not possibly appreciate. I need him! I want him here, and nothing you can say will make me change my mind.'

'Bella, please believe me, I do not wish to cross you or to make you unhappy. God knows we have had enough unhappiness to last us a lifetime, but what you suggest is impossible. We are going back to England soon, and when we leave here the villa will be let to someone else.'

Arabella looked him full in the face at last, and gave a triumphant little laugh. 'That's where you are wrong, Edward. You are going back to England, but I am staying here. Do you know why? Because the Bella Vista belongs to me! Yes, it's true. I signed the contract this morning. There, now you know.'

'I see. No wonder you made up that tarradiddle at breakfast.'

She turned on him angrily. 'Is that all you have to say?'

'No, Bella, it isn't. Why didn't you confide in me? I can understand your wanting to purchase the villa if it means so much to you, but staying on here with Florisent is out of the question. You must see that. Why, those so-called friends of yours would turn their backs on you and ostracise you completely if you attempted it, and while I should not care twopence if I never set eyes on their idiotic faces again, I imagine that you would.'

'I don't see that at all.' She began pacing the floor like a woman demented, picking at her shawl, tearing holes in the delicate fabric.

'Listen to me,' Edward spoke in a low voice, 'There are questions to be answered here. I can forgive your deceit of today, but I must know – is Florisent your lover?'

She turned like a tigress, her lips drawn back in a travesty of a smile, 'No he is not. He is my – saviour! He has given me new hope, new life!'

'Bella!' Grayston strode towards her and caught her by the shoulders.

'It's the truth, I tell you. Stephen has brought Catherine back to me. I have actually seen her; heard her voice. She is not dead after all. She is out there on the island!'

'Oh my God,' Edward muttered, torn between anger and compassion. 'So that's it. The island. That's where he practices his trickery. That's the hold he has over you. And how does Mr. Florisent get to the island? Does he levitate and fly there?'

'That's cruel and wicked of you, Edward!' She began to cry hysterically.

'Yes, I suppose it is. But you must make allowances for my feelings. Cathy was my daughter too. How did you think I would react to hearing that Florisent has not only fed upon your grief, but has tricked you into believing her still alive, God damn him!' Hatred of Florisent welled up inside him, 'I'll thrash the young pup within an inch of his life!'

'Where are you going?'

'Where do you think I'm going? To Malcesine, to settle this matter once and for all!'

'No!' Bella gave a cry of terror as she seized his arm, and collapsed, half fainting, against his breast. 'Don't go! Don't leave me! If you leave this house, I swear I'll kill myself!'

Edward had no choice but to heed his wife's threat, and swung her up into his arms.

'Where are you taking me?' she sobbed wildly.

'To your bed,' he said, striding towards the stairs. 'You are hysterical. I will call a doctor first thing in the morning.'

He laid the trembling, overwrought woman on her bed and covered her with an eiderdown, then he sat beside her, smoothing her tangled hair until at last she fell asleep.

It rained heavily during the night. Mountain streams descending from the Alto Adige tumbled with force into the lake. Edward rose at seven, paced the terrace for a while, then he went upstairs to Bella's room and knocked. There was no reply. When he opened the door he saw that the room was empty.

He strode to the kitchen. 'Where is the signora?' he demanded.

The old woman making coffee stared at him with dark, unfriendly eyes. 'She's gone to Malcesine,' she muttered. 'I heard her give instructions to Carlo.'

'Malcesine? Are you sure?'

'Of course. I may be old, but I am not deaf.'

So Bella has gone to Florisent, he thought dully. That was her intention all along, to go to that wretched garret of his; to warn him. Sick at heart, he pondered the situation.

At one o'clock, Arabella had not returned. Alone in the dining-room Edward toyed with his food, then pushed his plate aside and stared out at the lowering clouds and the slate-grey water of the lake whipped to peaks by the rising wind.

An hour later, Edward went to his room and flung himself on his bed. Rain was driving in torrents against the windows. Where is she? he wondered. What is happening? An hour later he awoke to the sound of carriage wheels and strode on to the landing, expecting to see her in the hall below, but the hall was empty, and yet he could have sworn he'd heard the carriage.

'Bella,' he called, 'are you there?' But there was no reply.

The wind seized him as he rounded the corner to the coach-house; tore at his hair and moulded his shirt to his body. Rain lanced his face; drenched his clothing. 'Carlo,' he shouted.

'Yes, signor?' Edward pushed open the door of the stable to find Carlo unharnessing the horses. So he was right, the coach had returned, but where was Arabella?

'Where is the signora?' he asked, grasping the coachman's arm.

'I – I cannot say, signor.'

'Cannot or will not?'

'A thousand pardons, Signor Grayston,' Carlo said unhappily, 'but madam told me that I am now answerable only to her, and I dare not risk losing my employment. I have a wife and three bambini to think of.'

'Your loyalty is commendable, but how would you feel if your wife were missing?'

The man blinked uncertainly. 'Please, signor, understand my dilemma. I am a good Catholic. If I break my word I must confess it on Sunday, and the padre will not be pleased with me.'

'And if harm comes to the signora, what then? Come, man, speak out.'

Carlo rolled his eyes heavenward. 'She went to Malcesine, Signor Grayston. I drove her to the house of the poet.'

'Did you go in with her?'

'Oh no, signor, she told me to wait. An hour or so later, they came out of the house together. The poet was carrying a valise. Then, after they had talked together for a while inside the carriage, I drove them to the house of the notary, Signor Claudinalle.'

'Go on.'

'It was almost noon when they left the notary's house. The signora seemed very excited, and the poet looked pleased with himself. Then I drove them to the Ristorante Tintoretto on the way from Malcesine. The signora gave me some money to buy food, and told me to go round to the servants' entrance, but I finished my own meal long before they appeared. When they did . . .' Carlo hesitated.

'For heaven's sake speak up, man. You need not be afraid to tell me.'

'A thousand pardons for saying so, but it seemed to me that they had drunk too much wine.'

'And where did they go after that?'

'Why, I brought them back here to the villa, Signor Grayston.'

'Here?' Edward glanced round uneasily, 'Then where are they now?'

'I heard the signora say that she did not care two figs for your opinion, that they would go to the island and be damned to everyone else. I did not understand what she meant, but it was not my place to ask. All I know is that, when they dismounted from the carriage, they made their way to the landing-stage.'

Fear lent wings to Edward's feet. Surely they would not have ventured out in a rowing-boat in this gale.

Carlo, hurrying behind him, made the sign of the Cross on his breast when he saw that the boat had gone from its mooring place.

Throwing himself flat on the landing-stage, Edward cupped his hands to shield his eyes. Funnelled wind whipped furiously down the open throat of the crags. 'I see it,' he cried, 'out there. The boat!'

'Where, signor? I can see nothing!' Carlo wrung his hands in despair.

'There, near the island! They are in trouble!'

'What are you doing, signor?' Carlo babbled. 'No! You cannot swim in that torrent! Mother of God, think what you are doing!'

But Edward did not stop to think. He stood upright and then plunged into the lake.

Entry in Lizzie Godolphin's diary:

February 17th, 1845

The stable clock chimed three. Three thin strokes of a stable clock. What did they convey to me at that moment? Nothing. And yet, as the clock struck, I felt a strange tingling of my flesh; an uneasiness, an awareness that something was wrong – not within the house, but somewhere beyond my own being. A warning note, a danger signal.

I was standing in the kitchen of Crossways Grange, making a hot drink for Miss Theodora, when my hands fell uselessly to my sides. Then unrelated images began to flash through my brain, brightly-coloured pieces as bewildering as those seen in a kaleidoscope.

I saw a woman's cloak; green fingers of rain-soaked branches, a sky as heavy as slate, a house built of rough pebbledashed stone with a roof of yellowish pink pantiles; steps leading down from a broad, arcaded terrace, a garden full of exotic-looking shrubs, a path leading to a landing-stage, and blue-grey water churned to anger by the wind.

Then I saw the woman who wore the cloak. Her movements were as jerky as a puppet's as she ran. The shrubs caught at her clothing, but she tugged at her cloak impatiently to free it from the impeding branches. With a wild, careless gesture, she tore off her bonnet and tossed it aside. Her hair streamed about her face, but her face was a blur; a faded canvas seen through rain, through the mists of time, through screens or silk; her features as indecipherable as inscriptions on forgotten tombstones.

She seemed to me to be a mad woman; Ophelia incarnate, scattering half-formed blossoms and showering raindrops in her wake – sweet ornaments to self-destruction. I knew her not, and yet she was familiar to me. Rain beat down upon her laughing face, but her laughter froze my blood. I cried out to her to go back, but she did not hear me.

Then I saw that she was not alone. A dark shape hurried after her, that of a young man dressed all in black, a prancing, dancing figure as impervious to the storm as she was.

I cried out again as I perceived the angry flood and the foolish woman hurrying towards it. Then my brain seemed filled by a ghastly rushing and roaring, and I fell to my knees and began to crawl forward on all fours, whimpering to her to turn back before it was too late.

She sprang into the boat, the man following closely behind her, and cast aside the lifeline to the shore. The boat lifted and then plunged forward into the waves, but she laughed, and beseeched the man with her to row faster, faster, faster . . .

Then, as the boat spun round in the trough of the waves, she stopped laughing and began screaming for help. I saw her lift her arms in supplication. She reached up to grasp the bow of the upturned boat, slimed with mud and moss, in her last, supreme effort for survival. Then her cloak spread, as dark as a night without stars, upon the surface of the water.

Even as she sank, I heard, through the clamour of the storm, my master's voice calling, 'Arabella, where are you?'

I crawled on, my palms bloodied and tingling from their contact with the stone-flagged kitchen floor, grasping at the stairs leading up to Miss Theodora's chamber, but those stairs seemed to me as towering waves coming at me like Titans, and my arms felt the agonising pull of the current which bore me under.

When I came to myself, Amelia was holding me in her arms, rocking me like an infant in her warm embrace.

'What is it, Lizzie?' she asked tenderly. 'Whatever has happened?'

'I think that the master and mistress are dead,' I said dully, and then I turned in her arms and sobbed as if my heart would break.

CHAPTER NINETEEN

Winds of April scoured the streets of London, and yet there was a brightness in the air, a scent of spring, the chattering of nest-busy sparrows.

Lettie Railton regarded her reflection with more than a little satisfaction, smoothed her dark shining hair, and sighed. Her morning gown of fine green wool, trimmed with moire, enhanced the creaminess of her skin, and the matching jade rings on her fingers emphasised the delicacy of her hands, but she could not forget Edward's rejection of her for a mere servant girl. The long winter months had fed her resolve to make the 'workhouse slut' pay – and yet she still wanted Edward.

Crossing to the fireplace, she thought that she had behaved like an hysterical child that night on the balcony at Wood's Lodgings. She should have realised that Edward was not a man to be netted like a herring, but angled for with skill and patience – and that she had misjudged his taste in women. When next they met, she would stand as patient as an angler on a river bank; wear a grey dress and pearl earrings. She would be utterly artless and charming; she would talk to him of ship-building – if he preferred that subject to any other – then surely he would come to her.

'Mamma!' Julia waltzed into the room, an opened letter in her hand, her wild rose cheeks flushed with excitement, 'I have heard from James!'

Lettie smiled indulgently, 'Oh, what does he say?'

'All manner of foolish things. He really is an absurd young

man.' Julia hugged the letter to her bodice. 'Oh, mamma, I wish with all my heart that we were back in Scarborough. I love the Spa promenade, the clean even sweep of the sand, the concerts and exhibitions, and the old town near Uncle Eddie's shipyard. Do you remember the day he took Cathy and me to see the finishing touches put to one of his vessels? It was so stimulating. Cathy and I pretended to be sailors.' She laughed, 'Mr. Mainfaring lent us an old telescope, and we leaned our arms on the bows and imagined that we saw a desert island with palm trees. The workmen looked up at us, and laughed, and Cathy danced a hornpipe to entertain them.'

Julia pirouetted. 'We walked, afterwards, to the church on the hill to see where Captain Smith is buried, then Uncle Eddie showed us the grave of another sea-captain, a man whose body was washed ashore after his ship capsized in a gale . . .'

'Really,' Lettie shuddered, 'I think your uncle might have turned your thoughts to happier things.'

Julia stopped laughing as she remembered her dancing companion of that day. 'I still cannot believe that Cathy is dead,' she murmured, her eyes filling with tears.

'Come, child, you mustn't grieve over the past. You still haven't told me what James Hennessy has to say in his letter.'

'Why, simply that he longs for the Scarborough season to begin. Life at Hutton Buscel is little short of boring at present, he says, and his father has not been well. Also that he has spent a good deal of time at York with Sir George and Lady Egmonton, but the house does not seem the same without me. I told you, didn't I, that he is an absurd young man?'

'Young men in love often are, my darling,' Lettie replied, reflecting that her daughter might one day become the Lady of the Manor at Hutton Buscel – a mere stone's throw away from Scarborough. The thought filled her with pleasure. Senningford Hall was a magnificent house, and James Hennessy such a handsome, wealthy young man. She was imagining Julia's future there when Percy blundered into the room.

'What's the matter, papa?' Julia asked in alarm, seeing the stricken look on his face.

A – letter. I have just received a letter from Italy. Oh, my

God.' He sank into a chair and covered his face with his hands.

'What has happened?' Lettie demanded.

'I – I don't know how to break it to you. It's Arabella . . .'

'What about Arabella?' Lettie took a step forward.

'I'm afraid that poor Bella is – dead.'

'Bella – *dead*?' Letti's eyes widened. A tiny flame of elation flickered momentarily.

'But that is not all.' Railton lifted his head. 'Edward is dead, too.'

'Edward?' The flame was extinguished. '*Edward*! I don't believe it!'

'It's true.' Railton ran his fingers through his hair. 'Dear old Edward. I liked him, you know. Would have given my right arm to be like him. I'll never forget how good he was to me the night of the storm when my horse broke a leg. I cried, you see. Now he's gone, the poor fellow. Drowned trying to save Arabella.'

Julia began sobbing wildly. 'I still don't believe it,' Lettie said stiffly.

'It's true, my dear. I have a letter here from the Italian Embassy. They regret to inform us that a body taken from Lake Garda on the seventeenth of February was identified as that of Arabella Grayston of Scarborough. Her remains were buried in the cemetery at Malcesine a week later.'

'And – Edward? What of him?' Lettie spoke thickly, feeling that her entire body had turned numb with cold.

'His – body was not recovered,' Percy said, 'or had not been recovered at the time this letter was written. An eye-witness, a man employed at the Bella Vista as a coachman, testified that he was with Edward on the landing-stage before the accident, and begged him not to enter the water. Conditions were bad apparently, and even the strongest swimmer could not have survived for long in that flood.'

To stunned to speak, Lettie remembered the swirl of Edward's cloak as he handed it to a footman; the way he had bent over her hand; the pale ghost of Arabella coming downstairs holding up her black dress.

'And to think,' Julia sobbed, 'that we were talking about Uncle Eddie before papa came in.' She glanced up fearfully, 'I should not have spoken of that poor drowned sailor. It was unlucky; an omen.'

Railton's letter fluttered to the carpet. Lettie stared down at it, a white oblong lapped by green moire. How cruel life is, she thought, how damnably unfair. If Arabella was stupid enough to fall into the lake, Edward should have let her go. Be damned to her!

Suddenly a thrush outside the window burst into full-throated song. The sound was almost ludicrous; a trilling note of hope and springtime in a frozen world of death and disaster.

This room, Lettie thought objectively, looks like the setting for a melodrama. Percy weeping in a chair, Julia at his feet, her rose-pink skirts awry.

She crossed to the side-table and poured herself a glass of brandy. The raw spirit burned her throat, made her eyes sting horribly, and brought her brain back to life. With Bella dead, who would inherit Crossways Grange and Grayston Lodge? Apart from me, she thought, there is only Theodora.

'Have you thought,' she said, 'that someone must inform our solicitor? That someone must go at once to Scarborough and to Haworth to see to things there?'

Railton looked up at his wife. 'Why no, such a thought never crossed my mind.' Hurt and baffled by his wife's mercenary attitude, he added, 'And I must say that I am shocked by your lack of feeling.'

'Don't, papa,' Julia cried. 'Can't you see that mamma is not herself?'

'You're right, my darling,' Railton conceded. 'It is all my fault. I am a clumsy fool to have broken the news so abruptly.'

'Please go now,' Lettie poured herself more brandy. 'I will see you at luncheon.'

'Very well, m'dear.' Railton rose to his feet.

'Come, papa,' Julia said, taking his arm.

When they had gone, with anxious backward glances, Lettie moved to the window and held back the starched curtains with a jade be-ringed hand. A nursemaid's ribbons streamed like seaweed in the square below. Birds chattered anxiously in the branches of the trees; crocuses were dying, daffoldils pushing up sturdy green spikes.

Shivering, Lettie replaced the curtain. Eddie will never see me now, she thought, in my grey dress and pearl earrings. He will never notice the quiet angler on the river bank.

Her grief broke suddenly in harsh sobs.

Amelia went slowly to Lizzie's room. The girl turned away from the window as she entered.

'It's my vision, isn't it?' Lizzie said. 'It has come true, hasn't it?'

Amelia held out her arms. 'Yes, my dear, I am afraid so. Miss Blakeney has just received word.'

'I have been expecting it for weeks now, but thank you for coming to tell me.'

'Is there anything I can do to help you, Lizzie?'

The girl smiled faintly. 'I should like to be on my own for a little while.'

When the weeping Amelia had gone, Lizzie sank down on her knees, searching every corner of her mind for memories of her master; the slightest word or look he had ever given her. But the most persistent memory of all kept coming back over and over again; the way his boots shone that day he strode into the long, cold workhouse room in Waterhouse Lane. Those boots of his that had always reminded her of newly-fallen chestnuts on a bright autumn morning.

How could she think of him as dead when he came striding from the recesses of her mind with all the strength and vigour he had possessed in life?

Anne left Thorp Green Hall in June. Life there had become increasingly difficult to bear. No sense of duty to her pupils, or loyalty to Branwell could outweigh her decision to return to Haworth. Mr. Robinson's health had begun to fail, and his increasing bedfastness prompted an even more flagrant flouting of moral conventions by his wife and Branwell, so that the children became even more unruly and, aware of the liaison, threatened to 'tell papa about Mr. Brontë' whenever their mother reprimanded them.

When the summer vacation came round, Anne packed her trunk and turned her back on Thorp Green, accompanied by an ebullient Branwell who, truth to tell, looked forward to his summer in Scarborough without her. On Branwell's return to Thorp Green, however, to make preparations for his summer idyll at Wood's Lodgings, he received notice of his dismissal as young Edmund's tutor.

In July, Lizzie received a letter from Anne asking if she could meet her somewhere on the road between Haworth and Keighley.

On the day of that meeting, Lizzie ran forward to embrace Anne. Both knew that they would not chat lightly on this and that; that their paths had run parallel in suffering since their last farewell in Scarborough.

'How strange it seems,' Anne said, as they walked along together, 'that fate has brought you within two miles of Haworth. I had hoped to ask you to the p-parsonage, but the house is scarcely the place to entertain anyone at present. We are having a sad time with B-Branwell.'

'Branwell?' Lizzie looked up in alarm. 'Why, what is wrong with him?'

'He has been given his m-marching orders from Thorp Green, and Mr. Robinson has c-charged him to break off instantly and f-for ever all communication with every m-member of his family.'

'Then Mr. Robinson knows . . . ?'

'About Branwell and his wife? But how did you know, Lizzie?'

'I guessed from the moment I saw them together on the Cliff Bridge in Scarborough. What he felt for her was written on his face.'

'Oh, I am not trying to excuse his conduct,' Anne said, 'we are all well aware of his fault in the situation, but how can we pile all the blame on his shoulders? A man does not bestow his heart where it is not welcome. You know Branwell. Could you believe him so wanting in sensitivity as to embark on an affair of the heart without some sign of reciprocation?'

'No Anne. I do not believe that for one moment.'

'Neither do I. Nor does Emily.'

'And what of Charlotte?'

Anne hesitated. 'Charlotte cannot bring herself to excuse

B-Branwell's conduct, and it grieves me to see her so set against him. They were so c-close as children. I try to keep an open mind, but it is not always easy. Now the house seems divided against itself, and yet I think that p-poor Charlotte, despite her uncompromising attitude to Branwell's misfortune, is the one most deeply hurt by it. She b-blames Mrs. Robinson, but Branwell will listen to no word of criticism ag-gainst her. His love for Lydia Robinson remains unaltered; his faith in her is absolute.'

'I'm so sorry, Anne. So very sorry . . .'

Anne smiled bravely. 'We are all downcast at the moment. All, that is, except Emily, whose clear-sighted philosophy enables her to accept the hard knocks of life. I wish I p-possessed Emily's strength of character, but I don't.'

As they turned back towards Crossways Grange, Anne said, 'Oh Lizzie, you cannot believe how narrow the parsonage seems to harbour so much suffering and intensity; how the quiet rooms throb with the violence of Branwell's grief. He is like a man demented, and our n-nerves are strung to concert-pitch lest papa should hear the commotion when Branni comes home late at n-night from the Bull Inn.

'I think that is the worst burden of all to bear. I often think how terrible it must be for that gentle, scholarly man, locked within the lonely spheres of his b-blindness, to be so helpless in this emergency.'

Lizzie stared out of her bedroom window at the unfamiliar hills surrounding her. Never once, since she came to Crossways Grange, had she ventured into those hills.

Since the death of her master, she had felt little inclination to stray far from hearth and home. Winter and death had held her heart in a grip as hard as iron, but now spring was well past, and the summer tints of the moors beckoned to her.

Opening the lattice, she leaned on her elbows and breathed in the warm, sweet-scented air, yielding to a strange desire to walk where larks rose among green bracken. She had harboured a foolish notion that she must await the call of the moors before venturing there. But now the moors were calling to her with an insistent voice which she could no longer ignore.

Putting on her bonnet, and pulling the veil over her face, she slipped silently from the house and turned her footsteps towards Haworth.

When she came to the signpost, she stared up at the cobbled street leading to the village, stifling a wild notion that no houses could possibly crown that preposterous ascent, and wondering why the thought seemed familiar to her.

Heavily-built houses appeared; weavers' cottages and wool-combers' sheds with long upper windows and exterior stair-cases. It was a stiff walk. The setts of the road were uneven, placed horizontally to give purchase to horses. There were open channels by the roadside, cut to runnel sewage and rainwater.

Lizzie panted as the hill curved on. At the summit she saw the solid bulk of a tavern, a chemist's shop on her right, and a church on her left.

The air in the valley had seemed still. Up here, Lizzie felt the wind clutching at her bonnet. She lifted her face to it, sensing a sudden sweetness, a feeling of home; the scent of open moorland and wild spaces.

So that was the tavern where Branwell drank? The Black Bull! How aptly named. It appeared to her as black and immovable as a grazing bull in a field. Then she noticed a narrow path winding away between flat tombstones to a house roofed with heavy slate flags – a house with long windows, two by two, flanking an apexed front door, and a garden enclosed by a low, stone wall.

Although she had never in her life before seen that house, she felt she knew it as well as she knew Grayston Lodge or Crossways Grange; knew as intimately as she knew her right hand, the flagged passageway behind the front door, and the stairs facing it; knew all the rooms – the dining-room to the left, and Mr. Brontë's study to the right. She knew the kitchen beyond the archway in the hall, the shallow stone sink in that kitchen, and the black-leaded grate with its side-ovens. Then she noticed that a second path led to the church door, near a lane with a Sunday school and fronted with humble, slate-roofed cottages.

Inside the church, all was cool and dim. Light filtered down on the massive three-decker pulpit and velvet-covered lectern, on the high wooden pews of blackened oak, and on the names of worshippers painted in white letters on every door.

As she passed the communion table, she heard, in the recesses of her mind, a familiar melody played on the strings of a violin, and then the name Maria.

'Maria,' she whispered, 'who are you? Why are you calling me?'

There is something here I must find, she thought, but what is it?

The church door opened. Behind her veil, Lizzie Godolphin saw Charlotte Brontë leading her father towards the pulpit to find some notes he had left there.

'Shall I help you look, papa?' Charlotte asked in a low voice enriched with a faint Irish accent.

'No, no, my dear. I can manage well enough on my own.'

Charlotte waited patiently near the steps leading up to the pulpit, but Lizzie sensed that her mind was in a turmoil despite her calm exterior, and knew as clearly as if someone had told her, that Anne Brontë's sister was a desperately unhappy woman.

Charlotte is in love, Lizzie thought, and doomed to disappointment. The person she is in love with will never answer the letter she plans to write to him.

Mr. Brontë found what he was seeking, and descended from the pulpit, searching blindly for the rail to give him support.

'Take my arm, papa,' Charlotte said, reaching out to guide him.

'Thank you, my dear,' Mr. Brontë replied. 'My eyes are troubling me more than usual today.'

Together, the two walked slowly from the building. But even when they had gone, Lizzie sensed that she was not alone. It seemed to her that a sudden warmth invaded the cold church; that quick, light footsteps echoed on the stone flags.

With a shock, she saw, to the right of the communion table, a mural tablet bearing the inscription:

Here lie the remains of Maria Brontë,
Wife of the Rev. P. Brontë. A. B., Minister
of Haworth. Her soul departed to The Saviour,
Sept. 15th 1821, in the 39th year of her age.

As Lizzie stared at the tablet, the music grew stronger. 'So it is your music that has haunted me throughout the years?' she murmured. 'Oh, Maria. My dear, sweet Maria. But what do you want of me?'

The girl rose slowly to her feet, her veil wet with tears. Poor Maria, she thought, so close to home and yet so far away from it.

The church door creaked softly on its hinges as she closed it behind her, and walked up Church Lane towards the parsonage, hearing, close at hand, the whisper of other skirts upon the cobbles, and quick, light footsteps keeping pace with hers.

And now Lizzie's foot was on the heath. Lifting her veil, she looked about her at the wide expanse of rolling hills shimmering in the clear light of a summer afternoon. A lark rose up singing as two dogs came bounding towards her, one a great lion-coloured creature, the other a liver and white spaniel with a plumed tail, like Cathy's Dido.

They leapt at her with every sign of affection and, when it was too late to adjust her veil, Lizzie saw a figure striding towards her – that of a young woman, a tall person, very slender, with a curiously proud carriage, and dark hair blown in tendrils about her face.

'I thought you had gone to Keighley, Anne,' she called, 'to fetch that dress you were having dyed.'

'I – I am not Anne,' Lizzie replied, her heart thumping in her chest. 'I am Lizzie Godolphin, companion to Miss Blakeney of Crossways Grange.'

The woman stared at her. 'Well, you appear to have won my dog's approval,' she said coolly. 'Keeper does not take to everyone, and your resemblance to my sister would not have guaranteed your safety had he not done so.'

So this was Emily Brontë. Remembrance of a soft sighing wind breathing that name in the very air around her brought tears of joy to Lizzie's eyes, but in that very moment, Lizzie understood Emily's character; sensed her proud reserve which only love could conquer; knew that to speak now would be to lose Emily for ever.

Emily grasped Keeper's collar, nodded briefly, and went on her way.

How different she was from her sisters, Lizzie thought. There was no resemblance to Anne or to Charlotte in those dark eyes and planed cheekbones. And yet she reminded Lizzie of someone.

Unable to resist the temptation to look back, Lizzie saw Emily striding down the path to the parsonage, her skirts swinging about her ankles, the dogs bounding along in front of her, and then Lizzie knew who Emily reminded her of. Cathy. Cathy Grayston.

CHAPTER TWENTY

Lizzie retired to her room early, excited by the news that Miss Blakeney was sending Tom to Scarborough to fetch Dido, for Joseph had sent word that the poor creature was fretting.

'Poor Dido,' Lizzie said softly when she was told.

'Yes, poor Dido,' Miss Blakeney echoed. 'You know, Lizzie, I often think that animals are endowed with a sixth sense which we mortals do not possess. Not every mortal, that is. But I find animals too boisterous as a rule. They do, quite literally, sweep me off my feet!'

'I'll make certain that she does not disturb you, ma'am,' Lizzie's eyes shone.

'*If* she survives,' Miss Blakeney said. 'I understand that she is a very sick and sorry little dog indeed.'

'She will survive, ma'am. I will *make* her survive somehow,' Lizzie promised.

Tossing in her bed, Lizzie heard one o'clock strike, then two before she fell asleep and dreamt that she was in a rough hut with three other people, two men and a woman. One of them was lying on a couch, his eyes closed, his head bandaged.

The woman's dress consisted of a colourful skirt and a white blouse gathered into a frill about her shoulders. Her skin was swarthy, her hair tied back loosely with a ribbon. She wore hooped earrings and her feet were bare. The other man was sitting at a rude table, whittling a Cross, his lips pursed with concentration.

The woman pattered to the fire where cooking pots were suspended on hooks above the blaze, and threw into them bunches of herbs, and salt from a stone jar on the hearth. Presently she brought wooden bowls and spoons from a cupboard and set them on the table. 'Come, Mario,' she said, 'put the Cross away. The food is almost ready.'

As she spoke, the man on the bed groaned and struggled to sit up. At once the man called Mario strode across the room and knelt beside it. 'Praise be,' he cried excitedly, 'his eyes are open at last. Quick, Constance, fetch some broth! The stranger is coming round!'

The woman at the hearth ladled soup into a bowl, and hurried towards the couch. 'Make him eat,' she said in a low voice. 'His life depends on it.'

Mario lifted the stranger tenderly in his arms. His hair was matted, his beard unkempt.

In the dream, Lizzie picked up the Cross from the table and put it into the sick man's hands; saw him clasp it to his breast. At once the wild, puzzled expression left his face. 'Lizzie,' he murmured, 'is it really you?'

'Master!'

She woke with the word on her lips, saw the clear light of early morning shining through the window, and stumbled from her bed, scarcely able to believe, when she saw the dawn-misted fields of Yorkshire, that she was not in that other room; that she had not spoken to Edward and seen his fingers close round the Cross.

Sinking to her knees she prayed, 'Dear God, let it be true. Let my master be alive. Somehow, oh Lord, bring him back to me.'

Emily bent over her desk. She was sitting in her bedroom – a slip of a room over the front entrance of the parsonage – which she had claimed as her own. Keeper and Flossie – Anne's little spaniel – were with her, and the book into which she had copied her poems lay on the chest beside her.

It was October, and the bright day was beginning to fade. The last rays of the sun touched the distant hills with a mellow light. Emily glanced up now and then, seeing in her mind's eye Top Withens, the long low farmhouse on the moors which she had chosen for the setting of the book she was writing. Now she was thinking of the name she had chosen for that isolated house standing four square to the winds of heaven – 'Wuthering Heights'.

Ideas flooded into her mind, some drawn from the characters she and Anne had created in their make-believe kingdom, Gaaldine; others from stories she had read in *Blackwood's Magazine*; yet more from ghost stories and legends told by Tabby Aykroyd on winter evenings round the kitchen fire, all centred on the theme dear to Emily's heart – love which outlives all earthly bonds.

Presently she laid down her pen. The light had faded and she could scarcely see the page. She put the manuscript away in a drawer and called to the dogs. Leaving the room in darkness, she went downstairs and looked in the dining-room. It was empty and the lamp not yet lit. Anne and Charlotte must be in the kitchen. Flinging a cloak about her shoulders she went out of doors, the dogs following closely at her heels, and turned her footsteps to the heath, muttering the words she would put into the mouths of her characters; planning to return to her work after supper, for the scene she was writing was more real to her than the grass beneath her feet. She was no longer Emily Brontë but the wild intractable Catherine Earnshaw with the firelight shining on her face, and her brainchild, Heathcliff, skulking in the shadows.

At the parsonage, Charlotte lit the dining-room lamp and set the table for supper, then went upstairs to see if Emily was in her room. Branwell's door, she noticed, was shut. He had slept all day like an infant in its mother's womb.

Emily's room was empty. Charlotte set down the lamp, thinking of Branwell who knew nothing of her own misery. Emily alone knew the full story of her unrequited love for Monsieur Heger. Only Emily was aware of the ceaseless, silent, hopeless battle she had fought since her return from Brussels, with no victories, no action, no drums, bugle-calls and battle honours.

Oh, to be lifted from her present desolation; to find some source of strength, hope and courage. Her hand trembled on the lamp as she picked it up and turned to go downstairs. Then the lamp's wavering beam fell on Emily's book of poems.

> I'll come when thou art saddest,
> Laid alone in the darkened room;
> When the mad day's mirth has vanished,
> And the smile of joy is banished
> From evening's chilly gloom . . .
>
> Listen, 'tis just the hour,
> The awful time for thee;
> Dost thou not feel upon thy soul,
> A flood of strange sensations roll,
> Forerunners of a sterner power,
> Heralds of me?

Charlotte could not put the book down. Knowing that she was committing an unpardonable folly, she read on.

> Then dawns the Invisible,
> The Unseen its truth reveals;
> My outward sense is gone,
> My inward essence feels . . .

She had prayed to be lifted up from her desolation, and God had heard her prayer. 'These poems must be published,' she murmured, 'they *must*, and I shall see to it that they are.'

Trembling with excitement, she took the book to the dining-room and awaited Emily's return, knowing that her sister would be angry – but totally unprepared for the storm that broke over her head.

'You *dared* to pry into my personal belongings! You went like a thief to my room and stole what was mine!'

'Emily, please listen. The book was lying open, I could not help seeing it.'

'But you could help reading it! Tell me, did you also search my cupboard while you were about it?'

'I admit my fault, and I am sorry, but that is beside the point. Your poetry is exquisite. I urge you to publish.'

187

'Never! Give me my book! I tell you, Charlotte, I will never forgive you!' She stormed from the room.

Charlotte and Anne faced each other when the explosion was over. 'I must go up to her,' Charlotte said, 'make her realise that those poems must be published. All our lives we have cherished dreams of one day becoming authors. Heaven knows how we have worked at our writing. It has proved a mutual bond since we were children, and Emily's poems are not common effusions; not at all like the poetry women usually write. They are terse, vigorous and genuine, possessing a wild melancholy music both elevating and beautiful.'

'It would be unwise of you to go to Emily now,' Anne said. 'Wait until her anger cools. You know that even those nearest and dearest to her cannot intrude upon her secrets with impunity. Meanwhile, dear Charlotte, would you like to look at some of my poems? I know they cannot match Emily's, but I should welcome your opinion of them.'

Anne slipped from the dining-room as Branwell lurched downstairs.

'Branni, are you coming in to supper?' she asked.

'Supper? No,' he muttered thickly.

'But you have not touched a bite all day. Please B-Branwell. You are not going out, are you?'

'For Christ's sake stop babbling, and let me pass.'

Stifling a sob, Anne watched her brother stagger from the house. So intense was Emily's anger that she could not bear, in the ensuing days, to speak or be spoken to. Ignoring her family, she strode out upon the moors whenever possible as an alternative to remaining under the same roof with Charlotte. Anne said nothing. No one knew better than she did about the humiliation Emily endured or the futility of trying to console her. All she could do was pray that some solution would be found to end the state of war between her sisters.

One day, when Miss Theodora had gone to Keighley to visit friends there, Amelia said it would be a good opportunity to visit her sister, Abigail, at Haworth, for a change of scenery would benefit them all. 'You will come too, Lizzie, won't you?' she asked. 'I daresay a run on the moors will do Dido good, now that she has regained her strength and appetite.'

Lizzie smiled as she bent to caress Cathy Grayston's spaniel, and the little creature rolled over in an ecstasy of delight at her touch.

'There's no doubt about it,' Amelia observed, 'you saved the dog's life. It was you she was fretting for.'

'No, I don't think so,' Lizzie replied. 'She was ever Cathy's dog. It is simply that she associates the pair of us in some way. But if Cathy walked through that door now, she would spring up at her as if they had never been separated.'

Thus it was that Lizzie came upon Emily Brontë hunched upon a rock, staring at the landscape of the moors, her hands clasped round her mud-stained skirts.

Seeing her, Lizzie drew back, uncertain whether to continue, for Emily's expression was sullen. Then suddenly, with a yelp of pure joy, Dido began straining at her leash, tore herself free of Lizzie's restraining hand, and launched herself at Emily, fairly knocking her from her solitary perch, licking her face and hands as she used to Cathy Grayston's.

Unable to resist the advances of a dumb animal, Emily bent down to pick up the struggling dog in her arms, soothing its frenzied outburst of delight with soft words.

'I – I beg your pardon, Miss Brontë,' Lizzie faltered. 'I think that you reminded her of someone else.'

'Oh? Who?'

'Her mistress, Cathy Grayston.'

'Indeed?' Emily frowned. 'And is this Cathy Grayston so insensitive to the needs of her own animal that she cannot exercise it herself?'

'Cathy's dead,' Lizzie said.

'I'm sorry. Who was she?'

Lizzie sank down on a hillock, thinking how strange it was that regret over a dead child and a little dog, had broken down Emily Brontë's barrier of reserve.

'Cathy was my late master's little girl,' she said quietly.

'How old was she when she died?' Emily's beautiful eyes were full of compassion.

'Almost twelve.'

'The same age as my sisters, Maria and Elizabeth.'

'Yes, I saw their tablet in the church, beneath that of your mother, and the words carved there. "Verily I say unto you, except ye be converted and become as little children, ye shall not enter into the kingdom of heaven."' She fancied she heard the distant music of a violin as she spoke, or perhaps it was just the soft wind bending and ruffling the heath.

The words affected Emily deeply. Lizzie noticed that her lips were trembling slightly. The girl seemed troubled.

I am close to Emily now, Lizzie thought. Help me, Maria, not to waste this opportunity of speaking the right words to her. But what were the right words?

'I think that Maria would not wish you to let the sun go down on your wrath,' she said.

'Maria?' Emily lifted her head sharply. 'What do you know of – Maria? Who *are* you?'

'Branwell once called me a doppel-gänger,' Lizzie said. 'Perhaps he was right. Perhaps that is what I am – a phantom, a wraith, a shadow. A Shadow of the Brontës.'

Summer had brought a new curate to Haworth, the Reverend Arthur Bell Nicholls. October brought to Theodora Blakeney a letter from her niece, Lettie Railton.

My Dear Aunt Theodora [Lettie wrote],
. . . I know how troublesome has been the question of inheritance; how the lawyers have puzzled the problem of the division of Bella's property between us – her aunt and cousin – in these distressing circumstances.

Now I have received a letter from a notary at Malcesine in Italy informing me that, on the very day of her death, Arabella signed certain documents – the deeds to the Bella Vista amongst them – and a new will naming me as the sole heir to this and to all her other property. This means that the vexed question of Crossways Grange has been settled at last. Naturally dear Arabella entrusted to me the continuance of her father's wishes concerning yourself and your tenancy of the Grange during your lifetime.

A codicil to that will puzzles me. In it Bella set aside a sum of money to the use of one Stephen Florisent, and specifies that the villa must remain his home for as long as he wishes to remain there, which seems to me a very unsatisfactory arrangement.

I have no wish to live in Italy, and intend to go to the villa to sort out the tangle as soon as possible.

Meanwhile, I am sure that you will be overjoyed to hear that dear Julia has become engaged to the Honourable James Hennessy of Hutton Buscel, and that her wedding will take place next May at St. Mary's Church, Scarborough. Naturally Percy and I would have preferred a London wedding, but Julia has decided otherwise.

In any event, I trust that nothing will prevent you, dear aunt, from attending the wedding, and that you will believe me, ever your affec. niece, Lettie.

Theodora folded the letter thoughtfully, having read much between the lines. How strange, she thought, that she had never liked or trusted Lettie for all her charm and beauty, and that Arabella, for all her faults, was ever the softer of the two.

Bella, if she had been spared, would never have sold Crossways Grange, her old family home, but Lettie would sell it to the highest bidder as soon as her own coffin was safely buried in the churchyard at Keighley, and Theodora felt sorry for the luckless Mr. Stephen Florisent -- whoever he might be – as a stumbling-block to Lettie's disposal of the Italian villa.

Then Theodora smiled to herself. At least pretty little Julia Railton had inherited none of her mother's inborn snobbery. A London wedding indeed! Theodora knew instinctively why the girl wanted to be married in Scarborough; because of dear little Cathy Grayston. In Julia's simple, unaffected way of thinking, she would want her wedding to take place close to where Cathy was buried.

CHAPTER TWENTY-ONE

The two men worked side by side in the clearing, swinging their axes, sawing and chopping wood in companionable silence. They were Mario Gambetti and the man he knew as The Stranger, whom his children had discovered, half dead, six months ago.

Little Pepita had run into the house one afternoon. 'There's a man out there in the woods,' she cried, pointing her finger.

'A man? What man?' Constance Gambetti's voice was shrill with fear. 'Mother of God! Where is your brother?'

'With the man.'

'Take me to him!' Constance snatched a knife from the table. 'If he has harmed my son, I will kill him!'

'The man could not harm him, *madre*. Pepe says he is dead.'

Constance made the sign of the Cross. 'Go and find your father. Tell him to come at once.'

The man lay in some thick undergrowth where the children had built a rough shelter. His face was ashen, a blood-stained gash lay open on his forehead. Constance hurried forward and knelt beside him.

'Is he dead?' Pepita began to whimper.

'I don't think so. If I make haste, we might yet save him.'

Constance Gambetti's only remedies were the herbs growing near the cottage. She made a thick ointment which she spread on the wound, and tried to force a little broth between the stranger's lips, but the man could not swallow it. He lay on the rough couch they made for him in a corner of the living room, deeply unconscious.

She and Mario were beginning to despair of saving him when, one evening, the stranger opened his eyes and stared wildly about him. Then Mario had called excitedly for her to bring food, but the man's eyes had fallen on the Cross lying on the table, and he held out his hands towards it in supplication.

It was nothing but a trifle Mario had whittled from an olive branch, but when the stranger held it in his hands, he muttered something in a foreign tongue, and that was the start of his recovery.

When he was well enough to talk, he spoke in Italian, but when they asked his name and where he had come from he could not remember, and that puzzled him.

As he grew stronger, his gratitude was touching, and he adored the children. The Gambettis treated him with deference. This was obviously no peasant used to wresting a meagre living from the soil, but a gentleman. The quality of the clothing they had been obliged to strip from his bleeding body had testified to that, but the stranger was not above turning his hands to work. He insisted upon helping Mario with his woodcutting, and when the day's work was done he would sit by the fire, a child on each knee, allowing them to pull his hair and his beard as they pleased.

'What is the name of this place?' he asked one day.

'Alconi, Signor Stranger,' Mario replied, 'but it scarcely merits such a fine-sounding name. It belongs to the Count Alconi whose villa lies further inland. The Count allows me to live on his land in return for keeping his household supplied with wood for the fires.'

'Which is the nearest town?'

'Why, Malcesine,' Mario scratched his head, 'but that is a good way off; twenty-five kilometres at least. We go there four times a year to sell my goods in the market-square, but it is a long, hard walk there and back.'

'But how do you live, Mario, apart from your woodcutting and carving?'

'I fish, signor.'

'Fish, where?'

'In Lake Garda. That, thanks be to God, is but three kilometres from here. But you have heard of Lake Garda surely?'

The stranger shook his head. 'I cannot understand it, Mario. Who am I? Where did I come from? I remember nothing of my past life. Only, sometimes, when I look up at the stars, I wonder if I might have been a sailor, for the heavens at night seem to me to be a chart to steer by.'

It was evening when Lettie and Julia arrived at the Bella Vista, and their only welcome a snapping snarling dog which bounded up at the carriage until Dickinson, the coachman, kicked it so savagely that it slunk away whimpering.

'Go and find out what is happening,' Lettie called angrily. 'The wretched place seems deserted. Where are the servants?'

Julia looked up at the peeling façade and shivered. 'Perhaps we should not have come,' she said. 'I cannot bear to think that this is where Aunt Bella and Uncle Eddie died.'

'You know we were obliged to come. There is some trickery afoot which I intend to unmask. But you need not worry, my darling. Your trousseau is all that need concern you. I've set my heart on Italian silks and laces for your wedding dress. Well, Dickinson, what's to do?'

'I scarcely know, ma'am. I went round to the servants' quarters, but all I found was an old crone who does not understand English, and a young man who bolted at the sight of me.'

'Well at least open the gates and let us get inside. We can't stay here all night.'

Dickinson put his weight against the iron gates, and drove the carriage up the drive to the front entrance of the Bella Vista. As they dismounted, a young man in black came to meet them, hurriedly donning a black velvet jacket. 'I am Stephen Florisent,' he said. 'A thousand pardons for this poor welcome.'

'And do you intend standing there apologising for what you rightly term a "poor welcome" or show us in? We are tired and hungry after our long journey.'

'Of course, Mrs. Railton, do come in – though I hardly think the accommodation will be to your liking. I did not receive word of your visit until this morning.'

Lettie glanced round with distaste at the eyeless busts filmed with cobwebs; the vast gilded salon with the ashes of a long-dead fire in the grate, a marble staircase leading to rooms mouldering for want of attention, and urns crammed with dead flowers.

'I will instruct Dotrice to prepare some food,' said Florisent, glancing at Julia who stood shivering near the door, 'and to light a fire.' He pushed back a lock of lank fair hair as he spoke, and smiled ingratiatingly.

'You'll do no such thing,' Lettie said coldly. 'I have no intention of spending a night under this roof. The place reeks of damp. You cannot think very highly of your property to have allowed it to fall into such a state of disrepair.'

'There is a reason for that, Mrs. Railton. Lack of money. I have not yet received the portion due to me under Bella's will.'

'We will not discuss my cousin's will tonight, Mr. Florisent. Have the goodness to direct my coachman to decent accommodation.'

'The Red Boar at Malcesine is the nearest. I trust that you will pass a comfortable night there, and that we will meet againt tomorrow.'

'You may rely on that!' Lettie's eyes sparkled angrily as she swept out to the carriage followed by Julia and a disconsolate Miss Skinner, carrying madam's jewel-case.

Morning dawned fair and clear. Malcesine came to life to the sound of the angelus bell ringing from the church tower across the cobbled square. Carts and awnings appeared as rough peasant hands set up their stalls and piled them with produce; caged birds, flowers, poultry and vegetables. Live goats and kids were tethered to stakes; pigs squealed as they were herded into pens. Black-frocked priests paced the square towards the church, looking for all the world like a flock of carrion crows.

Julia stared from the window, overwhelmed by the strangeness of a foreign country, worrying about the fate of the squealing pigs and tethered goats. 'You are not going to leave me here alone are you, mamma?' she said anxiously.

'Of course not, my darling.' Lettie put on her bonnet as she spoke. 'Skinner will stay with you.'

'But you will not be gone long, will you?'

Lettie smiled. 'I have business with the notary, Signor Claudinalle. That, I imagine, may take some time, then I am going to the villa. But don't look so woebegone, my treasure. I will be back this afternoon. Go and do some shopping.'

Smoothing on her gloves, Lettie kissed her daughter lightly on the cheek, and then swept down to the waiting carriage.

'Ah, Mr. Florisent. Have you a decent room in which to receive me?' Lettie's smile was disarming as Dickinson handed her down from the carraige.

'Yes, indeed.' Florisent led the way into the salon where a fire burned and fresh flowers had been arranged. 'Did you pass a restful night, ma'am?'

'Not very,' Lettie said amiably, 'for I had a great deal on my mind, but I have passed a very interesting morning with Signor Claudinalle and,' she smiled enchantingly, 'with a man who was once employed here as a coachman. Now what was his name? Ah yes, Carlo Medici.'

'Carlo?'

'Why yes. A most pleasant, informative young man. You know him, of course.'

'I – I don't understand.'

'Don't you, Mr. Florisent? What a pity.' Lettie removed her gloves. 'You struck me as a fairly astute person from the moment I set eyes on you, and it does take an astute mind, does it not, to plan ways of making a living without working for it? Oh pray, sir, don't interrupt me. I shall not, of course, go into the matter of how you came by your fare to Italy in the first place, or how you managed to live by your wits until you met my cousin – that would prove not only tedious and boring, but unnecessary, seeing that I have already made extensive enquiries into your background – but I am curious to know how you managed to worm your way into Bella's confidence, and the precise nature of your relationship with her.'

'As to that,' Florisent replied uneasily, 'it was a deeply emotional relationship compounded of her search for truth and of my ability to provide that truth.'

'My cousin was ever a fool,' Lettie stared into the crackling boughs in the fireplace, 'but I am not, nor was Edward Grayston. Did he see through you, Mr. Florisent? Is that why you killed him?'

Florisent's head jerked up. 'Killed him? Are you mad? I did not kill him. I was in the boat with Bella. Carlo must have told you that.'

'Ah yes, now I remember. So it was Bella you killed? How very convenient. A storm, a tipsy woman, a rowing boat, an island. It cannot have taken much persuasion to get my cousin into that boat, and when you were far enough from the shore, and believed yourself unobserved, how easy it must have been to push her overboard.'

'I did no such thing! I swear before God that Bella was swept away whilst I was struggling to save my own life. Why should I have killed her? Bella . . .'

'Bella had just signed a will highly favourable to yourself, and well you knew it since you had just accompanied her to the notary's office. Does it not strike you as odd that my cousin met her death a few hours after signing that will?'

'You can prove nothing. Nothing!' Trembling, Florisent sank down on the edge of a chair.

'I do not intend to do so, Mr. Florisent. I will leave that to the proper authorities. I imagine that they have not delved too deeply into the matter so far, but a word in the right quarters will soon draw attention to the fact that you were with my cousin when she met her death, and that you had a great deal to gain by her demise.'

'What do you want of me?' Florisent muttered.

'Want? I want you out of here for one thing. I want your signature on a document renouncing your entitlement to your so-called inheritance, and then, my dear sir, you may go to the devil.'

Skinner was fast losing patience with Julia. Why doesn't she splash out, the woman thought, I would if I had her money. Engaged to marry an Honourable and there she is diddling about in pennies and ha'pennies. A yard of ribbon here, a bobbin of thread there. Now where's she off to? Surely not to buy flowers for the girl was standing near one of the stalls in the market-place admiring the blooms.

'I thought, miss, as how you were going to choose some lace for your wedding veil,' Skinner said boldly.

'I was,' Julia confessed, 'but my heart's not in it. I keep thinking of my poor uncle, and Aunt Arabella.'

'It don't do to dwell on the past, miss,' Skinner replied. 'The dead are at peace, and life is for living.'

'I daresay you are right.'

'Cheer up, Miss Julia. Shall we go back to that shop where you bought the ribbon? They had some lovely lace there – as fine as cobwebs.'

'Not today, Skinner. I think I'll buy something for James. Look, there's a stall with wood-carvings. Aren't they beautiful? Oh, there's a horse carved from olive. He'd like that, I know.'

As the girl edged her way to the front of the crowd, she looked up and met the eyes of a bearded man standing near the stall. In that moment she felt that she knew him, and she half expected him to recognise her.

It was a foolish notion, of course, she told herself. How could she have met him before?

'The signorina wishes to buy?' he asked easily in fluent Italian.

Julia shook her head. 'I am not certain,' she said haltingly in the same language. 'May I look?'

'But of course. Take all the time you want.'

He was dressed in peasant style, she noticed, with cord breeches, a loose shirt and a bright neckerchief, and yet he was not a peasant, she felt sure of that.

She picked up the carved horse and traced its smooth outlines with her fingertips. A woman came forward. 'You like it, signorina?' she asked. Julia nodded. 'It is very reasonable,' the woman smiled, 'considering the time it took to carve.'

'I'll take it, then.' The girl fumbled for her purse, aware that the man in the cord breeches was watching her intently, whistling softly to himself. 'I – I beg your pardon,' she said, 'but did you carve this?'

'Alas no, signorina, I am not skilful enough for that,' he laughed.

'Then what do you do for a living?' the girl blushed at her own boldness.

'I am a woodcutter, signorina.'

'Come away, miss.' Skinner, who possessed an inborn snobbery peculiar to servants of the rich, tugged anxiously at Julia's sleeve. 'It is not seemly for a lady to exchange chit-chat with peasant folk. Whatever would the mistress think?'

Julia turned away from the stall, a puzzled frown on her face. 'That man,' she said, 'didn't he remind you of anyone?'

Skinner sniffed. 'Certainly not, Miss Julia. A common Italian peasant? Who would such a person remind me of?'

'My uncle, Edward Grayston!'

'What, that bearded lout?'

'But he was not a "lout", Skinner, and he certainly was not a peasant. He had none of the peasants' servility for one thing.'

'No, he was rather too bold if you want my opinion, whistling like that in front of a lady. Now don't look back, miss.' But Julia did look back to see the bearded stranger staring after her.

When Lettie returned to the inn later that afternoon, Julia attempted to recount the incident. 'I saw someone today who reminded me of Uncle Eddie,' she said awkwardly.

'Edward?' Lettie glanced up sharply.

'Oh, it was just a foolish notion of mine, I suppose,' Julia sighed. 'My mind was full of him and Aunt Bella at the time.'

'Go on, my darling.'

'It doesn't matter, mamma. How did you get on with Mr. Florisent?'

'It's a long story, and I am far too tired to recount it.' Lettie poured herself a glass of wine. 'Now tell me, did you buy the lace for your wedding veil?'

'No, mamma,' Julia's face fell, 'I simply could not do so.'

'No matter,' Lettie smiled, 'we will do it tomorrow. It would seem a pity to have come all this way for nothing.'

'There's just one more thing,' Julia murmured. 'Before we buy the lace . . .'

'What, darling?' Lettie yawned.

'Could we not visit the cemetery? I should so like to put flowers on poor Aunt Arabella's grave.'

CHAPTER TWENTY-TWO

1846

Once Emily had given her consent to the publication of her poems, Charlotte's thoughts became centred less on Constantin Heger and more on the preparation of the manuscript which, the sisters had decided, would contain a selection of all their poems. Charlotte set about the task of finding a publisher as a general marshals his forces before an attack, but nothing would induce Emily to publish under her own name.

'I will call myself Ellis Bell,' she said.

'Very well.' Seeing the stubborn set of Emily's chin, Charlotte was obliged to agree. 'What about you, Anne?'

'I choose Acton Bell as my nom-de-plume,' Anne replied, intent on keeping the peace between Emily and Charlotte.

'And I'll dub myself Currer Bell,' Charlotte adjoined, 'so that all our initials will remain the same.' But it was February before Charlotte found a publisher, and the last week in May before the book appeared – the very day that Julia Railton was married to James Hennessy.

Theodora had wintered badly, but she insisted on going to the wedding. Lizzie sat upright in the carriage beside her, plagued by bitter-sweet memories as Tom Stonehouse turned the horses in the direction of Grayston Lodge.

'The last time I drove along this road,' Miss Theo said softly, 'was from Cathy's funeral. Now I'm going to a wedding. Life is strange, my dear, is it not?'

'You are not too tired, ma'am, are you?' Lizzie arranged the rug over Theodora's skirts.

'No, and I shall bear up well enough as long as you are with me.'

'But I can scarcely attend the wedding, ma'am.'

'What nonsense, child. As my companion, you shall and must,' Miss Blakeney retorted. 'I will not stand for strangers meddling with me and treating me like an elderly child. You never fuss over me, Lizzie, and that is why I intend having you with me in church. Now tell me, are we almost at our journey's end?'

'Yes, there's Grayston Lodge!' The very words brought back vivid memories to Lizzie of a day seven years ago when she had driven from the workhouse and the driver had pointed his whip; memories of scurrying clouds and a feeling of apprehension as the carriage turned into the drive.

How much I have changed in seven years, Lizzie thought as she stepped down from the carriage. Now I have neat shoes, a blue dress and a matching bonnet, a blue brooch and a fashionable cloak – but how I wish that I might turn back the clock to that April afternoon and find my master waiting for me.

A strange servant answered the bell. 'I am Mrs. Railton's aunt,' Theodora said briskly, 'pray tell your mistress that I have arrived.'

'Step inside, ma'am, if you please.' The girl curtseyed and scurried off upstairs.

'Well, Lizzie, what do you think?' Miss Theo demanded.

'The house has changed, ma'am. Everything looks different, though I can't explain why.'

'My niece has a way of changing things when it suits her purpose to do so,' the old woman replied shrewdly.

Lettie appeared at the head of the stairs. 'Aunt Theodora,' she cried, hurrying down, 'I am so pleased to see you.'

Theodora allowed herself to be kissed. 'You have put on weight, Lettie,' she observed, 'have you taken to drinking too much brandy? No matter. How are you?'

'Quite well,' Lettie replied coolly nettled by the old woman's remark which came too near the truth.

'Old and crotchety, and well aware of the fact. Have you met my companion, Miss Godolphin?'

Lizzie stepped forward and met Mrs. Railton's look of shocked disbelief.

Spiders' webs were etched in crystal along the hedgerows, matching Julia's diamond coronet. Blossom hung heavy and sparkling after an early shower as her white slippered feet fairly danced to the church door where her bridesmaids spread her veil of finest Italian lace on the cold grey stones of St. Mary's Church. Tapers glimmered in dim side chapels as she moved forward down the aisle on her father's arm.

If Cathy had been alive, Lizzie thought, she would have looked over her shoulder and smiled at me. But then, if Cathy had lived, I would not have been standing here beside Miss Theodora in the family pew, aware of Mrs. Railton's hostile glances in my direction. I wonder why she so dislikes me?

Later, Lizzie slipped across the stableyard to visit Peggy and Joseph.

'Ay Lizzie, it's grand to see you again,' Peggy cried, 'although I'm half afraid of you in those grand clothes of yours.'

'Grand clothes?' Lizzie laughed. 'Well I admit they're better than my workhouse rags, but I'm no different underneath. Don't you remember when those rags of mine had to be thrown on the fire with a pair of kitchen tongs?'

'I do that!' Peggy threw her arms round Lizzie's neck. 'I was just a bit afraid that you might have forgotten now that you're a companion, and looking so bonny.'

After the excitement had died down, Peggy grew more solemn. 'Nothing's the same since the master went,' she admitted, 'and we're dreading tomorrow.'

'Why?' Lizzie asked sharply. 'What's happening tomorrow?'

'Tell her, Joe.'

'The master's shipyard's to be sold, lock stock and barrel,' Joseph said, lighting his pipe, 'The sale was advertised in the *Scarborough Gazette*, and that means an end to Zach Mainfaring and all the other men who have worked so hard to keep it going.'

'You mean that the shipyard will not be sold as a going concern?' Lizzie asked anxiously.

'Nay,' Joseph said, 'shipbuilding's not what it used to be in the old days, more's the pity. In my opinion the sale will be nought but a selling off of the timber and such in job lots, and her over there,' he jerked his head to indicate Mrs. Railton, 'will sell the land separately at a handsome profit. It makes my blood boil to think of it.'

'Lettie, are you there?' Percy Railton came into the library to find his wife sitting in a chair by the window. 'I've been looking everywhere for you. But you're not going to sit here in the dusk, are you, with a house full of guests to entertain?'

'Of course not. I'll be along presently.'

'What's the matter? Tired, are you?' Percy leaned over to kiss her.

'Oh for God's sake,' she said wearily, 'must you paw me?'

Railton drew back, abandoning his playful attitude. 'Paw you? I'm your husband, in case you've forgotten it.'

'Do you ever let me forget it?'

'No, and I don't intend to. I want to know what is the matter.'

'I'm tired, that's all.' Lettie drew in a deep breath, 'Tired to death if you must know. The wedding has been a strain, and now Julia has gone away . . .'

'What's unnatural about that?' Railton poured himself a glass of wine. 'Brides usually do go away on their honeymoon, but she'll be back in a month. Quite frankly, my dear, I can't see why you are so upset, especially in view of the fact that you appear to have taken up permanent resident here at Grayston Lodge, and that Hutton Buscel is not a stone's throw away from it. You'll make a very solicitous mother-in-law to young James Hennessy, I shouldn't wonder, driving over there every other day to keep an eye on things.'

'Don't be ridiculous, Percy.'

'Am I being ridiculous?' He stood beside her, breathing heavily. 'Oh, I admire your subtlety, the clever way you have managed to cast me aside thinking that I would never notice, but the fact remains that you have done so, and I don't like it. I am obliged to spend most of my time in London since my business interests are tied up there, but where is my wife? My friends are beginning to ask questions, and so am I.'

Lettie rose from her chair and turned on him furiously. 'How dare you throw accusations at me?'

'Because I know you, m'dear; have always known you. Do you imagine for one moment that I have been unaware of your indiscretions all these years? Your one abortive entanglement with a creaking member of the aristocracy; that furtive affair with Sir Edgar whatever his name was. No, Lettie, I knew all about them, and I managed to convince myself that this was the price I had to pay for having married a beautiful woman, but things are different now.'

'How are they different?' she interrupted, taking refuge in her anger.

'Because you are drunk with power; a mad desire to make money on your own account! First that villa in Italy; tomorrow Edward's shipyard, and I daresay you cannot wait for poor Theodora to die to sell Crossways Grange to the highest bidder.'

'It is none of your business,' she cried. 'It is my property, and I shall dispose of it as I see fit!'

'But have you ever given a thought to the poor devils who will lose their livelihood because of you? What would Edward think if he knew the work of three generations is to end in nothing?'

'Aren't you forgetting, Percy, that Edward is dead?'

'You needn't remind me of that, Lettie. I know it all too well, and life is the poorer because of it. But does one simply relinquish a man's ideals because he had the misfortune to die?'

'You've changed your tune, haven't you?' Lettie sneered, 'You whose whole life has been concerned with making money!'

'It is true that I have made money,' Railton said slowly, 'and I now see what an attraction that must have been when you married me, but I still possess a sense of loyalty to Edward which you apparently do not. At least postpone the sale of Eddie's yard long enough to go into the matter more thoroughly. Won't you please reconsider?'

'No, Percy,' Lettie said coldly, 'I will not.'

Railton went along to Theodora's room. 'We haven't had much time to ourselves lately,' he said.

'No, my dear boy, we haven't. But sit down and talk to me now.'

'How are you, aunt?'

'I'm old and tired,' she replied, 'as you very well know.'

'But you have a very charming and capable companion, it seems?'

The old woman glanced at him shrewdly. 'Lizzie? Why yes, but you must have seen her before? She was here in the old days.'

'Which "old days", Aunt Theo?'

'When Edward brought her to Grayston Lodge as a scullery-maid.'

'I don't believe so. If I had ever seen her before, I would have remembered her.'

'Why are you so interested in her?' Theodora asked roguishly, 'Don't forget that you are a married man.'

'There is little fear of forgetting that, I assure you.'

'You are unhappy, Percy,' Theodora's roguishness softened to compassion. 'Won't you confide in me?'

'Yes, Aunt Theo, that is why I came to see you.'

They were men, mainly, who crowded Sandside that May afternoon to see the old Grayston shipyard sold up, although a few of the fishermen's wives had come along to watch out of respect for Edward Grayston whom they had known and liked, and they stood silently on the edge of the crowd in their aprons and shawls. Zach Mainfaring and John Howard, Edward's designer and lifelong friend, were there, and alongside them many of the other shipyard owners and their workmen. Hammers stopped ringing as the men filed through the high wooden gates, silent and grim-faced, seeing perhaps the end of an era in Scarborough, thinking that what they were about to witness was tantamount to a public hanging, something harsh and cruel and unnecessary.

But for every friend of Edward Grayston, there were a dozen or more strangers intent on bargains; sharp-eyed dealers from Newcastle, Blythe and Merseyside. Ships' chandlers from Hull,

Filey and Bridlington, waiting for the chance to outbid each other; assessing the worth of every lot, weighing up in pounds, shillings and pence, the profit they might make in sailcloth, timber and tar – at the right price.

The shipbuilding fraternity of Scarborough watched, with a sense of guarded hostility, as they picked their way between the lots – thick ropes coiled like cobras, barrels of tar, piles of timber, some of it already steamed and curved into shape, even the tall, branch-stripped trees which had formed the stocks and launching cradles, manhandled from the harbour and still bearing traces of the thick mud and slime from the harbour bottom.

Zach Mainfaring laid a restraining hand on John Howard's arm as a rough-looking fellow carelessly handled the delicate instruments of the designer laid out for inspection on a trestle, and flicked through a pile of drawings with dirt-grimed fingers.

'This is monstrous,' Howard muttered. 'The only consolation, so far as I'm concerned, is that poor Eddie is not here to see this happening. My God, if I could lay my hands on that Railton woman, I would tell her exactly what I think of her.'

'If the master had been alive,' Zach said heavily, 'it wouldn't have happened at all.'

'What that blasted woman doesn't understand is that selling Edward's yard in job lots puts paid to a lifetime's work and endeavour. I can't stay any longer, Zach. It is like watching the living heart being torn from a body. Bundled into lots, all this stuff is virtually worthless, and when it is dissipated and carted away, nothing will remain but an acre or so of empty ground, with a few outbuildings and rusting padlocks.'

A platform had been erected near the gates for the auctioneer and his assistants. At two o'clock precisely, the men mounted the platform and the crowd fell silent.

Zach Mainfaring listened dully to the auctioneer's opening announcement. Well, this is it, he thought. It's come at last, Mr. Grayston, the end of all your hopes and dreams. But at least, sir, we built some of the finest ships ever to sail out of Scarborough.

'One moment, sir if you please!' A man in a checked cape

departed as suddenly as he came, leaving a scrap of paper in the auctioneer's hand.

'Ladies and gentlemen,' the auctioneer scratched his head and cleared his throat, 'I have here a bid of ten thousand pounds for this shipyard as a going concern.'

A ripple of disbelief surged through the crowd. Zach noticed that the fishermen's wives in their aprons and shawls were smiling at each other, and that John Howard, pushing his way towards the gates, had turned back to listen.

The auctioneer beat a tattoo with his gavel. 'Quiet, if you please. *If* you please! What I now require is a bid over ten thousand pounds for the Grayston shipyard as a going concern. Is anyone prepared to make me such an offer?' He stared at the sea of faces below him. 'No one? Then I have no choice but to withdraw from this rostrum and declare the Grayston yard sold to a consortium of London businessmen at the price stated.'

CHAPTER TWENTY-THREE

'Lizzie, do look!' Anne Brontë's voice held a hint of pride, her eyes sparkled with excitement. 'I have something for you.'

The two girls were walking together on the turnpike road near Haworth.

'Why Anne, what is it?' Lizzie caught her friend's enthusiasm at once. 'I have seldom seen you so happy.'

'It's a book of poems,' Anne produced a slim volume bound in dark green cloth, 'by Ellis, Currer and Acton Bell. Does that provide a clue?'

Lizzie frowned. 'No, I'm afraid it doesn't.'

'Think of the initials!'

'You don't mean . . . ?'

'Yes! It is our book! Our very own book! This is one of six complimentary copies sent to me by Aylott and Jones, the publishers. Look at the fly-leaf.'

'For Lizzie Godolphin,' Anne had written, 'Affectionately, A. Brontë.'

'Oh Anne! I knew that you were never meant to spend your life as a governess,' Lizzie cried, 'and here is the proof!'

'I pray that you are right,' Anne said softly, 'for Charlotte, Emily and I are hard at work writing novels. Do you really think that they may also be published one day?'

Lizzie smiled. 'I haven't a doubt of it,' she said.

Anne's happiness was short-lived. A month later, Lizzie received a letter in the nature of a *cri de coeur*, and knew at once that something was seriously wrong.

The pair had taken to meeting on the turnpike road, and Lizzie hurried there the next afternoon.

'What is it? What has happened?' she asked, as the forlorn figure of Anne walked towards her.

'Mr. Robinson is dead,' Anne said flatly, 'and Branwell . . .'

'Don't cry, Anne. Tell me, what is wrong with Branwell?'

'Oh Lizzie, I have never seen anyone in such a state before. I am so frightened.'

Lizzie slipped a comforting arm round her friend's waist. 'But why? I thought that . . .' But she could not continue. How could she possibly say that she believed that Branwell had 'looked forward' to the death of his former employer?

'Because Mr. Robinson's death has put the "finishing stroke" to my poor brother's hopes. The words are his, and he does nothing but repeat them over and over again. "I am finished," he says, "Done for".'

'I don't understand,' Lizzie said.

'Neither do I.' Anne buried her face in her hands, 'I always thought, as Branwell did, that when her husband died, Mrs. Robinson would send for my brother – that they would be married, and although I could never r-rejoice in Branni's affair with a woman so much older than himself, and on a d-different social plane, I was obliged to honour his unwavering d-devotion to her.'

Lizzie's thoughts returned to the day she had seen Branwell's eyes fixed on the beautiful woman in the cherry-coloured dress.

Anne continued, 'Soon after Mr. R-Robinson's death, his widow sent her coachman, Gooch, to Haworth, and word was d-delivered that he awaited Branwell at the Bull Inn. I have never seen a man in such a state of euphoria. Emily and I watched him d-dance down the churchyard to hear the news he had been expecting – that Mrs. R-Robinson desired his presence at Thorp Green Hall; that their path was clear at last, and that all lay smooth and serene before them.

'Charlotte was reading to papa in his study. Emily and I were together in the dining-room, but we felt no real joy at seeing Branwell so exuberant. Indeed, he looked little short of c-clownish as he tripped and stumbled down the path to the tavern.

'Poor Charlotte, how she kept her voice steady I shall never know, or how my father composed himself to listen as she read to him. Both knew where Branni had gone, and for what purpose.

'How time dragged as we awaited his return! Emily and I sat by the fire, talking in low voices, jumping at every sound, our eyes s-straying constantly to the window.

'Then, "he's coming," Emily cried, starting up. We r-rushed to the window to see Branwell weaving and staggering like a d-drunken man. Emily ran out to meet him. I watched her take his full weight as he leaned against her, his head lolling forward on his breast, his eyes rolling, his lips c-covered horribly with a kind of foaming saliva.

'I ran out to help her, but she said that she could manage by herself. By that time she was almost carrying Branwell. Then the study door opened and Charlotte appeared with papa. Emily lifted Branni into the passage. I think he had suffered some kind of a fit. The sound he made was like no other sound I have ever heard from a human throat – he was b-bleating like a newly-born calf.

'Emily hoisted him up and carried him along the passage to the stairs. Sweat was pouring from her. Then Martha Brown, the s-servant, came out of the kitchen, wiping her hands on her apron, and sprang forward to take Branni's legs. Between them, they c-carried him up to his room. The dogs tried to follow, but I called them back and bundled them into the kitchen. Charlotte was trying to comfort papa.

'There were two heavy thuds as Branwell's b-boots fell to the floor. I will never forget my father's face as he stood there, seeing nothing, a poor blind old man in a sea of c-confusion. All he could say was, "My son. What has happened to my son?"

'When Emily and Martha came downstairs, we were all standing in the passage like ghosts. "He'll sleep now," Emily said. Then I noticed that she held a scrap of paper in her hand. "Martha, make some tea. Charlotte, take papa back to his study," she directed.

'I stood looking at Emily, knowing that she was very angry. "It is just as I thought," she said, "that woman has let him down."

'She strode into the dining-room. "Read that," she said, handing me the paper. "I might have thought more of the Robinson woman if she had written to Branni herself, but to have sent a statement through trustees deterring him from ever again seeking to communicate with her is nothing short of cruel, knowing his feelings for her. But there is more to this than meets the eye. What that coachman said to Branwell to send him into a fit, I cannot think. I'm sure of one thing, however – this whole business is a tissue of lies, trickery and deceit."

'I started to cry, and she held out her arms to me. "Don't weep, Anne," she said. "It is not ourselves we should think of now, or even Branwell, but papa. Dry your tears and put on a brave face for his sake."

'Thus it is with Emily. She sees into the heart of things; gives courage where it is lacking; shores us up, not only with her physical energy, but something far b-beyond that. It is her clear-sightedness which brings hope and a sense of direction. I clung to her for a moment then, encouraged by one of her rare smiles, I went to the study to comfort papa.'

'I am truly sorry.' Lizzie held her friend's trembling hand in hers.

'The sorriest part of it is that papa is faced with a visit to Manchester in August for an operation on his eyes, and the oculist has warned us that there can be no anaesthetic to relieve the pain.'

'And what of Branwell? Did you discover what the coachman had said to him?'

'Oh yes,' Anne said bitterly, 'we heard the entire story later – not quietly or lucidly – but in a frenzied outpouring of grief. It appears that Mrs. Robinson has persuaded Branwell that she is half insane with worry. Her husband, it seems, altered his will before he died, and effectually prevented all chance of a marriage between his widow and Branni by stipulating that she should not have so much as a shilling if ever she communicated with him again.

'Now he is excitable, downcast, violent and maudling by turns; he has threatened suicide, and gives poor papa no peace by day or by night. The only place on earth where he finds comfort is in the bar-parlour of the Bull Inn.'

'And what of Emily?'

Anne smiled tenderly. 'Emily is our strength and stay at the parsonage. Never once has a word of blame for Branwell passed her lips. She holds fast to the belief that Mrs. Robinson's story is a tissue of lies from beginning to end, and says that t-time will p-prove it so.

'She keeps her hands busy from morning till night; says little, and seems shored up by some inner, shining faith which uplifts us all.'

CHAPTER TWENTY-FOUR

The birth of a son to Julia, now Lady Hennessy, gave Lettie reason enough to remain at Grayston Lodge, and stilled the wagging tongues of acquaintances busy speculating on a rift between herself and Percy.

James and his pretty young wife attracted a wide circle of friends to Senningford Hall – and Julia was thoughtful enough to invite people of her mother's generation to their house parties – the Bravingtons of Holl Beck, the Egmontons of York, and Lydia Robinson who had positively bloomed since the death of her dour husband. Indeed, since Lydia's return from Great Barr Hall in Staffordshire where she had been staying with her relatives, Sir Edward and Lady Scott, she and Lettie had struck up a particularly close friendship.

Lettie was now a wealthy woman in her own right. The Italian villa had been sold to a French nobleman at a price which had far exceeded her wildest hopes; Edward's shipyard to that mysterious consortium of London businessmen, and now it seemed likely that Crossways Grange would soon be hers to dispose of, for Theodora Blakeney was failing rapidly, and the house set in the heart of a thriving industrial region would bring a small fortune.

But if Lettie's concern over Theodora's illness was purely mercenary, Lizzie's was not. It grieved her to see the mistress so stricken, for the old lady was confined to one room, too crippled with rheumatism to cut up her own food. A heart condition gave further reason for concern, but her mind was as lucid as ever.

Lizzie's days were long and arduous in caring for Theodora, and the bond of affection between them strengthened as time went by. The girl slept in a room adjoining Miss Theo's, to be on hand if the mistress needed her during the night.

'Don't you think we should have a nurse?' Amelia said. 'Look at you! There isn't a picking on you, nor a scrap of colour in your cheeks.' But Lizzie wouldn't hear of it. 'It pleases me to nurse Miss Theodora,' she said with a smile, 'as long as I can manage on my own. Besides, what else would I do with my time?'

'That's just what I'm getting at. You're young, child, and life is passing you by. Don't you ever wish to get about and make friends of your own age? And have you thought what will become of you when the mistress passes on?'

Later, in her room, Lizzie looked at herself in a mirror. Never a vain person, she had not realised the changes the years had wrought. Her hair was darker than it used to be, and much tidier. Steam from the pans and kettles had once fluffed out curly tendrils on her forehead, and she would push them back impatiently with a wet hand. Now her hair was neatly braided, but Amelia was right, she was pale and thin – a different person from the comely second cook of those far-off days at Grayston Lodge when the master and Cathy were alive.

What would she do when Miss Theodora died?

The Reverend Patrick Brontë walked slowly down the path of Haworth parsonage, a tall erect figure in black relieved only by the high white stock folded impeccably about his clerical collar, his sight mercifully restored by a painful but successful operation.

Nothing about his appearance suggested that he had spent a sleepless night ministering to his son. Nothing indicated, as he passed through the gate to the church, that he seemed to have come face to face with the Devil during those long weary watches by the light of a flickering candle which cast weird shadows on walls and ceiling, as he listened to Branwell's demented ravings and low animal noises of despair.

In that eerie light, Patrick Brontë had been reminded of those tormented souls writhing eternally in Hell, shut away for ever from the light of the living God whom he served. What if Branwell, his beloved son, should die unabsolved, condemned to eternal darkness? But the old man showed no sign of his inner conflict, exhaustion and despair, as he walked unflinchingly towards the church he had served conscientiously for the past twenty-eight years.

Emily Brontë watched from her window until her father entered the church, and then went quietly downstairs to the kitchen, pausing at the foot to listen, with ears attuned by love, to every movement within the house – the gentle closing of a door, the ticking of the clock on the landing, the creaking of a floorboard – sounds as dear and familiar to her as the singing of wild birds on the moors.

The house pulsed gently with the heartbeats of those she loved. What she listened for was the sound of footsteps from the room Branwell shared with their father, but there was no sound save the grunting, indrawn breath of someone sleeping. Then she heard Charlotte's footsteps on the landing overhead; the soft padding of Keeper's paws on the stairs beside her, and the crackling of the kitchen fire.

The small bright kitchen reminded Emily of happier days when life at the parsonage had been pleasant and carefree. Clear in her mind was a day fourteen years ago when Sally Mosley, one of the village girls, had been doing the washing, her brawny arms red from the scalding water, her hair tucked under a white mob-cap. Suds had spilled over from the tub as Sally rubbed away on her washing-board, then she had rushed out to the yard to peg out the clothes, singing lustily at the top of her voice.

Anne had been kneeling on a stool, peeling apples, and the pair of them had dallied over their tasks until Tabby came in. 'Eh, what's to do?' she cried, 'What ya pitter-pottering there for, ya daft things?'

They had laughed at Tabby until the far more authorative figure of Aunt Branwell had stalked in, her pattens making a clicking sound on the slabs, to scold Anne for kneeling on the stool. Emily had dived out through the back door at the first 'click-clack', and had met the astonished Sally Mosley face to face in the scullery.

When Aunt Branwell had gone back to her room, declaring that the house was completely disorganised, Emily crept back into the kitchen laughing fit to kill herself, then she and Anne had finished their work in exemplary fashion; thrown their arms round each other and run out into the garden. 'What if the dinner boils dry?' Anne clapped her hand to her mouth, 'We never thought to look in the pot.'

Everything had seemed so funny; so inconsequential. 'Never mind,' Emily said, 'we shall grow more sensible as we grow older. I wonder what we shall be like in – in 1874!'

'Eighteen seventy-four?' Anne said in alarm. 'But that's a lifetime away.'

'I know. Just think, Annie, by that time I shall be fifty-six, Branwell fifty-eight, and Charlotte fifty-*nine*!'

'And I shall be fifty-four! Oh Emily, we shall all be old and grey and toothless!' She gazed fearfully at her sister. 'I wonder if we shall all be well and happy then?'

Now Emily knew that Branwell would not live to see his fifty-eighth year; never grow old and grey and toothless as Anne had suggested. His days were already numbered in the prime of his young life, and she watched his decline with a deep sense of compassion, and a sense of bitterness that Charlotte had withdrawn her sympathy at a time when Branwell most needed her help and understanding.

There were times when her own insight seemed more an affliction than a blessing. It was as if a powerful light shone clearly from her own mind into those of her family, illuminating with a terrible clarity their inmost thoughts. But it was impossible to condemn what she understood so well. One might just as well blame an animal for being born deformed, or a stream running downhill in a certain pattern, for forming its own way between rocks and stones in its very existence as a stream.

She paused to look out of the kitchen window at the dovecote in the yard, observing the way the dainty birds beat their wings, and thought, with a deep, inner peace, of the moors.

She longed passionately to be alone there among the solitude of rocks and glowing bracken with only the curlews for company, and she walked to the back door to breathe in the scents and sounds of the morning, recalling the sound of laughter borne on other winds, when Branwell was a little boy, and Charlotte a solemn child in a white pinafore; when she herself had climbed the double cherry tree outside papa's study window one Oak Apple Day, and had sent one of its boughs crashing to the ground.

The accident had brought Tabby on the scene, wailing and wringing her hands. 'Ay, t'maister'll niver forgive 'ee for ruinin' 'is tree,' she cried. 'Coom dahn this minute, tha limb o' Satan!' Then the faithful Tabby, whose bark was ever worse than her bite, had sent down to the sexton's cottage for a bag of soot to daub over the tell-tale scar.

How is it possible, Emily thought, for life to have robbed that marvellous closed circle of childhood of all its happiness and adventure? Why is Branni lying in a darkened room, the bright light of his existence dimmed beyond reluming? Why has Charlotte grown into a sharp, managing critical woman, apportioning blame, withholding mercy?

Why has dear, enchanting little Anne become so nervous and resigned? And why have I turned inward upon myself? There was always that tendency, but now I cannot bear to think that weak human flesh should hold the spirit in thrall, for when the demands of the flesh come uppermost the spirit seems cast down to the brink of disaster.

In Nature alone suffering holds its appointed place. In Nature the eagle takes the lamb without pity as an act of self-preservation. Nature reveals itself as the only yardstick for human existence.

This I believe, and yet the simple facets of my creed evade me time and time again when I am called upon to succour those I love. They evade me even now as I hear Branwell calling to me, and I cannot ignore his cries for help.

While writing fulfilled the sisters' spiritual needs during Branwell's headlong rush towards self-destruction, the physical application to their craft, night after night, by lamp and firelight, proved exhausting. And yet, as the stories and characters took hold of them, and the manuscripts grew even bulkier, they created a reason for living, and when Branwell's excesses seemed too much to bear, they withdrew to the worlds of their imagination, taking mental refuge in the next chapter, the next scene, the next page of dialogue.

Their poems, to Charlotte's chagrin, had not sold, but undeterred by that failure, she wrote to Aylott and Jones regarding three works of fiction by the 'Bell Brothers'.

Aylott and Jones's reply indicated that they were not publishers of fiction, and so began the wearisome task of packing and posting the completed manuscripts to other publishing houses – and the bitter pill of rejection when the package was returned repeatedly to its source.

It was not until the midsummer of 1847 that a letter from Messrs. Thomas Cautley Newby was received, agreeing to publish the novels of Ellis and Acton Bell, but declining that of 'Mr' Currer Bell.

The letter came as a blow to Charlotte, and the tender-hearted Anne admitted to Lizzie, during one of their nowaday rare meetings, that she felt disinclined to accept Mr. Newby's offer from a sense of loyalty to her sister.

'According to Mr. Newby,' Anne said wearily, 'Charlotte's book, *The Professor*, is too short to fall into any fictional category. But I cannot bear her work to go unrecognised, for she is a far better writer than I could ever hope to be.'

'Is there no ray of hope?' Lizzie asked.

'Only one. Charlotte has another book on the point of completion. A novel she started last August when papa was undergoing his eye operation in Manchester. A novel called *Jane Eyre*.'

Jane Eyre was accepted and published in eight weeks, and Charlotte's sun was in its ascendancy when Emily's novel, *Wuthering Heights* and Anne's *Agnes Grey* were still gathering dust in Newby's office. Now the boot was on the other foot, and it was Charlotte who felt the need to go into battle on her sisters' behalf. Anne was grateful, Emily less so – and Lizzie understood Emily's reasons, confided one afternoon on a lonely moorland path with the dogs bounding along in front of them.

Their meeting was purely coincidental. Amelia had insisted on Lizzie taking a breath of fresh air, and Emily happened to be out walking. There was never an affectionate greeting between the two women, no linking of hands, and seldom a smile from Emily. At times they seemed more like enemies than friends. Not for Emily the honeyed words of social intercourse. She would have fled in horror from sickly sentimentality. Whatever she felt for Lizzie sprung from the girl's quick intellect, her ability to 'fence' with words, and the knowledge that Lizzie often looked 'beyond the stars' as she did.

Lizzie was well aware that Emily had never quite forgiven Charlotte's well-meaning interference in her life, and now resented her sister's efforts to get *Wuthering Heights* into print.

Emily reminded Lizzie of a wild creature caught in a trap. And that, she thought, is exactly the way I felt when I was sent to work at Grayston Lodge, the reason why I told my master that I was obliged to go where I was sent. One part of me knew that my words were likely to bring down the wrath of God upon my head, another part of me cared nothing if I was thrashed for speaking my mind. I was trapped then just as Emily is trapped now. One part of her longs to see her novel in print, another part of her rebels against the publication of her innermost thoughts and feelings.

'I wish that Charlotte would let me be,' Emily cried, striding along the path. 'I do wish that she would let me be. I wish that she would drop the whole matter between Newby and myself. Let her see to Anne if she wants to, but I wish to God that I had never sent that manuscript to be haggled over as a couple of dogs haggle over a bone!'

'I understand,' Lizzie said softly.

'Do you?' Emily rounded on Lizzie. 'How convenient! But *you* understand everything, don't you?' Her smouldering eyes regarded the girl intently. 'I envy your understanding of every situation. But have your ever poured yourself on to paper? Have you ever known the humiliation of waiting for some mercenary-minded publisher in a dusty office to decide whether or not your work is good enough to print?'

'No, but I have known other humiliation equally devastating.' Lizzie threw back her head and laughed; snatched off her bonnet and revolved, arms outstretched, as if drunk with the sweet moorland air. 'I have known the humiliation of *your* disapproval, and I cannot imagine anything more terrifying than that.'

'You idiot!' Emily flared. And then she smiled one of her rare and lovely smiles that reminded Lizzie of an April day when the sun comes out briefly behind the rain clouds.

CHAPTER TWENTY-FIVE

1848

> When we, our thoughts seemed weaning from the sky –
> That pang which wakes the almost silenced pain!
> Thus, when the sick man lies, resigned to die,
> A well-loved voice, a well-remembered strain,
> Lets Time break harshly in upon Eternity.

Trembling with emotion, Branwell let the pages of his sonnet flutter to the ground. He lay fully dressed on his bed; tears coursed down his cheeks.

'Lydia,' he murmured, straining to catch one echo of that 'well-loved voice' to cheer his existence, but there was nothing save the wind whining across the gravestones.

He lay, too hard to die, too wretched to live, cut off from his childhood companions once so dear to his heart, unable to work himself up to face life's battle, his mind crowded with hobgoblin images; certain that the Devil lurked with bright glittering eyes to bear his soul to those vast drear regions where no light ever pierced the illimitable gloom.

His isolation was complete. Lydia, whose warm glances had opened up visions of heaven, was gone away from him for ever. Every channel seemed closed to him, except one – the narrow path leading down to the Bull Inn. There, and there only, fortified by fivepenny squibs of gin and surrounded by merry companions, could he hope to find consolation.

He got up unsteadily, felt in his pockets, jingled thankfully a few pence in the palm of his hand, then opened the door and went downstairs, terrified lest his footsteps were heard, in agony in case Charlotte should open the dining-room door and see him. He experienced a sensation in which his brain seemed to race with the power and noise of a high waterfall, and that roaring and pounding caused his slight frame to shake from head to feet. In his agitation to be gone from the house which seemed to him a trap rather than a home, he began to blubber like an ailing infant, knowing he could not bear to face his sister.

Turn the key, he thought, Oh God, how it scrapes in the lock. Now turn the knob. Curse these flags, how they echo my footsteps. She will surely hear me. Light will shine out suddenly from that door, and Charlotte will stand there, not speaking but thinking ill of me. Oh, that look of hers. I remember that day I came home from visiting a sick child for whom I felt an urge to pray – only I was not good enough. How dare I pray for another who has forgotten how to pray for myself?

Oh Lord, let the door open quietly! There! I know Charlotte thinks me unfit to live, and I shall never forget the look she gave me that day if I live to be a hundred – which I never shall. Her look said quite plainly, 'You felt like praying? You felt inclined to read a psalm to a sick child? Did my ears deceive me?' Then came that painful, baffled expression which was worse than all. It said, 'I wonder if that's true.'

I spoke not a word in my own defence, I was much too cut up. She will never know how she wounded me, and when she had gone I decided to make a night of it. Why not, when she couldn't even credit me with speaking the truth, and trying to be good?

That's better! The air feels cool on my face. What if the Old Man is looking out of the window? I shall fight him if he attempts to restrain me. I will shoot myself with that pistol he keeps by his bed. What will they think when I am stark and cold? Will Charlotte mourn me then, and what will Lydia think when they tell her that Branwell Brontë blew his brains out?

They think ill of Lydia, I know. Oh, Christ Jesus, Saviour, how could they think so of the sweetest being ever created? If I could live again one moment in her arms and gaze once more into that heavenly face, the Devil and all his legions could not harm me.

How I hurried between these slabs the day Gooch, the coachman, came from Thorp Green. I had waited so long for news of Robinson's death, then to be sent for so soon after reading his obituary in the *Leeds Mercury*! How could I restrain myself from running and skipping all the way, but I knew the minute I saw the coachman's face that he had brought me bad tidings. This path, I believe, witnessed my last happy moments on earth. Would that I might run down it just once more in the blessed anticipation of a message from *her*. To think of my beautiful Lydia so weighed down with sorrow, brought to the verge of madness, and threatened with poverty if ever she set eyes on me again is past bearing. Oh God damn Robinson's soul! May his flesh roast in Hell!

The light shines out a welcome. The only welcoming lights I perceive in this blighted universe are those on the cobbles by the Bull. Push open the door. Ah, the fire burns brightly in the hearth . . .

On August 4th, Lettie Railton received a letter from her friend Lydia Robinson.

My dear Lettie,

It is over at last! The unhappy Lady Scott is dead, but one can only feel thankful that her sufferings are at an end. Sir Edward is naturally distressed after his long ordeal, but he thanks providence that I am here to help him bear his bereavement, and I know that he holds me in the warmest regard. Indeed, we are devoted to each other, and I believe that our marriage will take place as soon as propriety allows.

I cannot help, therefore, despite the sad circumstances of Lady Scott's demise, but regard the future with a certain joyous anticipation. Great Barr Hall is a noble house. You will be as enchanted with it as I am when you come to visit Sir Edward and the new Lady Scott after our wedding . . .

It was a bright September morning when Amelia broke the

news to Lizzie that Branwell was dying, and saw with infinite pity the girl's stricken expression.

'Branwell, *dying?*' Lizzie clasped her hands together. 'Oh surely not, Amelia?'

'I'm afraid so, and from what my sister tells me it will be a happy release for the poor lad.'

'But I had no idea that he was confined to his bed.'

'He's not, child. Abigail tells me he's dying on his feet. She saw him yesterday staggering from the Bull tavern, and doubts if anyone realises how close his end has come. But my sister is never mistaken in such matters. It seems certain that Branwell will not last more than a few days at the most.'

'Then I must go to him,' Lizzie said.

'Eh, don't talk so daft, love! What could you do for him?'

'Nothing, I suppose. But I once made him a promise.'

'What sort of a promise? When?'

'Oh, a long time ago when he was in Scarborough. I met him near the museum. He was ill then, and very low-spirited. I'll never forget our conversation. He said that no one except Mrs. Robinson would come to him in his hour of need to give him succour and support. I told him he was mistaken, that I would go to him.'

'Ay, that sounds just like Branwell,' Amelia said, 'but I'm thinking his fine Mrs. Robinson won't give a tinker's curse if he lives or dies.'

'I guessed that at the time, and that is why *I* must go to him now.'

'That's all very well, but do you think Branwell will remember that promise now?' Amelia was troubled as she recalled Abigail's words, 'The lad's nobbut a ruin; even the locals are frightened of him. Why, I hear tell he carries a carving-knife up the sleeve of his coat to stab the Devil with, and he's raving mad with drink and drugs.'

'No, Amelia, Branwell will not remember, but I do, and I must keep my promise.'

'You'll do no such thing,' the housekeeper cried. 'You don't what you're up against. Branwell could be dangerous!'

'Dangerous or not, have you forgotten that I once believed myself in love with him; how he enchanted me with his bright

224

personality? How could I live with my conscience if I failed him now?'

Amelia sighed. 'You're a stubborn lass, Lizzie Godolphin, always were and always will be. But how do you intend to see Branwell? You can't very well walk into that tavern.'

'No, but I could wait outside for him. I'll go tonight.'

'Not on your own,' Amelia pursed her lips. 'Nay, it's no use arguing with me this time. Tom will go with you, or you'll go not at all!'

There was no moon, and no one abroad to notice the two dark figures huddled in the church doorway. The only light came from within the tavern, the only sounds were those of revelry whenever the door of the Bull opened; that and the hooting of an owl in the graveyard.

Tom turned up his collar and glanced at Lizzie uneasily. Why was he reminded of Christmas Eve, the Star and the Stable; the three Wise Men coming from the East? Was it the sense of drama as they waited for the parson's lad to leave the tavern; the dim and distant stars burning in an inky sky; the church and the winking fireglow that touched the tavern windows? He shuddered. For one split second his common-sense approach to life deserted him, then the door of the Bull Inn was flung open and he saw Branwell stagger out into the night.

'There he is!' Tom's voice was low and hoarse. 'Take care, Lizzie, he will pass close by us.'

The shambling form of a man, seen first in silhouette, came closer, clawing at the railings for support.

Oh dear God! Lizzie's cry of despair was uttered deep within herself. That shuffling scarecrow could not be Branwell! She heard his strange mutterings and laboured breathing as he stumbled up the steps near the church. He was hatless, and a mat of unkempt red hair hung raggedly about his face like the mane of a wild beast. His eyes were sunk deep in their sockets; his mouth had fallen like that of an old man and his lips trembled. His cheeks seemed hollowed out of marble; his limbs had wizened and bent so that his clothes seemed too big for him.

'You'd best come away, lass,' Tom whispered. 'You can see that state he's in.'

'No Tom, I must go to him.'

'But he might be armed; dangerous.'

'I am not afraid. Please Tom, will you wait here for me?' The girl slipped from the church door and moved along the path calling softly, 'Branwell, Branwell.'

'Who's there?' His trembling mouth fell open, then he cried out in anguish, 'Is it you, Lydia? Have you come to take me home?'

'No, Branwell, I am not Lydia.'

'Then you must be the Devil,' he gibbered, 'the Devil in disguise, come to fetch my soul at last! I don't care! Take me. Take me now!'

'I am not the Devil, Branwell, I am your friend.'

He drew in a soft shuddering breath. 'You?' he said drunkenly, and giggled – a mirthless cackle more terrifying than abuse.

'Take my arm,' Lizzie said compassionately, 'hold on to me.' She stepped forward, took his hand and guided it into the crook of her elbow. He resisted at first, smiling foolishly, then he mumbled, 'You're a good girl, Anne. You don't preach. You and Emily don't preach. You haven't turned against me.'

'No one has turned against you, Branwell.'

'Charlotte has.'

'Surely not?'

'She has, I tell you!' He reeled and would have fallen but for Lizzie's supporting arm. 'She thinks I am not fit to live!' He began to sob and to pull away from her; his legs buckled beneath him and he fell to his knees, retching.

Lizzie bent down, straining with all her might to lift him. 'Come,' she urged, 'put your hand on my shoulder; try to stand up.' He staggered against her as helpless as a new-born calf, slavering and moaning.

'I am damned,' he said thickly. 'I know that I am damned.'

'No. You must not say that.'

'But I *am*! There is no way out for me except to die!' Then, 'Do you think ill of her? *Do* you?'

'Think ill of whom, Branwell?'

'Of – Lydia.'

'No, my dear, of course not.'

He clutched Lizzie's arm, bruising her flesh and sobbed, 'Her miseries are all my fault. All mine! I betrayed her, my sweet Lady of Grief.' Tears streamed down his sunken cheeks.

'Come home, Branwell,' Lizzie said softly, 'come home.'

'See!' He stopped abruptly and pointed a trembling finger in the dark. 'See – Emily has set her lamp in the window to guide me.'

Slowly Lizzie led Branwell up the path between the gravestones, then she pushed open the garden gate and led him to the front door of the parsonage. I shall never see him again in this life, she thought, never again hear his voice or touch his poor, wasted hands.

A soft wind ruffled the grass; a nameless melody sighed through the branches of the tree. 'I have kept faith, Maria,' she whispered, 'I have brought your son safely home.'

Branwell lurched forward and sank down on the doorstep. 'I do feel sick, Anne,' he mumbled.

She leant over his prostrate figure, pressed her lips against his matted hair, and prayed for his immortal soul. 'Grant him, dear God,' she murmured, 'peace in Thine eternal kingdom. Take him to Thy heart and make him whole again. Restore to him the golden gladness of youth and, if it pleases Thee, let him know that he did not die unloved.'

Pressing one more kiss upon his cold cheek, Lizzie stood up, knocked at the door of the parsonage and heard footsteps in the passage beyond the door as she hurried away into the darkness.

Haworth Parsonage
September 28th, 1848

My dear Lizzie,

I write to impart the sad news of Branwell's death. That poor tormented soul has found peace at last. Five months of the utmost agony ended at nine o'clock last Sunday morning.

His end was preceded by a period of calm during which he opened his heart to a conviction of the existence and worth of those religious principles which he once ceased to believe in.

The knowledge of this change has brought a measure of

comfort to all of us. Charlotte and I heard with joy, Branwell praying softly in his dying moments, and his final fervent 'Amen' to the prayers my father offered up at his bedside.

Now, alas, my sister Charlotte, overcome with grief, has suffered a collapse. The noble face of our dead brother wrung her heart with pain beyond her strength to endure. But I feel that her real sorrow lies in the recollection of a long misunderstanding which broke the magical link of their childhood affinity. She grieves now for the squandering of an amazing talent; the extinction of a bright and shining light.

I know that you, Lizzie, recognised Branwell's worth, and loved him as we all did, despite his very human faults and failings, and I know that there is forgiveness for him in Heaven.

Charlotte summed it up thus: 'Had his sins been scarlet in their dye, I believe now that they are as white as wool'.

My own belief is that the black sheep has returned to his Loving Shepherd.

Your affectionate friend,
Anne Brontë.

CHAPTER TWENTY-SIX

The Stonehouses attended Branwell's funeral, and set off for Haworth in the gig, huddled in winter clothing, for the weather had changed suddenly and the first raw, icy winds swept down from Haworth Moor.

Lizzie watched them go, then went back into the house to minister to Theodora, whose doctor had warned the household of her approaching end.

'It could be days or weeks,' said Dr. Wheelhouse. 'Miss Blakeney has always possessed a strong will, and that is what is keeping her alive now. It's a great pity, but at least she has enjoyed a long and happy life.' He shook his head, and Lizzie knew what he meant – that the death of an old woman was different to that of a young man torn from life by his own folly.

Theodora was in no doubt that her end was near. She lay propped on her pillows considering that end, in no way troubled by it. She had made her peace with God, all that remained was to dispose of her earthly possessions as she saw fit. A nurse was now in attendance since it became impossible for Lizzie to lift the old lady by herself, and to nurse her day and night, but the woman was in the kitchen preparing gruel for the invalid, the house was quiet, and she and Lizzie were alone.

Miss Blakeney lifted a frail hand and beckoned the girl to come nearer the bed. 'Go to the bureau,' she whispered, 'open the top left-hand drawer, and bring me an envelope you will find there. Then get out my jewel-case. There is something I wish to settle.'

Smiling to herself as the girl complied, she said softly, 'That is what I like about you, Lizzie. That nurse would have thrown up her hands in horror and told me not to worry my head about such things, but I should worry a great deal more if I died before I had given you this.'

She handed the bulky envelope to Lizzie. 'Would you believe, my dear, that I am a "consortium of London businessmen"?' She chuckled, 'At least one of them! Percy Railton is the other. Between us we bought Edward's shipyard. Lettie was determined to sell it and, without Percy's intervention, there can be little doubt that the contents of the yard would have been sold separately, and many men would have been thrown out of work. Poor dear Edward would not have liked that.'

The old woman's eyes twinkled. 'Percy made me a proposition which I accepted, and although Lettie became richer by ten thousand pounds, at least we were able to keep faith with Edward. But the investment has proved a sound one – trust Percy for that – and the value of the land will be worth double what we paid for it in years to come. Lettie has no idea of this, and I fancy that my will, when it is read, will come as a shock to her. Here are the deeds to the Grayston shipyard, my dear. They belong to you, as my last will and testament will verify.'

Lizzie stared at the envelope. 'But I . . .'

'Now, child,' Theodora patted her hand, 'don't disappoint me by protesting. You are as dear to me as a daughter. I know your worth, and I intend seeing that you are provided for. What you do with those deeds when I am gone is entirely your own affair. Percy will honour his side of the bargain – but watch Lettie!

'Now hand me my jewel-case. I want you to have my mourning brooch and rings. The necklace is for Amelia, and my brother's watch is for Tom Stomehouse. I have left them a little money, too, and my silver tea-kettle and cutlery. As to this house, Lettie will sell it at the first opportunity, and she is entitled to do so, but I bequeath to you, to the Stonehouses, and to Percy Railton, something that Lettie will never own – my undying love and gratitude.

'Take my brooch and rings now, Lizzie. I have made no mention of them in my will because they have little monetary value, but they contain locks of hair which have meant a great deal to me. I know that you will love them equally for my sake. Ah, there's that wretched nurse! Kiss me, Lizzie, before you go, and may God bless you always.'

Amelia was in floods of tears when Miss Theodora gave her the jet necklace. 'That poor old soul,' she wept. 'Look what she's given me.'

'I know, Amelia. She gave me her mourning brooch and rings.'

'Yes, she said so,' the housekeeper sniffed.

On the twenty-seventh of November, Miss Blakeney died peacefully in her sleep.

'That's two,' Amelia said drawing the curtains. 'Poor Branwell Brontë, now the mistress, so there's bound to be a third, and my heart quails when I think who that third one is likely to be.'

'Who?' Lizzie asked fearfully, closing the door of Miss Theodora's room.

'Why Emily, Emily Brontë. She caught a chill at Branwell's funeral, and I'm not surprised. It was a bitterly cold day, and the poor creature looked as if a breath of wind would blow her away. Fair nithered, she was, not that she let on, mind you, but I was standing just behind her as the coffin was lowered into the vault, and I saw that she was shaking from head to foot. So thin she looked, too, with all the worry of her poor brother's illness, sitting up half the night waiting for him to come in from the Bull, and lugging him up and down those stairs at the parsonage. Tabby tells me she won't have a doctor near her; won't speak or be spoken to, and refuses to admit that anything's the matter with her. But it's consumption, Tabby says.'

Emily? Oh dear God no! Not Emily! Lizzie's hand trembled on the door-knob. But she said nothing, merely walked out of the room and went upstairs, understanding at last the terrible emptiness of her own heart; the utter weariness which weighted her own limbs; the feeling that she herself was dying.

'Maria,' she whispered, kneeling to pray, 'what would you have me do now? I am helpless. Helpless!'

Cerements of snow, soft as a bridal veil drifted across the moor at Haworth, imparting a fragile beauty of what lay sombre, grey, withered and dead beneath. Ponden Kirk, delicately frosted, towered against a pewter sky, each dent and hollow beneath that mighty crag levelled with snow, smooth and untrodden save for the claw and paw marks of birds and wild animals. There curlews wheeled and called their unanswered notes to the ice-still air. Called to Emily who could no longer come to them.

Dressing was torture for Emily Brontë, and yet she rose as usual, her will stronger than her dying body. Emily knew that she was dying – she needed no poisoning doctor to confirm the fact – neither did she seek to get well. Life no longer called to her, as wild and free as the curlews circling against the sky over Ponden Kirk. Life had narrowed to the shell of her own suffering body.

The living world held no hope for her. Interfering eyes had laid bare her soul; uncaring critics had dismissed her life's work; her prose, her poetry. Drained of inspiration, she now perceived the folly of submitting herself to the will of others.

Branwell was dead. Her grief manifested no outward signs, no tears, no lamentations. There had been no recoiling from the sight of his savage young face ironed free of the lines and ravages of living; sculpted white as a saint's, wiped clean of every emotion which had made him the man he was; lying cold against white linen; strangely impersonal, as if he had never suffered, never sinned or loved; never existed.

She could not weep for him. Sorrow for Branwell's sins, his squandered brilliance and youth; remembrance of his quick and ready wit, his boyishness and charm had cut too deep for tears; had carved within herself a spiritual tomb, a dungeon which no earthly light could ever penetrate.

Panting on her narrow bed, pressing her hand to her side where the pain was most acute, Emily looked out at the view framed by the high Georgian window; she saw how the dreary waste of granite slabs had been made beautiful by the newly-fallen snow, and perceived with an old passion how the slanting roofs of the village fell away down the hillside to the valley.

Someone was walking up Church Lane. A man in black. Mr.

Nicholls, her father's curate, exercising Keeper and Flossie.

Emily listened, sensing the loneliness. Branwell had filled the parsonage. His lunatic ravings and mutterings, now silenced for ever, had left no peace but emptiness. Anne was coughing – a hard, dry persistent cough so like her own. What if Anne, too, should die? What would become of Charlotte then?

She heard the closing of the front door. Mr. Nicholls had returned. Flossie yapped in the hall, then Keeper padded upstairs. She heard his soft whine outside her door, and got up slowly to let him in. The creature's dumb adoration brought a faint smile to her lips, and she remembered how, when he was young and untrained, he would slink up to Aunt Branwell's room and fall fast asleep on her bed. Her aunt's prim voice echoed back to her over the years, 'Emily! If you cannot keep that animal under control, he must be chained up in the yard!'

There had been no alternative, she had thrashed the dog for his own sake. Charlotte had been aghast as she pummelled him with her bare fists, screaming out that he would bite her. But Keeper had known, with some deep animal instinct, that she was acting for his own good. Afterwards, when she had bathed his swollen eyes and jowl, she had whispered soft words of affection into his sagging ears. 'I had to do it, Keeper. Could you have lived in chains?'

There was a light tap at the door. Emily's mask fell back into place. Pray God it wasn't Charlotte to worry her with talk of sending for Dr. Wheelhouse. She would see no doctor, take no medicine. But it was not Charlotte. Anne came into the room with Flossie at her heels.

'Won't you come down to the fire?' Anne asked. 'It's so cold up here.'

'Presently, when I am ready.'

Flossie leapt on to Emily's bed; licked her face, wagged her feather-duster of a tail.

'You have not buttoned your collar,' Anne said. 'Shall I do it for you?'

'No, I can manage.'

Anne turned away, hurt by her sister's brusqueness; yearning for the old closeness and rapport which had always existed between them, yet understanding Emily's silent, inner conflict, knowing what agony it must be for her to be confined to the house and unable to stride out upon the moor breathing in the fresh air. She longed to throw her arms about Emily, but she knew she must not. Her last gift to her sister was that of understanding.

'Go down, Anne,' Emily said more kindly, 'You should not have come upstairs when you are so short of breath.'

'Charlotte told me not to,' Anne turned her head and smiled, 'but I paid her no heed. I wanted to come. Flossie, get down, you bad dog!'

Their eyes met. It was a look that said all there was to say. Both understood. Anne said simply, 'I miss Branni. I keep thinking that I shall see him in another room, but whichever room I enter, he has just left it. Come down to the fire, Emily. Martha has drawn up the sofa, and Charlotte is going to read to you.'

Anne closed the door behind her and stood pressing a handkerchief to her lips to muffle her sobs. She heard Charlotte calling insistently from the foot of the stairs, and stumbled forward, gripping the banister.

'How is she?' Charlotte looked old and very tired. 'Do you think she is – worse?'

Anne stared at the stone-flagged passage beyond the archway, seeing phantoms from the past – two happy children running out to play in a sunlit garden, their arms intertwined. How could she bear it? How could she equate that happy past with this terrible reality? How could she live without Emily – the breath of her body, the motivation of her thoughts, the light of her life?

How remote God seemed to her now. How futile the prayers uttered endlessly, 'Don't let Emily die, dear God. Don't let Emily die!'

Charlotte's face swam before her, not beautiful but infinitely sweet and dear to her, a compassionate face etched in grief; curving mouth, brilliant intelligent eyes – but not Emily's face. Not that exquisitely-planed countenance, changeable as an April day, shining with an inner, unconquerable, unquenchable light; whose smile broke as infrequently, as beautifully as the sun through rain clouds, changing the mood of the day;

234

whose being exuded such magic, such mystery. Emily who seemed stubborn and proud, and yet gave to those she loved the passion and power of her incomparable spirit.

'I must go up to her,' Charlotte said.

'No! No, you must not! You – we – must let her be!'

'But Anne, if she should fall?'

'She will not fall! Anne cried. 'She will not fall! Not Emily!'

In the narrow room above, Emily Brontë rose unsteadily to her feet and made her bed, smoothing the sheets and pillows as well as she could, scarcely able to draw her breath.

Was it wrong to say goodbye to a bed? An iron frame which had given her body repose? When the task was done, she leaned her hands on the window-frame, the dungeon chains heavy about her dying flesh.

> Death is the veil which those that live call life;
> They sleep, and it is lifted . . .

A sad, low cry escaped her. Life, she knew, was ebbing away, as Branwell's had ebbed, and the tide carried all before it – joy, laughter, the inconsequentialities of youth, love and pain. She stood, a wanderer with no star to guide her faltering footsteps in the dark, clinging with all her might to the Strange Power; that Messenger of Hope once perceived in the mysterious midnight hour when her soul had pastured with the stars.

Where was her Messenger of Hope now? Where the visions conjured in the clear light of heaven that brought the thickest stars, filling her soul with such ecstasy, such desires that her being had seemed drawn to spheres beyond the world? Then her creative powers had burned equally with her belief in an eternal brooding power. Now that power seemed spent in her present agony.

What if, when her final breath was drawn, her soul cried out like Catherine Earnshaw's to return to all that she had held most dear on earth? What if her soul could find no rest beyond the stars, and her tormented spirit broke its heart with weeping to return to Haworth, her sisters, the wild moorland, and the crying of the lonely curlews on Ponden Kirk?

Emily staggered against the window and sank to her knees.

Keeper came to her, whined softly, and padded his great paws upon her skirt. She put her arms round his neck. Never again would she feel the dog's rough tongue upon her cheek; never again lie in the sun-warmed grass of summer watching the great white clouds billowing over Haworth Moor.

She dragged herself to her feet and looked her last at the tiny room which had harboured all her shining visions; all her hopes and fears, joy, passion and creative power.

Somehow she must cross the room, then the wide landing beyond, and walk downstairs. Summoning all her strength of mind, every ounce of willpower, she stood up straight and rested her hand on Keeper's neck.

The dog, sensing that he was to be her guide and support, trod softly beside her, turning his great brown head now and then to see that all was well with her.

Burn then, little lamp; glimmer straight and clear –
Hush! a rustling wing stirs, methinks, the air;
He for whom I wait, thus ever comes to me;
Strange Power! I trust thy might; trust thou my constancy.

CHAPTER TWENTY-SEVEN

Lettie's anger was at white heat when she discovered her husband's perfidy in the matter of Edward's shipyard.

'To think that you and Theodora of all people conspired against me,' she raged, but Percy merely smiled. 'Business is business, Lettie,' he reminded her, pouring himself a glass of brandy, 'and if you choose to deal with men, you must accept defeat like a man.'

'Faugh! I am your *wife*!'

'I reminded you of that at the time, my dear, but you chose to ignore it.'

'Clever words, Percy, but don't you see what you have done?'

'Of course I see. I paid you an excellent price for your property – and it has proved a worthwhile investment.'

'I am not referring to that. What you have done is made a rich woman of a mere servant.'

'If you mean Miss Godolphin, you are wrong. Theodora did that when she willed her holdings to the girl . . .'

'*Miss Godolphin*!' Lettie turned on him in a fury. 'Is that how you address a workhouse slut?'

'Workhouse slut?' Percy said mildly. 'Is she? I had no idea. She strikes me as a very charming educated young woman.'

'Does she indeed? Well she was scarcely that when she became Edward's mistress!' The words were out before Lettie realised it, but nothing, it seemed, could shock Percy out of his mood of gentle amiability.

'Was she Eddie's mistress? Well if that's true – which I doubt

– I must say that he displayed remarkably good taste. But why are you so heated? If a "mere servant" has inherited a little money under your aunt's will, I cannot see why that should so incense you. I wonder why you dislike her so? Could it be that Eddie looked twice at her and not once at you?' He yawned and finished his drink. 'Coming to bed, my dear? No, I thought not. Never mind, I'm used to sleeping alone, and I must confess that it does not worry me unduly.'

When the door closed behind him, Lettie stared into the fire. Percy had come to the truth of the matter. She must be more subtle in future. Then an old adage sprang to her mind – that flies are trapped with sugar, not vinegar.

Lizzie's world lay in ruins about her feet. Crossways Grange was on the market to the highest bidder, Tom and Amelia intended to retire from service and remain at Haworth, Branwell and Emily Brontë were dead, and Henry Godolphin had gone to America.

'Stay at Haworth with us,' Amelia begged, but the girl could not bring herself to make a decision. The security she had so treasured was gone for ever, her physical strength was at a low ebb, and she would never more be able to look at the moors without thinking of Emily.

'What are you going to do, then?' Amelia asked anxiously.

'I don't know, Amelia. I really don't know.'

At that crucial moment of indecision, Lettie Railton sent for her. 'Sit down, Miss Godolphin,' she said sweetly.

'Thank you, ma'am.' Lizzie noticed that the fine edge had gone from Mrs. Railton's beauty. Her features were coarser than they used to be, her chin was slightly blurred, and her waist had thickened.

Lettie sighed. 'These past few days have been distressing for all of us, have they not?'

'Indeed they have.'

Lettie regarded the girl coolly, loathing this thin, whey-faced creature who had been Edward's mistress, and hating the slim set of her shoulders, her delicately-marked eyebrows, and her neatly-braided fair hair. 'You do understand that I am obliged to sell Crossways Grange, don't you?' Her hands fluttered like two small white butterflies, 'Not because I *want* to, but simply because I have another property to maintain, and the upkeep of a second would be impracticable.'

'Yes, ma'am, I understand.'

'But I am concerned about you, Miss Godolphin – Lizzie. Oh, I know that you are now a person of independent means, and that pleases me. You were a kind and loving companion to my dear aunt Theodora, and you deserve the small inheritance she bestowed on you, but I perceive that you are not entirely well at the moment, and I wondered if you would consider coming back to Scarborough – to Grayston Lodge?'

Lizzie lifted her head. 'Grayston Lodge?' she murmured.

'Yes. My husband and I are spending Christmas there to be close to our daughter, Lady Hennessy. You could come with us if you like.'

Relief flooded through Lizzie. Home, she thought, I am going home.

'Well, Lizzie, what do you say?'

'Oh yes, Mrs. Railton. Thank you.' If a warning bell jangled momentarily in her brain, Lizzie was too tired, too thankful to heed it.

1849

The patient invalid sat quietly in Emily's chair. The garden looked so pretty. The currant bushes were in bloom, and the double cherry tree outside papa's window was thick in bud.

Charlotte, as neat as a grey squirrel, came into the room bringing Anne's dose of Gobold's Vegetable Balsam, prescribed by Dr. Wheelhouse in place of the sickly cod liver oil and carbonate of iron mixture which had so nauseated her sister.

'Thank you, Charlotte,' Anne could not help pulling a face as the physic went down, 'but why don't you rest for a while? You have been busy since daybreak.'

'Presently,' Charlotte said, 'but I must see to Tabby's potatoes first.'

Anne smiled. Poor Tabby's potatoes! The old woman would have a fit if she knew that Charlotte whisked them away every morning to remove the 'eyes' which the old woman could no longer see, and returned the bowl to the sink without her knowing.

How hard Charlotte worked to keep everyone happy, but what havoc such vigilance had wreaked on her far from robust constitution. With Emily gone, it was Charlotte who now shouldered the domestic burdens at Haworth parsonage, despite her own afflctions – pains in her chest and back, accompanied at times by a sore throat, headache and depression.

After dinner, Charlotte returned to the dining room and sat down to write to her friend Ellen Nussey. As her sister's pen scratched over the paper, Anne thought about Scarborough – and Lizzie. Keeper and Flossie were beside her chair, the spaniel curled up asleep, and the big dog lying with its head sunk on its front paws – waiting for Emily's footsteps on the stairs and her clear ringing voice calling his name. But Emily will never come again, Anne thought. Poor Keeper, you wait in vain, and so do I. No matter how much we might long for her, she will never come again.

As Charlotte's pen flowed on over the pages, Anne was reminded of those evenings when, after supper, she and her sisters gathered round the fire to write their novels. She could see, even now, Emily's dark head bent over her compendium, her brows concentrated upon the written word, her lips twitching over that pious old reprobate Joseph; her eyes kindling over the love scenes between Catherine Earnshaw and Heathcliff; such love scenes as to make the blood race and one's spirits to surge upwards to the stars.

If only I had possessed the tiniest part of Emily's genius, Anne thought, but how milk and water seemed my own poor romances compared to her one sublime novel, and yet I tried to set down the truth in *Agnes Grey* and *The Tenant of Wildfell Hall*, and I think that, in the second book, my pen took strength from Emily's. But I needed her to lead me. I always needed her strength to shore up my own weaknesses.

Charlotte peered short-sightedly at the pages of her letter, reading over what she had written. And as she did so, Anne remembered Scarborough; remembered the houses she had described in *Agnes Grey* – that row of respectable houses on each side of a broad white road with narrow slips of gardens, trim-handled doors and venetian blinds to the windows, and that feeling of freshness and vigour on the sands when the grooms came down to air their horses. She longed for that freshness once more; to gaze at the castle where she had set her last scene; to come close to Willie Weightman again, for she had sublimated all her secret hopes and dreams in the character of Mr. Weston . . .

Charlotte looked up anxiously. 'Are you all right, Anni? Shall I make some tea?'

'No, don't trouble yourself on my account. I was just thinking of Scarborough, and how much I should like to be there.'

Charlotte frowned. Her first impulse, when Anne was taken ill, was to remove her sister to a warmer climate, but Dr. Wheelhouse forbade any such thing. Anne, he said, was not to stir from the house; she must be kept in an equable temperature, for her lungs were affected.

All very well to say, but as the winter months dragged by, Anne's desire to go to Scarborough never wavered, and the prospect of so doing was all that cheered her.

A week of intensely cold weather in March had taken a further toll of Anne's strength, and yet she held fast to the idea of travelling to Scarborough when the chill wind ceased blowing; spoke of it constantly and with so much hope that Charlotte dared not attempt to dissuade her from making the journey.

If Charlotte felt that a tide of calamity was running against her, she must not betray her feelings. She believed that her cup of trial had been drained to the dregs when she lost Emily, now she trembled whenever Anne coughed, fearful that there might be more exquisite bitterness to taste. If there were no hope beyond this world, Charlotte thought, no eternity, no life to come, Emily's fate and that which threatens Anne would break my heart. Of the fate which had engulfed Branwell she dared not think at all.

'I think you would like Scarborough,' Anne said wistfully. 'It is so beautiful in May when the lilacs and laburnums are in bloom, and I know the place I would wish to stay at – a small house near Wood's Lodgings. No. 2, The Cliff, a clean little house with nicely starched curtains and sandstoned steps.'

241

'But do they board, Anne?' Charlotte kept to practicalities as an alternative to weeping, and her voice was sharper than she intended. 'Providing for oneself is such an insupportable nuisance. I hate keeping provisions in a locked cupboard with the prospect of it being pillaged. It is a pretty wearing annoyance.'

'I'm sure they do, but what harm in finding out? Would you write to the landlady, Charlotte? And do you think that Ellen would come with us? I am very fond of her, and I think she would be a great comfort and support to both of us.'

May 1849

Lizzie opened her eyes in the stillness of the early morning. There it was again, Maria's music.

She slipped from her bed and knelt on the windowseat. Pale and luminous shone the meadows of home; fields pearled with mist and sparkling with dew. The first bird sang. Dido whined softly and padded to her side; sprang to the seat and licked her cheek, understanding her grief.

Lizzie held the dog in her arms. 'How shall I live without her, Dido?' she murmured. 'How shall I face the future when Anne is gone?' She bowed her head and wept. The little spaniel thrust its body close to hers in an ecstasy of love.

'You are so like Flossie,' she whispered. 'Do you remember that day on Haworth Moor when you ran to Emily and licked her? She was proud and angry that day. We were two of a kind, Emily and I, when it came to standing on our dignity – and equally soft and foolish when it came to a dog's rough tongue on our hands.

'Do you remember her, Dido? The way she had of striding along the path with that haughty expression on her face, and how a minute later that expression would soften when she saw a bird or a rabbit? So few people understood her, Dido – understood that her haughtiness was a façade, something she wore as a mask to cover up what lay beneath it. But Anne – Anne is different. She wears no mask. What she is shines clearly for all to see, and yet deep within her lies a core of steel which matches Emily's.

'Oh, Dido, would that I possessed their courage, and that of

242

poor Charlotte. What will she do when she returns to Haworth alone? The emptiness of the rooms, the ticking of the clock, the silence of the house, the interminable longing for all the old familiar faces?

'Go back to bed now, Dido. Sleep your little sleep. Dream your little dreams of Emily, of rabbits and a wild moorland path. In Heaven, I wonder, will there be a place for animals? For dogs who give so much comfort to the human race? If not, then I think that I would not wish to go to Heaven.'

Lizzie went back to bed, not to sleep but to read again Anne's letter saying that she and Charlotte, with Ellen Nussey, were coming to Scarborough to stay at No. 2, The Cliff.

Anne's trunk stood next to Charlotte's. Shaking out a cambric wrap bought in Keighley long ago, Charlotte remembered when she, Branwell, Emily and Anne had gone there to shop; remembered the shopkeeper wrapping the garment in brown paper, snipping the string with a pair of scissors attached to the counter, smiling and taking the money – two shillings and elevenpence – and handing over a penny change.

What then? Why yes, they'd gone to the stationers. Did that shopkeeper ever wonder what his four laughing customers did with all the paper they purchased? He might have done so, but Charlotte doubted if it had ever crossed his mind that the three women were Currer, Ellis and Acton Bell, whose novels had set the literary world agog with curiosity. Now Ellis Bell, the undoubted genius of the trio, was dead and so was the red-haired Branwell whose loquacity had so amused the man, while Currer Bell had rubbed shoulders with the literary lions of the age in London, and had returned to Haworth more than ever convinced of her own plainness and ineptitude.

How strange, Charlotte thought as she packed the trunks, that the quietest member of the family, the most pious and outwardly the most orthodox, had dared to present in *The Tenant of Wildfell Hall* men and women at their most bestial. Even she had felt obliged to tell Anne that she considered the theme ill-chosen. Then it occured to her to wonder if Anne had ever been as 'orthodox' as she had supposed.

The journey which she herself was about to undertake with

243

so much apprehension, held none for her dying sister whose arms were no thicker than those of a little child. The drive, force and initiative behind the setting forth were not hers but Anne's, and there existed, in her sister's wasted frame, a life-force which matched that of the indomitable Emily.

Glancing at Anne, Charlotte could scarcely believe that this was the girl who had written, not only a controversial novel, but a Preface to that novel defending her reasons for having penned it.

In my own mind, I am satisfied that if a book is a good one, it is so whatever the sex of the author may be. All novels are, or should be, written for both men and women to read, and I am at a loss to conceive how a man should permit himself to write anything that would be really disgraceful to a woman, or why a woman should be censured for writing anything that would be proper and becoming for a man.

That was because the veil of secrecy concerning the identities of the 'Bell Brothers' – Currer, Ellis and Acton – had been broken, and the three authors revealed as women. Nevertheless, Anne had not hesitated to defend her book, and the writing of it now seemed to Charlotte like a rearguard action fought against tremendous odds.

Unaware of Charlotte's precise thoughts at that moment, Anne said, 'I am so glad that we shall stay overnight at York. We shall need to buy bonnets, dresses, and several other items.' And if the buying of bonnets seemed a dreary mockery to Charlotte, she kept her thoughts to herself, and thanked God that Ellen was going with them to Scarborough.

But the long awaited journey planned for May 23rd, had to be postponed at the last minute. Anne was so ill on that day that it was impossible either to proceed or to let Miss Nussey know of the predicament.

This last circumstance seemed the final straw to Charlotte, for Ellen, she knew, would be waiting at Leeds station for passengers who were destined not to arrive, and that brought on one of her nervous headaches.

And yet Anne would not give up the idea of going to

Scarborough. The next morning she arose early, dressed and made ready for the journey. Charlotte, standing near the front door, watched her sister walk slowly downstairs, and turned away to hide her tears as their father held his youngest child to his heart and blessed her.

The tableau, framed by the archway, touched Charlotte deeply. Flossie, in Martha Brown's arms, whined to follow her mistress, but it was Tabby's grief which most affected her, for the old woman wept openly, drying her faded blue eyes on the hem of her apron. Then came a flurry of dark blue skirts at the parsonage gate, and the small plump figure of Ellen Nussey hurried up the path.

'I simply had to come, Charlotte,' she said. 'I waited at Leeds yesterday and feared the worst.'

'My dear Ellen, how glad I am to see you. Anne was far too ill to travel yesterday – and indeed, she is too ill to travel today, but the chaise is waiting, and she is determined to set off.'

'What on earth are we to do?' Ellen's face puckered with anxiety.

'There is nothing we can do but to support her as best we may – and trust to God to help us.'

When Haworth, scene of Anne's five months long incarceration, was out of sight, she seemed borne up on a resurgence of hope. The radiance of early summer spilt like sweet warm honey over the gaunt landscape, and help came from all sides. At Keighley Station, strong arms lifted her from the chaise to the train, and at York appeared another stranger, a broad-shouldered young man, who carried the pretty invalid from the railway carriage to a waiting cab.

Anne, smiling and patient, seemed bemused by memories of the city where she and Branwell had once bought exercise books for the Robinson children. She could almost see his slight, jaunty ghost stepping quickly along the pavement on Lendal Bridge, and when they arrived at the George Hotel in Coney Street, she ate her dinner with an appetite sharpened by fresh air and excitement before setting out to buy the bonnets, stockings, gloves and ribbons she had set her heart on.

The warmth of the day, the animated street scenes, and the

charm of the city with its ancient Minster, cheered Anne. It mattered little to her that she must ride in a hired bath-chair, pavements she had once lilted along on her own two feet. But the majesty of the Minster almost overcame her, and it was Ellen who urged her away from it into a haberdasher's shop, and threw a grey silk shawl about her shoulders, saying, 'What a pretty thing. You must have it. It goes so well with your new bonnet and lavender dress.'

'But Ellen,' Anne protested, 'it is far too expensive. Real silk!'

'Nonsense,' Ellen laughed.

'B-but I have never owned a g-grey silk shawl . . .'

The words trembled and spread like ripples on a pond, awakening memories of a long-gone summer day near Wood's Lodgings, and Lizzie's words, 'I saw you in the summer of 1839. You were driving on the sands in a donkey-carriage. You wore a lavender gown, very like the one you are wearing now, a similar bonnet, and a grey silk shawl.'

I am going to die, Anne thought, certain now that what Lizzie saw that day was not a visitor to the town whom she had mistaken for herself, but truly herself, seen through the mists of time by a person close to her whose clairvoyant powers she had no reason to doubt. And then she remembered, with a certain wistful regret, that Branwell had once referred to Lizzie as 'the doppel-gänger'.

Number 2, The Cliff, Lizzie thought, reading Anne's letter in the stillness of a May morning. No. 2, The Cliff. That neat little house sandwiched tidily in the terrace where the phantom carriage stopped ten years ago.

The pattern tightened, warp and weft. Memories shuttled back and forward through her tired brain, weaving the whole, intricate inevitable design.

The scent of the sea was borne to Anne long before the railway carriage jolted to a halt at Scarborough Station, and every mile that brought her nearer to her journey's end imparted a sweeter smile to her lips.

But why? Charlotte wondered as they dismounted from the train and helped Anne to a waiting carriage. Anne's days in

Scarborough were not all happy ones, so why the inner radiance; the smile, the sense of homecoming? And yet her own heart lifted as the horse turned at last into an open space with a central garden, and a seagull wheeled joyously against the blue sky.

Mrs. Jefferson, the landlady, answered the bell and showed her visitors to their apartments – a sitting-room on the ground floor and a large bedroom on the first landing. Both overlooked the sea, with high windows set wide to catch both air and sunlight. These rooms, Charlotte thought, are like the deck of a ship, so high above the ocean that all I can see at first glance is blue water.

The beds were clean and billowy, the furniture polished with linseed oil and beeswax; armchairs were covered with rose-sprigged material; small tables laden with shell-boxes and framed miniatures. There was a marble fireplace in the sitting-room with a polished brass fender and gleaming fire-irons, and a high-backed sofa upholstered in blue velvet.

Crossing to the sitting-room window, Charlotte knew at once why Anne was so drawn to Scarborough. The view was breath-taking. Before her lay the mighty sweep of the South Bay, the Castle and the harbour, and a long rugged escarpment of green-topped cliffs – a scene so far removed from the austerity of Haworth that, in different circumstances, she would have revelled in it.

CHAPTER TWENTY-EIGHT

'Eh Signor Stranger, life is good, no?' Mario laughed as he entangled his friend's fishing line, 'But what is the matter, my friend? Your thoughts seem far away.'

The two rocked together gently in Mario's boat on Lake Garda. They had fished together before, but today the stranger seemed deeply preoccupied, and it was not like him to have tangled his line.

'What is the name of that house over yonder,' the man asked suddenly, 'the one with the terrace and the belvedere? I have never noticed it before.'

'That?' Mario glanced over his shoulder. 'I believe it is called Bella Vista. A good choice of name, eh?' He shrugged, 'Some people are luckier than others. The view must be beautiful indeed to those rich enough to enjoy it.' He laughed. 'But I am not envious, Signor Stranger, my own view of the lake, even from a rowing boat, is not to be sniffed at.'

'Bella Vista,' the stranger frowned, 'did you say *Bella* Vista?'

'Why yes,' Mario teased. 'Don't tell me that you have become hard of hearing all of a sudden.'

'Who does it belong to?' The stranger's eyes held a curious light.

'Belong to?' Mario scratched his head. 'I am not sure. To a French nobleman, I believe. How should I know? Ah, I have hooked something! A whale by the feel of it!'

'Answer me, Mario! Who does that Villa belong to?'

'I have already told you, to a Frenchman.' Mario felt aggrieved because his 'whale' had escaped from his line. 'Why are you so interested?'

'Because I know that place, only I cannot remember why I know it.' His line slipped from his fingers and floated away. 'Oh, God damn it! Trying to remember is like groping through a fog! I'm sorry, Mario, but you cannot know what it is like to have no recollection of one's past life. Only sometimes the unlikeliest things strike a chord. There was a girl in the market-place at Malcesine, for instance, who seemed familiar to me, and yet I could not remember where I had seen her before. Or perhaps I had never seen her before at all. Now that villa, and the name Bella strikes a chord, and that terrace, and the belvedere . . .'

For God's sake, man, sit down!' Mario cried. 'Do you intend to have us both in the water?'

'In the water?' The stranger looked down in sudden horror at the glassy wavelets sucking the sides of the boat. 'No, not that!'

'What did you say?' Mario's eyes held a dumb appeal, for the stranger had spoken in a foreign tongue, his eyes were glazed, and perspiration stood out in beads upon his forehead. 'Signor Stranger, I am your friend, remember?'

'Yes, Mario, I remember.' The stranger spoke in his customary Italian, 'But you must row back at once! The matter is urgent. I must go to Malcesine without further delay.'

'You have remembered, haven't you?' Mario said dully, 'who and what you are? I can see it written upon your face.'

'Yes, Mario.'

'And we are no longer friends? No longer brothers?'

'No, Mario, you are wrong if you think that. I owe you far more than I can ever hope to repay. I owe you my life. Now I owe you my memory.'

'But what did I say, Signor Stranger, to make you remember?'

'You told me the name of that villa. The Bella Vista. Bella was my wife's name.'

Mario shuddered. 'To tell you the truth, signor, I have always hated that villa. It is an evil place, an unlucky place.

The last tenants were drowned. The woman was buried in the cemetery at Malcesine, but the man's body was never recovered from the lake.'

'Wasn't it, Mario?' Edward Grayston said.

If Percy Railton was surprised by his wife's adoption of the 'workhouse slut', he chose to accept Lettie's assurance that she wished to make amends for the way she had treated the girl, by inviting her to Grayston Lodge. But Percy was nobody's fool, and he insisted that Lizzie should be given employment suited to her station in life.

'Station in life!' Lettie cried, betraying her true motives, 'I don't understand you.'

'Then let me put it another way, m'dear. If you had thought of putting her to work in the kitchen – and I am sure that you had thought of doing so – forget it. The girl is worthy of something better, and I intend to see that you treat her properly.'

'Really, Percy,' Lettie snapped, 'I shall begin to think that you have designs upon her!'

Railton laughed outright. 'Perhaps I have. I am not quite in my dotage, you know. But would she give me so much as a second look? I doubt it, seeing that my own wife finds me so physically unattractive. The fact remains that you must give her employment which allows plenty of scope for her intelligence.'

'Oh, and what might that be?'

'Cataloguing Edward's library. If you really have her welfare at heart, which I doubt, that task would prove fascinating and not too arduous for a charming heiress. Do remember, Lettie, that the girl is not a pauper, nor is she a servant.'

'Well, Percy,' Lettie replied icily, 'she has obviously found a champion in you. I wonder why. Could it be that you hope to persuade her to hand over those deeds to Edward's shipyard to you?'

'No, Lettie.' Railton seemed genuinely amused. 'Persuasion is your speciality. I shall never forget how you "persuaded" Mr. Florisent to part with his inheritance. Not that I felt any sympathy towards him. But just remember that if you attempt to hoodwink Miss Godolphin, you will come up against a deal more opposition than you did then.'

The ensuing months passed peacefully enough for Lizzie. Guests to Grayston Lodge came and went, and so did Mrs. Railton – first to York, then to Hutton Buscel, afterwards to London to attend to domestic matters at Well Walk, and finally to visit Sir Edward and Lady Dolman Scott who had just returned from a honeymoon cruise on Sir Edward's yacht.

On May 26th, Mrs. Railton returned from a visit to York, bringing with her Sir George and Lady Egmonton and a bevy of others besides. Fashionable folk intent on pleasure; women in fine dresses which they changed three times a day, and men who constantly wandered into the library to interrupt Lizzie's work with fatuous comments and compliments upon her appearance.

Lizzie, at work in the library, passed a weary hand across her brow. Her hand shook so much that she could scarcely write; the titles of the books danced before her eyes. Suddenly the door opened, and her closely-written pages fluttered to the floor as a group of women swept in.

'Oh dear, I suppose we are in the wrong room,' said a laughing woman in blue. 'What a confounded nuisance!' She turned abruptly, knocking a pile of books off the desk, and departed without stopping to apologise.

With a cry of distress, Lizzie bent down to retrieve the books. Two of them were badly torn – two old and valued friends from the past – the poems of Mr. William Wordsworth.

Unable to concentrate upon her work, Lizzie took the books upstairs to her room and locked the door behind her. Laying them on her dressing-chest, she attempted to mend them, but it was no use. Anne was calling to her.

Leaving the books where they were, she put on her outdoor things and slipped out of the house, almost too weary to walk the long miles into Scarborough, not knowing where she would find Anne, trusting in God to lead her footsteps.

Anne held the reins of the donkey-carriage in her wasted hands. The boy in charge of the poor beast had driven it too hard for her liking, whacking its rump with a bamboo cane. She leaned forward to remonstrate with him; begged him always to be good to the animal, then she took the reins herself. She wore a lavender dress, a dove-grey bonnet and a grey silk shawl.

She had begged Charlotte and Ellen to leave her alone. The beach shone golden in the afternoon sunshine. Her faded eyes perceived the moss-covered rocks where the little governess, Agnes Grey, had walked in the glory of a peerless summer morning long ago, and she knew that she had done her best, in that novel, to write all that she had truly felt and experienced; her love for Willie Weightman for one thing, and her loathing of the careless children who had once destroyed a bird's nest in the grounds of Blake Hall.

The donkey trotted obediently as if it knew that it must not overtax the strength of the driver. Anne peered anxiously over the wide stretch of sand. If only Lizzie would come to her. If only Lizzie would come . . . She had waited so patiently all winter long for the sight of her dear face, the warm, comforting presence that reminded her of Emily.

The hurrying figure seemed no more than a speck at first. Anne's fingers tightened on the reins as she watched that speck coming towards her.

Lizzie ran. Sand crunched beneath her feet; tears blew across her cheeks, the sun dazzled, almost blinding her. The figure in the carriage was no more than a silhouette at first – but Lizzie knew. She knew! 'Anne,' she cried, '*Anne!*'

They clung to each other. 'I knew you would come, Lizzie! My heart has cried out for you! I longed to see you just once more – before the end. All winter long I have prayed that my strength would hold out for this moment!'

'Oh Anne, my darling!'

'Don't weep for me, Lizzie. I am not afraid to die. If I have any regrets they are not for myself but for those I must leave behind me. Papa is old and frail, and Charlotte is not as strong as she pretends to be. But what of you, Lizzie? I cannot bear to think of you alone in the world, and poor, when it lies in my power to help you.'

'But I am not poor, Anne. Miss Blakeney left me the deeds to

Mr. Grayston's shipyard – though I have scarcely thought of them.'

'Then you must think of them, Lizzie. You must think of the future. Your future! You could start a school here in Scarborough. You are so clever . . .'

Lizzie shook her head. 'I'm not. But you look exhausted, my darling, and you must not waste your strength on me.'

Anne smiled. 'Waste my strength? No, dearest, if I can use these last hours to persuade you to look beyond the present, then I shall die happy. I want to help you as you have helped me; as you helped Branwell and – Emily.'

'It was the other way about,' Lizzie cried. 'Branwell and Emily helped me! Branwell made me aware of other dimensions to living – a world of art and poetry I had never known before, and Emily . . .'

Anne leaned forward in the carriage intently. 'And Emily . . . ?'

'It is hard to explain. Her spirit was ever with me; her name was in the very air about my head; her voice spoke to me in every bird that sang. She was the first evening star; the cold moon radiant in a winter sky. Oh we quarrelled at times, we fenced with words, but I loved her.'

'I knew it,' Anne said. 'I think I always knew it. Emily never mentioned your name to me, but that was her way. She guarded fiercely what she loved most. Charlotte is different, she needs to speak freely, to let her emotions flow unimpeded. That was the bond she had in common with Branwell, but poor Branni lacked Charlotte's control. If he had possessed that, he might be alive today. As for me, I have never quite understood my own role. I was always the weak little sister. I had none of Emily's genius, none of Charlotte's business acumen and initiative, none of Branwell's talent . . .'

Lizzie pressed Anne's hand to her cheek; her tears ran unchecked as she said, 'Perhaps not, but you possessed one sublime gift that outweighed all the rest – that of humility!

Time was running out. Anne's frail and wasted frame could not sustain so much emotion. That knowledge tightened Lizzie's clasp on hands so dear to her.

A light breeze ruffled the sea to a sudden, almost blinding

radiance. A lone gull drifted on white wings as the two women clung together for the last time. Then the little donkey-carriage turned away.

Lizzie saw a delicate hand raised in farewell; the fluttering of a grey silk shawl.

The lone gull circled higher and higher, then dropped on eddying currents of air until it skimmed the surface of the sea.

CHAPTER TWENTY-NINE

Lettie Railton awaited Lizzie's return. 'Will you come into the library?' she said coldly.

'Yes, of course, ma'am.'

'You evidently believe that you are privileged to leave this house whenever you see fit?'

'I don't understand, Mrs. Railton. I am sorry if I have inconvenienced you, but I was obliged to go out this afternoon.'

'Obliged? Without permission. I should like an explanation!'

'I am sorry, but I cannot explain why I went out.'

'Then perhaps you can explain how you came by these books? They were found by my housekeeper, Mrs. Piercy, on the chest of drawers in your room.'

Lizzie stared uncomprehendingly at the two volumes of poetry she had taken upstairs to mend. 'Why yes,' she said, 'as you see, ma'am, they are damaged, and I . . .'

'And you thought that a good enough reason to steal them?' Lettie interrupted.

'*Steal* them?' Lizzie cried. 'Why no such thought ever entered my head! I was going to mend them!'

'But you went out instead?' Lettie tapped a pencil against her teeth.

'Yes, but . . .'

'Don't trouble to lie to me! When my housekeeper discovered these books, I asked her to search your chest of drawers. I was scarcely surprised when I discovered this jewellery belonging to my late aunt.' Lettie uncovered Theodora's brooch and mourning rings. 'Perhaps you will be good enough to explain how my aunt's personal property came into your possession. They were not willed to you, were they?'

'No. Miss Blakeney gave them to me before she died.'

'I do not believe you. Why not admit that you stole those articles from a helpless invalid?'

'Because I did not, and I can prove it.'

'Indeed? And can you also prove that you did not coerce my poor aunt on her deathbed?'

'As to that,' Lizzie said with dignity, 'you had better consult her lawyer since he drew up the will.'

'Will or no will, you came into possession of those deeds before my aunt's death, did you not? You must have done so, for they were not with her other papers.'

'I did not take them, ma'am, as you infer. They were given to me at the same time as the jewellery.'

'How very convenient. And did she also give you those books?'

'Why no. How could she have done so? The books did not belong to Miss Blakeney.'

'Exactly. And they do not belong to you. Am I correct?'

'Yes, but . . .'

'Please!' Lettie raised her hand in protest. 'Don't trouble to continue, for you condemn yourself with every word you speak. The fact is that you have taken advantage of my kindness and stolen from me. I really have no other alternative except to call the police.' She paused to assess the effect of her words, but the girl seemed undismayed.

'You are very silent all of a sudden,' Lettie snapped. 'Does the thought of prison frighten you so much?'

'Watch Lettie!' Suddenly Miss Theo's warning came home to Lizzie. How could she have been so foolish as to ignore it?

'Well, why don't you speak?' The girl's silence was beginning to unnerve Lettie.

'There appears to be little that I can say, Mrs. Railton, as you have already judged and condemned me.'

'You are impertinent, miss! How dare you speak to me in such a fashion? My coachman is outside that door. One word from me and he will lock you in your room.'

'Then I think you had better call him, ma'am, don't you?'

'You are a fool, Lizzie Godolphin, an arrogant, ill-bred fool whose scheming has come to nothing. But I am a reasonable woman, and I am prepared to strike a bargain with you.' She stared at the girl nonplussed. 'Well, don't you want to know what it is?'

'No, Mrs. Railton, because I can guess. You want me to sign a paper waiving my right to Mr. Grayston's shipyard, but I won't do it.'

'Dickinson!' Lettie's voice was shrill with anger. The man entered the room without enthusiasm. 'Take this person upstairs at once! Lock her up! And, Dickinson, lock up that wretched dog of hers in the stable! Give it a dose of poison for all I care!'

Locked in her room, Lizzie cared nothing for herself, it was Anne she grieved over, Anne and – Dido. Hunger and thirst were nothing compared to the mental anguish she suffered.

Anne was dying; poor little Dido might already be dead for all she knew. She wrenched fruitlessly at the doorknob; beat her fists against her prison door; cried to be let out, but no one came, no one heard.

She prayed for a while, and then she grew angry; pulled open a drawer and saw her doll lying there; Cathy's 'magic' doll, and it was Cathy's dog that Lettie Railton had taken away from her.

Drying her tears, Lizzie thought how spineless she was, how quiescent. The time had come to take action. Tearing the sheets from her bed, she began to knot them into a rope, anger lending a certain precision to her movements. Lettie would never take the deeds to Edward's shipyard; she would never take her, and she would never have Dido. But, ah God, what if Anne and Dido were already dead?

She heard the scrape of the key in the lock and stood back, panting, ready to spring like a tigress.

Peggy's tear-stained face appeared round the door. 'Oh Lizzie,' she cried, 'I've been waiting my chance all day.' Her arms were warm and comforting. 'Look, I've brought you some food. Have you any money?'

'I've got a florin.'

257

'You'd best go quickly, then. Oh Lizzie, to think things have come to this. But where will you go, what will you do?'

'I must go to my friend Anne Brontë,' she said, 'she is dying, Peg. She may be dead already for all I know. But what of Dido? I must take her with me if she is still alive.'

'Dido's in the stable,' Peggy whispered, 'and Joe's in the yard ready to pole-axe that Bert Dickinson if he interferes, but I don't think he will. I heard him grumbling that he's employed here as a coachman, not a jailer. Oh, Lizzie, you will keep in touch with us, won't you?'

'Yes, Peggy, and – God bless you.'

'God bless you too, dear Lizzie.'

Hastily the girl put on her outdoor things, then with a faint smile she bundled up her doll and her Bible, felt in her pocket for her florin, and stole quietly downstairs.

It was the hour of sunset when Lizzie walked past the cottage near Wood's Lodgings. She longed to walk up the front steps and ask to be allowed to see Anne, but some inner sense of proprietry would not allow her to do so.

Her weary footsteps led her on to the Castle Hill where she ate the bread and cheese Peggy had provided for her, sharing her frugal meal with Dido, who soon fell asleep, her head resting on her paws.

Poor Dido, Lizzie thought, how little she knows that we are homeless. We can never go back to Grayston Lodge. True, there were the deeds to her master's shipyard, but what did money matter when her whole world was surrounded with death and disaster? She would tear up those deeds and cast them piecemeal into the sea if that would bring Anne and her master back to her; if only God would give some sign that He had not forgotten her.

Suddenly a massed army of cloud battalions stole from the west, and moved like chariots of fire across the sky. Then the sable clouds broke to reveal their softer edges; glorious tints of gold and turquoise, spreading the heavens with a map uncharted by any human pen; coves of amethyst lapped by pure tides of unsullied gold; lilac mountains and deep indigo valleys; rose-tipped heights blending to the exquisite tints of blood-red

258

peonies, sinking then towering upwards in spirals of gold-edged splendour to limitless horizons beyond the power of any human to describe.

The glorious sunset touched with fire, buildings, sea, cliffs, chimneys, roofs, grass, stones and human beings alike: bewildering the eyes with its sublimity; touching the heart with its awesomeness yet deep simplicity.

Impossible to believe that the Lord of Hosts had painted His sky with such colours to comfort her sad heart, and yet Lizzie felt comforted, and prayed that Anne had seen the colours of that sublime sunset.

It seemed to Charlotte Brontë, as evening fell that her sister had already passed beyond the pain and suffering of this world to a wider world of peace and beauty. But had she done the right thing in bringing Anne to Scarborough?

She believed so, but Ellen Nussey thought differently. In her heart of hearts, Ellen had never wanted to come to Scarborough; had done so from a sense of duty and loyalty to Charlotte and a deep affection for Anne, but she was out of her depth; painfully aware of her lack of vision; her stolidity and pragmatism which tied her firmly to the ground, which made her worry about the practicalities involved – doctors in a strange town, how one would set about registering a death and finding an undertaker; how they would break the news of Anne's death to Mr. Brontë, and how the landlady might react to a funeral from her boarding-house.

Anne was the first up the next morning, as if her final hours were so precious to her that she could not bear to let one moment pass without making the most of it, but although her spirit was willing, her strength proved unequal to going downstairs alone, and Ellen found her clinging to the newel, totally exhausted.

Breakfast was a silent meal. Ellen was painfully aware of her own shortcomings; Charlotte guessed that Anne's hours were numbered, but Anne was thinking, not of herself, but her two companions. Was she being very selfish in giving them so much trouble? Would it be easier for them if she died at Haworth? If she made one supreme effort, could she possibly reach home alive?

It was Ellen who set off in search of a doctor, and when a little after eleven o'clock, the landlady showed him into Miss Brontë's sitting-room, he found a neat, fair-haired young woman with dark blue eyes, almost transparent hands, and dainty feet resting upon a footstool. There was about her a disturbing ethereality, as if her tender, childlike spirit was already beyond his power to recall.

Ellen Nussey drew forward a chair. The doctor seemed at a loss for words. Then he found himself smiling at the pretty invalid who seemed intent upon putting him at his ease rather than the reverse.

'I believe that you are a visitor to the town,' he said, lifting her hand in his.

'Yes, sir, and that is why I seek your advice. My home is in the West Riding of Yorkshire. I wonder – if I travelled today or tomorrow, is it possible that I might reach home alive?'

'Why, Miss Brontë . . .' His professional calm was shaken in the face of such courage.

'You need not fear to speak the truth, sir,' Anne said.

'In that case, I – I would say not.' He forbore to add that, in his opinion, she would never leave that room alive; her consumption was far too advanced for that.

'I will call again,' he said to Charlotte as he took up his hat, 'but there is nothing I can do for her. You do understand that it is merely a question of time? A few hours at the most.'

Donkey carriages were astir on the sands. Lumbering carts pulled seawater to the baths. Anne gazed intently at the scene before her. Her chair was drawn up to the window, the sun was warm on her face, and now the tide was beginning to turn. She had seen it turn so many times before; had walked by the water's edge when the sand was wet, and bent to pick up shells left stranded by the tide.

Smiling, it seemed to Anne that soon, very soon, she would run to the sea's edge once more, and stand there to catch the bright ribbons of a summer afternoon. Suddenly a white gull cut through the shining air.

'I feel a change coming over me,' she murmured, and through the veil of peace enfolding her, she heard the sound of weeping. Charlotte was crying.

Gentle hands lifted her from the chair. She felt the comfortable length of the blue sofa beneath her, a pile of billowy cushions at her head, and the softness of the grey silk shawl about her feet.

Faces swam before her, and the soft sound of weeping pulled her back momentarily from an all pervading drowsiness to a pressing need to give comfort to a suffering heart.

Poor Charlotte, she thought. Poor dear Charlotte, she must not weep for me.

She felt the pressure of her sister's hand, and understood, in her final moments, that it was Charlotte, not herself, who needed comforting.

Smiling her last smile, she fixed her clouded eyes on the figure beside her.

'Take courage, Charlotte,' she whispered. 'Take courage!'

CHAPTER THIRTY

'There's someone asking for Miss Brontë.'

Mrs. Jefferson, the landlady, hardly liked to intrude on Charlotte's grief, for the poor soul had taken her sister's death very badly, and sat motionless in the chair by the window, staring out at the sea.

Ellen Nussey rose at once, 'I will attend to it, Mrs. Jefferson,' she said in a low voice. 'Do you know who the person is?'

'No ma'am, she came to the door to enquire about Miss Anne, and seemed likely to faint when I told her the sad news. She seems a very respectable person, and quite young – although I couldn't see her face for a veil.'

'Very well, I'll speak to her. Where is she?'

'In my private sitting-room. I thought it best to make her sit down as she seemed so upset. I hardly liked to keep her standing in the hall.'

Ellen felt unequal to the interview, and yet she believed it her duty to support Charlotte in every way possible. Squaring her shoulders, she entered the sitting-room. The past few days had taken their toll of her own health and strength, and she could not help wishing that Charlotte had not declined the doctor's kind offer to be present at the funeral, for he had been a tower of strength during Anne's final hours, and his presence would have proved a comfort to herself if not to her friend.

Ellen saw the figure of the caller sitting in the chair in the darkened room, for Mrs. Jefferson had drawn the blinds as a mark of respect and mourning. The little spaniel she held on a lead wagged its tail as Miss Nussey stepped forward, and the woman rose unsteadily to her feet. She was neatly dressed in black, Ellen noticed, with a black cloak, about her shoulders, and yet she was shivering. 'I am sorry to trouble you, ma'am,' she said faintly.

'I am sorry that Miss Brontë is not well enough to see anyone at present,' Ellen said. Her voice faltered – there was something strangely familiar about the woman to whom she was speaking. 'But pray sit down, I can see that you are not well either.'

'No thank you, ma'am, I cannot stay, but I would take it as a kindness if you could tell me just a little about – about Miss Anne Brontë.'

Ellen turned her head away, overcome with emotion at the memory of Anne's last day on earth; her amazing courage and fortitude in the face of death, and found herself speaking of it in a low voice.

'Even the doctor wondered at her fixed tranquillity of spirit which, he said, gave evidence of no common mind. Her passing was a triumph of that spirit. She knew no fear, of that I am certain. Indeed, her last words to her sister – to take courage – were an indication that she felt living, not dying, had proved the more difficult.'

It would have seemed harsh to Ellen to withhold details of Anne's funeral from the young woman in black, despite Charlotte's wish to keep it private. Usually ready to defer to her friend's wishes in all things, Miss Nussey could not really understand why Charlotte had asked her permission to use her address – Brookroyd, Birstall – in registering Anne's death.

'The funeral is to take place tomorrow,' she said, naming the time and the place. 'It had proved less harrowing were it possible to have held the service at St. Mary's, but it is closed for repairs . . .'

Lizzie, the woman in black, did not need to ask Miss Nussey where Anne's funeral service would be held. Clear in her mind was the memory of that April day when the hired cab had struck a pothole near Christ Church, and she had seen shadowy veiled figures on the steps leading to it.

'Thank you for your kindness,' she murmured, turning to leave.

Miss Nussey touched her arm as she did so. 'Forgive me, but I cannot help feeling that we have met somewhere before, and I should like to ask if you knew Anne Brontë well,' Ellen faltered. 'It is strange, my dear, but even the little dog you are holding is very like Anne's spaniel, Flossie.'

'We're in for trouble, Peg,' Joseph Franklin whistled softly under his breath and tied a clean kerchief at his throat. 'The missis wants to see us in the library. Bert Dickinson's just told me. Madam's in a right old temper it appears. She's given him a roasting over Lizzie and the dog, and I daresay we're in for one as well.'

Peggy's head came up proudly. 'I don't care! I'm glad I helped Lizzie to escape. Mrs. Railton had no right to treat her like a criminal, and as for telling Bert to poison poor Cathy's dog, well I'd have fought Bert Dickinson tooth and nail if he'd tried it!'

'Oh, Bert's not as bad as all that,' Joseph flattened his hair with water. 'But if Mrs. Railton's on the look out for trouble, she's going to get it this time. Come on, love, let's go and hear what she has to say.'

Anger had etched ugly lines on Lettie Railton's face, and yet it was not merely anger she felt but something far deeper than that, something she had never known before and felt powerless to deal with – fear allied to frustration, unhappiness bordering on despair, a sensation that her world was collapsing about her head and that she possessed none of her old swirling, dancing magic to recreate it.

How ironic it seemed to her that now she was a rich woman in her own right, money could not buy any of the things she wanted – it could not give back her lost youth, love, or beauty.

The mirror drew her like a magnet. Shocked beyond belief she saw the blurred contours of her face as those of a stranger, a middle-aged woman whose ability to turn men's heads at the merest smile and the lowering of her lashes was gone for ever.

She drew her fingers over her cheeks, lifting and smoothing the skin, and narrowed her eyes until the pale reflection in the glass swam before her like a dream of remembered beauty. Ah, that was better. Reassured, she thought that when this night-mare was over she would go abroad to one of the German spas, Baden-Baden perhaps, or even to Italy, take a cure, meet new and amusing people.

How could James Hennessy have been so cruel as to suggest that she had kept Julia tied to her apron-strings too long, and that she was spoiling her grandson? But even more cruel were Julia's words, 'I think James is right, mamma'.

The scene was etched deeply in Lettie's memory: the long drawing-room at Senningford Hall, windows opened to the terrace, fields with grazing cattle in the distance, sunlight and the sound of birds, lilacs and laburnums in full bloom, a Chinese vase on the polished sideboard, tapestries in blue, gold and red, colours echoed in the furnishings.

'How can you speak to me like that, my darling? I am your mother. Surely I am allowed to make little suggestions now and then regarding my own grandson's upbringing?'

'I know that you are my mother, but James is my husband, and little Jamie is my son.'

Julia linked her arm in her husband's as she spoke, and it was then Lettie realised that she had never thought of Julia as anything but her daughter, and Senningford Hall as an exten-sion of her own home, a place to visit every day if she felt so inclined without being invited to do so. Quite rightly so, she believed. How could a child like Julia be expected to manage a house the size of Senningford Hall, and a baby all by herself? Wretched James Hennessy, whom she had regarded as her own son, had shown himself in his true colours at last. Why, he was nothing but a young bully at heart, and Lettie lost no time in telling him so before putting on her gloves and sweeping out to her carriage.

She had expected Julia to run after her, but when she turned her head to look back at the house she saw that the footman had already closed the door behind her.

And where was Percy when she needed him? In London of course, having left her alone to manage a house full of guests on her own. One would have thought that he might have come up from town to play the host. In any case, he would have to be sent for to give James Hennessy the dressing down he deserved, for she would not set foot in Senningford Hall again until she had received an apology.

She poured herself a glass of brandy – the third since breakfast – and swirled the amber liquid against the light. How tired she felt, how utterly jaded and weary. How cruel and thoughtless of people to have brought her to this pass – Julia, of all people, and James. She dwelt on that aspect of her unhappiness with self-pity, seeing herself as a martyr to their selfishness. Then as she waited for the Franklins to arrive, her mood changed from self-pity to anger against Lizzie Godolphin and those who had engineered her escape.

Joseph, dressed in cord breeches and a shirt with sleeves rolled up to the elbows, entered the room, followed by his wife, white-faced and nervously smoothing her apron.

'You know why I have sent for you?' Lettie had finished her brandy and was now sitting behind Edward's desk.

'No ma'am,' Joseph said boldly, 'though I imagine you won't take long to tell us.'

'Oh don't, Joe,' Peggy murmured, 'you'll only make things worse than they are already.'

'I don't see how that is possible,' Joseph replied.

'Indeed? You are very outspoken all of a sudden.' Lettie got up and crossed to the window, feeling herself at a disadvantage sitting down with Joseph's dark eyes boring into her. Turning to confront the pair of them, she said, 'Well, you can pack your things and leave this house at once, do you hear me?'

'But where shall we go? What shall we do?' Peggy began to cry. 'We have two children to think of . . .'

'You should have thought of them when you aided and abetted Lizzie Godolphin,' Lettie said coldly. 'Now you may go to the Devil for all I care.'

Joseph took a step foward. 'We shall not do that, Mrs. Railton, although I would rather beg my bread in the streets of Scarborough than stay one minute longer under a roof where servants are treated as animals rather than human beings. You are a hard, cold unfeeling woman.'

Lettie stared at him as if he had struck her in the face. 'I?

266

Hard, cold and unfeeling? How dare you speak to me in such a fashion?'

'Because it's the truth. Come on, Peg. Don't cry, love, she ain't worth your tears. Best leave her to her Maker. But you know the old saying ma'am. "The mills of God grind slowly but they grind exceedingly small".'

'Joe's right. You treated Lizzie shamefully, locking her up like a criminal, and telling Bert Dickinson to give that poor dog a dose of poison. Poor Miss Cathy's Dido! I wonder what the master would say if he was here . . .'

'I *am* here, Peggy,' said a quiet voice at the door.

No one moved or spoke as Edward Grayston, followed by Percy Railton walked into the room.

Swaying on her feet, Lettie heard the clink of a glass and felt the swelling contour of the brandy balloon Railton pushed into her hand. The room began to spin. Edward, she thought dully, but it can't be Edward. He's dead.

'Oh sir!' She heard Joseph's voice as if from another planet. 'I have never been so pleased to see anyone in my life. We thought for certain you were dead, didn't we, Peg?'

Why is the fool making such a fuss? This man is certainly not Edward. I should have known him at once if he were. Oh Christ! My face, my hair! Did he hear what I said to the Franklins? No, he couldn't have done so. Grey! I should have worn my grey dress and pearl earrings!

'Is it really you, Mr. Grayston?' Peggy was smiling now. 'Why, I wouldn't have known you with that beard.'

He appears to find that amusing. Ha, Bella said he was ever too familiar with the servants. But why is he telling Joseph to take his wife to their apartment? Doesn't he comprehend that I have just dismissed the pair of them for insubordination? Who is this man to countermand my orders? Doesn't he realise that Grayston Lodge belongs to me?

And what is Percy doing? Why is he standing there by the fireplace with his arms folded? Why should he be smiling? God, I wish I had worn my grey dress! Oh, heaven help me, I must pull myself together! My face, where is my face? Not the one I saw in the mirror just now, but my real face? Is my dress straight? Is the fichu fluffed out just so? Why didn't I get my maid to dress my hair in curls on my forehead? That is what is wrong with my appearance! Pulled back hair never suited me even when I was a girl! All men like curls best! Is he really Eddie? I must step forward to greet him, then, very charmingly and gracefully, with my hands outstretched, and I must smile. I must smile and raise my eyebrows, then lower my lashes. But why don't I feel anything for him now?

Railton stared at his wife dispassionately, amazed at her resilience, wondering what was going on in that scheming brain of hers, and saw, with the tiniest ripple of inward applause, a touch of her old coquetry towards Edward. What a consummate actress the woman was to be sure.

'Oh my dear Eddie,' she murmured, 'I am so glad to see you again. But I want to know what has been going on behind my back. Where have you been hiding yourself all this time? And why, Percy, did you not tell me what was happening? It was rather cruel of you, was it not, to spring such a surprise on me?'

'You mustn't blame Percy. He had no idea that I was alive until I contacted him at his London office a few days ago, since when he has done all in his power to help me.'

'But why are you both so serious?' Lettie laughed suddenly in an attempt to disguise her rising panic as she looked enquiringly from one man to the other. 'Surely this is a cause for celebration? Percy, do pour some more brandy.'

Why doesn't Percy do as I ask? she thought. Why will they persist in looking at me as if I had committed a crime? Oh Lord, I suppose Eddie – if he is Eddie – thinks I have no business to be here! I don't care for his beard at all. I wonder why he grew it? It changes his appearance entirely. He looks so much older. She turned to the decanter and attempted to pour the brandy herself, but her hand shook so that she spilled it.

'You had better let me do that for you, Lettie,' Edward said.

'I asked Percy to do it,' she snapped as Edward handed her the glass. 'Perhaps you can explain why he is standing there like a graven image when we should be celebrating your return from the dead. Well why don't you speak, Percy?'

'Perhaps you would not care to hear what I have to say.' Railton's pale blue eyes were strangely compassionate.

'What do you mean? If you have anything to say get it over and done with. You too, Edward.'

'Very well, Lettie. I realise that my return must have given you a shock, and I'm sorry for that,' Edward said.

'I should think so too. It was unkind of you, I really think that . . .'

'Lettie,' Edward interrupted her chatter. 'My main concern is for Lizzie Godolphin. Where is she? What have you done to her?'

'So that's it! I might have known!' Coquetry forgotten, Lettie's anger blazed. 'So you have come here seeking your workhouse slut? Well she isn't here. She's gone, and she will never come back, I can assure you of that.'

'There you are wrong,' Edward picked up his travelling cloak from a chair. 'I shall find her wherever she is, and when I do I shall bring her back to Grayston Lodge as my wife – if she will so honour me.'

'Percy! Did you hear that?' Lettie sought refuge in her husband. Hurrying across the room to him, she laid her hand beseechingly on his arm. 'Oh it is too cruel of Edward to speak to me in that tone of voice. What have I done to warrant such hostility? You must take me back to London with you at once, do you hear me?'

Oh God what have I done to make everyone turn against me? First James, then Julia, now Edward. Tears of self-pity streamed down her face. There is only Percy left to me now. Percy . . .

'I will escort you to London with pleasure, m'dear,' Railton said. 'That's the least I can do.'

What on earth does he mean? 'That's the least I can do'? The man's my husband!

'What I wanted to say to you is that it is all over between us. Finished and done with. I'm sorry, Lettie, but I can no longer live with you. Do you understand?'

'No, I do not understand! You are my husband. It is your duty to live with me! If you leave me, where shall I go, what shall I do?'

Railton sighed. 'You will think of something, my dear.'

CHAPTER THIRTY-ONE

Charlotte Brontë drew on her gloves, and arranged her veil over her pale, tear-stained face – an all too familiar ritual. The third time in less than nine months. First Branwell, then Emily, and now Anne.

But if I do not smooth my gloves just so, she thought, my heart will break. As long as there are rituals to be observed, then I will observe them. But afterwards, oh God, be with me in my loneliness, my bitter regrets for my follies and my failures.

'The carriage is here, Miss Brontë.'

'Thank you, Mrs. Jefferson. I will be out directly.'

Oh papa, she thought, have I done the right thing in leaving Anne here in Scarborough? Will you feel for ever separated from her? And yet it seemed the kindest thing of all to leave the fallen flower where it lay.

'I am the Resurrection and the life, saith the Lord; he that believeth in me, though he were dead, yet shall he live; and whosoever liveth and believeth in me shall never die.'

The parson's words rang out in the still air; his surplice fluttered in the light breeze stealing in from the sea.

'I know that my Redeemer liveth, and that he shall stand at the latter day upon the earth.'

In the roadway, black-plumed horses stamped and snuffled in the air of a May morning.

Standing alone on the edge of the wide meadow, holding Cathy's dog in her arms, Lizzie saw Anne's coffin borne to its

270

last resting place; remembered her as she had been in life, so gentle, meek and mild, yet tempered like the finest steel. Remembered the warmth of her hands, the slim set of her shoulders, her shining hair and deep blue eyes. But far more than that, her tender love of animals, her compassionate concern for all those people she had so loved in life; her vision and her fortitude.

'For I am a stranger with thee; and a sojourner, as all my fathers were. O spare me a little, that I may recover my strength; before I go hence and be no more seen.'

'Forasmuch as it hath pleased Almighty God of his great mercy to take unto himself the soul of our dear sister here departed, we therefore commit her body to the ground; earth to earth, ashes to ashes, dust to dust; in the sure and certain hope of the Resurrection to eternal life, through our Lord Jesus Christ.'

Lizzie saw Charlotte and Ellen turn away from the graveside. Ellen slipped a comforting arm about Charlotte's waist, then the two lonely figures in black walked slowly towards the churchyard gate. The black-plumed horses tossed their heads, the carriage creaked slightly as the two women got into it. Harness jingled, sounds faded.

It is all over, Lizzie thought, lifting her veil and turning her face to the sea. Anne is gone. My destiny is fulfilled.

Faint with hunger, for her florin was long since spent on food for Dido, Lizzie walked to the Castle Hill, sank to her knees on the grass, and covered her face with her hands.

'For I am a stranger with thee,' she murmured, 'and a sojourner, as all my fathers were. O spare me a little, that I may recover my strength before I go hence . . .'

A light breeze ruffled the grass. She heard the distant music of the sea and the crying of the wild birds overhead. Then, above all, came the faint sound of a violin.

'Maria,' she whispered, lifting her face to the sky. 'Oh, Maria, do not leave me now. Show me what to do, for the world seems a mighty stranger to me.'

Suddenly Dido lifted her head and snuffed the air ecstatically, and her tail thumped the ground. Then she began to whine and fret as she used to whenever she saw Cathy Grayston.

Struggling free of Lizzie's arms, the little creature raced across the meadow and flung herself at a tall bearded man who seized her as eagerly, as lovingly, as Cathy herself would have done.

Half blinded by tears, Lizzie looked up to see the sunlight glinting on a pair of boots which glowed as brightly as horse chestnuts on an autumn day.

A pair of strong hands reached down to her and pulled her gently to her feet.

'Well, Lizzie,' said a well-known voice, 'I thought I should never find you! I have combed this town from end to end looking for you.'

'Master?' she whispered. 'Master!'

'Ah, my poor little girl! My darling, sweet Lizzie! Your bonnet is awry, as usual, and your poor little feet are so weary with walking. Come, now, Joseph is waiting with the carriage to take us home.'

'Home?' Lizzie murmured. 'Home?'

'Why yes, my heart's darling. You know where home is, do you not?'

She smiled and leaned drowsily against Edward's shoulder. 'Oh yes,' she said contentedly. 'Home is wherever you are.'

As they moved together across the grass, a cloud of linnets rose up and swept across the sloping meadow to the sea. A single gull dipped and wheeled on eddying currents of air. Suddenly all was movement again after the long stillness of despair, all was sweetness after pain. All was life and energy. All seemed possible once more. All was love that knew no boundaries.

Lizzie glanced back over her shoulder.

'What are you looking at, my darling?'

An ineffable sense of gladness filled her heart as she whispered, 'They are all safe at last – with Maria'.